"Kasischke could have . . . gone a hundred different ways: backwoods thriller, social satire, meditation on family, or pastoral love story. Instead, she craftily combines all these genres, creating a farcical, dark, resonant near-future world. . . . Lurking in the background is a chilling sense of foreboding straight out of *Deliverance*, swirling around a dysfunctional accidental-family dynamic that's as familiar as it is flawed. Kasischke . . . writes with worldly-wise profundity and sudden beauty but also sly humor . . . Her brevity actually enhances the story's propulsive quality. Reading *In a Perfect World* is like watching *The Birds* or another eerily vague tale of inchoate dread. We never really get answers, but we're helplessly drawn in by a slew of burning questions, with this one foremost: When can we expect a sequel . . . or is that nothing but a doomed hope?"

—*Elle*

"Although Laura Kasischke's novel is frighteningly timely with its backdrop of a pandemic flu, it is also touchingly timeless. From its haunting opening image to its riveting end, this is a tale of beauty, resilience, love, sacrifice, and even grace found in the most unlikely of places. In a truly 'perfect world' every book I read would inspire me like this one."

—**Katrina Kittle,**
author of *The Kindness of Strangers*

"One of modern literature's harshest explorations of married life with kids."

—*Detroit Free Press*

"*In a Perfect World* reveals astonishing and tender insight into human nature while exposing a terrifying, yet believable, world I'd never before imagined. This story will grasp onto your heart before swiftly carrying you away. . . . If you were going to pitch this book for a movie you'd say something like, 'A great Anne Tyler story meets a great Margaret Atwood story with a little bit of Ann Packer mixed in.' But, really, it's even better than that: terrifying, brutally honest, and totally believable."

—Jessica Anya Blau,
author of *Drinking Closer to Home*

"It is not enough to say that Kasischke's language is 'poetic,' a word that has come to mean 'pretty.' Rather, her writing does what good poetry does—it shows us an alternate world and lulls us into living in it. . . . [T]he language catapults us into another plane of existence, one of facade and reflection."

—*New York Times Book Review*

"Kasischke's verses walk that perfect Plathian line between the everyday—making macaroni and cheese, getting pulled over for speeding—and the eternal, the plainspoken and the lyrical, the comfortable and the abyss of loss that lies just beneath it."

—*Time*

The Raising

ALSO BY LAURA KASISCHKE

Fiction

In a Perfect World

Feathered

Be Mine

Boy Heaven

The Life Before Her Eyes

White Bird in a Blizzard

Suspicious River

Poetry

Lilies Without

Gardening in the Dark

Dance and Disappear

What It Wasn't

Fire & Flower

Housekeeping in a Dream

Wild Brides

The Raising

A NOVEL

LAURA KASISCHKE

HARPER  PERENNIAL

NEW YORK • LONDON • TORONTO • SYDNEY • NEW DELHI • AUCKLAND

HARPER PERENNIAL

P.S.™ is a trademark of HarperCollins Publishers.

Designed by Janet M. Evans

ISBN 978-1-61129-469-9

For Bill

We are enmeshed in a sad dilemma
when we ask if these apparitions
are natural or miraculous.

MONTAGUE SUMMERS,
The Vampire: His Kith and Kin

And all the winds go sighing,
for sweet things dying.

CHRISTINA ROSSETTI

The Raising

Prologue

The scene of the accident was bloodless, and beautiful.
That was the first word that came to Shelly's mind when she pulled over:

Beautiful.

The full moon had been caught in the damp bare branches of an ash tree. It shone down on the girl, whose blond hair was fanned around her face. She lay on her side. Her legs were pressed together, bent at the knees. She looked as if she'd leapt, perhaps from that tree or out of the sky, and landed with improbable grace. She was wearing a black dress, and it was pooled around her like a shadow. The boy had already climbed out of the smashed vehicle and crossed a ditch full of dark water to kneel by her side.

He seemed about to take her in his arms. He was speaking to her, pushing her hair out of her eyes, gazing into her face. To Shelly, he did not appear panicked. He seemed stunned, and rapturous with love. He was kneeling. He was just beginning to slide his arms beneath her body, to cradle or lift her, when Shelly came to her senses long enough to honk the horn of her car. Twice. Three times. He was too far away to hear her no matter how loudly she might shout, but he heard her honk her horn, and looked up. Startled. Confused. As if he'd thought that he and the girl were the last two creatures on earth.

He was far from Shelly, on the other side of the rain-filled gash, but seemed to wait for her to tell him what to do, and Shelly was somehow able to tell him, as if they could speak to one another without bothering to speak. As if they could read one another's thoughts. (Later, she would consider this. Perhaps she hadn't spoken to him at all, she'd reason, or maybe she'd been shouting and hadn't realized it.) However it had happened, Shelly managed to tell the boy, calmly, so he would understand, "If she's injured, you don't want to move her. We need to wait for the ambulance."

This was the one thing Shelly knew about accidents, about injuries. She'd been married for a few years to a doctor, and that detail had stuck.

"The ambulance?" the boy asked. (In Shelly's memory his voice was clear and close. But how could it have been?)

"I called them," Shelly said. "From my cell phone. When I saw what happened."

He nodded. He understood.

"What happened?" he asked. "Who was that? In the car without headlights? Why—?"

"I don't know," Shelly said. "You ran off the road."

"Help," he said then—a statement, not a cry—and the bare monosyllable of it was heart-wrenching. A cloud passed over the moon, and Shelly could no longer see him.

"Hey?" she called, but he didn't answer.

She turned off the engine. She opened her car door. She took off her shoes and waded carefully into the ditch.

"I'm on my way," she called. "Just stay where you are. Don't move the girl. *Don't move.*"

The water was surprisingly warm. The mud on the soles of her feet was soft. She slid only once, climbing up the opposite bank—and that must have been when she cut her hand on some piece of chrome torn from the wrecked car, overturned ten feet ahead of them in the road, or on a shard of broken glass from the windshield. But Shelly didn't feel it at the time. Only after the twin ambulances had flashed and wailed away from the scene would she notice the blood on her hands and realize that it was her own.

When she finally climbed out of the ditch and reached the boy and girl, the cloud had passed, and Shelly could see clearly again:

The boy was lying down beside the girl now, his arm wrapped around her waist, his head at rest in her blond hair, and the moonlight had made them into statues.

Marble. Perfect. Rain-washed.

Shelly stood over them for a few moments, looking down, feeling as if she'd stumbled onto something secret, some symbol in a dream, some mystery of the subconscious revealed, some sacred rite never intended for human eyes, but which she had been singularly and mysteriously invited to see.

Part One

1

There was a sad landmark on every block of that town:

The bench they'd sat on, watching the other students walk by—with their backpacks, short skirts, iPods.

The tree they'd stood under during a downpour, laughing, kissing, chewing cinnamon gum.

There was the bookstore where he'd bought the collection of poems by Pablo Neruda for her, and the awful college sports bar where they'd first held hands. There were the pretend-Greek columns that pretended to hold up the roof of the Llewellyn Roper Library, and Grimoire Gifts, reeking of patchouli and incense and imported cloth, where he'd bought the amber ring for her—set in silver, a globe of ancient sap with a little prehistoric fruit fly trapped in it for eternity.

And the Starbucks where they went to study, and never opened a book.

Craig's father cleared his throat and slowed down at an intersection when a girl in tight jeans, flip-flops, and a low-cut tank top walked in front of the car without even glancing over. She was nodding her head in time to something she was hearing through the white wires plugged into her ears. Craig's father looked over and said, in a voice thick with emotion, "You okay, buddy?"

Craig nodded solemnly, straight ahead, and then looked over at his father. They both attempted to smile, but to someone seeing it through the Subaru's windshield it might have looked like two men grimacing at one another, each gripped suddenly and simultaneously by chest pains or intestinal discomfort. Sun slid through the car windows in the slanted, distant way of a bright day in early autumn; obviously, their side of the planet was tilting away from the sun. The girl passed, Craig's father stepped on the gas, and the car moved through the green shade of the huge, leafy oaks and elms that lined the road through campus, and which had been greeting new and returning students to the university for nearly a hundred and fifty Septembers.

"Take a left here, Dad," Craig said, pointing.

His father turned onto Second Street. On the corner a girl with an old-fashioned bike was stomping at the kickstand near the curb. Her hair was so blond it glowed. It was the kind of hair that Craig had always distrusted—too seraphic, almost God-fearing—on girls.

Until Nicole.

But this girl at the curb with the bike was nothing like Nicole.

This girl had seen too many music videos, and was trying to look like one of the straggly, anemic blondes dancing behind the band. Her hair was greasy. Her nose was pierced. Her jeans sagged down over the sharp blades of her hipbones. She was the kind of girl Craig might have dated for a few weeks back home. Back then, before Nicole.

"Take a right now, Dad," he said.

His father slowed down on narrow King Street. It was still cobblestone, somehow. Some strange nineteenth-century leftover. (Had they simply forgotten to pave it?) The tires of the Subaru rumbled over the stones, and the rearview mirror rattled.

Here, on King Street, the trees made a canopy overhead, and the houses sagged with their decades at the edges of the sidewalks. These decrepit mansions must have been, at one time, inhabited by the town's elite; Craig could picture women in bustled skirts, men with handlebar mustaches and bowties, rocking on the front porches, being brought glasses of lemonade by servants.

But it was a student slum now. The thudding bass of someone's stereo served as a heartbeat to the whole block. Couches sat on the porches and on the lawns. Bikes appeared tossed into piles, leaning into each other, locked up to wrought-iron fences. There were hitching posts for horses at the ends of the driveways, most of them painted the school's colors: crimson and gold. Two shirtless guys standing several lawns apart threw a football between them with what seemed like malicious force, while a girl in a bikini on a lawn chair watched it fly back and forth in front of her. Against the sky that football looked like the pit of some piece of bright blue fruit.

"It's this one."

Craig's father slowed down in front of the house, which had once been painted white but had weathered to gray. There were ten mailboxes beside the front door—the number of apartments—and there was Perry.

Good old Perry.

How long had he been standing there, waiting?

Eagle Scout. Altar boy. *Best friend.*

The realization of that fact filled the back of Craig's throat with something that tasted like tears. He swallowed. He lifted his hand to wave.

Perry was wearing a Pittsburgh Pirates cap, a clean T-shirt, and khaki shorts. New tennis shoes? Had his mother ironed that perfect crease in the shorts?

Perry saluted—sadly, ironically, the perfect gesture—and Craig's father's chuckle sounded vaguely like a sob. "There's your pal," he said, and pulled up to the curb, and Perry strode solemnly over to the car, yanked open the passenger door, and called in, "Hey, asshole, welcome back," and then bent down and looked past Craig to his father. "How are *you*, Mr. Clements?"

Dependable, presentable, sociable Perry. Just profane enough. Just polite enough.

"*Great*, Perry," Craig's father said in a voice full of gratitude and relief. "It's really good to see you."

C raig and Perry's apartment was on the third floor. Perry had picked it out for them back in July. "It's not the Ritz," he said as they climbed the stairs behind him. "But it has indoor plumbing."

Craig's father carried a box of books and a tangled mass of USB cords. Perry had Craig's duffel bag slung over one shoulder and a trash bag full of sheets and pillowcases over the other. Craig carried his laptop, towels, and another trash bag—boots and shoes and his down jacket—up a narrow staircase carpeted in dust and dirt, to the left, past the closed doors of two other apartments. One of the doors had a whiteboard nailed to it and *I went to Good Time Charlie's! meet us!* written in purple Magic Marker on it, a big smiley face for the *o* in *to.*

"This is us," Perry said, nodding at number seven. He pushed open the door with his sneaker.

"Great!" Craig's father said again, stepping in behind Perry, exclaiming it so loudly that his voice echoed off the bare floors and walls, sounding even more falsely bright the second time.

The apartment was, of course, immaculate. Perry had moved in a few weeks before, having worked as an orientation guide for new students over the summer, and he'd obviously done his thing—swept, dusted, arranged a collection of books in alphabetical order on the narrow bookshelf next to the couch. Craig carried his things through the dark little kitchen with its freshly scoured sink, past Perry's bedroom, to his own, and stood in the middle of it.

A bright whiteness. The windows looked freshly washed—something Craig felt pretty sure their slumlord hadn't done—and the bed was made in crisp-looking blue sheets, a plaid bedspread.

"My mom did that," Perry said, nodding at the bed, "and that," he added, nodding at a bouquet of daisies in a clear vase on a scratched-up plywood dresser. "I like you, man, but not enough to buy you flowers. *Yet.*" He raised and lowered his eyebrows in the way that only Perry could, and Craig felt what might have been a chuckle start in his chest, but he suppressed it, just in case it might turn into something else.

"Well," Craig's father said, clapping both guys on the back at once. "This looks *great!*"

The year before, his freshman year, Craig's whole family had rolled onto campus together to bring him to Godwin Honors Hall. Craig's father had been laying on the horn the whole way through town, startling pedestrians and causing the drivers of the other vehicles to swivel their shocked faces at the Subaru. "Don't they teach people how to drive in the Midwest?" he had growled.

Craig's mother had just stared out the window, taking it in. Her silence made her dissatisfaction with the place palpable—a kind of thick green mist filling up the car. "It's *pretty*," she'd said, tapping her finger in the direction of the library's ridiculous faux-classical columns, as if it weren't the most damning praise she was capable of giving. Beside Craig in the backseat, Scar maniacally twiddled at the Game Boy in his hands, breathing heavily through his mouth as if he were alone at the control panel of a spaceship that was about to spin out of control.

Finally Craig's father pulled the car up to the curb right under a sign that read, NO PARKING HERE TO CORNER, and asked, "This it?" as if it might not be, despite the name chiseled into the stone above the entrance, GODWIN, and the crimson-and-gold sign posted near the gate, GODWIN HONORS HALL, and the banner strung between two trees in the courtyard, WELCOME TO GODWIN HONORS HALL, and the student standing outside with a poster board sign that read, GODWIN HONORS HALL.

"I think so," Craig said.

Godwin Honors Hall was the oldest building on campus, and looked it. It was the campus's only "Living Learning" facility, a dorm in which selected students slept, ate, and attended classes all in one building. On a campus that covered two hundred and fifty acres, if you were allowed into the Godwin Honors Hall program, it was implied by the brochure materials, the farthest you would ever have to walk was to the library, and you would never have to take a class or share a meal with any non-honors student for your entire four years at the university.

The whole thing had started as an experiment in 1965—a way, mainly, for some hippie activists to keep the decrepit building from being torn down, Craig would learn later the proposal being to create a private little liberal honors college (Oberlin? Antioch?) right there at the dead-center of one of the country's biggest public universities. It would appeal, they'd implied, to students who didn't want to get lost among the unwashed hordes.

Or who'd applied to Oberlin and not gotten in.

To Craig, it had sounded claustrophobic, a rat-in-a-maze kind of experiment that should have failed by 1966 due to rat insanity, but his father had insisted that the prestige of getting into the program would confer some sort of magical properties on Craig's future. And once Craig got his acceptance letter, which had shocked them all, the subject was closed for discussion.

The windows of Godwin Honors Hall were of the tiny diamond-paned variety, one or two of them cracked, glittering in the sun. The heavy wooden doors—gouged and shellacked, gouged and shellacked—shone with the sad decay of having been abused by thousands of students for a century and a half. The tiles of the entranceway were blood red and cracked, chipped, ice-picked away in places and sloppily replaced in others. Inside, there was the smell of mildew and disinfectant. A guy leaned against a wall of mailboxes, wearing a baseball cap on backward and a football jersey. He might have taken a long soaking bath in stale beer that morning. Someone had spray-painted, misspelled, the great philosophical advice "KNOW THYSEFL." Scar tapped Craig on the shoulder and mouthed the now-familiar and maddeningly annoying joke: "It's not Dartmouth."

Four flights up, through a maze of old carpet and blasted rap music and flyers taped to cinderblock warning the residents about STDs and inviting them to church jamborees and library orientations, they dead-ended at Craig's room, number 416, opened the door, and found Craig's roommate sitting at one of the two desks, reading a textbook of human anatomy.

That was Perry, back when Perry was a stranger.

His hair was shaved down to a millimeter of his scalp, and he was wearing khaki shorts and a fluorescent orange T-shirt that looked brand new, but which Craig would learn later wasn't (Perry's mother starched his T-shirts, per Perry's request), that read, EVENT ASSIST, on it in alarmingly large black capital letters. What event? What assist? Craig would also learn later that this was the standard T-shirt worn by Perry's Scout troop when they helped out in the parking lots of state fairs and Civil War reenactments. He just liked to wear it, whether he was assisting any events or not, and at the moment, it struck Craig as disorienting.

"Hello!" Perry said, closing his book.

"Hey," Craig said, and then, "I guess I'm your roommate," shrugging, feeling noncommittal, but Perry stood up quickly and offered his hand to Craig, shook it firmly, and then went around the room shaking the hands of each of Craig's family members—even Scar, shaggy bangs falling across his face, who stood openmouthed before this new breed of human being. Had Scar ever seen a person under the age of twenty-five shake another person's hand, except on television, or as a joke?

Had *Craig*?

"Welcome," Perry said, and then, without a hint of irony, gesturing around, "Sorry the place is such a mess."

They all looked at the room at once:

Four bare walls, a dustless linoleum floor, two closets with doors closed. Perry's bed was made. (A green comforter. A pillow in a plaid pillowcase.) Where was the mess?

"Where are you from?" Craig's mother asked Perry in a tone that suggested she fully expected Perry to admit that he'd been assembled in a laboratory, or that he'd grown up on the moon.

"Bad Axe," Perry said, as if everyone would be familiar with "Bad Axe."

"No way," Scar said, sounding sincerely astonished.

"Yeah," Perry said. He held up his hand and pointed at his thumb, as if that might explain something. "What about you?"

"New Hampshire," Craig's mother said. "Via Boston," she added, as she always did, and Craig's father stiffened, as he always did—but Craig could tell, by looking at Perry, that none of this meant anything to him.

Now, obviously, a year later, Perry had given Craig the better room in the apartment. The closet was large, and the window faced the backyard instead of the street.

"Don't you think?" Craig's father asked. "I mean, that it's a great apartment? A lot better than the dorm?"

"Yeah," Craig said, trying hard to sound appreciative. "It's great."

"We were pretty lucky," Perry said. "Leaving it so late. It's got a good view." He walked across Craig's room to the window and gestured out. Craig and his father followed, looked down into the backyard, where two girls of the bed-head-and-belly-button-ring variety were lying in bikinis on towels. Glistening in the sun. Their hipbones seemed to glow under their tanning skin. Craig looked away fast. His father and Perry looked at him, and then both cleared their throats at the same time.

"So. Shall we get something to eat?" Craig's father asked. "Before I head back to New Hampshire?"

"You're going back already?" Perry asked. "We can put you up for a night, Mr. Clements. Or for as long as you like."

"No. No," Craig's father said, shaking his head, making the expression of someone who'd just been offered a lifesaving drug but who didn't want to bother anyone to go to the cupboard to fetch it. Clearly he wanted to escape. "I really need to—"

Perry nodded, pretending Rod Clements had finished the sentence with something that explained it—although Craig knew that there could be nothing his father needed to get back to New Hampshire for so fast. His father was a writer. He was in the middle of writing a one-thousand-page sequel to his last novel. He hadn't sat down at the computer to work on it since Christmas.

Craig knew precisely why his father wanted to get out of there as quickly as he could. If there was anything Rod Clements couldn't stand, it was to see anyone he cared about suffer. Even as a child, Craig had intuitively understood that it would have been easier for his father to shoot him, like a racehorse, than to drive him to the hospital screaming in pain with a broken leg.

It had happened once—the broken leg—and Craig's mother had done the driving, Craig's father insisting that he should drive behind them, separately, just in case her car broke down, and even in his writhing agony Craig had picked up on the sneer of contempt his mother shot at his father's back as he trotted away from her car, huge sweat stains spreading out in the armpits of his gray shirt.

This time, Craig knew, his dad would probably drive a couple of hours east, as quickly as he could, and take a room at a Holiday Inn.

"That's a lot of driving, Mr. Clements," Perry said. "But, okay."

For the bite to eat, they went to the fanciest restaurant in town, Chez Vin. Chez Vin was where the Clements-Rabbitts had dined as a family the year before, overdressed and exhausted after their long drive, the four of them shoulder to shoulder at the hostess's podium as Craig's father announced to the toothy redhead that they were meeting a friend.

"Oh!" she'd said. "You guys are here to meet Dean Fleming!"

Craig's mother rolled her eyes behind the hostess's back and mouthed "you guys" to Scar. She'd been complaining about this phrase since they'd passed through Ohio, where, at every gas station and fast food place, someone addressed them as "you guys." At a 7-Eleven in Dundee, Michigan, when the ponytailed twenty-something at the cash register chirped, "How are you guys today?" Craig's mother had finally snapped and said, "Do I look like a *guy*?" She'd gestured toward the family she obviously thought looked far more dignified than they were being given credit for, and said, "Are we *guys*? What's this *you guys* thing?"

Craig had turned with his Tic Tacs and hurried out the electric doors into the parking lot as quickly as he could, listening to the girl at the register giggle in panic. Hopefully, she thought it was a joke. Hopefully, Craig's dad would get his mother out of there before she disabused the poor girl of that.

But, that first night at Chez Vin, standing at the hostess's podium, Craig had looked away from his mother, away from Scar, and away from the redhead, and had stared hard at the side of his father's face while registering for the first time that his father's friend from college, the one they'd come to meet for dinner, this friend from way back, was the dean of the Honors College—the *incredibly selective* honors college they'd all been so astonished that, "with your low-achiever grades and unambitious test scores," Craig had been so lucky, so *honored*, to get into.

"What?" his father had said to Craig, sensing his stare and turning around with both his hands up, as if to prove that there was nothing up his sleeve.

This year, the hostess was an older woman, who nevertheless said, "Hi, you guys," to which they all three nodded as she directed them to a corner table. Only Perry had bothered to wear a long-sleeve buttoned shirt and dress shoes. They ate all the bread in the basket before the waiter arrived with their mineral water. Craig's father and Perry talked about weather and the relative merits of certain kinds of mountain bikes as Craig watched the candle at the center of the table surge and recede—now a perfect diamond shape, now a teardrop, now a fluttering fingernail followed by a crescent followed by a dog tooth followed by a burning vertical eyelid.

Perry," Craig's father said later, in front of the apartment house, pressing both of Perry's hands in his own as the boy bid them farewell, "I'm so glad Craig's—"

"Craig will be fine, Mr. Clements," Perry said.

"Son," Rod Clements said, turning to Craig, "I—"

"Be careful driving, Dad."

They stood in the middle of the sidewalk. A few feet away from them a couple kissed with abandon under a dead streetlamp. A sad foursome of ugly guys parted around the couple, and then around Perry, Craig, and his father.

"Love ya," Craig's father said, and clapped Craig to him, patting him hard on the back.

"I love you, too," Craig said.

They held the embrace for at least three seconds, long enough for Craig to notice, just beyond his father's shoulder, hanging above the couple kissing, far over the place where the streetlamp should have been shining, the moon, which appeared to be made of either solid rock or the softest of human flesh, floating in an ink-blue sky.

2

Shelly Lockes called the newspaper after the first article, full of inaccuracies about the accident, came out, and although the reporter to whom her call was forwarded assured her that he would "set the record straight on the details of the accident as reported in our paper right away," no corrections ever appeared.

After that, Shelly asked to speak to the newspaper's editor, and her call was passed on by a receptionist, who said, "Well, *he* doesn't take calls from the public, but this person is *one* of our editors, and she could speak to you."

On the phone, *this person* sounded like a child:

"You mean, like, you were the first one at the scene of the accident?"

"Yes. I was. Why hasn't anyone spoken to me? My name's part of the public record. The paramedics and the police took all my information. I'd like to correct the record."

The editor stammered a bit before she said, "Wow. Okay. Well, I'll have someone call you this afternoon."

No one called, and the next day, again, there was a front-page story that described how the girl had been found in a "lake of blood" in the backseat of the car. How she'd been thrown there by the impact. How she hadn't been wearing a seat belt. How she'd already bled to death before the ambulance arrived, and that she was unrecognizable. That her face had hit the front windshield, and then the rear window. That her roommate had identified her at the morgue from the black dress and jewelry she'd been wearing that evening, and that the boyfriend who'd been driving the vehicle was found hours later wandering down a rural road, covered in his girlfriend's blood.

The newspaper said that medical professionals could only wonder at how he'd managed to stumble so far with a broken arm, a dislocated shoulder, a closed-head injury, and a ruptured spleen.

But Shelly Lockes had *been* there.

She'd called the ambulance herself within minutes of the accident. She'd waded through a ditch full of water and stood above the boy and girl. The girl had been thrown into the grass. She was not in the car. The light of the full moon had been plenty bright for Shelly to see it all—and she knew for a fact that the only blood at the scene had been her own.

The gash to her hand.

Admittedly, it was a nasty gash. She'd needed stitches, and bandages, and if she'd ever played handball or mandolin, she'd probably never be able to play again. The scar still surprised her every time she looked at it. How had she not felt the cut when it happened? It wasn't until she was in the Emergency Room, holding it up, wrapped in her own sweatshirt, that her hand had started to hurt like hell.

But it had not created a "lake of blood."

There had been no *lake of blood.*

"Maybe they're all like this," her friend Rosemary suggested. "Maybe every goddamn article about every event in the local newspaper is completely made up, but we don't know because we didn't witness most of them. 'A lake of blood' sells a lot more newspapers than *no* blood."

The next article described the "first person at the scene of the accident" as a middle-aged woman who came upon it hours after it had happened, and made a call to 911 but left the scene before the paramedics arrived, and could not be reached by police. After that article, Shelly called the newspaper *and* the police.

"Not one word of what's being reported is accurate. This needs to be looked into. For the record. There are implications here, for all of us."

The officer in charge of the case assured Shelly that he had all her information, that her help with this was invaluable, that he himself would contact the newspaper and make the correction. But he also said,

"It's a rag, you know. I wish I had a dime for every time they slaughtered a story. I'd be a very rich man."

The managing editor of the paper promised Shelly that a correction would appear the next day: "We have so many sources of information, ma'am. I'm sure you understand that with so much effort put into each story by so many people, mistakes can and do occur."

Shelly waited for the correction—scoured the next week's newspaper, every day—and never found it.

3

"Her name's Nicole Werner," Perry told his roommate, whose mouth was open, staring at her. Perry was hoping that if he distracted him with information, Craig would close his mouth and quit leering. "Her whole family's from Bad Axe, for generations. She's got about four hundred cousins. Our elementary school was called Werner Elementary."

"Farm slut?" his roommate asked. "Dumb blonde?"

"She was our valedictorian," Perry said, sounding more defensive than he felt. He had no particular stake in Nicole Werner per se, but everything Craig Clements-Rabbitt had said about *everything* since spreading out his high-tech sleeping bag on his bare mattress in their dorm room on move-in day had been either annoying or infuriating.

"Huh. Valedictorian? I thought that would have been you, Perry-my-man. What the hell happened?"

"She was the better student." Perry nodded with what he hoped looked like sincerity, not bitterness.

There'd been, certainly, a period of bitterness. Nicole Werner, in addition to being valedictorian, had also gotten the Ramsey Luke Scholarship—the first time in Bad Axe High history that it hadn't been given to the president of the senior class, which had been Perry. But Perry had told himself that they couldn't really give the Ramsey Luke and the E. M. Gelman Band Scholarship to the same student, and he'd clearly been the leading candidate for the latter.

They were in the cafeteria. It was the end of their first week in Godwin Honors Hall. Craig was eating chili piled so high with chopped onion that every time he put his spoon in the bowl, onions fell onto the laminate table. "What do her parents do?"

"They own a German restaurant in town. Dumplings."

"They make *dumplings*?" Craig let his spoon hover over the bowl for a moment, as if this were a bowl of absurdity itself. He shook his long dirty-blond rock-star bangs out of his face by whipping his face to the left—a kind of cool twitch Perry had seen on VH1 more than a few times.

"No," Perry said. "The restaurant's *called* Dumplings."

Craig snorted loudly and leaned back in his chair. This was routine for Craig as far as Perry could tell. Everything about the Midwest was one big joke to Craig Clements-Rabbitt—the food, the trees, the names of the streets, the girls.

"It's the most popular restaurant in Bad Axe," Perry said, again sounding, and wishing he didn't, as if he had some personal investment in this. Craig opened his mouth as if at news too astonishing to believe. Perry looked away, shaking his head.

One might think, from his attitude, that this Craig Clements-Rabbitt came from a huge city, but when pressed for the details it turned out that the town in New Hampshire he'd grown up in was, if anything, a bit *smaller* than Bad Axe.

"But it's not the same," Craig had said, sounding weary already, as if the whole subject would be too complicated to explain and he dreaded the task. This had been the first night in their shared dorm room, while they were still attempting to be polite to each other. Craig had left his duffel bag unpacked at the foot of his bed, and rolled out the technologically advanced sleeping bag onto his mattress. It was made of some sort of metallic material that even Perry, with a great deal of outdoor-gear expertise from the Boy Scouts, didn't recognize. No pillow.

"The town I live in is *small*," Craig said, "but nobody's *from* it. Everybody's got a place there because they work on the Internet, or only have to travel to Boston or New York every couple of weeks. Or they're independently wealthy, or they retired early. Except for a couple of people whose parents work at the ski resort. I guess *they're* sort of like small-town kids. But not really."

Perry imagined a few hundred families like Craig's: Mothers in slim beige skirts, rolling their eyes. Fathers in corduroy jackets and jeans.

In fact, while Rod Clements had been wearing jeans and a corduroy jacket earlier that day, he'd also been wearing bright green Converse All Stars and a couple of hemp bracelets around his wrist, as if he were in middle school, while the little brother, Scar, already looked like an old man, if old men had ponytails. The kid's face had appeared chiseled in stone, as if he hadn't laughed or frowned in his whole life—and although Perry had not yet asked Craig why his brother was called Scar, he felt sure there was some story behind it. Perry had only been in the company of the Clements-Rabbitts for an hour before they'd managed to share several seemingly amusing stories about Craig.

("Oh, Perry," Craig's mother had said, "I hope you can adjust to living with our son. We knew he was different when he was only three years old and asked, in all seriousness, if he could have for his birthday his own *agent*.")

And the family.

("Remember that time," his father had asked, looking around the dorm room skeptically, "when we thought we were renting a cottage on the beach in Costa Rica and it turned out to be a storage shed?")

"Dumplings," Craig repeated, trancelike, as he watched Nicole Werner cross the cafeteria. She was carrying her tray ahead of her as if it had something radioactive on it. Perry knew her well enough, after thirteen years of sharing classrooms with her, to know that Nicole was walking that way because she knew she was being watched, and she didn't particularly mind it. Her ponytail was swinging behind her like an actual pony's tail, the palest of blond, just like the hair of all the other Werners—except Etta Werner, who was Nicole's grandmother, a nice old lady who lived down the block from Perry's family and who always had on hand the most incredible homemade cookies you could imagine. *Her* hair was pure white.

"She looks like a milkmaid."

Perry didn't respond to this. He supposed it was intended as an insult. He might not have been Nicole Werner's biggest fan himself, but he couldn't help feeling protective. For one thing, he was pretty sure any insults Craig Clements-Rabbitt was going to think up for Nicole—hick, nerd, etc.—would eventually come around to him. When Perry had asked him about his last name, the hyphen, Craig had rolled his eyes and said, "Don't tell me you've never seen a hyphenated name before. Are the womenfolk in your town allowed to vote yet?"

In truth, Perry hadn't ever known anyone with a hyphenated name.

"I have two parents," Craig had said. "A Clements and a Rabbitt."

"I thought your dad was the Clements," Perry said.

"So you *have* seen hyphenated names—enough to know that my parents are so hip they decided to put my mother's name last."

Really, Perry hadn't figured that out himself. A guy on their hall had speculated that Craig's mother was actually R. E. Clements, because of the order of the names. His girlfriend had said, "No way. Have you read those books? No woman would write anything so stupid. That's testosterone-inspired schlock."

"So," Craig said, plunging his spoon into the chili, spilling more onions around the bowl, "in this town of yours, this *Bad Ass*, do all the girls look like that?"

"Like what?" Perry asked.

"Rosy-cheeked? Sunny blond? Strong but slender limbs? Big hooters?"

Perry thought about this for a minute, and then said, quite honestly, "Pretty much."

"Fair enough," Craig said. "So, when you go with your family to this"—he waved his free hand in the air—"this *Dumplings,* do you see Nicole Werner there?"

Perry had to think again, but then remembered that, yes, she'd started working as a waitress the summer before last. She was there, it seemed, mostly on Friday nights and some Saturday afternoons, moving quickly from table to table in her bustley skirt and frilly top. But usually his family went to Dumplings on Sunday, after church, with Perry's grandfather, who loved the sauerbraten, and although Perry saw Nicole in church, he never saw her at Dumplings those afternoons. Sundays must have been her day off.

"What's the uniform like?"

Perry described it. The wide blue satin belt. The—what'd-ya-call it?—peasant blouse. The pinstriped skirt.

"Oh, man, stop." Craig put up his hand and shook his head. "You're going to make me come."

Perry cleared his throat, and when Nicole looked over at him and gave him her usual polite (apologetic?) smile from across the cafeteria, Perry could feel himself blushing from his Adam's apple up.

How'd you get so fucking idealistic, man?" Craig asked one night a few weeks later, after their relationship had become openly hostile. Perry had come back from the library once again to find his roommate lying on his back in bed on top of the covers (he'd rolled up the high-tech sleeping bag he'd arrived with and put it in the closet), wearing boxer shorts and headphones. He had a paperback open on his bare stomach, a novel his father had published a few years ago and which, according to Craig at least, had been a big hit. *Brain Freeze*, by R. E. Clements. A lot of the other students in the Honors College seemed to know who Craig's father was, and not to hold him in very high regard, but Perry had never heard of him.

It was an achingly beautiful autumn. Clear and dry, skies so blue day after day that somehow it was possible to see the moon hanging there above the library, as if all the atmosphere had been scoured away. And the brightness of the changing red and gold and russet leaves of the big trees that lined Campus Ave seemed more like cinema than nature in so much light.

"You should see Dartmouth," Craig had said to him one morning as they walked down the staircase to breakfast. "Dartmouth was founded before there was even a *dirt path* hacked through this state."

Perry had heard about Dartmouth from Craig already a couple of times, and he'd already asked the obvious question, to which Craig had answered, "Because I couldn't get into Dartmouth. It's a real college. At Dartmouth I'd have gotten a real roommate, too."

"Fuck you," Perry had said, not for the first or last time.

"Thanks," Craig said, "but I'm not horny right now."

It had never crossed Perry's mind to go to college anywhere but here. All the smartest kids from Bad Axe had come to this university over the decades, and only three of them had gotten in this year—Perry, Nicole, and an obese girl named Maria, who played the harp and hadn't spoken a word to anyone except the school psychologist, as far as Perry knew, since eighth grade, when her mother had committed suicide.

His parents, both of whom had gone to a smaller university closer to Bad Axe, were nearly beside themselves with pride. His father had painted the big cement squares of their patio crimson and gold a couple days after Perry got his acceptance letter. "This is the big time," he'd said. "You did it, kiddo."

It was hard for Perry to imagine an older, more formidable looking college than this—the library's enormous pillars, the gold trim around the ceiling of Rice Auditorium, the leafy Commons with its marble benches. What could Dartmouth have that this school didn't?

"It's *selective*," Craig had said. "It's private. Not a jock-ocracy," waving his hand around at the walls of their room.

But for Perry, this was like a dream of being in college. The heavy books with their translucently thin pages. The gregarious professors and the unsmiling ones. The fat columns of the library, and the crammed stacks of books inside it.

The smell between those narrow walls of books was, Perry felt, the smell of rumination itself. Decades of reason and reflection. He checked out books that had nothing to do with the classes he was taking, just to be able to bring the heft and the scent of them back to the dorm with him. *A Handbook of Classical Physics. A History of the Anglo-Saxons.*

"Huh?" Craig asked. "How'd you get like this, man—all romantic about it all?"

"I don't know, *man*," Perry said, dragging out the *man* in imitation of that East Coast accent. "How'd you get so fucking cynical?"

"Native intelligence. Born with it," Craig said without missing a beat. He never missed a beat. He had a whole encyclopedia of comebacks on the tip of his tongue at all times.

"Is it a burden," Perry asked, "being so much better than everyone else? Or is it pleasing?"

"I'm so used to it by now," Craig said, "I really couldn't say."

Perry sat down on his own bed and unzipped his backpack. You could have drawn a line straight down the center of the room. Every time some piece of Craig's laundry or a magazine or a discarded protein bar wrapper inched over onto Perry's side, he carefully pushed it back over to Craig's side with his foot.

"Your mom called," Craig said. "I told her you were out trying to score some heroin, but you'd be back in an hour or so."

"Thanks."

"Here," Craig said. "You can call her from my cell in the lounge if you want some privacy." He tossed the phone, slightly larger than a matchbook and just as thin, to Perry. It had been a source of endless surprise to Craig Clements-Rabbitt that Perry didn't own a cell phone and was dependent on the antique mounted to the wall of their room. Craig did not, himself, even know their phone number, and had only touched the telephone in the room to take calls for Perry.

"Thanks," Perry said. He took the phone, stood, and closed the door behind him.

M om?"

There was no one else in the second floor lounge, so Perry lay back on the blue couch, careful to keep his shoes from touching the cushions.

He and his mother talked about his classes, his grandfather, his father's business—a lawn mower shop, the best one in town—and about the weather, which had been beautiful. The leaves in Bad Axe had changed dramatically already, she said, and were starting to fall, and she joked that she supposed she was going to have to do the raking now, with Perry at college.

"I can come home for a weekend," he said, "if I can get a ride."

"Don't be ridiculous," his mother said. "We can handle the *leaves*. You just get good grades."

Perry was an only child—except that there'd been another, a sister before him, who'd died at birth, a baby his mother had never once spoken of to him. The only reason Perry knew about her was because his grandmother, when he was nine, had decided Perry needed to know.

Since he'd been a toddler, Perry'd had an imaginary sister whose name was Mary.

He was getting too old for imaginary playmates, his grandmother told him one day, and God knows what it must be doing to his parents, listening to him in his room, talking for hours to that imaginary girl. Unlike the other adults in Perry's life, Grandma Edwards pulled no punches just because he was a child. She was the one who'd told him that his grandfather had been an alcoholic, and that his Uncle Benny took after him, a slobbering drunk, and that's why he was never invited for Christmas dinner. She was the one who would, eventually, tell him that she herself was dying of bladder cancer, not "recuperating" in the hospital, as his parents had said.

So Grandma Edwards took him to the grave—a flat, shining stone engraved with "Baby Girl Edwards," and a date that meant nothing to Perry—and that very day, his imaginary friend Mary had vanished, as if the imaginary could die as easily as the actual. Perry almost never thought about her again, except on the rare occasion that her translucently pale skin would come back to him, and the way her soft, cool, imaginary hand had felt on his, guiding it across a piece of paper, teaching him how to draw a dinosaur.

And the scent of her hair—that red tangle of curls—like warm earth.

I love you, Mom," Perry said before hanging up.

"I love *you*, Perry," his mother said.

"Tell Dad I love him."

"He loves you, too."

A few more good-byes, back and forth, and Perry snapped Craig's snazzy cell phone shut, rose from the couch, and headed back. A few students passed him on the way—strangers, but strangers he recognized now from the hallways, from the cafeteria. One guy, with wire-frame glasses, Perry recognized from a class, although he couldn't remember which one. They nodded seriously, politely, to each other.

The stairwell was empty when he got there. He could hear his own steps ringing around him, and as he climbed to the fourth floor, he suddenly was struck with a terrible grieflike longing for his mother, home alone in their two-bedroom bungalow. What would she do now that their phone call was over? Call her own mother? Watch television?

And there was grief for his father, too, still at the shop. He might be trying to fix something, or sell something, or schedule some kid to work on Saturday now that Perry was gone.

He thought about his grandfather, too, sitting on the bench in the hallway of Whitcomb Manor, already looking forward to Sunday, when Perry's parents would pick him up to go to Dumplings.

And then he was feeling sorry for the whole town of Bad Axe. The drugstore. The pizza place. The brick façades of the few, desperate businesses downtown. The strip malls at the edge of everything. The cemetery with its little flags and flowers stuck into the soft, green ground. The women at Fantastic Sam's, staring out at the parking lot, waiting for someone with too much hair to come inside.

Homesick. Now he knew what *that* was. And as soon as he stepped out of the stairwell, eyes fogged with emotion, Perry realized how stupid he was being, and rubbed away his ridiculous, homesick tears. Sentimental crap. The only other Eagle Scout from his troop in Bad Axe was already in the Marines, sent off to Afghanistan. *That* guy had something to get teary about, not Perry.

A girl in a miniskirt rounded the corner of the hallway, laughing hysterically into her cell phone. She didn't even glance at him. When Perry rounded the corner himself, he saw that the door to his dorm room was open, and someone was standing in it.

And then he saw who it was.

The bright blond ponytail. The perfect posture.

Nicole Werner.

She turned when Perry came up behind her, and she said, "Hi!" in that voice so bright and girlish it sounded like it was coming out of a piccolo.

"Hi," Perry said back, sounding like a party pooper in comparison, but who could compete with Nicole Werner when it came to congeniality? He saw Craig, still in his boxer shorts, no shirt, standing a few feet in front of her.

"I came by to see, you know, how it's going," she said to Perry, but glanced back at Craig as if trying politely to include him in the conversation. "You know, see if you'd want to set up a study time . . ."

"Oh. Yeah," Perry said. He'd forgotten. They'd talked about this back in Bad Axe—after they'd both gotten their acceptance letters, but before she'd been awarded the Ramsey Luke. They'd said they'd keep up the ritual, the weekly study marathons. "Okay," he said, and shrugged.

Craig caught Perry's eye then, and Nicole looked from Perry to him. "You're welcome to join us," she said to Craig.

Craig nodded, appeared to consider it, and then said, "That would be helpful. I could use the support, you know, to keep up the good study habits."

Nicole nodded. She'd obviously missed the false note, and the fact that Craig Clements-Rabbitt was half-naked, having been lying in bed with an iPod and *Brain Freeze* at eight o'clock on a Tuesday night. "Great!"

she said. "So, now we just need a time and a place." She whipped her academic planner out from under her arm in a flash, and slid out a pen conveniently tucked into her ponytail. She stuck the pen in her mouth as she scanned the pages of the planner.

"I'm free anytime," Craig said.

Perry rolled his eyes.

4

M aybe her students thought she was deaf. They could chase her down a hallway for half a mile calling out, "Professor? Professor?"and it did not occur to Mira to turn around.

Professor?

That couldn't be her.

But here she was, a professor at one of the largest universities in the world. They called her a cultural anthropologist, as if that were an occupation. She was an "Expert on the Treatment of Human Remains in Preliterate Civilizations"—the way her father had been an Insurance Salesman, or her mother, a Homemaker.

She was thirty-three, the mother of two-year-old twins, the wife of a Nice Guy who happened to be content in the role of Stay-at-Home Dad. She'd gotten her Ph.D. with honors and kudos and special awards: a Fulbright to Croatia, and even the unheard-of Guggenheim for a graduate student. Her dissertation, *Traditional Burial Practices and Their Folk Origins: Fear, Fantasy, and the Cults of Death*, had been published by a major academic press just a few months after she'd finished it. There'd been positive reviews in the specialized journals, and even a quick notice in a newspaper or two because of popular interest in her subject.

So, why, when they called out, "Professor!" did Mira not assume they were calling out to her? Why, day after day in that place, did she feel like such a fraud?

Because, perhaps, she *was* a fraud?

Mira Polson had ridden into her position as an assistant professor at the Honors College on the merit of that first book, and the "promise" the college saw for her future publications. That was three years ago, and now she was two years away from her tenure review, and there was no doubt—the department chair had made sure she had *no doubt*—that she would not receive it, and would not be kept on at the university, if she did not publish a book between now and then. And, so far, in the last three years allotted to her by the university to write and publish that book, Mira had produced nothing beyond some scrawled notes on a legal pad—notes that had become, in the year and a half since she'd scrawled them, illegible even to her.

And if she did not get tenure, then what?

Then she would be far worse than a fraud. She would be an unemployed expert on an obscure subject with two toddlers and a husband to support.

This Mira had considered as she closed the apartment door behind her and headed off to Godwin Honors Hall, trying not to listen to the twins scream after her, or to Clark's impatient shushing on the other side of the door. It took every ounce of fortitude she had to keep walking down the hall toward the stairs.

They had been sick in the night. No fevers, but both had barfed over the sides of their cribs around two o'clock in the morning, Andy taking his cue from Matty, as he usually did when it came to vomiting. They had apparently gorged themselves on Doritos while Mira was at a department meeting the evening before. Clark had been dead asleep when she got home, although it was only nine o'clock.

"The twins sleep, you sleep," their pediatrician had advised at their two-year checkup when Clark complained that the twins were still waking up once or twice in the middle of the night. Clark had been doing that anyway—sleeping when they slept—as far as Mira could tell, but after the pediatrician's advice, Clark had made a religion of it. Sometimes he even slept while the twins were awake. Mira would come home to find him out cold on the carpet in the living room beside the playpen while the twins stood inside it, shaking the cushioned edges like bars on a prison door.

They were healthy, active, curly-haired boys who spoke to one another in a rapid chatter that, when she was being irrational, Mira thought might be some linguistic or genetic remnant of her Eastern European forebears in their blood. When they asked for milk, it was *milekele*; "byebye" was *gersko*; "mama" and "papa" were *meno* and *paschk*. Sometimes Mira caught herself wishing that her grandmother was still alive to translate. Even more irrationally, she'd gone to the Llewellyn Roper Library in the summer to look up the words for *milk, good-bye, mother, father,* in Romanian, Lithuanian, Russian, Serbo-Croatian, and cross-referenced them to everything—Latin, French, German, and all the dialects—to find, of course, nothing that indicated that her twins were actually speaking a foreign language.

Of course.

Walking away from the library that day—its stiff neoclassical columns pretending to hold it up—Mira had felt silly, at best. Slightly insane, at worst. So, less insanely, she consulted medical books and websites, but when she asked their pediatrician if the twins might be experiencing some kind of language development delay, he'd laughed and said, "You professors all think your kids should be delivering lectures a few months out of the womb. Look, if they're still babbling in a foreign language this time next year, we'll explore the possibilities. But I'm telling you, they won't be."

Clark was becoming more and more frustrated these days by the twins' refusal to speak his language, and Mira knew it was because he was the one at home day after day while she was doing research, going to meetings, teaching. He was exhausted most of the time, wired up with manic energy the rest. There were dark circles the size of half-dollars under his eyes, and in the last three years he'd gone from the horniest man she'd every met—hard inside her again before he'd even pulled out—to the kind of guy women called radio talk shows about: *I wonder if my husband's having an affair; he hasn't wanted to have sex for the last three months.*

An affair might have occurred to Mira, too, if she didn't know exactly how Clark spent his days, and how impossible fitting anything extra into them would have been. The twins woke at 5:00 a.m., and did not stop having needs or making demands in their foreign language until 9:00 p.m. If she didn't have class, Mira would get up with them in the morning and let Clark sleep. But when she did have class, which was most days, he'd be the one stumbling and swearing out of the bedroom and into the hallway. Mira would roll over and pretend to be asleep—even on the occasions when Clark seemed to take forever to wake up and roll out of bed—although her whole body would be screaming as she listened to the twins cry out. Their cries, always the same (*Braclaig! Braclaig!*), made it impossible to know whose attention they were demanding, but Mira felt certain they were calling for *her*. It made her feel as if an alarm clock were rattling inside her chest, sending vibrations through every nerve and into every nerve ending of her body.

There were *so many* nerve endings.

The year before, in the fall, she and Clark had gotten a babysitter and gone to the Body Worlds exhibit at the Natural History Museum in the city.

Dead bodies.

Her specialty.

It was why Clark had thought to buy the tickets. A birthday present. "Right up your alley," he'd said, holding them up.

Except that these weren't *historical* dead bodies. *Folkloric* dead bodies. These weren't the kinds of primitive embalmings Mira studied. Instead, these were plastinated, dissected corpses, standing right in front of the viewer, filleted and splayed. A dead guy was set up on horseback, holding his own brain in one hand and his horse's brain in the other. Another was lobbing a basketball into the air, all his muscles on display, stringy and red. There was a corpse reclining in front of a dark television set, and one kneeling in prayer, literally holding his heart in his hands. The worst, the one that haunted Mira for weeks afterward, was the pregnant woman lying on her side like a centerfold—nothing left but tissue and bone and a net of blood vessels, but still with her baby floating eerily in her womb.

Maybe it was because Mira was a cultural anthropologist and had never had the vaguest interest in biology or physiology, but standing in the moving line of gawkers at the Natural History Museum that day, all of them together shuffling past that woman and her child (both of whom looked unborn and undead at the same time), Mira had urgently wanted to know how that woman had died. The brochure they'd been handed when they turned in their tickets insisted that the people who'd donated their bodies for the exhibit had requested anonymity, had donated in the interest of science, and that to reveal the mundane details— age, race, nationality, dates, and circumstances of their deaths—was to muddy the waters, lessen the message of the exhibit, which was to show the human body in all of its glorious detail.

Bullshit, Mira thought. The *only* important thing here was who that woman was and what she had been doing on the day of her death. Had she known she would die? Had she lingered for weeks, or had she simply failed to look both ways as she crossed the street? Had she had her throat cut by a husband who suspected the baby she was carrying wasn't his? Had she been stoned to death in some dark corner of the world for some supposed crime—maybe she'd flirted with a man of another religion, or sold some book to his wife that women weren't allowed to read?

"They were executed," Clark whispered into her ear as they stood in line waiting to view the dead Madonna, as if he'd gotten the news firsthand from someone who'd threatened to kill him, too, if he passed it on. "The men at least. You can tell. They're all Asian. They're shorter than Americans. Chinese prisoners."

Clark hadn't liked the exhibit either, but he said it was because he'd found it dull. It reminded him of high school health class, Mrs. Liebler. "I shouldn't have wasted the money," he'd said, but there was an edge of bitterness in it as if he'd expected Mira to love it even if he hadn't.

Instead, Mira had agreed—not that it was dull, but that they shouldn't have wasted the money. God knows they did not, at the moment, have money to waste. And they so rarely hired a babysitter that Mira felt they should have used the free time to do something more important, like bathe, or sleep.

Still, she *had* learned something from looking at those corpses. She had learned that nerves were not the invisible, semi-imaginary forces inside the body she'd always thought they were.

No.

Nerves hung off the body in dangling cords, draping like willow switches. They looked damp and heavy. Humans were tangled in them like ropes and pulleys.

No wonder she felt as if every inch of her had been electrified as she lay there listening to the twins cry in the mornings, Clark taking his time shuffling out of the bedroom to meet their demands. She was, Mira realized, wrapped in a curtain of nerves! She was wearing a web of them. She was strung with them, like a Christmas tree in lights.

So, why didn't she get up?

Because that was his job.

His *only* job.

She had an *actual* job.

Mira wasn't, she thought, a feminist. Not exactly. If she had been, she wouldn't have married a man like Clark—not with his lascivious admiration of women's legs, and his belief in the supremacy of men in all things requiring logic or mechanical inclinations.

But she also felt it would be a terrible precedent to take over these tasks for him on the days she was teaching. It would take away the last thing he seemed to be contributing to the running of the household—attending to the children when she had to work.

Work in the world. For pay. An activity Clark, it seemed, had no plans to engage in again anytime soon.

And then she felt terrible for thinking this.

If Clark were a woman, a housewife, and Mira had heard some man say that the work of caring for two children wasn't *real*, Mira would have been the first to stand up, waving a banner, shouting the chauvinist down. *Of course* it was a full-time job. A job she should have been grateful he was doing so that she could do hers.

So why, now, did she wish she were the one staying home with the screaming twins? Why, now, did she resent Clark for not having to get up in the morning, find his notes, pack his briefcase? She'd known exactly what his plans were when she'd married him, and bread-winning hadn't been one of them. Mira had been the one who'd bristled when her father had asked if Clark planned, maybe someday, to go to law school, and proudly explained to her father that they both valued their "freedom to pursue intellectual endeavors" too much for either to take on such a mundane endeavor as law school.

Still, Mira had finished her doctorate, and Clark had dropped out of his master's program in comparative philosophy, finding it to be another "mundane endeavor." Now they were in their thirties, with two children, living in an apartment complex full of undergraduates, many of whom drove much nicer cars than the clunker she and Clark shared. Sometimes, Clark let his beard grow for days before shaving, and Mira occasionally wondered, from the smell of his breath, if he was taking sufficient care of his teeth. She knew he was bathing, because he would spend a long hour every night in the claw-foot tub with the door latched while she put the twins to bed. Once, she'd mentioned to him that their electric bill, $125, might be so high because of the hot water heater, and he'd turned to her with wide, desperate-looking eyes and said, "The fucking *tub* is the only thing I have to look forward to *all day.*"

"What about the gym?" she'd asked.

They'd joined the nicest one in town because Clark insisted he needed a place with Nautilus machines and childcare. Mira rarely got to this gym herself, but on the occasions she did, she couldn't help noticing that the parking lot was full of BMWs. *You cannot afford this membership*, the BMWs said to her.

"And what about Espresso Royale—?" where Clark met a gaggle of stay-at-home mothers many afternoons, and where, as far as Mira could tell, they just let their children climb around on the upholstered cubes in the Kid Corner while they drank coffee and complained.

Clark looked at her blankly. "I need the *bath*," he'd said.

Professor Polson?"

This time Mira turned around, recognizing, finally, even in her sleep-deprivation and distraction, her own last name.

How long had he been running after her? The boy was sweating. He had the clean-shaven, buzzed-head look of an ROTC student, or maybe a member of College Students for Christ. But these kids could fool you. Sometimes the conservative look was an ironic statement, right down to the pressed khaki shorts. He could be the lead guitarist in some bad college band. She'd seen flyers around Godwin Hall for an upcoming performance by the Motherfuckers.

"Professor Polson," he said. "I saw you, and I wanted to ask—" He gasped for breath. "I wanted to ask if I could get into your seminar."

"I'm sorry. It's full," she said, and started to turn from him as quickly and unsympathetically as she could. She always felt bad, sending students away, but these late registers would keep demanding entrance into the class for weeks into the semester if she didn't stand firm. This was a first-year honors seminar, and Mira couldn't teach it well with more than fifteen students in it because of the amount of writing and discussion she required. The seminar was called Death, Dying, and the Undead. A *lot* of students wanted in. It was the most popular seminar in the college. This was, Mira supposed, because they were only eighteen, so the death and dying part didn't faze them—what eighteen-year-old believes in death?— and because they wrongly imagined that the "Undead" part would mean vampires, when that was only the thinnest (and, in Mira's opinion, the least interesting) thread in the vast tapestry of Undead material.

"But—"

"I have a waiting list," Mira said. "Twenty-seven students are on it before you, and there's not a chance that any one of them will get in, but I'll add your name to the bottom if you insist."

"Can I just tell you one thing?"

Mira inhaled, but stopped walking. She looked at a spot over the boy's shoulder so she wouldn't seem to be encouraging a long explanation of his scheduling problems or credit deficits or financial aid requirements. They were the only two people in the hallway, and the stone floors beyond him were gleaming in the September sunlight as it shone through the windows. Godwin Hall was the oldest building on campus, and where it showed its age most was in its windows, which were an intricate crisscross of glass diamonds and molten lead. The panes were multicolored, warped, and one or two had been cracked and not yet replaced—but these cracked ones added to the prismatic blues and golds when the sun hit them and made dazzling patterns of light and shadow on the walls and floors.

"I'm a sophomore," the boy said.

"Well," Mira said, no longer as reluctant to reveal her impatience. "In that case, you're not eligible for a first-year seminar anyway."

"But I don't want to take the class for credit. I just need to sit in. For personal reasons."

This time Mira looked at him, directly into his eyes, which were dark brown and long-lashed. His hair was so short it was impossible to know what color it was, but she imagined it must also be dark, although his skin was fair. His cheeks were still flushed from him running after her.

"Why?" she asked, but then she stopped herself—why bother to encourage his explanation or excuse?—and held up a hand. "Just so you know, I'm against auditors. I find they're an intrusion in the closed circle of a seminar, and often they have very little stake in the class. And, the class is *full.*"

Still, she tilted her head, to show him she was listening. It was rare, but there were the occasional students who took Death, Dying, and the Undead because of a trauma in their backgrounds. A car crash involving high school pals. An older sibling who had committed suicide. Twice, she'd had students who'd had childhood leukemia and been cured, but the experience of it had left a strange gray haze over the landscape of their lives. The year before, there'd been a girl in the class who'd revealed, only a few weeks before the end of the semester, that her mother had been murdered by her father:

That, in itself, was enough of a story, but this girl had been in utero when the murder took place, and had been delivered two months prematurely at the Emergency Room in the same hour her mother had died. The girl had been raised by wealthy grandparents who'd told her that her parents had been killed in a tragic car accident when she was a baby—of course, is there ever any other explanation for such things?—but the student discovered the truth on the Internet, her grandparents being of a generation that hadn't anticipated that one day, thanks to Google, no family secret would be safe.

The boy was still breathing heavily. He said, "I would participate fully, Professor. I'm a straight-A student. I've—" He stopped. A cool, rose-colored diamond passed over his eyes through the broken windowpane—a cloud traveling across the sun—and he blinked it away. "I've never gotten a grade lower than an A."

"That's impressive," Mira said. "But it's a first-year seminar, and if you audit you won't get a grade anyway, so your special interest in the subject is . . . ?" She waved her hand through the air to indicate that he needed to continue, and then shivered. She was wearing a silk dress—catalog stuff, deeply discounted—and it had short cap sleeves. She knew it looked good on her because Jeff Blackhawk, the poet-in-residence in the Honors College, had nearly spilled his coffee when he saw her walk into the faculty lounge. He was the kind of man who was completely undone by a woman in a sexy dress, or a low-cut blouse, or a nicely tailored pair of black slacks, and Mira was glad, almost relieved, that she'd caught his attention. Still, the dress was too light without a sweater, a cool-weather one, and autumn had come on before she'd expected it—only the first week of September, and that morning the sky had been full of the kind of fat blue clouds Mira associated with snow.

The student inhaled, and wiped a hand across his brow. He said, "I was good friends with Nicole. Nicole Werner. I grew up with her. And Craig Clements-Rabbitt was—*is*—my roommate."

Nicole Werner.

And that horrible rich boy who'd killed her.

Mira had known neither of them personally, but of course she knew the story. Everyone did. It was last year's Tragic Incident. Most years, there was at least one, and this year the victim had been perfect for the leading role: Virgin. Girl Scout. Sorority pledge. A devout Christian from a small town. Two married, devoted parents. The youngest child. The baby. A straight-A student, but full of goodwill and vivacity, too. In her spare time she tutored illiterate children. She'd been beloved by her professors and her classmates alike. Until the end of the spring semester, the whole of Godwin Hall had been draped in black.

Mira hadn't, herself, attended the memorial service in the auditorium, but another professor at the college told her that the girl's mother had wept so piteously throughout the service that no one could help but join her in sympathy until the four hundred and fifty people gathered around the high school senior portrait of the dead Nicole Werner were sobbing.

And then they'd let her murderer back into the university. Despite the public protests, the outrage, the letters to the editor of the student and local papers, the university lawyers had concluded that since no criminal charges had been filed against him, they had no grounds for keeping him out. Only the Honors College had the balls to ban him, and everyone knew that was only because the dean, who was old pals from Dartmouth with the boy's father, had bent all the rules to admit him in the first place, and didn't want that getting any more press than it already had.

There were goose bumps on her arms now. Wrapping her arms around herself, Mira realized that not only had she shivered, but now she was trembling. She worried that her teeth might begin to chatter. It was truly autumn. The sun had clearly slipped a few notches down on the horizon, and the light on the leaves was amber now, not white, not even golden, as it had been the week before, and a breeze seemed to be pouring through the centuries-old windows of Godwin Honors Hall despite the fact that they were all closed. That cold breeze seemed to pour in a steady stream down the hallway, bathing her.

"I know you're an expert on death," the boy said to her, "and dying, and the undead. All I know about is Nicole and Craig. But there are . . . circumstances. I could tell you, but you might think I was nuts. Basically, I just need to know more, and I thought your seminar might help me with that."

5

Perry had—on purpose, most likely—picked out an apartment for them that was as far from Godwin Honors Hall as you could get within the boundaries of the same circumscribed college town. And since Craig no longer had any classes at the Hall, he had no reason to go there. Still, he found himself standing outside of it within an hour of the dismissal of his first class of the semester, staring up at the window of the room he was certain had been hers—fourth from the end, facing East University Avenue.

The window was open. The curtains were closed. They rippled a little, without parting. A flock of starlings circled the roof, landing and rising over and over in a mass that managed to look both fluid and nervous. The wrought-iron gate around the courtyard was freshly painted. Black. And the grass was emerald green. The branches of the walnut tree near the entrance were bowed under the weight of big green fruit, and every few minutes one of those walnuts fell from the tree and onto the lawn with a muffled thump.

Craig didn't know how long he stood there, but for whatever period of time it was, no one entered or exited Godwin Hall. No one passed him on the sidewalk. No one parted the curtains and looked out a window. And not a sound came from anything except for those occasional thuds of a walnut, and the starlings—but only their wings, very swift and distant, churning up the air around the roof.

It could have been, he realized, a year to the very day that he'd opened the door on that Tuesday night, thinking it would be Perry, who'd left for the lounge with his cell phone to call his mother (did he think he'd locked himself out?), and found *her* standing in the hallway instead.

"Hi. Is Perry here?"

Her hair was pulled back in that ponytail, and he could see how a few brilliant threads had worked loose around her face, and how they were lifting and falling weightlessly with her breathing.

Later, he'd remember the exchange as having taken place in slow motion:

Nicole Werner turned her face away from Craig, and looked down the hallway—for Perry, presumably, but also probably so she wouldn't have to look at him, naked except for the boxers—and the trick of light on those loose blond strands made him feel as if he, too, were floating brightly in the air around Nicole Werner.

"No," he said, sounding underwater to himself. By then she'd already raised her hand to Perry, who was walking toward them with Craig's cell phone in his hand and a desolate expression on his face, as if he'd just gotten news that the love of his life was imprisoned in Turkey.

It amazed Craig then how casually Perry nodded to the heavenly creature who'd come looking for him. As if she were his sister, or as if, in Bad Axe, girls who looked like her grew on trees.

At Craig's high school in New Hampshire there'd been only seventy-one students in his class at the time of his graduation, and only twenty-nine of them had been girls. Occasionally there'd be a new one, but usually she stayed only a few months, half a year—maybe she'd flunked out of her boarding school or come to town from Boston or Manhattan to live with the noncustodial parent for a while.

Otherwise, Craig had known those twenty-nine girls since he was in kindergarten. His parents knew their parents. He'd taken skiing lessons and swimming lessons and tennis lessons with them. He'd called them names, and had been called names by them. He'd seen them emerge from the girls' bathroom with eyes swollen red from crying, or dashing into the girls' bathroom in their prom dresses to vomit up vodka and Fruitopia. He'd fooled around with a few, had sex with a few, been slapped in the face hard by one of them. And he had *never* seen anyone like Nicole Werner:

The pink cheeks, the serious expression, the sincerity radiating off of her so nakedly he wanted to close his eyes, or throw a coat over her.

She was the All-American Girl.

Eventually, he'd had to take a step back.

Y ou hate chicks, don't you?" his best friend Teddy, his only *real* friend back in New Hampshire, had said to him in the high school cafeteria once—and then stuttered, "I-I-I mean, not like you're a fag, you j-j-just—"

"I like chicks," Craig had said. "Just not *these* chicks. Not *here.*"

He'd meant Fredonia High, and he'd believed it to be true—that they were, all of them, a special breed of brainless, or bitch.

Except, he had to admit, he didn't like the chicks at the Quaker camp he went to in Vermont every summer, either. And he didn't particularly care for the tourist girls who passed through town with their parents. Or the girls his cousin in Philadelphia had introduced him to over winter break.

"Ah," his father had said once when Craig tried to draw him out on the subject of females. "The war between the sexes. It's as old as time." He went on to tell Craig a story about a nurse he'd met in Vietnam. The Perfect Woman. She'd ended up marrying his buddy. "I set it all up," his father said wearily. "I knew if I had anything to do with her, it would ruin her."

"What happened to her? To them?" Craig asked.

His father shook his head. "Don't know."

When Craig's little brother, Scar, turned thirteen and asked Craig for advice about girls, the only thing Craig could think of to say was, "Just forget it, man."

"Thanks, man," Scar had said, without irony, and wandered back to his own room, where, it seemed to Craig, the kid had proceeded to take the advice:

By the time Craig left for college, Scar was fifteen, and spent most of his time at the computer, blowing things up. Craig had been waiting for the last two years for one or both of his parents to say something to Scar about the "productive use of time," or the "mind-numbing soul-sapping" nature of video games, but they never said a word. Maybe they'd used up all their parental energy on Craig.

Or maybe it was because, by the time Craig graduated from high school, *they* seemed to spend all of their time, too, in front of their computers. His father, Craig knew, was writing, or trying to write. His mother, he guessed, was doing something she also considered work, but wasn't. She'd taken to answering her cell phone by saying, "This is Lynnette Rabbitt," as if someone besides her friend Helen or her personal trainer might be calling. Occasionally Craig considered asking her what she was doing on the computer, but he always ended up following his father's advice when it came to his mother:

Don't ask, Don't tell.

Still, he sometimes had a bad feeling—jealousy? apprehension?—when he heard her on the other side of Scar's closed door, talking to his little brother in a tone that, even muffled by oak, sounded alarmingly, like confession.

So, is she your love interest?" Craig had asked Perry as the door closed on Nicole Werner's retreating form.

(Corn silk. That was the color and texture and general impression of the girl's hair.)

Perry shook his head, and turned his back on Craig.

"Well, she seemed pretty anxious to find you," Craig said.

"Superstitious."

"Huh?"

"She's *superstitious*," Perry said, louder, as if Craig hadn't heard him.

There was a bitter edge to his voice when it came to Nicole Werner—
something Craig had noticed in the cafeteria when he'd first asked Perry
who she was. Craig assumed it was the result of unrequited love, or at
least unrequited lust.

"Care to elaborate?" Craig asked.

Perry sat down at his desk and opened his laptop. To his computer
screen, he said, "We studied together in high school. She always thought
that when we did she got A's, and that when we didn't, she didn't."

"*So*," Craig said, "you're the Magic Man? The Buddha? All the girls
gotta rub the lucky boner before their tests?"

Perry made a disgusted face, and then shrugged. "Whatever."

"Have you slept with her?"

Perry looked at Craig for a long time, but from a distance, as if he
were counting to ten or twenty before speaking.

"No," he finally said. "Why?"

"Why not?"

This time Perry turned around and kept his eyes on his computer
screen for a long time, waiting for something to materialize, gigabyte by
gigabyte, on it. Craig gave up and lay back down, stuck the iPod buds
back in his ears.

But that night, waking from a dream in the darkness of the dorm
room, he remembered something his brother had said years before at
the Petrified Forest. They'd gone there with their father, who was speaking at a writers' conference in California.

They hadn't set out to go to the Petrified Forest at all, or even
known about it, but on their way to Napa Valley, they'd passed the
place, along with six or seven signs urging them to turn left, to see the
WONDERS OF THE PREHISTORIC PAST! STEP BACK IN TIME! 3 MILLION YEARS! "Hard
to say no to that," their father had said, slowing down, slapping on
the blinker.

Craig was fifteen that summer, and he hadn't wanted to see the Petrified Forest. He'd wanted to get to the hotel where they were staying, to
lie down in a dark air-conditioned room, maybe watch MTV, definitely

check his text messages, jerk off in the bathroom if his father and brother went out for burgers. But the next thing he knew, they were standing in a gift shop surrounded by shining rocks and plastic dinosaurs, waiting in line to buy tickets, and then they were walking the red, dusty trail into the Petrified Forest.

It was just past noon, and there was an unnerving insect drone taking place somewhere overhead and, at the same time, all around them. The shadow of a bird crossed the path in front of their own shadows, and made Craig jump backward. He was tired from the drive up from San Francisco, and that insect drone was like having your head inside a computer that was perpetually booting up, or like the feeling you had after a blow by a basketball to the ear. It made him think of bad sleep, the kind of nap you wake up from on a summer afternoon, realizing you're sick. They stopped in front of a plaque nailed to a post beside a fenced-in pit. The plaque explained that the log lying in the pit had been, millions of years before, a towering "Redwood Giant" that had been knocked down and buried in ash by a volcanic eruption.

Big deal.

After three more pits like it, with logs like the first lying at the bottom, Craig said, "I've got to find the crapper."

His father, standing before a plaque, reading closely, waved him away without looking at him. "Go," he said.

But Scar, who was eleven then and not yet nicknamed Scar, turned with big kid eyes to Craig and said, "Don't you think this is cool?"

Craig shook his head. Maybe he rolled his eyes. He said, in a voice that he remembered consciously trying to make sound adult, "Looking at logs that have turned to stone doesn't seem much different to me than looking at logs."

As he walked away, toward the gift shop and, hopefully, the restrooms, Scar said to his back, "That's because you always decide what you think about things before you see them."

Craig's father chuckled at that and rested his hand on Scar's head as if the kid had just performed some good trick. It was how Craig knew his father thought Scar was right, and it crossed his mind then that, possibly, the thing Scar had said was something he'd overheard their father say about Craig to their mother, or to one of his writer buddies: *That son of mine, his problem is he always decides what he thinks about something before he sees it.*

Craig had turned his back to them both and muttered, "Fuck you," under his breath, and didn't bother to go back out to the path and find them after the bathroom, just waited for them at the rental car, leaning against the burning hot chrome, every once in a while yanking on the handle of the door as if it might spontaneously decide to unlock itself. He didn't speak again until that night, over dinner at some fancy restaurant in St. Helena, when some beautiful woman leaned across the table and asked him what it was like to have such a famous writer for a father.

"It sucks," Craig had said, and everyone at the table laughed as if that were a really witty response.

But that night, the night after Craig met Nicole Werner up close and personal at the threshold of his dorm room, those words of his little brother came back to him, as if on a dusty California breeze over the miles and years—and, with them, the sight of that giant redwood, turned to rock, at the bottom of that pit.

In truth, a log that had turned to rock looked nothing like a log.

The million-year-old trunk of that tree had appeared to be laced with diamonds, had seemed to be bathed in powdery pink-and-green gems. It was as if the volcanic ash, burying it, had turned it into something celestial, instead of arboreal. The pressure and the time and the isolation of death had entirely changed the nature of the thing. Had made it *eternal.* Had made it not just rock, but *space.*

Craig had already decided that Nicole Werner was a bitch, hadn't he? A dumb blonde. A tease. An empty, pretty vessel. A single glimpse in the cafeteria, and he thought he knew what she was all about.

Lying in the dark, listening to his roommate's steady breathing,

Craig knew that if he wanted, he could still let himself think that—think it and think it all the way back down the path and through the gift shop to the men's room, so to speak. But he could also still see and feel the brilliant image of her in his doorway burning against his eyelids, like something so obvious it might blind you if you really let yourself look at it.

If he slept at all that night, he didn't remember it.

It was the screaming of a blue jay that broke Craig's trance. The jay was perched on the low branch of a crabapple tree in the Godwin Honors Hall courtyard, yawping unattractively, frantically, maybe even directing its harsh warnings at Craig, who looked up at the bird for a minute as it hopped mechanically up and down the branch.

He'd never seen them arrive, but now there was a cluster of homely girls standing around the bike rack, casting furtive glances in Craig's direction. And a guy was looking out of a second-floor window at Craig, one hand on the curtain, the other absentmindedly scratching his bare stomach.

The jay made a few more threatening noises, and Craig looked at it again. He could even see one beady little eye, seeming to shine with some inner bird light from the branch, trained on him.

Craig stepped backward, nodded to the bird, and turned away.

6

"Perhaps you could write a letter to the editor?" the unhelpful receptionist said to Shelly Lockes the day she actually went down to the offices.

"This isn't my *opinion*," Shelly told her. "These are *facts*. Doesn't your paper want to publish *facts*?"

The receptionist looked at her blankly, almost as if she were blind.

"Can I see someone? An editor?" Shelly asked.

The receptionist moved her fingers around on a phone, holding the receiver to her ear, before she looked back up at Shelly and told her that there were no editors in the building ("Big convention in Chicago"), but that she would call for a reporter. The reporter who finally met with Shelly, a girl who appeared all of twenty years old, took copious notes on a yellow legal pad and nodded meaningfully at every detail—but the next article repeated the same false information:

No one knew how long Craig Clements-Rabbitt and his girlfriend, Nicole Werner, lay there in the lake of Nicole Werner's blood, or how soon afterward the young man had fled the scene.

The middle-aged woman who made the cell phone call did not give adequate information about the location of the accident for the paramedics to find it until it was too late to assist the victim.

After that, Shelly Lockes quit reading articles about the accident, and not long after that, she quit buying the newspaper altogether.

Still, she imagined there would be a trial, or some sort of investigation having to do with Craig Clements-Rabbitt, and that she might have a chance then to deliver the facts.

But by the end of the summer, she'd quit expecting that as well.

7

Omega Theta Tau," their resident advisor, Lucas, said, nodding drunkenly at the house on the hill.

Lucas owned about fourteen flasks, and had four of them on him that night—one in each pocket, except for the one in his hand. He stumbled on a sidewalk crack, and Craig laughed like it was the funniest thing he'd ever seen. Perry just kept walking. The two of them kept falling behind, and if they stopped again to piss on someone's lawn, Perry had already decided he'd just keep walking back to the dorm.

"They're *virgins*. Every last one of 'em."

"No," Craig said, and slapped his hand onto Lucas's shoulder. "No," he said again.

"Yep," Lucas said. "And they're the most beautiful fucking bitches on this campus, too."

"*No.*"

"Yep."

"That oughta be illegal. That oughta be fucking against the fucking law."

"Yep," Lucas said.

Perry looked up at the house on the hill. It was a dark, tall, rambling, and formidable brick edifice—one of those turn-of-the-century mansions with a carriage house out back and hundred-year-old oaks and elms in the yard. A white banner with black Greek letters on it fluttered between the pillars that held up the front porch. There were lace curtains in the front windows, and maybe a candle flickering behind them. Otherwise, the house looked so quiet it might have been empty—completely different from most of the fraternity and sorority houses on the row, which looked used up, neglected. Plastic cups in the driveways. Towels hung in the windows.

Perry had been at the university for only two weeks, but he'd already gotten used to seeing the parties spill out of those houses and onto the lawns. The girls, wearing soft sweaters and miniskirts, would be stumbling drunk, sprawled on the grass or in the mud. He'd seen those girls hobbling down the sidewalk back to their houses after a party—one high heel in a hand, the other on a foot, laughing or crying. The week before, someone had set fire to a frat house with a barbecue grill. One of the frat brothers had been passed out on a couch on the porch as the Fire Department sprayed down the front of the house with water, and no one had realized he was there until the fire was out and he'd been burned over 60 percent of his body.

Perry had no interest, he already knew, in Greek life. He did not want to be a fraternity brother, or to have any. Still, this sorority house on the hill seemed a part of some better, older, more elegant tradition, he thought. He could picture the sorority sisters sitting around some large oak table speaking seriously of the traditions of their house. They'd be wearing dark and sober clothes. There would be some sort of Oriental rug on the floor, a Siamese cat asleep on it. Maybe a tapestry on the wall. That candle flickering he saw from where he stood on the sidewalk, looking up at the house, would be at the center of their circle. There would be a large ancient book on the table, opened to a page that held some message from the Founding Sisters. One of the girls, her long hair falling over the text, would be reading aloud in a respectful tone.

"Somebody better go *fuck* those sluts, don't you think?" Lucas asked.

Craig was fumbling at Lucas's back pocket, trying to retrieve one of his flasks, and didn't answer.

"I *said*," Lucas shouted, and then held a hand to his mouth, shouting toward the house on the hill, "Somebody better go *fuck those Omega Theta Tau sluts!*"

A porch light snapped on.

The front door opened.

A slim silhouette with cascades of hair stepped out and stood under the light in the doorway, looking in their direction.

Craig unscrewed the flask and tipped it into his mouth, leaning his head back. Perry turned and left them there just as Lucas was taking another deep breath to shout at the house again.

Are you having fun there, honey?" his mother had asked Perry on the phone that afternoon.

He'd said yes.

She'd asked if he'd gotten the cookies she'd mailed.

He had, a few days before, but had eaten only one before Craig and Lucas finished them off in a stoned frenzy on a Wednesday night. Standing over them with the empty wax-paper-lined shoebox in his hand, he'd said, "You fucking assholes." They'd looked up at him from the floor, where they had a chessboard without enough pieces on it between them. Their eyes were so bloodshot Perry had to look away. They'd fucking eaten his mother's cookies. Fucking assholes.

To be fair, they both apologized profusely then. Stammering, ashamed. "We *are* assholes, man. You should kick our asses."

Lucas, especially, seemed horrified by his own actions, but Craig, looking into the empty shoebox, also appeared appalled. "This is unforgivable," he said, without irony. Getting stoned seemed to rinse the irony right out of Craig, although it made him a jerk in about a hundred other ways.

Perry had tossed the empty shoebox down between the two of them, taken the towel off the hook inside his closet, and gone to the shower. By the time he got back, both Lucas and Craig were gone. Craig returned a few minutes later with a package of Chips Ahoy, handing them over to Perry.

"You like these, don't you?" he asked.

Perry held the package, shaking his head wearily.

"We fucked up," Craig said. "We were only going to eat one, I swear."

"Do you always smoke so much dope?" Perry asked.

Craig seemed to think about that question for a long time, his eyebrows knitted together. But, apparently, he forgot what he'd been asked; he stripped off his clothes and got into bed without ever answering.

Talking to his mother on the phone, Perry could picture her in their kitchen at home. She'd be wearing one of her heavy, old sweaters. Jeans. She never wore shoes in the house, and didn't like slippers, so he could see her polka-dotted socks. Or the green wool ones. It would be colder up there than it was down here. In the distance, if the window was open a crack, you would be able to hear Lake Huron churning in the wind. An undulating static. There would be the smell of fish and seaweed and the metallic air that skimmed for many miles across water.

She said, "Dad and I are taking Grandpa to Dumplings tomorrow. We'll miss you."

"Have a strudel for me," Perry said. "I'll miss you guys, too. Tell Grandpa hi."

"Do you ever see Nicole Werner down there? I saw her mom at the grocery store the other day, and she said Nicole was liking school."

"Yeah," Perry said. "I see her all the time. She lives one floor down, and we're in a study group. With our roommates. She's fine."

"Any other girls there, sweetie?"

Perry cleared his throat. "Well, there are a lot of other girls here, Mom."

Perry's mother laughed softly. "Ha, ha, smart aleck," she said. "You know what I mean."

Nicole's roommate, Josie, flashed through his mind—the kind of girl he didn't like. When she looked at you, she started with your shoes before deciding whether or not to bother with the rest of you. And why she was bothering with their study group, Perry didn't know, except that maybe she was interested in Craig. Every one of her classes was something she'd already taken at the private high school she'd attended in Grosse Isle. She just rolled her eyes at her textbooks when she opened them, and said, "*This* again."

"No. No girls, Mom," Perry said.

"Well, your mama loves you. Why would you need any girls?"

She laughed again, and Perry tried to laugh, too.

"I talked to Mary the other day," she said.

"Oh."

"Just on the phone. She called to say hi. See how you were doing."

Perry snorted.

"Now, Perry, really. That's the reason she called, and I can't just hang up on her, you know. I feel sorry for that girl."

"Yeah, well . . ."

"Yeah, well, what?"

"Yeah, well, she's the one who dumped *me*, Mom. Shouldn't *I* be the one you feel sorry for?"

"I would, Perry, if you weren't down there starting your whole life when she's up here, stuck forever, having ruined her own."

"And whose fault is that?"

"Well, I think we've had this conversation before, honey. I only told you I'd spoken to her because I thought you'd want to know."

"I do. I did. It's okay, Mom. How pregnant is she?"

"Four months."

"Oh, yeah. That's right."

Of course.

For *three years*, dating Perry, Mary had virtuously clung to her virginity, never wavering in her commitment to save herself for their wedding night. Within two months of dating Pete Gerristsen, though, she was having his baby whether Pete liked it or not.

The moon followed Perry all the way back to Godwin Hall, and caused him to cast a long foreshadow stretching so far ahead that it looked like a redwood or a telephone pole was meandering down the sidewalk. There was a smell to this town, completely different from the smell of Bad Axe. Carbon emissions maybe? Not that Bad Axe didn't have cars and busses and trucks, but not centralized, like this. Not blocks and blocks of cars, parking garages, bus stops.

Perry had spent his whole life in Bad Axe, and even the summer camp he'd gone to, deep in the Hiawatha National Forest, had been within eighty miles of his own front door. He'd traveled, of course. A trip every year with his parents. Nova Scotia. Gettysburg. Washington, D.C. They'd gone to Mexico for spring break a few years before. But he'd never *lived* anywhere else. And, already, after only a couple of weeks in this college town, he was beginning to see how some of the ways he'd assumed the world worked everywhere were not the ways they worked at all.

Perry kept walking at a steady pace, following his own shadow until he'd crossed the whole campus and was back at the dorm.

"Hey."

She was standing in the entryway of Godwin Hall:

Nicole Werner, wearing jeans and a dark, bulky sweatshirt. Her hair wasn't in the usual ponytail, and looked uncombed, a bit frayed at the ends around her shoulders. He hadn't recognized her as he walked across the courtyard, and had almost walked past her without noticing. A few other girls were sitting on the cement stairs. One was talking on a cell phone. Another was smoking a cigarette. They didn't seem to be with Nicole.

"Hi, Nicole."

She shifted her weight from one leg to the other, tilted her head, and said, "How are you, Perry?"

"Great," Perry said. "You?"

She shrugged. Her shoulders looked narrower than he thought he remembered. In high school, she'd played volleyball, and he remembered being surprised, seeing her in her uniform in the gym one afternoon their junior year, that she was so muscular—not in a bad way, just sort of sturdy, sinewy, which he wouldn't have expected from such a slender girl.

But tonight, on the front steps of Godwin Honors Hall, Nicole looked like a kid. Like a *waif*, he thought. And the baggy sweatshirt. What was with that? She'd been one of the best-dressed girls at Bad Axe High, which was saying something. You might think that in a small town like that, girls wouldn't have much fashion sense. But the Bad Axe High girls, most of them anyway, *did*. They'd drive every weekend the two hours to Birch Run to go to the outlet malls, and come back wearing Calvin Klein and those other designers, looking like models, and Nicole had definitely been one of those. And up until now, when he'd seen her around campus, she'd seemed to be carrying on the tradition. Even when they were just meeting in the lounge for study group, she'd been in a neat blouse or sweater. One night, she'd even worn a skirt and sandals with heels.

Nicole wrapped her arms around herself. She looked down at her feet, which Perry was surprised to see were bare.

"I'm not so great, I guess," she said.

"What do you mean?" he asked.

Perry thought maybe she meant she had the flu or something. She *looked* like she had the flu, but maybe that was just the harsh electric light over the stairs.

"I don't know. I guess I'm having adjustment issues," she said.

"To college?" he asked.

She nodded, and made a puckery little expression with her lips. Perry hoped she wasn't going to cry. What was he supposed to do if she did? He didn't have a handkerchief on him, and he couldn't imagine giving her his shoulder, or putting his arm around her. He'd have to just stand there like an idiot, saying stupid things, until she stopped.

Unable to think of anything else to say, Perry shrugged and said, "Yeah, well. It's not like high school."

"Not that high school was so great," Nicole said.

"You always seemed pretty happy."

"I did?" She looked up at him with what appeared to be genuine surprise.

"Well. I don't know," Perry said. "Weren't you?"

"Well, I guess it was better than this," she said, looking out at the courtyard of Godwin Honors Hall. "But I hated it."

Perry snorted a little. He couldn't help it. He pictured Nicole in that bright floral dress, accepting the Ramsey Luke Scholarship from Mr. Krug, then climbing the step to the lectern to deliver her valedictorian speech about the importance of being "first and foremost moral people."

Nicole seemed to have heard the little involuntary sound he'd made, and her eyebrows sprang up. "What?" she asked, locking her eyes onto his.

Perry looked away fast, down at his own shadow stretched between them. He cleared his throat. "Well," he said, running a hand over the top of his head. "It's just that . . . well, you were the queen of the school, Nicole. You did *everything*, or *won* everything, or were *president* of it. What wasn't to like?"

She let her arms drop to her sides. Her eyes seemed to be pooling with tears.

Shit, Perry thought. She *was* going to cry.

"Are you still pissed at me about the scholarship, Perry?" she asked in a trembling voice.

"What?!" Perry took a step back, and nearly stumbled down the stairs. The girls who'd been sitting there had left; now there was only a cigarette butt where they'd been. He put his hand on his chest.

"'What?'" Nicole echoed, putting her own hand on her own chest, mocking him. She said, "Don't you know I only got the Ramsey Luke because you got every *other* award?"

Perry shook his head. He felt he could actually hear something rattling around inside his skull. He said, trying hard to sound convincing, if only to himself, "I have no idea what you're talking about."

"Oh, get off it, Perry," Nicole said. "Why are you so competitive? I mean, haven't you won enough stuff? You still have to begrudge everybody else the few bones they tossed us?"

Perry stuffed his hands in the pockets of his jeans. He was pretty sure they were shaking. He said, "Why are we having this conversation? I was just on my way to bed."

"We're having this conversation because . . ." Nicole seemed to choke on whatever she meant to say next, and then, to Perry's horror, a few fat teardrops actually spilled out of her eyes and onto her cheeks. He opened his mouth, more in protest against the tears than to say something, and then she buried her face in her hands and sobbed, "Because we're *family*. We're like *family*, Perry. You're the only person in this whole place who knows me. You've known me *forever*. You're the *only one*, and you *hate* me."

The two girls who'd been sitting on the steps had wandered back, and were now openly staring at Perry as if he'd committed some crime and was thinking he could get away with it. He looked from them back to Nicole, and then took a step toward her as slowly as he could. She started to sob more loudly. A couple of people on the other side of the doors looked out the window to see what was going on.

"Um, Nicole . . ." he said. But she didn't say anything or take her hands away from her face. He could see now that a *lot* of tears were leaking out from between her fingers, and his heart began to hammer in alarm. He'd never been around a girl *really crying* before. Mary had never cried except a kind of teary nervousness the day she dumped him, handing him his class ring with an awful little shove. Even his mother only cried when she'd been laughing too hard, too long. Desperately, he patted his pockets, although he already knew he had no tissue.

The girls who'd been smoking were still staring at him, waiting. Perry looked around, as if someone else might be able to step in for him, but no one was going to—so, although his arm felt like it weighed five hundred pounds, he managed to raise it in Nicole's direction, and to put a hand on her shoulder. She seemed to sag a little when he did this, and then sort of hopped toward him and buried her head in his chest, and then Perry had no choice but to put his hands on her back and pat it.

8

How long had he been standing there in front of Godwin Honors Hall, staring up at the room that had been Nicole's the year before?

Had he been talking to himself?

Craig was walking fast back toward his and Perry's apartment now, staring at his Converse, trying not to look around him at the people he felt pretty sure were looking at him.

On the phone, his father had said from back in New Hampshire, "You call me, bud, the second you feel like you're losing it, you hear me? I'll get there, and if I can't get there fast enough, I'll find someone who can."

Losing it.

Even his father, the famous writer, had never been able to find the right words for it—that madness, or confusion, or fog that had enveloped Craig after the accident, and had lasted for months, only to mysteriously evaporate in July when Craig simply woke up one morning, looked around, and understood, perfectly, who and where he was again.

Who was that other person who had inhabited him during those months? Had he really believed that the rehab nurse, Becky, was his grandmother, raised from the dead and fifty years younger?

"Closed head injuries can take *years* to heal," Dr. Truby had said when Craig was Craig again. "You got lucky. A few months."

Lucky.

Was he?

Craig knew where he was now, but would he ever be able to shake the sense that the other world, the one he'd spent months living in, was still there? That back in that world, animals could talk, just not with their mouths? That if you stared at the grass, it spelled messages to you in the breeze? That every blond female was some perverted version of Nicole—face twisted, or wrinkled, or made insipid to torment him?

"Synapses," Dr. Trudy said. "Misfiring."

"You were bonkers," Scar had said. "You were livin' in Creepyville, man. Welcome back."

His mother had been horrified when she discovered that his plan was to go back to school in September if they'd let him back in. She'd said the words *relapse* and *what if* about five thousand times.

"No one in this family cares what I think, but I am stating for the record that he should not go back to that horrible school," she'd said to Craig's father. She was standing in the street talking loudly to the side of the Subaru as if no one were in it. "What if . . . relapse . . . or something *worse?*"

"What could be worse?" Craig asked from the passenger seat. "I killed my girlfriend." He even managed a laugh. Beyond his mother, he could see her new boyfriend's shadow moving around behind the curtains of his parents' bedroom.

"Lynette, you're right about one thing," Craig's father had said, rolling the car window up as he said it. "No one gives a flying fuck what you think."

Craig's mother started screaming at the Subaru as they pulled away from the curb, but his father had turned up his Vivaldi, and Craig didn't hear from her again until the next week, just before they headed back out to the Midwest, when she came by his father's apartment and said— subdued, choked with emotion, spilling tears all over the place—"Just

come back the second you can't stand it anymore," as if it were a fore-
gone conclusion that it would come to that. "If . . . relapse."

"And do what?" Craig had asked. "Come back and live with you and
Scar and 'Uncle Doug,' work at the ski resort?"

His mother turned her back then, and walked out the front door,
down the stairs, and crisply back to her car, sobbing openly the whole
way, as other apartment dwellers passed her in the parking lot and
Craig watched from the balcony. For a second it had crossed his mind
to run out there after her, tackle her, press his face into her chest, and
sob, too, but she was already driving away in her Lexus before he
could.

Now he was back, and wondering if she'd been right.

He shouldn't be here.

They'd let him back in, but that didn't mean he *belonged* here.

Even Dr. Truby had seemed worried, and Dr. Truby had been, from
the beginning, all about self-empowerment and complete recovery.

"You may . . . begin . . . to have frightening recall," he'd said. "Please
phone me if you do."

The last time Craig had met with the shrink it was a hundred degrees
outside and the air-conditioning in the office was blowing in the smell
of an overheated refrigerator. He knew Dr. Truby was about to ask him,
for the ten millionth time, the same question:

"Tell me, Craig, anything you can recall at this time about the
accident."

Craig had looked down at his lap, as he always did, and then rubbed
his eyes where he saw, against his lids, a woman's face.

Unfamiliar.

It was round as a moon. She was speaking to him in a foreign language, but somehow he understood what she was saying:

Don't move the girl.

Craig looked up at Dr. Truby. He said, "I think there was a lady there."

Dr. Truby nodded. His head was shaved, and so perfectly shaped it seemed to have been made with the idea of shaving it in mind.

"And this lady . . . ?" Dr. Truby moved his hand through the air, churning it in his own direction.

Craig thought for a minute, and then said, "She told me not to move Nicole."

"And then you . . . ?" Again, the paddling. Pulling him in.

Craig had looked down at Dr. Truby's shoes. Slippers? Loafers. They looked soft and suede, not like something you could wear to walk on pavement.

"And then . . . ?"

But Craig had no words for what came after that.

After that, there were hands on him. A blow to the stomach. His head and ears were ringing. And water. Was he being baptized? There was a needle in his arm. A man in a blue uniform shouting at some flashing lights. Someone kicked him hard in the ass, and then he was stumbling. And all the time, he was trying to ask about Nicole, but the words came out so garbled he knew no one could understand him. Someone wanted to know if Craig knew his own name, and where he was, but when Craig tried to form, in his mouth, the shape of the words of her name, some-one said, in a soothing voice, "You shouldn't think about that now. You should rest. Nicole is dead."

"I don't know," Craig had said, and Dr. Truby, who must have been waiting for a long time for Craig to say more than this, leaned back in his chair, looked at the ceiling, and sighed.

9

Mira always started the semester with the story of Peter Plogojo-witz:

In 1725, in the village of Kisilova, a peasant by the name of Peter Plogojowitz died of natural causes and was buried. Within a week, nine other villagers died, and Peter Plogojowitz appeared to his wife demanding his shoes. It was widely assumed that the dead man was "walking," and that he was the cause of the other deaths, so his grave was dug up and the corpse examined.

Except for his nose having fallen away, Peter looked as good as new in his grave. His hair and beard and nails had grown. His skin had peeled away, and what looked like new, pink skin had grown beneath it. There was fresh blood in his mouth. The crowd that had gathered at the grave became enraged. A stake was driven through the peasant's heart, whereupon he shouted, bled from the ears and mouth, and acquired an erection. After that, the corpse was burned and the ashes scattered.

Peter Plogojowitz walked no more.

Several of the girls in the back row covered their mouths. One, a dark-haired beauty with nearly translucent skin, covered her whole face. A couple of boys began to laugh nervously, and some others chuckled loudly. A few of the more serious students were taking notes. Perry Edwards, the only student whose name Mira knew already, since she'd had to sign his override form, was nodding, looking at her so fixedly she felt as if he were looking *through* her.

"So," Mira said. She clapped her hands together, turned to the blackboard, and picked up a piece of chalk. Holding it up, she said to the class, "What do we learn from this anecdote about the Serbian burial practices and superstitions of the eighteenth century?"

She wrote the number one on the board, a pale wisp of white dust rising from it.

Usually, no one had a word to say at this point. Perry Edwards had his hand raised.

"Yes?" she said, nodding at him to speak.

"Apparently they believed that a dead person could get out of his grave and back into it."

Mira nodded. Next to the number one, she wrote, *The dead can escape and reenter their graves.*

"Two?" she asked.

There was a moment of polite silence before, again, Perry Edwards raised his hand.

"The dead who can do this don't decay?" he asked.

Mira wrote on the board: *2. The "walking dead" do not decay as expected.*

"And they cause other deaths," Perry said without raising his hand this time. As Mira was writing this down, he continued. "They drink blood? They can be killed a second time, more completely?"

Mira wrote these down as well, and then: *6. These creatures are sexual in nature.*

As Mira knew they would, the girls in the back with their hands over their mouths giggled, and the boys who'd chuckled before chuckled again. But Perry Edwards just held her gaze so long that, finally, Mira was the one who had to look away.

10

Craig tried hard not to stare at Nicole Werner while she studied, but the way her hair slipped over her face when she cast her eyes down on her *History of the English Language* textbook, and the way the highlighter in her right hand flashed over the pages, and even the way her foot seemed to tap out some rhythm for four or five seconds, then stop, was so much more riveting than the book he was reading that he couldn't look away.

If she knew he was watching her, she was pretending she didn't.

Perry had found a study room for them in the basement of Godwin Hall—an old lounge tucked away behind a storage room, with dust-covered chairs and maroon carpeting. There was a brass plaque on the door that read, THE ALICE MEYERS MEMORIAL STUDENT STUDY ROOM, and although it looked like no one had used the room for years for anything but furtive sex (empty condom wrappers were stuffed into a glass vase that was otherwise full of plastic flowers), it was really a very comfortable room.

There were no light bulbs in any of the lamps, so they'd brought down their own desk lamps from their dorm rooms and set them up on the end tables. The dim, focused light was intense and relaxing at the same time. Perry sat at a table in the corner, one elbow on each side of an open book. Nicole was curled up in a cushioned chair with a battered ottoman. Her roommate, Josie Reilly, sat on the floor with her back to the wall, legs folded in the lotus position as if her body were made of clay. Craig lay on the couch, watching Nicole over the edge of his book as she flipped a page and bit her lower lip.

He had thought a study group would entail talking. Quizzing. The sharing of test-taking tips. Maybe flash cards. He'd never been in a study group before so had no way of knowing that it meant, simply, a circle of companionable silence, concentration—except for the occasional yawn, the clearing of a throat, Nicole's dainty sneeze, Josie's distracted "Bless you." It crossed Craig's mind, when the silence grew so thick that you could have reached into the air and grabbed a handful of it, to crack a joke. But he didn't know what the joke would be. It would have to be incredibly funny to warrant the interruption, and he wasn't really that funny unless there was something to be made fun of, and nothing here seemed stupid enough to make the kind of joke Craig usually got a good laugh out of—the kind of comment that got him in trouble in high school or had Scar snorting chocolate milk out of his nose at the dinner table.

Now and then, their desk lamps flickered. (Maybe one of the washing machines in the laundry room next to the lounge had started its spin cycle and sucked up all the electricity in the basement for a minute.) Briefly, Nicole looked up to the ceiling, and then back down. She highlighted something else on the page she was reading, and then she took the pencil out of the place in her hair where she'd tucked it and wrote something quickly in the margin.

You make me sick!"

Randa Matheson had screamed that at him in her parents' bedroom one afternoon after school. She was naked, standing at the edge of the bed, screaming down at Craig, who was lying on his back with a hard-on, wondering, What? What? Where did *this* come from?

"Huh?" he finally managed to ask.

"I said," Randa shouted, "that you *make me sick.*" She enunciated each word as if she were shouting to a foreigner, a retard. Her dark eyes were narrowed, and her lips, bloated and red from all the kissing they'd been doing, made her look exactly like her mother, whose face was well known to anyone who watched reruns of a very stupid sitcom from the late seventies.

"What? What did I do?"

"Just forget it," Randa snapped, pulling her thong up over her narrow hips, hiding her perfectly trimmed pussy, which made his hard-on throb even harder, before she turned and ran from the room, holding her jeans and her shirt against her breasts. Behind her, the door slammed so loudly Craig flinched and closed his eyes, thinking for a split second that maybe he'd been shot.

After a while, he got dressed and let himself out.

The Mathesons' house was immaculate, and enormous, and he got lost on his way out, finding himself in some kind of sunroom with no door. Randa herself was nowhere to be seen.

For months afterward Craig wondered what he had done, although it didn't really occur to him to call Randa or to stop her in the hallway and ask. The day after the "incident," his mother pulled her car up next to Randa's empty Jeep in the parking lot of the Trading Post. Craig slumped down in the passenger seat. "What's the matter with you?" his mother asked. Luckily, she realized then that she'd forgotten her purse, so they didn't stay.

But it was impossible not to cross Randa's path. In school. At parties. At the video store. At first, Craig tried not to look directly at her, hoping to avoid her eyes, but after a while it became clear that she was treating him as if he were invisible, so it wouldn't have mattered what he did anyway. In the stairwell one day between classes, just the two of them passed each other (she was going up, he was going down) and, stupidly, he sputtered out, "Hey."

She looked right at him, seeming to register nothing. Not the vaguest hint of an expression crossed her face. She was looking *through* his head, seeing nothing but the wall behind it.

He tried, now and then, to think about what could have happened, what he'd done or failed to do.

They'd been kissing, he was clear on that, and the shirts had come off, and then the jeans—around their thighs at first, and then around their ankles, and then on the floor—and then he'd eased that thong down her silky legs while she ran her fingers over one of his eyebrows. He'd stood up and pulled his own underwear off, and she'd sort of propped herself up to look at him, and asked, "Do you like me?"

Craig was fairly certain that his answer to the question had been yes (why wouldn't it have been?), but the question was followed by a long, fast series of other questions, and he was less sure of what his answers to those had been.

Do you think Michelle has better tits, who's the skinniest girl you ever had sex with, have you ever had sex with Melody, when did you first notice me, is Tess the one you really want, are you using me to get to her, did you just come over here this afternoon because you were hoping you were going to have sex with me?

Craig had gotten back into bed beside her and lay there with his throbbing hard-on, until finally he interrupted her, and said, "Are we going to fuck or what?" And that's when she'd leapt out of bed and screamed at him.

Craig had hardly been within a few feet of a girl since that day with Randa. The whole summer after graduation had passed without a flirtation, let alone a kiss.

Now he closed his eyes and let the image of Nicole Werner—only two feet away from him—linger on his lids for a minute. He tried to picture her in Fredonia, carrying on a conversation with someone's actress turned mother or millionaire father strutting around in a suit with nowhere to go but the Trading Post.

No.

He could not picture Nicole Werner anywhere he'd ever been before this minute.

Nicole Werner belonged *here*, now, in the lounge of Godwin Honors College.

Virgin valedictorian, daughter of the Dumplings's owners.

Probably that gold chain around her neck held a crucifix dangling somewhere down between her perfect, untouched breasts, in the powder-scented shadows of her plain cotton bra and flowery blouse. At night, she probably said prayers and probably cuddled up to her stuffed monkey. Maybe back in eleventh grade she'd let some asshole grope her ass and stick his tongue in her mouth, but she'd never sauntered out of her parents' hot tub stark raving nude, stoked up on Ecstasy, and invited every guy from Fredonia High at the party to stick his dick in her—a not-uncommon event back home.

Nicole Werner had never even been to a party like that. She'd never *heard* of a party like that. They did not, Craig felt certain, have parties like that in Bad Axe.

She sneezed again—a dainty sneeze, all consonants and *wheee!*—and Craig opened his eyes.

She was looking back at him with a tissue held to her nose.

I'm sorry, she mouthed.

God bless you, he mouthed back.

11

Shelly went over it again every morning in her mind, and every night before she went to bed. She thought about it as she drove to work and as she sat behind her desk. When the telephone rang, the sound sometimes startled her. She forgot she was in her office, that she had a phone on her desk that might ring.

First, she'd remember the car, solidifying her own description of it in her mind:

Dark colored. Two door.

Then, the familiar road:

A semirural highway. Two lanes, north and south, just on the outskirts of town. She'd driven that road a million times before, and had driven it a hundred times since.

That time, she'd been listening to a country station—a guilty pleasure. (If anyone she worked with at the Chamber Music Society knew her secret, she might not actually be fired, but she'd be chastised so relentlessly she'd eventually have to quit. Sure, it was a free country, but not when it came to certain aesthetic preferences or political opinions and you happened to work at the Chamber Music Society at the university.) One of her favorite country stars was singing about how great it was to live in the U.S.A., and Shelly was singing along.

She remembered the yellow line down the middle of the road.

She remembered noting the small, dark-colored car that was just far enough ahead of her that she didn't need to pay much attention to it. It wasn't going fast. There were no other cars on the road.

As she sang the words to the country song along with the radio, she realized for the first time (although she'd heard the song a hundred times) that the subtext of it was that if you didn't like it in the U.S.A., you should leave.

Personally, Shelly Lockes more or less agreed. Her big brother had been killed in Vietnam. Her parents had never gotten over it and had died young of the kind of diseases the grief-stricken die of: heart attack for her father, stomach cancer for her mother.

Still, Shelly was wondering to herself even as she sang the catchy lyrics at the top of her lungs, if you did decide to leave the U.S.A., where would you go? If you were able to think of a country that appealed to you more, would they be willing to let you in? What if, afterward, you wanted to come back?

Then the red lights of the car ahead of her swerved, and blinked, and seemed to dance in the air for a few wild seconds. And then they vanished.

How many hundreds of hours had she logged on Google by now, searching for information on the accident? The girl. The boy. The "investigation," which seemed to have ended before it ever began.

But every hit Shelly came across that wasn't the local paper's colorful misinformation had something to do with the cherry trees in the memorial orchard at the dead girl's sorority, or quoted sappy things her sorority sisters had to say about her purity. Shelly plugged in her own name, and found nothing. She plugged in the date and *accident* and, on a whim, *the truth*. Nothing. She plugged in *the truth* and the name of Nicole Werner's sorority, and came up with one surprising detail about a music school student, a violinist named Denise Graham, who'd disappeared in the spring, right around the time of the accident—and many of the same sorority sisters who were quoted as saying that Nicole was "the sweetest girl who ever lived" said of the disappeared violinist, "She was really aloof and strange. No one ever got to know her."

It almost seemed staged, this juxtaposition, as if to prove that Nicole had, indeed, been an angel in the guise of a sorority girl—the proof being that this other one's life was of such little concern to anyone. If she'd ever been located, there was nothing about it on the Internet that Shelly could find.

S helly?"

Josie was standing in the threshold, wearing her usual surprised expression. It had taken Shelly three months of working with this girl before she realized that Josie wasn't actually *surprised* by anything, ever. That the expression was some kind of amusement—perhaps at someone else's expense. Perhaps Shelly's.

"Yes?"

"Would it be okay with you if I went down to Starbucks? Espresso fix? I could get you something?"

"That's fine. Go ahead. But I don't need anything."

"You sure?"

"I'm sure."

After Josie had clipped away in her little hard-soled shoes, Shelly went back to the file she'd opened on her computer—numbers surging electrically, shimmering, seeming for the moment to be unrecognizable as anything but shapes and dots. She rubbed her eyes and leaned back in her chair, and after she thought it had been long enough for Josie to get down the stairs and out to the street, she looked out the window, found Josie among the hundreds of other students passing (between classes) on the sidewalk, and then watched her sway along the sidewalk with her hands tucked into the pockets of her cashmere hoodie, threading her elegant way toward Starbucks.

The girl's back was straight, and her long, dark hair whipped around her face. She was gorgeous. As Josie crossed the street, Shelly saw two guys turn around to watch her, and although Shelly was too far away to see their faces, she could see that they were nudging one another the way guys did when they were talking about a girl's body. Josie bent over and picked something up—a dropped coin?—and put it in her pocket, and then ran her hand through her beautiful hair. The two guys had a hard time walking straight while craning their necks around to observe her ass. Shelly turned back to her computer screen.

She dreaded it, but she was going to have to fire Josie Reilly, who'd worked in the office only since July. She was the most unreliable work-study student Shelly'd ever had, and had gotten hired because, frankly, it was hard to find work-study students living on campus during the summer months. Josie had also seemed so intelligent, so composed, during her interview, that Shelly had been genuinely impressed.

But now, nearly every afternoon, there were guys hanging around in the lobby waiting for her more than an hour before she was supposed to get off work—cracking jokes, talking about parties—until, finally, exhausted by her own annoyance, Shelly would say, "You can leave early if you want to, Josie," to which Josie never objected.

Then, each Monday, the one day Josie was supposed to come into the office in the morning, she never failed to stumble in an hour late, apologizing profusely but always with that amused look on her face.

And, inexcusably, a few weeks earlier, Shelly had found the expense-reimbursement form for the Marymount String Quartet, which was supposed to have been submitted a month before, collecting dust under Josie's desk. There was a doodle of a shoe on the back of the form—a high heel with straps and buckles. "Oh, my God!" Josie shrieked when Shelly waved the piece of paper at her, but she offered no real explanation, just a series of false-sounding self-recriminations, and there was always that look on her face.

It was true that all of Shelly's work-study students over the years had been bad, and she'd tried repeatedly to make a case to the dean that what she needed was a *real* assistant, but every year they foisted a new work-study kid on her. They were all sloppy, unreliable, and empty-headed, for the most part, but Josie Reilly was perhaps the worst. She barely even made an effort to *pretend* she was making an effort.

Shelly looked back out the window just in time to see her come out of Starbucks with a cup in each hand.

She always did that.

Shelly always told Josie she didn't want anything, and Josie always brought her something anyway. It would have seemed thoughtful if it didn't somehow also seem like an afterthought, as if Josie had gotten to the Starbucks with no recollection whatsoever of what Shelly had answered when she'd asked her if she wanted anything.

As Josie crossed the street back to the Chamber Music Society offices, she glanced up and Shelly ducked away from the window, looking back at her computer fast, feeling her cheeks flush, her heart beating in embarrassment.

Josie Reilly seemed to her to be precisely the kind of sorority girl who would assume that because Shelly was a lesbian she was attracted to *her*. She was, Shelly thought, precisely the kind of girl who went through the world assuming *everyone* was attracted to her.

Josie would assume she was being watched by her boss from the window of her office because she was so irresistible. She would come back into the offices bearing that paper cup of hot chocolate, or mint tea, or peppermint chai, and Shelly was going to have to look into her amused expression without batting an eye, and take it from her, and thank her, and offer to pay her the outrageous three or four dollars it had cost. And, this time, because she'd been caught watching the girl cross the street—horny old dyke in a position of power at a university so sensitive to such matters that the very air around them felt censored, as if it had actually become possible to neuter the *mind*—Shelly would now have to wait at least another week before she fired her.

12

The twins threw themselves onto the living room floor—Andy on his butt, Matty on his face—when Mira walked in the door. It was a part of the routine.

She came back from her teaching and her office in the afternoons, and they wept and screamed for a solid hour while Clark stomped around the apartment. When she asked him if they'd been fussy during the day, he shook his head with his lips sealed tightly, letting her know that this behavior had to do with *her*, and was, therefore, her problem.

But what, she wondered, did it mean? Were the boys weeping with excitement because she was back, or crying with their just-realized grief that she'd been gone? Mira's terrible suspicion was that they'd longed to cry all day, but because their father seemed either so unsympathetic in his weariness or so close himself to cracking, they'd suppressed it until she came home.

She pulled off her shoes and sat down on the floor, and gathered them to her. Matty opened his mouth and sucked onto her kneecap, sobbing. Andy grabbed a fistful of her hair, stuffed it into his mouth, and wept into her neck. "Clark?" Mira called to him over their sobbing.

She needed a glass of water but couldn't risk standing up yet, having to disengage the twins.

He didn't answer.

"Clark?"

Mira had grown up in a traditional family. Her father sold insurance all day while her mother slammed doors and screamed at the kids. Mira had little idea what her mother did with those precious hours when they were at school. Early on she'd imagined her lying on her bed staring at the ceiling, hands crossed over her chest until she heard the school bus pull up to the curb at 3:45.

Later Mira considered other possibilities: A secret life of some sort. Not a lover, surely, but maybe a group of friends to whom her mother confided, over neighborly cups of tea, the disappointments of her marriage, her difficulty with her children. Or maybe she read romance novels, bodice-rippers she kept hidden around the house. Maybe she pursued some passion Mira hadn't considered: bird watching, poetry-writing.

But no sooner had Mira turned twenty, the age at which she might actually have gotten to *know* this stranger who'd raised her, than her mother died, and the only genuinely revealing scene of her childhood she could remember with clarity was an afternoon when she'd had to stay home from school, suffering as she was from such debilitating menstrual cramps that even her mother, who had no patience at all for female-related troubles, had to admit that Mira looked green, and let her stay in bed.

That afternoon, Mira was fourteen. She'd gone straight back to bed after breakfast and slept until noon, and then she'd woken up to a silent house, and tiptoed into the hallway.

Why had she tiptoed? Had she *expected* to find her mother doing something she wouldn't want her daughter to witness?

Whatever the reason for it, Mira could still remember her sense of being on a furtive mission—the way she'd stepped gingerly over the floorboard that creaked, and then how she'd slid, rather than stepped, down the hallway in her socks.

Their house was small. There were only three bedrooms, one of which her brothers had to share (an endless source of conflict: *Why does she get her own room?*) She moved from the hallway's bare floorboards to the living room's orange shag with only the vaguest of whispered footsteps, and then peered around the corner, to the living room.

Her mother wasn't there.

She'd held her breath as she passed under the low arched doorway of the dining room, separated from the kitchen by a swinging door (one side of which would no longer swing, since either Bill or Frank—neither of whom would admit to it—had pulled it off the door frame by hanging from it, and because their father, who had no carpentry skills, also refused to hire anyone to do any work around the house.) If her mother was behind that door, she was standing too still to be detected.

Mira pushed open the side that still opened, and stepped into the kitchen.

Nothing.

Only her mother's half-empty coffee cup on the counter, with a bright red imprint of her lips on the rim.

Mira touched the cup. It was cold.

There were only two other places in the house her mother could be, Mira knew: the half-finished basement (except that Mira didn't hear the washer or dryer) or the walk-in pantry. They had only one car, and her father would have taken it to work, so unless her mother had walked into town (unthinkable, as she didn't even own a pair of real walking shoes, and it had rained that morning, so there would be puddles, and what would she do in their small town anyway?), she had to be in the house.

Perhaps, Mira thought, her mother was alphabetizing soup cans in the pantry or checking expiration dates. There was one bare bulb in the pantry, and the space was large enough, even crammed as it was with cans and jars and boxes of pasta and Pop Tarts and Frosted Flakes, that her mother might comfortably stand inside it or even sit on a chair if she wanted to, looking around, making lists.

Mira walked to the door and put her hand on the warm solidity of the fake brass knob, and had the sure sense of something beyond the door. But what? Not her mother, exactly, but some suppressed energy, some barely perceptible movement, some silent intense activity, like cell growth or furtive sex. It crossed Mira's mind that there might be someone behind that door who was not her mother at all—or that her mother might be in there *with* someone.

She hesitated, and then pulled the door open so quickly she felt a rush of wind on her face and neck, and the bright overhead light nearly blinded her after the darkness of the hallway, and she gasped when her mother turned around, seeming less bathed in that light than emitting it, standing as she was in the center of the pantry, directly under the one bare bulb, wearing what looked to Mira at first like some kind of white choir robe made of feathers, or giant wings wrapped around her body, eyes closed but lips and cheeks vividly, garishly, painted red (although in real life Mira's mother wore makeup only on Sundays, for church, or on the rare weekend nights Mira's father took her out to dinner). Her skin looked wet, coated with dew or sweat, and Mira got a quick but definite impression that her mother had just hatched or was in the process of hatching, or being born, or being reanimated after death.

Mira froze in the doorway, hand flat against her chest, heart pounding into her palm. Her mother slowly opened her eyes and said, "Mira?" in a voice a hundred times softer and more full of patience and motherly affection than Mira had ever heard it.

"Mama?"

"Yes?"

"Are you—?"

"What, sweetheart?"

Mira took a step backward, and her mother simply pulled the door closed again between them, and Mira hesitated for only a second or two before returning quickly to her room and getting back into her bed where she belonged.

As the years passed, like so many other incidents from childhood and adolescence, that moment became a confused vision in her memory, and often Mira would think she'd simply dreamed the whole thing, or hallucinated it. (Was it possible the Tylenol she'd taken that morning had codeine in it? Could she have had, in addition to her period, a fever?) But she also never lost the sense that she'd stumbled upon a deep secret that day, a secret in the pantry as well as in her mother, and the distant, irrational suspicion that her mother spent her days in the pantry regenerating, *reanimating*, shedding cells and making new ones, would make its way into Mira's dreams for years, until it eventually entered her conscious life, permanently, when her mother succumbed to the breast cancer she must surely have known she had that day in the pantry—must have known she'd had for *years*. (The physicians who were eventually rounded up to treat her expressed shock and horror that an illness that might have been successfully addressed had been ignored, or concealed, or borne in silence for so long.)

At the funeral parlor on a cool April afternoon, Mira looked down at her mother in the white coffin and remembered that glimpse of her in the pantry in the flush on her mother's cheeks, the ghoulishly painted red lips, the cool, waxy film of her skin, and the smell of the embalming fluid.

By then, it would seem like a century since that day in the pantry and the diagnosis that had followed a few months later. The breast cancer went on for what seemed like another lifetime, straight through Mira's high school prom, and then through her graduation (which no one had expected her mother to live to see), and then through her first and second years of college—during which there were four or five exhausting Greyhound bus rides home, because it seemed her mother was in her last days—until, in her sophomore year, just before final exams, Mira's father called to say that they again expected her mother to die within a few days and that she shouldn't *rush* home, but . . .

So, as it happened, her mother died while Mira was scrawling a response to question number eight: "In Jung's consideration of *synchronicity*, he establishes that *tertium comparationis* is *meaning*. Explain."

As her mother left this world, Mira was sitting hunched in an auditorium trying to describe the way an outer event and an inner event might bear equal significance, and the example she'd used was of a woman being reminded one day, by a song on the radio, of a boy she used to love but hadn't seen or thought of in many years, and then coming across his obituary in a newspaper she did not ordinarily read.

The next week, looking down at her mother in her coffin bathed in funeral home light, it would all come together—the memory and the precognition, the symbolism and the folklore, inherent in that day years earlier when Mira, in her own delirium and bleeding, had come upon her mother in the pantry, and had seen not only her mother's death in it but also, in a flash, the trajectory of her own career.

Within a few weeks of her mother's funeral, Mira had read *The American Way of Death*, and then, of course, eventually, she'd read every book ever written on the traditions and rites and superstitions related to the decomposition and reanimation of the body, until she finally ran out of books to read, and began to write one herself.

With his Nikes in his hands, Clark stood above Mira and said, "Maybe you could take care of their dinner tonight? I've had it. I'm going for a run."

"Clark," she said, looking up at him—that body, which, one lazy Saturday long ago, after a hot bubble bath, she'd licked the sinewy length of from the tip of the big toe to the crown of the head—and tried not to let her gaze linger on the belly, which was both slack and bulging. (How was it that Clark had recently taken on the physical attributes of a person who had given birth to twins when there was no longer a shred of evidence of it on Mira herself?) She tried to hold his eyes and to keep a steady tone of unexcited objectivity in her voice, even as Matty sank his incredibly sharp new teeth into the flesh of her thigh, as she said, "I have an Honors College thesis committee meeting tonight, Clark. I have to leave in an hour. I told you that this morning."

He turned from her then, and before she even realized he'd thrown them, the running shoes had sailed across the living room and knocked over their only nice lamp, which Mira could hear shattering even before it hit the coffee table, and the twins began to shriek with what seemed to be all of the hysterical energy of human history channeling itself through their lungs.

13

It was not a dorm known for its great parties, to say the least, but there was a tradition in Godwin Honors Hall of throwing one big blowout the Friday night after midterms.

Craig had, himself, only one exam (Political Science) and a paper due (Great Books). He'd already tracked down on the Internet a "model" for the paper, and had begun to sketch out some tentative plans for the model's rebirth as his own term paper. The Poli-Sci exam seemed like no big deal. He'd just make it a priority to go over the outline at the back of the book the morning before the test.

Apparently, his fellow students had harder schedules, or approached their studies differently. Beginning the weekend before midterms, Godwin had become a ghost hall, and Perry barely darkened the doorway of their room except to sleep for a few hours in the early morning before he was gone again.

("Where you been, man?" Craig asked him in passing, to which Perry replied, "The library. Studying," as if it were a given.)

Even the cafeteria was silent. Instead of the usual clusters, people sat separately, absentmindedly lifting forkfuls of eggs or baked beans to their mouths while staring intently into the textbooks open beside their plates. Craig watched as one kid accidentally speared the page of his book instead of the meatloaf on his plate, and then even brought the fork halfway to his mouth before realizing there was nothing on it.

Jesus Christ. No wonder his father had had to call on his old buddy Dean Fleming to get Craig into this place. These were not his people.

They were an entirely different species. Back in Fredonia there'd been professional students, for sure, but theirs had been such a casual superiority that Craig never bothered to pay any attention to how they were doing it. They just waltzed out of their Advanced Placement courses fluttering the A-pluses on their exams, sauntered down the hallway to the meetings of the clubs they were presidents of, or grabbed their violins and headed off to the orchestra room.

That these Godwin Honors College kids worked so hard both frightened and puzzled Craig, and made it even more impossible for him to imagine, somehow, joining them at the library. So far the only thing he'd done at the library was check out an armload of CDs, which he'd downloaded to his laptop.

"Are we going to meet this week?" Craig asked as Perry stumbled past him on his way to the shower in the middle of midterm week.

"Huh?"

"Study group?"

"We've *been* meeting," Perry said.

"When?" Craig asked.

"At the library," Perry said. "*Constantly.*"

"Why didn't anybody tell me?" Craig asked.

"I don't know," Perry said. "I guess we figured if you wanted to study you'd be at the library." The two of them looked at each other blankly, and then Perry grabbed his towel and was basically gone again until Friday night.

Craig's paper looked pretty good, he thought. He'd gone way out of his way to make sure no series of words in any given sentence could be Googled to reveal his source. He also thought his Political Science exam had gone well, though it concerned him a bit that he'd finished it so much more quickly than the other twenty-two students in the class, who were still chewing the erasers at the ends of their pencils as Craig handed his test in and grabbed his backpack (making as little noise as possible, but, still, a couple of girls on either side of his seat looked up from their papers and glared at him).

It had been a bright October afternoon. Blue sky, red and yellow leaves, green grass. A very distant and watery-looking half-moon was hanging over it all.

It was Thursday, so he went looking for Lucas, to get high. On Thursday afternoons they usually met in the arboretum with their stashes and smoked weed until it was time to go back to the hall for dinner, but this Thursday even Lucas seemed to be off somewhere studying, so Craig smoked up what he had alone, and then he went to Village Corners, flashed his fake ID at the fat man behind the counter, bought himself a fifth of Jack Daniels, and headed back to the deserted dorm.

He was feeling, for no reason he could pinpoint, the kind of vague depression he'd felt on and off for years, but which had lifted last summer (forever, he'd hoped). It had been bad, the few weeks right after graduation, when the sense that he should be happy, and proud of himself, somehow made him want to cry all the time (although he never did). It had been June, he'd graduated from high school, he was on his way to college, and his dad kept telling him he was going on to greatness and better things and should be excited, and the fact that he *wasn't* happy, proud, or excited made his arms feel tired all the time, as if he were carrying around a big block of cement.

The first "episode," as his family doctor would come to call these periods of depression, came on him when he was fourteen, in Belize. A famous movie director was trying to woo Craig's dad into selling him the rights to his most successful novel, *The Jaguar Operation*, and it was supposed to be his dad's special treat for Craig, taking just him along, leaving Craig's mother and Scar in New Hampshire.

Craig was only partly fooled by this. He knew his mother hated going on these kinds of trips with his father. She hated the drinking, the schmoozing, the phony bonhomie, and the competition from younger women smitten with the famous writer, leaning across the dinner table with their silverware held high so that their cleavage practically spilled onto his plate. His mother would have turned down the invitation to Belize anyway, and Scar didn't go anywhere without their mother unless he was forced.

Still, stepping out of the tiny jet that had been sent for them in Miami—just ahead of his father, a breeze wafting around them that was both fragrant and heavy with the smell of dead things rotting in seawater—when the famous director took off his straw hat and whooped, and an actress Craig recognized from a movie he'd seen the week before on HBO smiled with brilliant familiarity, Craig felt privileged, and thrilled.

He was the famous writer's kid.

"Hey," the director said, "you must be the famous kid!"

The Caribbean was an amazing blue backdrop to the director's resort. Twenty thatched bungalows lined the beach, a kidney-shaped pool behind them, and green miles of jungle behind that. Smiling people with beautiful bodies sauntered around the sand paths in bright little bathing suits, sipping drinks. A few fat gray iguanas dragged their tails between the bungalows, and in the jungly distance Craig heard the screaming of crazed-sounding birds. While the director led his father around, Craig sat poolside downing one after another of the rum punches a grumpy Belizean man old enough to be Craig's grandfather brought to him on a tray.

He was completely plastered by the time his father and the director came back, laughing companionably. The wind had picked up, and the thrashing of the jungle and the Caribbean surf together made a deafening roar around Craig's head, pummeling his ears, making it impossible to hear the conversations taking place around him at the dinner table. The meal itself was one unrecognizable dish after another, spooned up by the same angry-seeming black man, whom the director called Handsome Man.

No one else seemed deafened by the wind. There was a beautiful young woman on either side of the director, and one sitting across from

Craig's father, and the conversations they were having seemed both lighthearted and intense, as if they could hear and understand one another. But even when the Belizean man leaned down and spoke directly into his ear, Craig had to ask three times before he understood: "Are you finished? Will you want more? Cream sauce or broth?"

Craig's father shouted across the table to him, "Fred here says if it's not too windy tomorrow we'll go out to the barrier reef and swim with the sharks. What do you think about that?"

Craig had somehow managed to hear this proposition. "Wow!" he said. "Yeah! Sure!"

The director and Craig's father laughed.

"The boy wants to swim with the sharks!" The director raised his glass. The young women all laughed, and then stared at Craig for several seconds as their smiles faded. It was as if they'd just noticed he was there, that the fact of the writer's adolescent son had just occurred to them, and that they weren't necessarily happy about it.

Craig flushed. One of the women said something to him then, but over the wind he couldn't hear it. He shrugged. She laughed again, even less enthusiastically. He looked down at his plate. It was gone.

He woke the next morning with a throbbing headache and had to lie very still under the thwacking ceiling fan, willing himself not to open his eyes until the bed had stopped spinning. He could hear the wind rattle the thatch overhead and the sound of waves crashing in the distance. He sat up and heaved, once, dryly, before getting his hand around a bottle of water on the nightstand and drinking it down. After he'd managed to stand for a minute or two on his rubbery legs, he wove his way out of the thatched hut to find his father sitting at a glass table with the director, the old black man pouring coffee into their cups.

"Are we going to swim with the sharks?" he asked.

Both Craig's father and the director looked up. They had obviously been having a serious conversation, maybe a disagreement. Neither of them looked happy to see Craig.

"Sorry, kid. Too windy to get out there," the director said, holding up his hand as if offering the wind for proof. Over the Belizean man's head, a ferny tree was leaning so far over it looked like it would be torn up by the roots and blown into the sea.

Craig couldn't help it: He was far from home, fourteen, hung over, and exhausted, and the idea of facing a long day alone at the side of the pool being waited on by the black man, deafened by the wind, ignored by the director and his women, eating little muscled things in coconut sauce, hit him like a punch in the gut. (Why had his father brought him here? Maybe, it occurred to Craig for the first time, simply to placate his mother, to make it seem less likely that he was going to the famous director's resort in Belize for the attentions of the young women she knew would be there.) "Oh, *man*," he whined.

A grim shadow passed over the director's face. He said something to Craig that Craig couldn't hear again over the wind, and then looked up at Craig's father and said, more loudly, "Unless the Great American Writer here can do something about the wind!"

Craig's father strained to smile. He looked up to the sky. He tapped his fingernails on the glass top of the table, something he did when he was being criticized by Craig's mother, and then shouted, "Cease, wind! I command you!" The director guffawed and looked over at Craig with a genuine sneer.

It didn't happen right away, but it happened.

Within a half hour, the air had grown eerily calm. Craig was sitting cross-legged on the beach, staring glumly out at the crashing surf, when suddenly the churning bath of the wind around his head stopped. A pelican that had been pumping its wings strenuously through the air over the ocean began to glide effortlessly, and Craig could hear again. There was hearty laughter coming from somewhere behind him, and he turned to see the director clapping his father on the back hard enough that the impact of it registered on his father's face as annoyed surprise.

"Let's go, Miracle Guys!"

·············

The old black man drove the boat over the placid pale blue ocean while Craig's father and the director drank beer in the back. They seemed no longer to be on speaking terms. Craig sat up front, and the ocean sprayed him in the face with a fine, spitty mist. The Belizean man cut the engine in what seemed to be simply an undefined spot in the middle of the Caribbean, specific nevertheless, and then he turned to Craig and nodded. "Here," he said. "Put on your snorkel equipment."

"Have fun, pal," the director said, raising a brown bottle to him. "Been nice knowin' ya!"

Craig's father laughed, but looked uneasy. He stood up with his beer in his fist and looked over the edge of the boat, and Craig, struggling to pull his fins over his feet, felt his enthusiasm for swimming with sharks drain out of him as the Belizean man reached into a cooler, pulled out a handful of bloody fish pieces, and tossed them into the sea.

The chunks floated along the surface for a few seconds, and then there was a roiling of the water beneath them, and then they were gone, and Craig saw beneath the unearthly aqua blue two long black shadows, side by side, moving in awesome silence, each one longer than a tall man. The Belizean man threw another handful of fish into the water, and it never even floated, just disappeared in an instant into a mob of shadows.

"Is this safe?" Craig's father asked the Belizean man, who shrugged his bony shoulders.

The director said, "I've done it myself a million times. Never even been nipped."

There was, Craig realized now, something sinister about the director. (Was it possible that the irises of his eyes had no pupils?)

Craig looked away from him, swallowed, put on his snorkeling mask, and stood, but his father reached out and took him by the arm. "Whoa, wait a second there, son," he said.

"Let him go!" the director shouted. "The boy wants to swim with the sharks!"

It was then that Craig understood what was going on, that the director had cast him in a role: impetuous, spoiled, foolhardy boy.

The sharks rose closer to the surface of the water again, their shadows made of flesh circling over and around one another, and Craig instinctively took a step back, into his father's arms.

"Forget it, son," his father said. "You don't need to do this. I won't let you do this."

Craig turned around, and the Belizean man was looking at him with an expression that was impossible to read.

"Let's go," his father said, and the Belizean man started the boat, and Craig sat back down and took his flippers off.

Back at the resort, he drank rum punch by the side of the pool until everyone else had gone to bed, and got so drunk that the stars seemed to be blowing around in the completely windless black air over him, like moths or silvery ashes. He got up to replenish his punch only to find that someone had locked up the tiki bar, so he stood with his empty plastic cup under the stars and listened to the calm, distant pounding of the surf against its barriers. He tilted his head back and tried to drink the very last drops from his empty cup, lost his balance in the sand, and fell on his ass with a soft thud, and then he sat there for a few minutes and laughed at himself, held up the plastic cup to the stars the way the director had raised his beer bottle to him back on the boat. "Been nice knowin' ya!" he shouted, and waited for an echo.

It didn't come.

The tropical air was like cotton, soaking up his voice.

Craig shouted again, looking around to see if anyone was there to hear him, and saw then, at the edge of the boat dock, a light. He stood up, leaving the plastic cup on the sand, and stumbled toward it.

It was a kid. Maybe Craig's age. He had a flashlight at his feet and a net. He cast the net off the end of the dock, and Craig stood behind him, watching it float loosely in the clear water and then sink under, and then the kid pulled it out, heavy with thrashing small silver-dollar-size fish, which the kid dumped into the bottom of the boat in which the Belizean man had taken them to the sharks that afternoon.

"Hey," Craig said, feeling suddenly much drunker in the hallucinatory darkness. The boy was so completely ignoring him that Craig felt as if he might be dreaming the boy, or that the boy was dreaming him.

The boy cast his net back out into the water, although there was still a fish in it, caught in the strings, wriggling.

"What are you doing?" Craig asked, and then the kid turned to look at him. His dark skin made his eyes even brighter in the light shining up from the flashlight at his feet.

"Fishing," he said.

"Yeah," Craig said. "I guess so."

The kid turned back to the net, which was sinking into the water again, and the two of them were silent for what seemed like a long time before the kid said, "My father said you wouldn't swim with the sharks." He was looking at his net instead of at Craig. "Even after your own father stopped the winds for you."

Craig snorted with laughter, and began to walk backward, his legs feeling as if they were made of that wiggling fish stuff in the kid's net, and also the bloody, inert muscle of stuff the kid's father had tossed by the handfuls into the Caribbean. As best he could, he trotted away on those weak legs, laughing and snorting, back to the hut, where he dropped into bed and a waveful of stars and ocean closed over him. He slept like death. When he woke up, his father had already packed, and they left the resort without saying good-bye to the director.

It was back at home that Craig began to carry the cement block with him. He was so tired every morning from carrying it, and facing carrying it again all day, and utterly unable to articulate to his mother what was wrong and why he could hardly hold his head up at the breakfast table.

She assumed, of course, that he was on drugs, and she would scowl at him when he woke from the naps that lasted all day on the weekends and stretched from after school to dinner during the week. She sent him to a shrink, who prescribed some pills Craig never took because of the warning that he couldn't get a hard-on if he took them, but after a couple of months, the cement block simply lifted, on its own, returning now and then with a change in seasons but disappearing after he got used to the rain, or the snow, or the falling leaves, or the first brilliant days of summer. He hoped this wasn't the beginning of that again—here at school, in October, during midterm week.

Friday night Godwin Honors Hall was loud, and drunk, and full of good cheer. Girls—even the homely ones he'd never seen wearing anything but sweat pants—had gotten dressed up in short skirts and high heels and lipstick. Guys were stocking their dorm refrigerators with Michelob and Corona, and competing iPod playlists were blaring from speakers aimed toward open windows and into the courtyard.

Craig had woken up in the late afternoon with a hangover, and hadn't even realized that everyone was back from their weeklong absence, and that the beer was already flowing, until he stepped out into the hallway, headed for the shower with a towel wrapped around his waist, and walked right into the party.

Perry was there, leaning against the wall, holding a beer. He and some chick were comparing answers to an essay exam. The girl had buggy eyes but great calves and ankles. She and Perry were so absorbed in the shared vocabulary of their exam that neither one said hi when he passed them and said, "Hey."

When he came back out of the bathroom, he had to push his half-naked way through a crowd of guys in glasses who were silently nodding their heads to some bad old rock 'n' roll blaring from one of their rooms. One of them slapped him on his bare back, and Craig turned fast, ready to punch the asshole, until he realized the guy was just drunk, and happy. Perry was still in the hallway, and he and the buggy-eyed girl were still arguing the finer points of their comparisons and contrasts, and Craig was relieved to close the door to his room behind him. He was in no mood for a party. He *was* in the mood for some extra-potent stuff with Lucas, and maybe a trip to Pizza Bob's, he thought, and it wasn't until he was bent over, picking his jeans up off the floor, that he noticed a pair of long legs stretched out on his bed.

"Hey, Craig."

"Jesus Christ," Craig said. "How did you get in here?"

"I walked in the door."

Craig let the jeans slip out of his hand, back onto the floor, and stood up straight, hitching the towel tighter around his waist and looking at Josie Reilly, who was lying on his bed with her black hair spread out on his pillow, holding his *Maxim* magazine open in front of her but looking at him, not it. She was wearing a little skirt with orange flowers on it, and her legs and feet were bare.

"Um, Josie, can I ask what you're doing here?"

"Reading your dirty magazine."

"Oh," Craig said. "Okay. Well, I'm going to get dressed now."

"Okay," Josie said without taking her eyes off him.

"So . . ." He waved his right hand through the air while holding on to the towel at his waist with the left.

"So . . . ?" she said. She tossed the magazine onto the floor, and then swung her legs off the side of the bed and stood up. He felt the perfumey breeze of her pass him as she made her way barefoot to the door and locked it before turning back around. She stumbled sideways then, but caught herself on the edge of Craig's desk, and laughed, and then slid down it and sat hard on the floor with her ankles tucked under her butt.

"How drunk are you?" Craig asked.

"Just a"—she held her thumb and index finger an inch apart— "drunk," and then she held her arms up to him like a little kid wanting to be picked up.

"Josie," Craig said. "I'm wearing a towel."

"Take off the towel!"

"I think you're more than a little drunk," he said.

"I flunked," she said. "I know it. Didn't even study." She made the motion of erasing something on a blackboard in front of her. "*Shupe.*"

"Probably you didn't," he said. "You probably did better than you think you did." He had no idea if this was true or not, but what else was he going to say?

She started moving toward him on her knees then, and he backed up a couple of steps, but then she got on her hands, too, and scrambled toward him, grabbing his ankles.

"Shit, Josie," Craig said, sort of dancing away from her, but she was holding on tight. "Cut it out. It tickles. Shit."

He couldn't help laughing. It really did tickle. She was laughing, too, and spidering her way up his legs to his towel, and then she was standing with her whole clothed body pressed against his whole naked one, with her tongue in his mouth and his hair in her hands, and despite his reservations (honestly, he just wanted to find Lucas and get stoned), his dick was fully into it within half a second of the kiss, and then she had her hand on that and her mouth on his neck, and she was pulling him backward onto his bed.

14

Perry saw her coming out of Starbucks with a cup in each hand, and he ducked around the corner. The last person he wanted to see right now was Josie Reilly. The last time he'd seen her was in May, the end of the semester, at a memorial tree-planting ceremony for Nicole.

An entire orchard of cherry trees paid for by Omega Theta Tau had been planted around the sorority in Nicole's honor. A backhoe dug the holes, and then dropped the trees one by one into the soft earth. A crowd gathered to sing and pray all day, and then there was a candlelight vigil all night. There were eighteen trees, one for each of Nicole Werner's years. Their branches were actually in bloom.

("Do you know how expensive it is to plant an orchard of almost full-grown trees *in bloom*?" he'd overheard one student at Godwin Hall say to another over soggy pancakes that morning. There were a few bad jokes made about cherries, and the whole virgin rumor, with regard to the Omega Theta Tau house in general, and Nicole in particular.)

Somehow, in the crowd during the candlelight vigil, Josie had found him, snuggled up to him, and whispered dramatically, "She's still with us, Perry. Can you feel it? She isn't dead."

He'd backed away.

"What's with you?" she'd asked, offended, but he just shook his head, and she moved on to someone else. The candle some sorority girl had handed him in a waxed cup sputtered out. A few minutes later, when they started singing "The Wind Beneath My Wings," he tossed the waxed cup into a trash can and headed back to Godwin Hall.

Josie had hardly known Nicole, but you wouldn't have known that from all the mileage she got out of having been the dead girl's roommate and sorority sister for six months. She'd read a putrid poem at the memorial service, been interviewed for the newspaper, worn a tight T-shirt with Nicole's photo on it and a black armband all through April and into May, and managed to be excused not only from finals but also from having to turn in her essay for Classical Sources of Modern Culture because she was organizing the petition to expel Craig Clements-Rabbitt from the university:

"Drunk + Driver + Death = Murder."

She went to Houston, Perry learned from the school newspaper, to speak to the annual SADD convention "in memory of my best friend, who was murdered by a drunk driver."

To Perry, she apologized for whoever had splashed his and Craig's door with red paint and plastered that sad senior portrait of Nicole at the center of it:

"Nobody blames you for anything, Perry," she'd said. "We all know you just had the bad luck of being his roommate."

"He's not even *here*," Perry said. "Why are people messing with my door?"

"It's symbolic. You have to understand that."

When it happened again, the university housing department arranged for Perry to finish the semester in a vacant room on the other side of the dorm.

Now, glimpsing Josie Reilly, who was clipping purposefully out of Starbucks, Perry imagined she knew that Craig was back (it had been in the paper, after all), but he had no idea if she knew that Perry was living with him again, and didn't want to find out. He was on the way back to their apartment from the bookstore, where he'd bought the book Professor Polson had assigned for them to read that week: *The Body After Death*. The cover was white, the letters black, and on the back there was a quote from Professor Polson herself, saying that this book was the definitive text on folklore and the funereal sciences. Except for a four-subject notebook, it was the only thing in his backpack, which slipped around loosely between his shoulder blades as he turned the corner at State Street and Liberty as quickly as he could, ducking around a bagel place before Josie could see him and maybe try to talk to him about Nicole, or Craig.

By the time of the memorial service in April, Nicole had already been buried for two weeks. Four hundred people had crammed into Trinity Lutheran Church in Bad Axe for the funeral, and another hundred had spilled out the front doors and into the parking lot, where a late March blizzard was doing its best to bury them inch by inch. Some of the women were wearing open-toed shoes. Some of the men wore only their suit coats. A few people had put up umbrellas to keep the snow from soaking them. One of those umbrellas was decorated with smiley faces, and Perry found it hard to take his eyes off of it as he and the other three pallbearers passed it carrying Nicole's white coffin between them.

It wasn't so much the irony of the smiley faces as the banality. The simplicity.

And it wasn't just the umbrella. It was everything:

The shiny coffin. The white, cheap-looking cloth that had been spread over it near the altar, and Nicole's smiling senior portrait propped up on the lid. The coffin, of course, was closed. As the paper had reported over and over, Nicole had been identified only by the jewelry and clothes she'd been wearing because there was nothing left about her that was identifiable as *her*.

Not that perfect smile. Not that blond ponytail. Not those pink cheeks.

The last time Perry had seen her was two nights before the accident, when she'd passed him on the sidewalk on Campus Ave. She'd been holding on to some older guy's arm, wobbling in her high heels back to his frat, Perry supposed, hair soaking wet and plastered to her face, although it was a completely clear night and hadn't, in fact, rained or snowed for days. She had a red plastic cup in her hand.

Perry hadn't recognized her at first. She could have been any drunk sorority girl. When finally he did recognize her, he was shocked by how drunk she looked. The guy who was holding her up seemed both very pleased with himself and stone-cold sober.

Perry stopped in front of the two of them and said, "Nicole. Are you okay?"

It seemed to take her several seconds to realize she'd been spoken to, and then even longer for her eyes to focus on him. Finally, she hiccupped a little and said, "Oh, hi, Perry."

"You want me to walk you back to the dorm?" he asked. "You're looking like you need some help."

"Get lost, man," her frat guy said. "We're doing just fine here."

Nicole leaned into the guy's arm, tripped on the heel of her shoe, giggling, and the guy caught her, propped her up on his shoulder again. She raised up her red plastic cup to Perry. "No, I'm doing great. But thanks for being such a Boy Scout," she said, and the frat guy snorted, and Nicole stumbled away with him.

Perry had turned and watched them go, feeling uneasy, but what could he do?

At her funeral, in the photograph on her coffin, Nicole was wearing the dress Perry remembered from the Senior Class Awards Ceremony: pale blue with ruffles down the front. As she'd accepted the Ramsey Luke Scholarship with a little curtsy, that dress had shimmered under the gym lights. In the front pew of Trinity Lutheran Church in Bad Axe, as the funeral was coming to an end with weeping and prayers and organ music and the blowing of noses, Perry was thinking about that little curtsy—how it had infuriated him—and then Pastor Heine plucked the photo off the coffin and nodded at the pallbearers to come forward, to take Nicole Werner in her coffin out to the hearse that was waiting in the parking lot.

It was amazingly heavy, that coffin, even with the four of them balancing the weight of it between them. Perry was on the right side, at her head. As they passed down the aisle of the church, he stared in a straight line into the distance, having to work especially hard not to look at Nicole's sisters, who were tossed together in the first pew in a dark lacy heap of blond grief, or to glance in the direction of his own mother, although he could feel her red eyes on the side of his face.

Then they were stepping out of the church and into that cold rain beyond the doors, and the ushers motioned for the mourners to move off the church steps in order to clear a path to the hearse. The crowd parted for the pallbearers and the coffin, and that's when Perry saw the umbrella with the smiley faces. Maybe the other pallbearers saw it, too. They all hesitated at the same time at the top of the stairs, preparing for the precarious journey down. Nicole's uncle—in the front, across the coffin from Perry—seemed to be having trouble bearing the weight and weeping uncontrollably at the same time, but they took the stairs one at a time, slowly, until, on the last one, Tony Werner, Nicole's cousin and the guy who'd once punched Perry in the stomach for refusing to give him a ball on the playground, stumbled. Some salt had been thrown on the snow, but it had only made the cement slushier, more dangerous.

Nothing ridiculous happened, thank God. The other three pallbearers compensated by leaning backward, and Tony managed to regain his footing and get right back in sync with the others within a few seconds, and they crossed the parking lot and guided the coffin into the back of the hearse without further incident. Still, in those seconds, Perry had felt

Nicole's weight shift to his shoulder before settling down between them all again—and, now, he thought of that weight often.

On the other side of Bagels and Bites, he waited until he was sure Josie would be down the block, across the street, and then he turned around and headed back in the direction of his and Craig's apartment.

15

The night Shelly had come across the accident, she had been on her way home from the gym. It was the Ides of March. All day, a watery sun had been trying to creep out from behind the same sloppy, gray, and borderless cloud until finally, giving up, it just sank into the horizon. Of course, then it cleared, and hard little stars blinked on one by one as the sky grew darker, and a huge round moon rose over everything, tremendously bright, as if it had somehow managed to finally push the sun out of the sky.

Et tu, Brute?

It had seemed unfair that it had been such a cloudy dark day, only to be such a crystal clear night. By mid-March, Shelly was always weary of winter and its continuing, small injustices. She wanted spring.

Her arms and back ached. She'd overdone it again. Every night before she stepped foot in the gym, she told herself she wouldn't overdo it, and then she'd start hauling the heaviest weights she could lift off the rack and over to the bench.

Why?

She wasn't trying to impress the men, and there were almost never any women in the free weights corner of the gym.

She was, she supposed, trying to impress her own reflection in the mirror.

Often, she did.

Shelly was five feet, five inches tall and weighed a hundred and fifteen pounds, but when she yanked those forty-pound dumbbells off the floor, you could have counted the sinews in her biceps and triceps. You could have sketched the grainy fibers. She was a forty-eight-year-old woman *made* of muscle. "Whoa," some guy would almost always say from the other side of the weight rack. "You a bodybuilder, or trying to scare somebody?"

Usually, Shelly said nothing in response, but once she said, trying to make it sound like a joke, "I have a past."

She had sounded serious. The guy who'd been joking with her looked away, but a leering teenager on her other side said, "I bet you do."

Shelly knew she looked her age, but that she also looked good. Her stomach was flat. Her legs were lean. Her skin was smooth and pale. Her hair was long and strawberry blonde. Boys like this one—chiseled body, face full of acne—had been staring at her body her whole life, although, these days, the older men left her alone. More experienced, probably they smelled it on her.

Lesbian.

She didn't do men.

She wished she never had. She still had a scar that ran straight from her collarbone down to her hipbone, left over from the great heterosexual mistake of her life, and the last one of *those* she'd ever make.

Not that she was doing very well with women, either. The last woman she'd dated for more than a few weeks had moved to Arizona with the life partner she'd never bothered to tell Shelly she had.

"Good riddance to bad rubbish," Rosemary had said. But Rosemary had three teenage sons and a dashing brain-surgeon husband. It was easy for her to cast people out of Shelly's life without a backward glance. Except to go to work, Shelly herself had hardly left the house for a month after the break-up.

And now, to top off a whole lifetime of sexual misadventures, it seemed that early menopause had arrived. A few weeks earlier, she had found herself stripping off her jacket and sweater in the checkout line of the grocery store. Dripping, panting. What the hell? Had they turned the

heat up to three hundred degrees? Was the place on fire? She had a sudden nauseating memory of being placed by some beautician under a
steaming plastic hood in a sweltering hair salon as a child, and being
told to sit still as it poured stinking air from a hundred little holes onto
her hair and the chemicals burned their way into the skin on her scalp.

"Jesus," Shelly said in the grocery store, and the woman at the cash
register said in a cigarette-husky Midwestern drawl, "Yer havin' a hot
flash darlin'. Ain't ya ever had a hot flash before?"

No. She most certainly had not. But now she had one every other
day. "Oh," her doctor had said, "this is a little early, but might as well get
it over with, right?" Shelly wondered if he'd say this to her someday
when she came to him with a terminal illness.

Up ahead, someone seemed to be swerving around. Shelly rubbed her
left bicep with her right hand, holding the steering wheel with her left,
and then changed biceps and hands.

She was solid. She was aching, but her arms were hard as rock. She
was singing along with the radio. A country song about staying loyal to
the U.S. of A. If you didn't like it here, you could leave, the lyrics
twanged—and Shelly's brother's black-and-white high school yearbook
picture floated up out of the ten billion images in her unconscious.

He was smiling, getting ready to die in Vietnam.

Ahead, the red brake lights of the meandering vehicle seemed to be
making elliptical dashes across the centerline, into the shoulder, back
into the right lane, back over the yellow line. Kids, screwing around. Or
a defensive driver avoiding something in the road. Too far ahead to
worry too much about. Shelly was still singing along to the radio as she
still rubbed her aching muscles. She was thinking of how tired she was
of pretending to be everything she was not, and then wondering who
she might be if she stopped pretending not to be what she was, when
the car in front of her (fifty yards? Forty?) seemed to be plucked out of
the moonlit darkness by a gigantic hand.

Gone.

16

Nicole Werner was standing outside the library shivering. She had a book pressed to her chest. She was wearing a sleeveless white shirt over a pair of khaki shorts. It was the last week in October, but it had been a weirdly hot, hazy day—the sky purple and fuzzy-looking behind the changed leaves—and although the sun had seemed far away, it had still managed to turn Craig and Perry's dorm room into a sauna by two o'clock in the afternoon. They had a west-facing window.

Because it had seemed so much like summer, Craig, too, had left Godwin that afternoon in shorts and a T-shirt, but he'd been back to his room since then and gotten his jacket, which he was glad about, because as soon as the sun set, it felt like late autumn again. Obviously, Nicole Werner hadn't been out of the library since the temperature had dropped.

"Hey, Nicole. What are you doing?" Craig asked when he reached her at the top of the steps. He'd already told Lucas to get lost.

("Aw, man," Lucas had said as Craig veered away from him, a clear diagonal cut across the Commons toward the column Nicole was leaning against. "You gonna dump me for that bitch?")

Nicole looked up, and the light from inside the library fell on her flossy hair, which was pulled back in the usual ponytail but also looked mussed, as if she'd been rolling around in a stack of hay, or studying philosophy all night. Midterms had been over since the week before. Could she already be cramming for something else?

"I was waiting for Josie," she said.

"Oh," Craig said, trying not to display any particular reaction to the name Josie, but he couldn't help taking a quick look over both shoulders to make sure she wasn't there. "Here," he said to Nicole. He took off his jean jacket and handed it to her. He would have preferred to step around and drape it over her shoulders (a gesture he felt certain he must have seen made by men in movies, since it wasn't the kind of thing his father would have done for his mother), but he found himself unable to step into the circle of light in which Nicole Werner stood.

Nicole balanced her book on her hip with one hand, took the jacket from him with the other. "Thanks, Craig," she said. "Wow!"

"I'm not cold," he said, and then wished he hadn't. Instead of sounding chivalrous, now he sounded like he'd been looking around for a coat rack and had happened to run into her.

"Well, I'm freezing," Nicole said, stuffing her arms into his jacket. "I was so stupid leaving the dorm like this. I guess I thought I'd be back for dinner, but then I got obsessed with this stupid paper, and ended up just eating one of those disgusting sandwiches out of the vending machine. I had no idea how cold it had gotten."

"Yeah," Craig said. "When's your paper due?"

"Couple of weeks," she said.

He couldn't help opening his mouth and eyes in astonishment. "And you're working on it *already*?"

Nicole laughed, rolled her eyes, and then widened them, mimicking him. "*Yeah*," she said. "College is hard for some of us, Craig. Just because *you're* one of those guys who just sails through everything with no problems . . ."

Craig considered correcting her, but decided not to. He shrugged.

"Perry says you just sort of open your book, and close it, and you're done. Believe me, I wish *I* could get away with that."

Craig was ready to get this part of the conversation over with. He remembered the clammy handshake Dean Fleming had given him in Chez Vin that first night, and the few phony sentences the dean had managed to stammer out about how great it was to have his old friend's son in the Honors College, pretending it was a coincidence. Since then, on the few occasions Craig had passed Dean Fleming in the administrative hallway, the guy had gone way out of his way to pretend he didn't know Craig any better than any of the other students, and Craig felt pretty certain he was pissed he'd had to do that favor for his old Dartmouth pal.

"Well, I should probably study more than I do." He dragged a hand across his eyes. Was he mistaken, or was the light getting brighter the longer it lingered on Nicole Werner's hair and face? He inhaled, and said, "So, want to walk back to Godwin?"

"Like I said, I'm waiting for Josie. Want to wait with me?"

"No," Craig said. Too quickly. For a second there he'd forgotten about Josie. "That's okay."

He raised a hand in a gesture of farewell and took a step backward, but Nicole said, "What about your coat?"

She sounded alarmed, as if he were about to walk off a plane without a parachute—but maybe she always sounded alarmed. He remembered the way she'd waved Perry over in the cafeteria one night. *Perry!* she'd said. *I forgot to tell you! I went home last weekend, and I saw Mary. She said to say hi!*

Perry had just grunted. He hadn't even looked up from his tray. Whoever Mary was had seemed like a really big deal to Nicole, but when Craig asked Perry about it, he said, "Who cares?"

"Nicole seems to care," Craig pointed out. "She made this Mary sound like a long-lost cousin, or somebody risen from the dead."

"Well, Nicole always sounds excited."

It had occurred then to Craig, again, that Perry was nursing some unrequited love grudge, but he also thought he had a point. Nicole, and girls like her, *did* usually sound excited, or alarmed, or semihysterical, when they weren't. It was something about the hard vowels and the crisp consonants and the way most of their sentences ended with "you guys!" And sounding like a question: "I'm, like, so hungry, you guys?!" You'd think some girl was starving to death, but she might just mean she wanted to borrow some quarters for a roll of Lifesavers.

It's not a problem," Craig said, still backing away. "I'll get it from you back at the dorm."

"Wow!" Nicole said. "Thanks so much, Craig. You're so nice!"

"Sure," he said, trying to smile like a nice guy but imagining his own mug shot on a sexual predator website.

Josie had not, it seemed, told Nicole about the other night. Maybe, he hoped, she wouldn't. But why wouldn't she? Briefly he'd held out some hope that she'd been so drunk she didn't even remember the incident, but that hope had been dashed when he'd passed her in the courtyard on Sunday morning, and she'd stopped dead in front of him.

"Hi," he'd said.

"Yeah," Josie had said. Craig had tried hard not to look her in the eyes, but they just bored straight into his own, and then he couldn't look away. It was a bright morning, too, and his eyes started to water in the glare. He hadn't left the dorm since Friday. He'd been pretty much either stoned or sleeping since he'd last seen her. "So, 'hi' is all you have to say to me?" she asked.

About a hundred bad jokes flashed through Craig's brain, like having Eddie Murphy or Lenny Bruce shuffling a deck inside his skull, but he managed to keep his mouth firmly shut. The morning sun was making Josie's hair look so black and shiny and smooth it scared the hell out of him. He couldn't have spoken if he wanted to.

"You're a great guy, Craig," she'd said. "Really exceptional. I hope you rot in hell."

And then she was gone so fast he didn't know in which direction she'd left.

Shit, he thought. She definitely remembered.

He didn't see her again for at least a week, but that was mostly because he'd been staying away from anywhere she might be—avoiding the stairwells near her hall, slipping out the side entrance to Godwin instead of going through the courtyard—and when he did see her again, luckily she didn't see him. She and Nicole were together in the cafeteria, dressed up for some sort of Greek tea or soiree or salon or something equally feminine and mysterious and inane. (Rush Week started as soon as midterms were over, and half the girls in Godwin Honors Hall were joining sororities, appearing suddenly around the dorm every evening in pearls and skirts, while the guys who were rushing stumbled around looking disoriented and hung over.) As soon as he recognized Josie's black hair, he'd scrambled to the back of the cafeteria as fast as he could.

The next week, he didn't go looking for the study group on the night he knew they'd be down in the Alice Meyers Memorial Student Study Room, although he missed the group. He missed Nicole, and it pained him to think he'd never be in that room with her again, listening to her breathe through her nose as she read her textbook. By then, he assumed she hated him and that Josie had given her some ugly Cliffs Notes version of the events:

The way, in his bed, Josie had asked, "Are you wearing a condom?"

It was the first whole sentence she'd uttered since she'd stripped off her clothes and, standing shiningly naked in front of him, had whispered, "I want you to fuck me. I've wanted you to fuck me for a long time."

"Condom? No," he'd said, sounding more annoyed than he'd meant to. But when would he have put on a condom? Did she think he'd come out of the shower wearing one?

Her dark eyes, bleary as they were, shot open then, and Josie put her hands on his chest, shoving, and said, "Get off!"

"What?" Craig asked.

"I said *get off of me!*"

Craig rolled off of her, although every nerve ending and instinct he had—his brain having been turned into a kind of strobe light—was telling him to stay on top of her and to keep going.

"I'll get pregnant," she said. "Or a *disease!*"

"Huh?" Craig said. "Aren't you on the pill or something?"

"*No,*" Josie said. "Why would I be? I'm not even *sexually active* right now."

At this, Craig had snorted, and said, "I'd say right now you're pretty sexually active." He hadn't intended to sound so sarcastic, but the whole thing was just so fucking stupid. He'd been minding his own business when she'd come into his room and taken off her clothes and pulled him down onto her in his bed.

But at that point, she was already out of his bed, pulling her little silky panties up over her wildly lush and dark-haired pussy, and then she was looking around for her top, and Craig sighed, too loudly, and flopped down on his back and said, "I'll go see if somebody on the floor will give me a condom," before he realized she was crying.

"I can't believe this," Josie said, pulling her lacy tank top down over her breasts.

Craig sat up at the edge of the bed then. Luckily, he'd completely deflated, but he pulled his towel up off the floor and put it over his dick anyway. "Can't believe *what*?" he asked, but by then she was dressed, and she'd unlocked his door, slipped out of it, and slammed it behind her. For just a second, in the space she opened as she left, Craig could hear the party going on in the hallway—all the hardworking students celebrating the harvest. Somehow he pictured them in plaid shirts and gingham dresses—ruddy with good health, living their productive lives, while he searched the dresser for clean boxers, put them on, got back in his messed-up bed, and shoved the buds of his iPod as deeply into his ears as he could.

But now, as he rounded the corner, jacketless, to Godwin Honors Hall—which looked stately and decrepit at the same time under a low, bright moon—he was really hoping that maybe Josie wasn't so mad at him anymore, or at least had never told Nicole what had happened. Truly, he never really thought he stood a chance with Nicole anyway (because, for one thing, he knew he'd never have enough courage or imagination to figure out how to get together with a girl like that: every girl he'd ever hooked up with had made the moves on him first, and it seemed unlikely that Nicole would be that kind of girl), but it had surprised him how sad he was, after the shit with Josie, to think he'd blown that chance with Nicole without ever even actually *having* it.

When he came up the walk to the dorm, Lucas was smoking a cigarette under an elm tree in the courtyard.

"So!" Lucas called out. "Did you strike out again, young man?"

Craig held out his hand for a cigarette, but Lucas patted his pocket and said, "I'm out," and then, "She's not for you anyway, Craig. She's one of those girls who's waiting for marriage, and then she wants two kids and an SUV, and wants to stay home and bake cookies all day while you slave away at some shitty job. On the other hand, you've got 'fuck-'em-and-dump-'em' written all over you."

"What?" Craig asked, sincerely astonished by this assessment. "Go to hell, Lucas. I do not have 'fuck-'em-and-dump-'em' written all over me."

"Yeah, you do, Craig. You look at girls like you hate 'em."

"What? I do *not*."

Lucas shrugged, and tossed his cigarette over the wrought-iron fence and onto the sidewalk.

"Okay," he said. "Sorry. Whatever. But I just don't see you taking Little Miss Sunshine there on a walk through the park before you propose to her."

To this, Craig said nothing. He could think of nothing to say. He watched the shadows of other students pass on the other side of the tiny glittering windows of Godwin Honors Hall. *They* knew what the hell they were doing there. For one thing, they hadn't gotten into the Honors College just because their father was buddies with the dean.

"Besides," Lucas asked, "wouldn't you rather have a really great blow job than a really nice date? I mean, I just don't picture that little virgin on her knees with her sweet red lips wrapped around your massive man tool."

"Shut the fuck up," Craig said.

But there was no animation in it.

No energy.

Lucas was probably right, he knew.

Lucas was often right.

Craig had never, he realized, been on an actual date. And the idea of one—asking for one, going on one—seemed like another one of those ten million things that all the normal guys, wearing khaki pants and carrying bouquets of daisies, would know exactly how to do, but which would be about as easy for Craig as building a spaceship and then going for a zip around the earth in it.

"Hey, sorry," Lucas said to Craig's silence. "I didn't mean to—"

"Forget it," Craig said, more to himself than to Lucas. "Let's just go smoke a bowl."

"Splendid idea, dude," Lucas said. "Let us indeed go smoke a bowl."

17

Perry Edwards was waiting outside her office when Mira got there. She wasn't surprised. There'd been a look on his face when she dismissed the class at the end of the first session, and a hesitancy, as if he wanted to stay behind, had more to say. But Mira was already late for a committee meeting and had made a conscious effort to avoid eye contact, to gather her books and papers up in a way that would convey how rushed she was. She told herself that it was because she *was* rushed, but she knew there was something else, too—Perry Edwards's intensity during class combined with what he'd said that day in the hallway when he was imploring her to let him audit:

"I have some fundamental questions about death, questions I'm trying to find answers to," he'd said. "Because of Nicole. And not just philosophical questions. I have metaphysical questions. *Physical* questions."

There was such an urgency in the way he'd said it that Mira had signed his override without asking for any further explanation.

At best, she thought, this was a true philosopher—a metaphysician in the making, one of the rare twenty-year-olds she occasionally encountered who actually had a mission, and the mind with which to accomplish it.

At worst, he was just another morbid college kid, and Mira knew all about those. Who knew better than she the fascination people had with death? Every year she took her class on a field trip to the local funeral parlor and the university hospital morgue, where she had plenty of opportunity to observe their rapt attention to the embalming table, their hushed awe upon being led through the basement to the room with the refrigerators. When there happened to be no dead bodies at the moment, someone—often the most squeamish-seeming of the girls—would express bitter disappointment. And when they were ushered into the autopsy room to find a body still on the coroner's cabinet, there would be a rush of excited breathing, stillness, awe. Occasionally someone fainted, but no one ever left because they didn't want to look.

Still, Perry Edwards's interest seemed bigger than morbid fascination. During that first class he had an answer to every question. This material wasn't new to him. He'd been doing his own research, for his own reasons. That's what had made her think she might not want to talk to him after class—that she was not, perhaps, ready to hear about those reasons.

"See you next time," she'd said that day at the end of class, without looking up.

"Thank you, Professor Polson," he'd said as he stepped past her, out the door, and into the hallway.

Now he was standing outside her office door, and Mira cleared her throat so she wouldn't startle him when she came up behind him. There was no one else in the corridor this early on a Thursday morning. He was looking at something she'd tacked up two semesters earlier, a photograph she'd taken in the Balkans during her Fulbright year: a color image of a charnel house in a small village in the mountains.

It had been, in the nineteenth century, the custom in the village to exhume corpses from the local cemetery a few months after their burial, and to display the skulls and long bones, brightly painted with the names and dates of their former owners. Mira had taken the photograph from a distance, but with a zoom lens on a sunny day, and the effect, when the photograph was printed up, startled even her: A dizzying multitude of skulls stared from their dry sockets at a little gathering of tourists, staring back.

Below the photo, Mira had taped an explanation of how the villagers believed that the dead could escape from their graves, and that the only way to avoid this was to dig up the bodies, to make sure they were in their graves, and that the flesh had fully decomposed. That way, if they came upon a corpse on which the flesh hadn't rotted away (a potential "walker"), the villagers could go through the stake-through-the-heart ritual.

Once or twice, according to village folklore, they came upon an empty grave, and panic broke out. It was said that the village lost three quarters of its nonelderly population during one such panic. They packed up their wagons and moved, leaving behind any grandparents too enfeebled to come along. The year Mira visited the village it was little more than a field of a daisies with a stone church at the center of it, and its only attraction was the charnel house.

"Oh," Perry said, turning. "Professor Polson. I don't want to bother you. I just wonder if I could—"

Mira handed him the book she held in her hands, Nils Stora's *Burial Customs of the Skolt Lapps,* as she felt around in the darkness of her leather bag for her keys, coming up, first, with the purple nipple of one of the boys' bottles:

Despite everything she'd read or been told about what she should do, Mira still let the twins carry their bottles around with them when she took them to the store, or to the park. Sometimes the nipples were dislodged, or dirtied, or they wound up on the floor of the car. Who knew how long ago she might have stuffed this one into her bag? Perry Edwards looked at it, and then looked away, as if Mira had shown him something intimate—which, she supposed, it was.

She reached in again, and this time snagged the key ring, which was attached to a rubber heart that Clark had given to her years ago. ("Squeeze me," it read, and when you did, a little mechanical voice said, "I WUV you.") She unlocked the door and ushered Perry in, and he sat in the chair across from her desk, looked around, and then handed Mira's book back to her.

"Are you . . . ? Is this . . . time? An okay . . . ?" he stammered politely.

"It's fine," Mira said. She cleared the books she had piled on her own chair, stacking them on the floor at her feet, and then sat down at her desk, folded her hands in her lap, and said, "How can I help you?"

"I've been reading," Perry said, unzipping his backpack on the floor and leaning over it. He took out a book with the Roper Library's generic brown cover, and held it up as if it would explain something on its own.

She took the book from him. It was G. Melvin's *Handbook of Unusual Phenomena*—book twenty-four on the suggested reading list. It was a text Mira had put on loan in the Godwin Hall dormitory library several years before, but that, to her knowledge, no one had ever checked out. She kept it there for students who might want to explore Ukrainian death and burial superstition further—in particular an account (late for such an account) of a teenage girl killed in a farm accident circa 1952 in a primitive village in the foothills. The girl was said to have managed an escape from her tomb, and the proof of this was that, although she was not seen in the flesh, whenever a photograph was taken in the village in the year following her death, the girl's shadowy image could be seen in the upper left- or right-hand corner.

In the *Handbook* were several grainy photos of stiff and formally dressed peasants staring expressionlessly into the camera. In the corner of each photograph a dark-haired girl, blurred, seemed to be moving as quickly as possible out of the photographer's range. And as if that weren't enough, the girl had appeared to every man in the village, in the night, unclothed, demanding sex. Apparently, the men obliged her, however reluctantly, and during the act she bit them—a few on the neck, a few on the arm, and one, mercilessly, on the nipple, which she bit clean off his torso before disappearing. Each man died in a farming accident within a few weeks of the event.

But what Mira wanted the students to read was the part that followed this:

How the body was dug up, and how the body was found in her coffin, a year after the girl's death, good as new. Her flesh was pink. Her hair had grown luxuriously around her shoulders. Her mouth was red, filled with blood. Her teeth had grown, and they glistened. Only her clothes had rotted away, revealing, of course, her beautifully gleaming breasts.

The village then managed to engage, at great expense, a cement truck to back up to the grave and fill it in, and the girl, whose name was Etta, never walked through the village again, and the farm accidents mysteriously drew to a halt—a fact the villagers attributed to the cementing-in of this tomb, not to the fact that their agricultural lifestyle was, within a few years, completely eradicated when a cardboard box factory moved into the village.

Melvin, the author, had been an ancient professor at Mira's undergraduate institution and had given her the only B she'd ever received in college, but she still thought his was a brilliant analysis of the superstitions of the period and the move from an agrarian to an urban culture that fueled them. This story of Etta, he said in the *Handbook*, was the last real "vampire" story the world would ever know. In only another year or two, all the young adults who might have died tilling the land or harvesting the grain were working in that box factory or in shops in some Soviet metropolis, and the funerary traditions were forever changed. Instead of simple burials in wooden coffins in the churchyard, the whole commercial funeral business moved in, complete with embalming and sealed tombs and caskets that cost more than most families in the area made in a year.

"It's a good book," Mira said to Perry, handing it back to him. "I'm glad you thought to check it out."

"I've read all the articles," he said, "that you assigned, and—"

"Those aren't *assignments*," Mira said. "That's the suggested list. That's for supplemental research."

"I know," Perry said. "But . . ." He shook his head, and then he held up one of the photos of "Etta." He'd had the page bookmarked. Mira looked at it and nodded.

It *was* possible, she realized, that this student was mentally ill. It was far from unusual. There were always mentally ill students, especially in the Honors College. Intelligence and ambition went hand in hand, it seemed, with some kinds of delusion. These days, too, Mira found that students who were perhaps only minimally depressed (and how many smart twenty-year-olds *weren't* depressed?) had been medicated by their family doctors into a state of either apathetic insensibility or manic excitement. These kids carried their bottles of Klonopin and Xanax from class to class, and swigged their pills down by the handfuls with their energy drinks. Who knew what this particular kid might be taking, especially if he had, as he claimed, been close friends with Nicole Werner?

Mira nodded at the book, leaned forward, and considered the photo. The small gray girl in the corner was dashing out of out it while a grim-looking family stared solemnly into the camera, oblivious. Although it was 1952, this photograph was black and white, and there was an aura of antiquated severity about it that made it seem more like an image from the late 1800s. But Mira had been to villages near this one, and even in the mid-nineties, in broad daylight, in the spring, in real life, there was always something black and white about the places and the people, as if their joyless lives had drained the color out of the world around them.

She looked from the photograph to her student. His brow was furrowed. "Yes?" she said.

"I read the whole essay," he said, "and the author's analysis. And I understand what he's saying about the cultural context, and the societal changes, and the folklore, but—" He stopped, seeming to search for words. He closed the book.

"But what?" Mira asked.

He reached into his backpack again, and unfolded a copy of the student newspaper on his lap. It was the front-page article that had run about Nicole Werner a few days after the accident. On one side of the page there was the now-familiar senior portrait of Nicole with a warm halo of studio light pouring over her blond hair, and beside it a photograph of the memorial orchard-planting that took place at her sorority. In that photograph, a group of slender sorority sisters in black dresses and sunglasses held one another's hands, heads bowed, around one of the blooming cherry trees that had been planted. Perry Edwards pointed to this photograph, his finger on the tree—which looked, even in miniature and in black and white, like the lush icon of lost innocence it was meant to be. He slid his finger over the blossoms and then into the right-hand corner of the photo.

"Look," he said.

Mira did.

There was nothing there.

She moved her eyes slowly from the newspaper back to Perry Edwards's face, and shook her head.

"There's a girl there," he said.

Mira looked again, more closely—although by now she suspected where this was going, and that her hunch about mental illness had been right. She searched the grainy distance until, finally, just over the boy's clean fingernail, she *did* see what looked like a gray figure of a girl moving out of the photograph.

She looked back at Perry, and shrugged. She said, "Okay. Maybe. Yes?"

Perry let the newspaper drop onto his lap, and then leaned over his backpack again and took a manila envelope out of it.

"I scanned the photo," he said. "And then I enlarged it." He reached into the envelope, took it out—glossy, gray, eight by twelve—and handed the photo to Mira. Now only the right-hand corner of the whole image remained—a few petals on a bough at the bottom, like a cloudy carpet, and, in the left-hand corner, the shining bumper of someone's car parked in the sorority driveway—and, in the center of it all, the blurred girl.

She was wearing something filmy, either a mid-thigh-length dress or a shift over a miniskirt or shorts. Her arms were bare, and she was obviously in a hurry to get somewhere—one leg was bent behind her, like she was running. Her arms were swinging widely at her sides, or pumping. There was a flash of silver or gold around her wrist—a bracelet—and the side of her face had caught the sunlight, and the light obscured her features. Her blond hair was flowing behind her from her shoulders, lifted by a breeze or by her own momentum.

Certainly, from this distance, the girl looked like Nicole Werner, but so did half the other girls standing in the first photograph, in their black dresses, with their straight hair, holding one another's hands.

So did half the girls on this campus, especially the sorority girls.

"Yes," Mira said again, nodding, and handed it back to him.

She continued to nod as she tried to think carefully about what to say next. She'd made mistakes with students in the past, given them too much encouragement. She swallowed, and inhaled, and then said, "You've been through a terrible trauma. I understand that. I think, for that reason, this is not a class you should be taking right now. The material is too *relevant*, perhaps, at the moment, and it might be"—she used her hands to try to soften the word before it came out of her mouth, opening the hands on her lap—"*suggesting* things to you."

Perry Edwards nodded, but he didn't look away. He seemed to have expected her to say this, and was neither disappointed nor insulted.

He inhaled, bit his lower lip for a second, and then he said, "I understand what you're saying. But I've had this photograph since May. And there are other things." He looked up to the ceiling, as if searching for the words, and then back at Mira. "Professor Polson, Nicole's *here*. She's still on this campus. I was here all summer. I've *seen* her."

Mira sat back in her chair, a kind of recoiling she immediately regretted. The tone of his voice. It was so *certain*.

Perry Edwards reached into his backpack again, took out another envelope, and out of it, a second photograph—this one of a slender girl with shoulder-length brown hair emerging from one of the sorority houses on the Row. She was glaring at the camera. She looked ready to sneer an obscenity at the photographer, or raise her middle finger. He held the newspaper—the senior portrait of the blond Nicole Werner—up next to the photograph.

Mira looked from one to the other, and said, "I do see the resemblance, Perry, but, surely, you—"

"I know," he said. "I know these girls all look alike to people who don't know them. But, Professor Polson, I went all through school with Nicole Werner. We grew up in the same town. We went to Sunday school together. We were confirmed at the same church. I know what she looks

like. I see her. She's *here*. She's dyed her hair, but it's her. I don't know
how. And I didn't expect anyone to tell me anything except that I'm
crazy if I told them, so I haven't told anyone. But, I thought—well, I read
your book, *Traditional Burial Practices and Their Folk Origins*." He pronounced the words carefully, as if Mira might not recognize the title of
her own book. "And," he said, "I thought maybe, if you're working on a
new book, a book like it, what could be better than if you had a campus
equivalent of *this*?" he held up Melvin's book again, open to the photograph of Etta. "I mean, even if you just think we're crazy—"

"*We?*" Mira asked.

"That's the thing," Perry said. "There are two other guys who've seen
her. Lucas Schiff. He's a fifth-year senior. He was our resident advisor last
year—"

"I know Lucas," Mira said. Lucas Schiff. He'd been in her first-year
seminar her first year on campus. He'd been busted for possession of a
controlled substance then, but had gotten off on some technicality. He
was one of those politically active kids who used their political activism
as an excuse not to bathe, and to smoke a lot of dope.

"And also Patrick Wright."

"I know Patrick, too," Mira said. Patrick was clean-cut, from a small
town in the northern part of the state. Nothing like Lucas Schiff. "He's a
junior?"

"Yeah," Perry said. "He and Lucas—they've both been with her since
she died."

"Excuse me?" Mira asked.

"They've had sex with her."

Mira put her hand over her mouth. She wasn't sure if she was going
to laugh or cry. Perry seemed not to notice the gesture. He went on.

"What my point is, Professor Polson. I mean, couldn't you, maybe,
write, say, something comparing Etta to—"

"Nicole Werner?"

"Yeah. I mean, *if* you're working on another book. You wouldn't
have to believe us. Melvin doesn't believe what the villagers are saying
about Etta. He just listens. He analyzes."

Mira looked at Perry Edwards carefully. For a crazy second she wondered if he'd spoken to the dean of the Honors College about her, if he somehow knew she hadn't even *begun* the book she was going to have to have *published* in the next eighteen months. That she hadn't even come up with a solid *idea* for the book.

No, of course not. He was just a bright, passionate, or maybe crazy kid. She inhaled. She said, "Why, Perry? Why do you want me to do that? What's the point?"

"I need your help. There's something here. I need"—something seemed to catch in his throat, and he swallowed—"a grown-up."

"Perry," Mira said, and then stopped, literally biting her tongue.

Although, later, she would try to tell herself that it was this last appeal to her as a "grown-up" that had brought the two of them together in their search for Nicole, Mira could already see, in her office that September afternoon, the book, published by a major university press, in her hands, the bright, smiling senior portrait of Nicole Werner on the cover, her own name underneath that photo, and the letter to the dean from the department chair, and the recommendation it expressed for her tenure.

What, at this point, did she have to lose? Did she have any better ideas?

"Professor Polson?" Perry Edwards asked after Mira was silent for a very long time.

She held up a hand to keep him from saying anything else, and then she put the hand over her eyes and forced herself to count to five before she looked at this boy again, and said, "Okay."

Part Two

18

It was one of those soul-snatching, deadly dull days at the Chamber Music Society. The offices buzzed with it, literally. A fly caught between the window and the screen in Shelly's office was tossing itself between the two barriers with exhausted fury. She watched it from her desk, its electrical droning competing with the sound of her dozing computer.

It was the end of September, and the weather was making a concerted effort to change. The sky was closer to lavender now than blue, and there was a smell of leaves sweetening, softening, giving way, shifting into a lower gear. As always, the change from late summer to actual autumn brought back for Shelly every September of her life—the dust swirling around her kindergarten desk, bobby socks and shiny shoes, straight through to her last year of graduate school, lugging an expensive textbook back from the store to her little efficiency over the Beer Depot—along with all the Septembers since then, the years passing one by one outside the window of her office at the university's Chamber Music Society.

What, she wondered, was September like for people who didn't work at an educational institution? Did the melancholy reminiscence of September simply skip them?

If so, Shelly thought, it would be a little like skipping one of the Twelve Trials of Hercules: you'd still be stuck with the Christmas despair, but you wouldn't have to relive the end of every summer vacation of your life, that sad realization of your own mortality, year after year, as the kids swarmed back into your world with their freshly sharpened pencils and new sweaters.

No, she supposed, it wouldn't be like that. They'd all gotten that calendar engrained on their psyches so early. No one escaped the mortality of autumn.

"God, you depress me," her ex-husband used to say, and said for the last time on the day she left him, shaking his head sadly—and then, as if some switch had been flipped in his head, charging after her, fists whirling around them both as she stumbled out the back door, and he yanked her back in by her hair.

Shelly?"

"Yes?"

"Do you think, you know, since we're all caught up, I—"

"—could leave early?" Shelly tried not to let out an exasperated sigh.

"Yeah," Josie said. She was twirling a strand of silken black hair around her index finger. She had her face tilted at a right angle, like a sparrow. "It's Greek Week."

"You're in a sorority?" Shelly asked.

"Yeah," Josie said.

"What house?"

"Omega Theta Tau." Josie pronounced each Greek letter with irrepressible pride.

Shelly turned around in her chair to face Josie fully in the doorway, and asked, "Isn't that the sorority Nicole Werner was in, the girl who was killed?"

Josie began to nod slowly and melodramatically with her eyes half closed.

"Did you know her?" Shelly asked. How was it possible that she'd not only not known that Josie was in a sorority but in Nicole Werner's sorority?

Josie shrugged. She said, "We all knew her. She and I rushed and pledged at the same time. It's not one of the bigger houses—sixty girls— so, yeah, sure, I knew her. It was a huge shock."

Shelly stood up. She said, "Did you know—?"

"—that you were in a sorority?" Josie brightened. "Yeah. You were wearing that Eta Lambda T-shirt the day I ran into you outside the gym, so I looked you up on their Plaque Wall when I was over there for a party, and found your name! That's so cool. I mean, I'm sure it used to be a better house back when you—"

"No," Shelly said, shaking her head, dismayed to feel rising the familiar defensive self-consciousness related to sororities you'd fully expect a lesbian in her forties to be far beyond by now. "No. That's not what I meant. Did you know I was at the scene of the accident? Nicole Werner's? I was the first one there."

Josie bit her lip, and seemed to look upward, to scan her brain for this bit of information. Not finding it, she said, "No," and then, eyes widening, "That was *you*. The middle-aged lady, the one who didn't give directions to 911?"

Shelly felt her cheeks redden, burning, and her breath escaping her. She shook her head. She said, "No. I gave perfect directions. I was there when the ambulances arrived. I stayed until they took those kids—"

"Jeeze," Josie said. "That must've been awful. I had no idea."

Of course she hadn't.

How could she have?

Shelly's name had never even made the papers, where not a single detail of the accident had been reported correctly—except, apparently, that Shelly was middle-aged.

"They got the facts wrong," Shelly said. "I was there when they took the kids away."

"Oh. Wow. Okay. Well, this is a bummer. Would you mind, can I ask you, you know—"

"If you can leave early?"

"Yeah."

"Yeah," Shelly said, and in less than a second, the girl was gone. Shelly stood, looking at the threshold, empty now, and listening to the sound of the front door of the Chamber Music Society opening, then closing, and then the sound of Josie tapping down the stairwell in her black flats. Then, she sat back down, opened one of her desk drawers, and pulled out the file with Josie's name on it.

Her résumé, her application—Shelly scanned them for Omega Theta Tau. These girls never left their sorority affiliations off their applications. They were so impressed with themselves that they assumed everyone else would be, too.

But it wasn't on any of the paperwork, and Josie had given only her home address in Grosse Isle as her contact information.

Grosse Isle?

How had Shelly missed *that* detail?

The girl was getting financial aid for the "work" she was doing at the Chamber Music Society. Was there anybody in Grosse Isle who needed work-study funds to attend college? When Shelly herself had been at the university, one of her sorority sisters from Grosse Isle had invited her home for a weekend. The house the girl had grown up in had a helicopter landing pad, and her father's helicopter, on its roof.

Well, of course, Shelly had no way of knowing the Reillys' situation, even if they were from the wealthiest suburb in the state. A bitter divorce could have accounted for the need, or a family illness, or parental job loss. It wasn't Shelly's job to assess the candidate's financial situation. That assessment was sent over from the Financial Aid Office to the dean of the music school, who gave it his stamp of approval.

Shelly put the file back in her drawer and looked out the window. A white butterfly, seeming to try to land on the windowsill, was being jostled around by the breeze, buffeted away from the ledge each time it got close.

Shelly watched, feeling nervous for it—unable to look away and hating the spectacle of it. Her eyes focused on it, as her thoughts fluttered around:

Omega Theta Tau.

Those were the Virgin Sisters. Theirs was the house on campus that supposedly advocated chastity and sobriety. The press had made a big deal of that with Nicole Werner. It was another stratum of the tragedy, that she'd been such a good girl.

Back in Shelly's day, the eighties, there'd been a bit more cynicism than that—strange as it was to think that Americans were getting *more* innocent as time passed.

Back then, Omega Theta Tau had been the sorority of choice for the girls who wanted to go into politics, or marry into politics. It was the keep-your-record-clean sorority. Shelly was fairly certain the governor's wife had been an OTT here. And who knew who else? These more powerful houses had connections that crisscrossed the nation's most important people like telephone lines. Maybe every female judge in the nation had been one. Probably half the female lawyers with ambitions to be judges—or senators, or congresswomen—had been. Most likely some huge percentage of the senators' and congressmen's wives in the country could claim Omega Theta Tau sisterhood, and who knew how many First Ladies.

Shelly's sorority, Eta Lambda, had been nothing like that. Hers had been known as the Friendly Girl's Sorority. In other words, it was not as cool as the other houses; its sisters not as popular, not as pretty.

You might think that would have made it an easier house to live in—with more laid-back sisters, less pressure of all varieties—but you would be wrong. Being on the lower rung of the Greek ladder made the Eta Lambda sisters even more competitive, even more ruthless, crueler. Shelly's most vivid memory of those days was of coming down the stairs in her formal gown on Pledge Night, and watching as the girls already assembled below in their own gowns made eye contact with one another and then, in unison, it seemed, rushed their hands to their mouths to stifle their laughter.

Shelly's heart had begun to pound so hard she was afraid she would pass out. To this day she had no idea what they were laughing about. Maybe she looked fat, or her gown was too revealing. It could have been her hair, her makeup, her shoes, her little sequined purse. She would never know. She wasn't intended to know. There was not a single girl among all those sisters who would have been kind enough to tell her, or to reassure her. So Shelly simply continued to descend the stairs (what else could she do?) and then to move through Pledge Night in a cloud of shame, dashing away from the activities every chance she got to check herself in the bathroom mirror: Her teeth, the blond hair over her lip, her eyebrows. She sniffed her underarms. She sniffed her *underpants*. She checked the front of her dress, the back of her dress, her bra straps, and the worst thing of all was that she couldn't *find* it. Whatever it was, this thing they could all see on her, she was blind to it.

Shelly had moved through the next two years as an Eta Lambda *trying* to find it, to see it, to figure it out, unable to and determined, at the same time, to stay and face it, whatever it was, day after day after day.

A complete waste of youthful energy and time, she knew now— although, in truth, she'd made a couple of lifelong friends through Eta Lambda, friends who'd seen her through her graduation, graduate school, an abusive marriage, and a divorce, and who had then accepted her into the new life she'd taken on as a lesbian.

There was a special kind of loyalty born of that strange sisterhood. It wasn't blood. But it was like *some* kind of precious body fluid, spent and shared between them.

The butterfly seemed stuck to the windowsill by the force of the breeze now.

Really, it was unbearable to watch. The breeze, which would have been nearly undetectable to anything not made of tissue paper and thread, as that butterfly was, was crushing it into the bricks. Shelly watched for a few more seconds and then decided she had no choice but to open the window and let it in. Luckily she worked in one of the few buildings left on campus that had windows that could actually be opened, although she rarely did so, and she had to push hard and then hold the heavy pane up with one hand while attempting to gently pluck the butterfly up with the other.

She got it. She could have sworn she felt its heart beat (atomic whispering, and dusty little particles of time and terror) and *she* felt terrified, too, trying to shake it off her fingers and onto her desk, where it lay motionless (had she killed it, had she *killed* it?)

She was certain, then, that she'd crushed it, scared it to death, injured it past fixing, but after a few seconds the butterfly fluttered its wings, and then it rose into the air, and Shelly stood back, out of its way, as it flew past her and through her office to the door, and then into the outer offices, where it zigzagged from wall to wall, until she opened the office door, and it flew down the stairwell, to the propped-open front door, and disappeared back into the world.

19

It was Putrefaction Day. As they filed into the room, Mira wrote on the board:

> *He looks like he's asleep.*
> *It's a shame that he won't keep,*
> *But it's summer and we're runnin' out of ice . . .*
> —*"Pore Jud Is Daid,"* Oklahoma!

Perry Edwards was the first one in, already with his notebook open, jotting down the quote from the board (which was really intended more as a joke than something to include in one's notes).

He was wearing a somber-looking pair of black trousers and a white button-down shirt, as if he'd just come from a Glee Club concert, or a funeral.

"Perry," Mira said before the others were in their places, "would you mind working the slide projector?"

"No, Professor Polson." He rose from his seat and moved to the chair next to the projector.

"Okay," Mira said. "Today's the big day. I'm assigning you your first essay, which will be due next week. I didn't assign it earlier because I don't believe in giving students, as some professors do, a *month* to write a paper. The longer you have, in my experience, the longer you'll put it off. But, at the same time, as I state in the syllabus, I accept no late papers, so my suggestion is that you start working on this assignment *today*. It can be as long as you need it to be to make your points, but it will be no shorter than ten pages."

"Ten pages!" Karess Flanagan blurted, and then blushed and looked around as if trying to pretend someone else had said it.

Under what circumstances, Mira wondered, would a parent consider naming a child Karess? Of course, they'd had no way of knowing that their infant daughter would turn into a stunningly sexy dark-haired beauty with C cups and glossy pink lips, did they? Mira could only *begin* to imagine the jokes and riffs the name and the girl had inspired in boys' locker rooms over the years.

Karess continued to look shocked, whether by the number of pages of the assignment or by her own outburst, or both.

"Didn't you read the syllabus?" Mira asked. "Under 'Requirements' "— she whipped a syllabus out of the folder on her desk—"it says pretty clearly, 'five papers, ten pages double-spaced or longer, must receive a grade of C or higher to pass the course.' "

Karess managed to nod and shake her head at the same time.

"So, here's your paper topic," Mira said.

Out of the same folder, she took her stack of Xeroxed assignments and handed them to Karess to pass out to the class. As the girl stood up with them, every guy in the class except Perry (who was studying the slide projector) looked from her ankles to her breasts, and lingered there until she sat back down.

"I'll let you read this on your own," Mira said, "but let me go over the basics. In this essay, which is a Personal Reflection piece, you are to examine your own superstitions—personal and cultural—related to death. You might start with why it is you signed up for this class, but you might also examine your preconceptions regarding burial, cremation, funeral rites, and the other rituals practiced by your family and community. What is your experience with the dead? Have you been in the presence of a dead body, and if so, what was your reaction? What are your fears related to the dead? What are your *attractions*?"

There was a snort here and there, and a baffled huff. It was the same every year.

"Because," Mira said, without missing a beat, "you, of all people, can't tell me there's no such thing as an attraction to this subject matter, since you have, yourselves, enrolled in a class about death and the dead. You had twenty other classes to choose from. Although I'd like to flatter myself that it's my reputation as a stellar educator that makes this the most popular class at Godwin Honors College every year, I rather doubt it. There are other reasons, perhaps related to the fascination that, for instance, young women with almost no interest in poetry beyond Hallmark cards have for Sylvia Plath, and why Kurt Cobain, who barely lived long enough to write and sing more than a handful of decent songs, commands so many fans among teenage boys.

"These are the subjects," Mira continued, looking around, catching the eyes of the students who looked the least impressed, "that I want you to explore, in as much depth, with as much critical analysis and personal reflection as you're capable of, in this essay."

She turned and sat back down behind her desk, and said, in a less impassioned tone, "On the class website you'll find papers from previous years. Questions?"

The students were either looking at Mira or staring at their assignment sheets, some with their mouths hanging open. There were questions regarding font, and quotes, and the width of margins. Mira made it clear that ten pages meant *ten pages*. The frantic questions subsided when it became obvious that there would be no way around this, whether or not their high school teachers had counted the title page as a page, or allowed them to use two-inch margins and eighteen-point font.

"Okay," Mira said, exhaling. "Finally. Putrefaction."

There were titters, and a groan.

"I'm sorry," she said, "but I'm afraid we can't begin to understand the folklore and superstitions surrounding the dead until we understand the reality of death and decay. In our particular time and place, it's the rare person who encounters putrefied human remains, but it has been less than a century that the technology and professional services allowing us to avoid this nasty reality have been around, and in most places on earth, they still don't exist. So, the decay of the dead body remains a powerful psychic and cultural memory.

"I'm assuming you've all read the selection in your course packs from W.E.B. Evans's *The Chemistry of Death*?"

A few heads nodded. Mira flipped the lights and pulled the screen down over the blackboard. "Okay. Perry, can you turn on the slide projector? First slide."

The first image was a still from *Dawn of the Dead*. A "corpse" in ragged clothing was chasing a beautiful young girl across an emerald green lawn.

"You're probably familiar with this movie. I imagine most of you also know the story 'The Monkey's Paw,' in which a husband comes home to his wife with a monkey's paw he's been told will grant him three wishes. The first wish, which is for a sum of cash, results in their son's death in a mining accident, and a life insurance payoff of that exact sum.

"The wife, several days after the son's burial, in a state of unbearable grief, makes the second wish: for his return.

"She's about given up hope when, late at night, the couple hears something slow and heavy and scraping coming up the walk. The wife rushes for the door, but the husband stops her. He seems to understand, in a way his wife doesn't, what their son, returning after a few days spent in the grave, will be—so he uses the last wish to make his son go away.

"Now, let me ask *you*—this is your beloved only son, and you are responsible for his death. Would you open the door?"

There was a collective "No!" Karess Flanagan actually put her hands to her rosy cheeks, shaking her head.

"Well, why not?" Mira asked, pretending to be shocked by their callousness. "He's your *son*. Your loving child. What are you afraid of?"

"He's dead!"

"So? He's back!" Mira imitated their tones, and they laughed.

"He won't be the same," Miriam Mason said. "He's been *buried*."

"He'll be pissed as hell," Tony Barnstone said.

"Maybe not." Mira shrugged. "He'd probably understand that you just screwed up with that first wish, and then, after all, you used the next one to get him out of the grave."

"Dead people are *always* pissed," Tony said.

"Well, here's a question then—*why*?" Mira asked. "What would turn someone who has been, say, kind and shy before death into this kind of monster after?" She used her pencil to point to the raging zombie in the movie still.

There was no answer.

"Perry? Next slide?"

The next slide was a photograph Mira had taken herself in Bosnia during her Fulbright year. In it, an old woman in a black dress was walking backward out of the doorway of her little cottage on a hillside. She was sweeping the threshold.

"This is a Bosnian woman whose only daughter had died of pneumonia a few days before I took this photo. I'd been in the village and was invited to the funeral, where I saw this woman throw herself onto the casket of her daughter, clawing at it. She eventually had to be pulled away by her sons. During the funeral procession and service, the woman collapsed to her knees in grief five or six times. But what she's doing here"—Mira pointed with her pencil to the broom—"is sweeping the doorway while walking backward, exactly forty-eight hours after her daughter's death, to ensure that the girl won't come back."

Some of the students were chewing on their pencils.

"Perry?"

He flipped to the next slide, which was as provocative as Mira allowed herself to get this early in the semester—a black-and-white morgue photo of Marilyn Monroe, laid out on a gurney, covered to the neck with a sheet. Her face was completely slack, her cheeks sunken and discolored, mottled along the cheekbones and forehead and nose, her hair combed back straight behind her head, her lips a thin grimace.

"This is Marilyn Monroe's last photo," Mira said.

There were the expected *oh my gods* and muffled cries of horror as the students started to recognize in the corpse's distorted features the icon of sex and beauty with which they were familiar. Several students sat up and leaned over their desks to get a closer look. No one turned away.

"Perry?"

The next image was the famous shot of Marilyn Monroe standing over the subway grate, pretending to try to hold down the pleated skirt of her white dress.

"Thanks, Perry. You can turn the projector off," Mira said. "So, as you now know from your reading, within twelve to fifteen hours of death, if the corpse is left untreated and unrefrigerated, the following changes take place:

"The corpse changes in color, usually to a kind of pinkish-purple. This is called *hypostasis.*"

Mira wrote the word on the board.

"Even *earlier* than twelve hours, depending on the weather, there will be massive swelling due to the build-up of gases in the body, which renders the facial features unrecognizable. Blisters rise on the surface of the skin, and burst, due to the shedding of the epidermis. This is called *skin slippage.*"

She wrote the word *sacromenos* on the board.

"This," she told them, pointing, "is the Greek word for 'vampire.' Literally, it means 'flesh made by the moon.' You can imagine such flesh on the dead, can't you, after skin slippage?"

There were dazed-looking nods all around.

"So," Mira went on, "a few hours after skin slippage, there begins the escape of bloodstained fluids from the orifices and the liquefaction of the eyeballs. Within twenty-four hours—again, depending on the weather—there will be the presence of maggots, and in another twenty-four hours, the shedding of nails and hair, and then the conversion of tissue into a semi-fluid mass, which, along with the buildup of gasses, will cause the abdomen to burst, often in a noisy explosion.

"It may not surprise you to learn that the number one cause of 'shell shock' as we used to call it, among war veterans, or posttraumatic stress disorder as we call it now, is not actually due to the experience of shelling, or the fear of their own deaths, but by encounters had with corpses.

"It's why the old man in 'The Monkey's Paw', who perhaps lived in a time before the funeral parlor business got so big, and who might have been a war veteran himself, would not have wanted to open the door to find his three-days-dead son on the other side, and why the old woman in Bosnia swept the doorway to make sure her beloved daughter wouldn't come home. It's why the fear of the dead, and the conviction that they are evil—our utter aversion to them—has persisted and influenced so many of our rituals and beliefs. And, as with anything so feared, there are corresponding obsessions and fascinations. *That* will be the focus of our next class."

There were no questions. The students seemed vaguely disoriented, as they often did on Putrefaction Day, and Mira let them go ten minutes early. They gathered their things in silence. As they filed out past her desk, Perry unplugged the slide projector and wound the cord carefully. As she packed up her things, he asked, "Are we meeting this afternoon, Professor?"

Mira looked at her watch. It was Tuesday, and Clark would be eager to be relieved of the twins, who had been especially cranky that morning—tossing their Cheerios around the kitchen, hollering at Mira in their musical, unintelligible chatter. Clark had said, "Don't be late," as Mira hurried out the door.

"Clark," she'd said, stopping, turning, "I'll try not to be, but I have a job. I have students, and colleagues, and emails, and phone calls—"

Clark held up a hand, shaking his head. "No need to list all the things you have, Mira. I get it. See you when you can manage it."

"Clark," she'd said, holding out her hands—not as if she were reaching for him, she realized, but more as if she were offering him her wrists to slash. She'd said his name again, but he'd gone into the bathroom and shut the door.

She looked now at Perry.

All weekend she'd thought about their project. She had a hundred questions for him, and a strange bright spot of hope about the future. Despite herself (how well she knew the foolishness of putting the cart before the horse), she'd thought of a title: *The American Campus: Sex, Superstition, and Death.*

It was, she had to admit to herself, the first sense she'd had since the twins were born that she might have another book in her, and a continuing academic career.

"Well," she said to Perry. "Yes, we should meet. But I'll need to leave within the hour. Childcare."

She shrugged, but felt a soggy lump in her throat that she thought must have to do with the twins, and the way, that morning, the boys had looked up from their high chairs as she bent over to kiss them, their faces wet with milk and a few stuck-on Cheerios, and how she'd been too worried about what their reaction would be to her leaving (and what Clark's reaction to their reaction would be) to actually say good-bye. They were babbling in their sad foreign language, and she had to push down, as she always did, her fear that there was something wrong, that this was not just your routine "delayed language acquisition," and as perfectly normal as the pediatrician had insisted, but something much larger, much more predictive of future horrors. Clark refused to talk about it except to say, "You blame me, I suppose?"

"Why would I blame you?"

"Because I'm the one raising your kids, I suppose."

Everything, even the sounds that came out of their toddlers' mouths, was a minefield between them now.

She couldn't say good-bye. Instead, she'd waited until they were busy with their plastic airplane spoons again to sneak out the front door, pulling it closed behind her without making a sound.

20

I'm in love, man."

Craig was sitting at the edge of his bed. It was a Saturday night, mid-November, and Perry had just finished writing a paper on Socrates' belief that rational self-criticism could free the human mind from the bondage of illusion. He didn't want to talk to his roommate about Nicole Werner.

"Great, man," he said.

"I'm serious," Craig said. "I know you think I'm an asshole, but—"

"Well, who's to say an asshole can't fall in love?"

Perry deliberately kept his back turned to Craig's side of the room, hoping he'd take the hint.

"You're not fooling me," Craig said.

Perry couldn't help it. He turned around. "Okay," he said. "So, what is it I'm not fooling you about, Craig?"

"You're in love with her, too. You've probably been in love with her since kindergarten or something. It galls you that I'm dating her. You're going nuts."

"Jesus Christ," Perry said, leaning back, looking at the ceiling. "You're so full of shit, Craig. You'd be saying that about anyone you were dating. You think the whole world's just watching you, burning with envy. But you know what? News flash: We're not."

Craig snorted, as if Perry had confirmed his suspicions by denying them. It was one of the many, many infuriating things about his roommate. You could not win with Craig Clements-Rabbitt. You either confessed or you were lying.

"Look," Perry said, and inhaled. "Even if I'd been madly in love with Nicole Werner since kindergarten, I'd have fallen out of love with her by the time I realized she was stupid enough to date someone like you— not to mention this sorority bullshit, which seems about as stupid as it's humanly possible to get."

"What's that supposed to mean?" Craig asked.

Perry shook his head.

"Huh?" Craig prodded.

"Forget it," Perry said.

"So she likes her sorority, Perry. I think it's cute. You have to admit, she looks incredible in a string of pearls. And that was one helluva float they decorated for Homecoming."

"If you say so."

"I say so. And you *know* so."

"What happened to all your cynicism, man?"

"Well, then I fell in love with Nicole Werner. Just like you did, back in Bad Ass."

"Jesus Christ," Perry said. "Why do we have to talk about this? Why do we have to talk *at all.*"

"Because you won't admit it to me, or to yourself. You're in love with Nicole."

Perry tossed up his hands. "Okay, Craig. Okay. If I 'admit' I'm in love with your girlfriend, will you shut the fuck up? Will that make you feel like a Big Man? Like the Big Campus Stud with the girl we'd all die to get our hands on?"

"How about you admit it first, and I'll decide after that?"

"Okay," Perry said, and cleared his throat, rolled his eyes heavenward. "Let me see. The first time I saw Nicole Werner in Mrs. Bell's kindergarten classroom, clutching a crayon in one hand and a piece of construction paper in the other, I thought to myself, There's the only girl I'll ever love. I sure as hell hope she doesn't end up dating my roommate in college, because then I'll have to kill myself."

Craig nodded. "I knew it," he said.

"So, you're going to shut up now?"

"No," Craig said, and he went on to tell Perry about their date that night. Pizza at Knockout's. Hours afterward at Starbucks, holding hands. A long walk across the Commons in a bright, sparkling snow. He'd walked her back to her room, and kissed her outside her door.

"Did I tell you yet that I'm in love?" he asked Perry.

"I think you might have mentioned that," Perry said.

21

Craig knew it was a bad idea to walk by the sorority. He'd promised Perry he wouldn't, and his father, and he'd managed to get through the entire month of September without doing so, without visiting any of the old haunts, except that one day he'd stood outside Godwin Honors Hall in September. Now, it was October.

Where had September gone?

Craig had simply sleepwalked through it, it seemed. He woke up in the mornings and realized that, somehow, he'd done his homework. He'd have only the vaguest recollection of doing it, but there it would be on his laptop: an essay on the Ptolemaic strategy waiting to be taken to the lab to be printed up. The notes he took in his classes were in his own handwriting, so he had to have taken them himself, but it was like that story "The Elves and the Shoemaker." Craig just woke up and found all the work had been done, as if by elves, or some other self.

That morning he woke to hear Perry running water in the kitchen, nuking something. Through the other wall he could hear a thudding bass from the neighbor's stereo. Outside, the masses of blackbirds that had taken to roosting in the trees outside their apartment windows were already cawing and squawking. The black arrow of one's shadow passed over his window shade. He was going to have to get out of bed, he knew, and he knew that once he did that, he was going to walk by the Omega Theta Tau house.

P_{al}," his father had said on Saturday when he'd called. "You don't sound right. Are you depressed? Are they harassing you there? Any problems? Memory? Et cetera?"

"No, Dad. No one's harassing me. And, yeah, I guess I'm a little depressed. I wouldn't be any less depressed anywhere else, though. And I think I'm okay in the head. As good as I'm going to be again, I guess."

"You're sure no one's giving you a hard time?"

"No one," Craig said, realizing, not for the first time, that maybe he'd hoped they would. Maybe he'd come back here hoping to be hounded off campus, ridiculed, killed. Where were the outraged sorority sisters? Why hadn't they chased him down on the Commons and ripped him limb from limb? Had they forgotten about Nicole? Shouldn't there be daily protests outside the administration building?

How could they have let Nicole Werner's killer back in?

But Nicole's death, it seemed, was last year's news. He hadn't overheard a word about it anywhere. If people recognized him, they didn't show it. If his professors made the connection between Nicole's death and his name, they kept it to themselves. Maybe back at Godwin Honors Hall there were still some flyers posted to the bulletin boards, or a memorial in the lobby or something, but there wasn't anything else anywhere else on campus.

He dragged himself out of bed. He was packing up his laptop, pulling a sweatshirt over his grungy T-shirt, saying, "See ya later," to Perry, and trying to get out of the apartment quickly enough that Perry couldn't ask him where he was headed.

He was headed *there*. He hadn't even glimpsed it, he realized, since that last night in March. Back then.

Back then, Craig had hated the Omega Theta Tau house and the way, each time he walked across campus to it, the front door would open for Nicole and swallow her whole. There was always some blonde standing in the shadows beyond the threshold, and the door would swing closed, and Craig knew he wouldn't get her back until whatever party, or pledging, or tea, or secret meeting, or special election of floral arrangement committee members, or selection of the menu for the next Founders Formal that night was over.

How many times had he walked by the Omega Theta Tau house (its brooding brown and blond bricks, the wraparound porch, the long windows, the eaves crawling with ivy) after he'd started dating Nicole, just to see if the candles were still flickering in the rooms beyond the windows?

And the guys hanging around.

Those frat guys with their handshakes and their collars turned up. Tossing a football, hard. The smack of it hitting their hands.

"Maybe you could think about a house, you know, for next year? It's not too late. Plenty of guys rush their sophomore years," Nicole said one night as he was walking her from Godwin Honors Hall to the Omega Theta Tau house.

"Why?" he asked.

"I don't know," she said, sweet and pouty. "It would just, maybe, make things easier, you know."

"What's hard now?"

"I don't know. I mean, there's a lot of social stuff. The sorority likes it, you know, if your dates are Greek. When I'm living in the house next year, there might be a bit more, I don't know, pressure or something to be dating a frat guy."

"Nicole," Craig said, speaking slowly, as if to a child, humoring her, but, he hoped, radiating affection at the same time. "I'm not going to be one of those assholes. I mean, I think your whole sorority sister stuff is cute. But you're a *girl*. It's all about hair and makeup for you, and shaving chocolate onto gelato, and decorating floats. But if *I* joined one of those things I'd have to, I don't know, wear a beanie propeller or shave my pubic hair or something."

"*What?* Is that what you think?"

"Okay, not *that* maybe. But something equally dumb, and obnoxious. Those guys are all about dumb and obnoxious. I'd rather die than live in a houseful of those kinds of guys."

Nicole hadn't said anything. She'd grown quiet.

Sometimes, when she sulked, Craig glimpsed a single dimple at the right corner of her mouth, and he could imagine her as a toddler then, mad about something: A teddy bear. A lollipop. It made him want to give her anything she wanted.

"But I'll think about it," he said. "I understand why you think that would make things easier."

"Really?" she asked, turning to him, taking both his hands in hers, kissing them.

He'd hated having to let go of those hands—soft and white as little cashmere mittens—and watch her walk away from him, sway up the paving stones to the front door of that house in her silver sandals, some meaty frat guy watching her ass from the porch of the frat house next door.

Now he walked across campus as quickly as he could, long strides, without looking up. He had a reason for going to the Omega Theta Tau house today, although the reason was only a half-formed idea in his head, a kind of dreamy inclination that had begun at the Roper Library a few days earlier. He'd gone there to check out a book his Western Mind professor had put on reserve, but the book had already been checked out, so Craig had found himself at a computer instead, plugging Nicole's name into the friendly Google rectangle and coming up with about four hundred and twenty hits—mostly local newspaper accounts of the accident, which he'd read a hundred times already, and a few reports from the Bad Axe Times, including an obituary, and a couple of articles from the school newspaper calling for his blood, and then lamenting his readmittance to the university, all of which he'd also seen and gotten used to.

But then he came upon one with a photograph of the Omega Theta Tau house: an entire orchard of cherry trees being planted in the two acres that stretched between the south end of their property and the Presbyterian church next door.

The Nicole Werner Memorial Cherry Orchard.

How, on his many Google visits, had he missed *this*?

Fifteen, *twenty* trees, and a line of sorority sisters in black dresses and black sunglasses holding hands before those trees as if they were worshipping them, their gleaming sorority hair lit up by the sun, their heads bowed.

In the branches of the trees were bright blossoms. In the background, some shining cars.

Craig had zoomed in on the photograph, leaned forward until his face was only a few inches from the screen. With the photo enlarged, he was able to recognize some of the sorority sisters who were holding one another's hands. Nicole had introduced him to some of them while crossing campus, or standing in line at the Bijou, or looking up from their milkshakes at Pizza Bob's.

("Craig, this is my sister Allison. This is Joanne. This is Skye. This is Marrielle.")

Back then, they'd all looked the same to him. Whether blond (mostly) or dark-haired, they each appeared to Craig like cheap knockoffs of Nicole—girls who were trying hard but could only dream of being as bright-eyed, as pink-cheeked, as purely beautiful as she was.

Nicole had accused him of being unfriendly. It was December by then, and they'd been together for two months (which to him seemed like a lifetime, by far the longest he'd ever dated a girl), and she'd said, "You don't make eye contact with my sisters. They think you're un-friendly." He agreed to try harder, albeit reluctantly. But the only time he met any of her sorority sisters again after that was when he'd already pissed them off by pushing his way into a Greek-only party:

Two a.m., and Nicole had said she'd meet him outside the Omega Theta Tau house at midnight. Craig had stood around for what seemed like long enough, and then he'd sat on the front stoop, calling her dorm room over and over. (Like Perry, Nicole didn't own a cell phone. Verizon, it seemed, had not yet made its sales pitch to Bad Axe.) He was thinking that eventually she'd pick up, and explain that she'd waited outside the OTT house but hadn't seen him, and so had walked herself back to God-win. He was thinking she'd say how sorry she was, and ask if he would come by to give her a good-night kiss. The worst-case scenario would be that Josie would answer and sound pissed off to hear his voice, but at least she'd offer some explanation for what had happened to Nicole.

But there was no answer at all in Nicole's dorm room, and not a single girl came out the front door of the sorority house. Craig could hear the music thumping away inside, along with the occasional burst of wild laughter, the occasional girlish scream, sounding as if someone was being tickled with something surprisingly sharp. He'd already tried to look in the windows a few times, but they were high, tall windows, and the party seemed to be taking place in the basement, out of sight.

The only partiers he'd managed to glimpse were some guy passed out on a couch and two girls appearing to be trying to read each other's palms.

There was a hired thug at the door: some hulking guy in a black shirt and black pants, holding a walkie-talkie in his hand, who did not look as if he were now or had ever been a college student. The thug would stand up and shrug his shoulders menacingly each time Craig came around the front door, and then shake his head, looking at Craig. When Craig went to the *back* door, there was always a sorority sister there—a different one each time—who would cross her arms over her breasts as if Craig were about to grab them, and, in this pretzel shape, manage to say something into a walkie-talkie while watching Craig warily until he went away.

He pretended to be walking back to the street, but then veered back through the shadows and managed to find a spot at the side of the house where he was able to crawl between a couple of shrubs and peer through a toaster-size window into the basement. The shrubs were of the thorny variety, and Craig could feel them ripping through the thin material of his T-shirt. He knew he was going to have scratches and welts, but he managed to creep to the little window anyway, put his face up to it, his hands around his face.

Down there, in the basement, they had a strobe light going. It seemed to be hooked up to the throbbing bass of the music they were playing, flashing to the beat. What Craig saw in the spasmodic intervals of light was dancing—girls' bare arms lifted, girls' bare midriffs and hipbones swaying, girls with their arms around each other's necks and shoulders, tossing back their heads, seeming to be howling, or screaming, or laughing, a few girls holding hands and dashing around in a wild circle, falling onto the basement floor, limbs and hair and bra straps and bare skin, and a keg in a corner, and a line of girls at it, and then, in another corner, what looked to him like Nicole (he pressed his face hard enough against the glass that he thought he might crack it in half), holding a plastic cup, taking a sip from it, her arms around the neck of some beefy older-looking guy in a sweat-stained light blue shirt—and then, long before he knew he was doing it, Craig was barging through the back door past the sorority girl, who started swearing into her walkie-talkie, shouting at his back, "You're not allowed in our house, asshole!"

He took the stairs down to the basement two at a time, finding his way to them by pure instinct, slipping on the last one into a small smoky crowd dancing to some crappy Beyoncé song, and found himself looking straight into the face of a girl with long black tears of sweat and mascara dripping down her face. "What the fu—" she said, and then the sorority sister who'd been chasing him since the back door grabbed his arm and started shouting, and the bruiser from the front door had him by the collar, and in the corner where he'd been sure he'd seen Nicole, there was no one.

"Nicole?! Nicole?! Nicole?!"

He screamed her name over the music, over and over again, in the direction of the empty corner as the bruiser pulled him out of the crowd of girls and toward the basement stairs, at the top of which Nicole stood looking down at him with a shocked expression on her face.

"Craig . . . ?"

"Nicole?"

"Who *is* this jerk?" the girl with the walkie-talkie asked Nicole, scowling in Craig's direction. "Do you *know* him?"

When he reached the top of the stairs, the bouncer behind him gave Craig a shove, and Nicole said, "Yes," as if she regretted having to admit it. "This is Craig. He's my friend. I'll walk him home."

The girl glared at Craig. Her eyes were too blue to be real. Those had to be contacts, Craig thought.

The girl looked from Craig to Nicole. She was wearing so much lip gloss she looked like she'd recently been kissing an oil slick. She said, "Don't ever let him come around here again. *Ever.*"

"Okay," Nicole said, sounding like someone who'd slipped into shock. "Come on, Craig."

"Don't you have a coat or something?" the girl asked Nicole.

"I'll get it tomorrow," she said, guiding Craig back out into the cool darkness, where the temperature had dropped since he'd first walked her to the OTT house. Now he could see their breaths puffing into it as they walked in silence, quickly, in the direction of Godwin Hall. Nicole was shivering and shaking her head at the same time. When Craig tried to put his arm around her, she shrugged it off.

"What were you *thinking?*" she asked, staring straight ahead, not looking at him. She was walking so fast he practically had to jog at her side.

"Nicole, you said you'd be out of that party at—"

"Okay, Craig, but I never told you to pick me up. I told you I was going to walk back with Josie. Why did you come back to the house?"

"Because I was going to make sure you got back to Godwin Hall. I was worried. I was worried about you. *Sorry.*"

It sounded whiny and pathetic, even to him.

"Well, I was helping with the party. You know, picking up empties, making sure people put their cigarettes out, tossing out cups. Do you know how bad this is Craig, to have a friend crash the party, and make a scene, and—?"

"Is that what I am to you, Nicole? Your *friend?*"

"Of course," she said, as she if were consoling him.

"Gee," he said, "I sort of thought I was more than that." He felt something behind the bridge of his nose—his sinuses?—fill up with the sarcasm, the self-pity implicit in it, like . . . Jesus Christ, was he getting ready to cry?

"Well, I mean, we're dating, sure. We're more than friends. But I think *friendship* is really valuable, maybe the most important thing in the world next to family. I *want* to be your friend, Craig. But—"

She'd slowed down and put her cold hand in his. She squeezed his hand. She was shivering, and so he put both arms around her and pulled her to him, and said nothing, just happy to have her close to him.

He couldn't have argued with her anyway. He already knew from experience not to argue with her when she was dealing in abstractions: friendship, God, love, patriotism, chastity. He loved that about her.

"Okay," Craig said, happy enough to lose this argument. "Me, too. That's not what this is about. I saw you dancing with some guy."

"No, you didn't!" Nicole shouted, as if she'd just caught him in a brazen lie, jumping backward out of his arms. "I did *not* dance with *any* guys. I danced a little with Josie, and with Abby one time, but when guys asked me to dance, I said, 'Sorry, can't,' and held this up."

It was the ring he'd bought her from Grimoire Gifts two weeks ago—a little globe of amber, with something ancient, some little black bug, trapped in it forever. She wore it on her right hand, because she wore a ring her father had given her on her left. He'd have preferred the left, but Nicole had made it clear that there was no room for debate.

She stopped walking and turned to him with a stony, hurt expression. Her teeth had actually begun to chatter loud enough that he could hear them—like fingernails tapping across a keyboard, or dice being rattled in a can. "Oh, Jesus," he said, moved by the sound of those teeth, and her shivering, even though he knew she didn't like him to say Jesus. "Oh, Nicole." He unbuttoned his shirt—he was wearing a T-shirt underneath—and wrestled the button-down off his arms, draping it over Nicole's shoulders and then helping her put her arms through the sleeves, as if she were an invalid, or a toddler. She limply accepted his shirt, his help, and he wrapped his arms around her again and hurried her back to Godwin Hall, whispering words of apology desperately in her ear as they walked.

When they finally got into the dorm, and he'd told her he loved her so many times that she finally started laughing, and she wasn't shivering any longer, she leaned back against the foyer wall and pulled him to her, and they leaned there kissing one another for a very long time, long enough that time seemed to have stopped, and maybe a hundred people had passed them going up or down the stairs—but it wasn't long enough for Craig, who was always the one who said, "Just another minute or two," a hundred times, until Nicole, laughing, finally left him, shaking her head at him, throwing him kisses as she went up to her room. *Forgiven.*

It was the first thing Craig saw when he rounded the corner of Seneca Lane and West University Avenue: the Omega Theta Tau house casting a shadow down on that orchard that hadn't been there in the winter, the last time Craig had walked by.

There was a stone angel at the center, lifting her concrete wings and bending over at the same time, as if the wings were what had forced her down to earth in the first place.

It didn't take much imagination to guess what the brass plaque at the feet of that garden statuary said.

Tomorrow, Craig supposed, there would be mounds of roses, a teddy bear, that sort of thing.

Tomorrow would have been her nineteenth birthday.

22

Clark was asleep when Mira got home. It was two o'clock in the afternoon, but he lay on his back on their bed with his hands folded on his chest, so deeply asleep he never heard her come in the house or the twins' deafening squealing upon her arrival—the usual tearful reunion, the clinging, the sobbing against her chest. By the time Mira had finally calmed them down enough to stand up from the floor and go looking for Clark, there were two spreading damp circles of their tears on her red silk blouse.

Ruined, she thought. Her mother used to have a trick for getting water stains off silk, but Mira hadn't been paying attention then, and certainly didn't remember now what the secret method might have been. Maybe, she thought, as she headed for the bedroom in search of Clark, she could research it on the Internet if she ever found the time— the Internet, which had become the mother lode of folk remedies and feminine advice for those without mothers to consult.

"Clark?"

Clark sputtered, blinked, coughed like a man surfacing in shallow water, and then he gasped and sat up fast. "*What?*"

"Are you okay?"

He rubbed his eyes, and then he scowled at her with half his face. Somehow, the other half of his face still looked familiar. She recognized the blank expression from a photo in their wedding album. "What the hell is that supposed to mean? Of course I'm *okay*."

"Well," Mira said, "you're in here dead asleep at two o'clock in the afternoon while the twins are hungry and sitting in dirty diapers on the kitchen floor. I thought maybe you were sick."

"Fuck you, Mira," he said, and lay back down, staring straight at the ceiling, folding his hands over his chest again, closing his eyes with such finality that Mira almost thought she could hear them click shut with the neat precision of Swiss pocket watches.

She turned around and pulled the bedroom door closed hard behind her.

The poop in the twins' diapers seemed to have been there a long time. It was hard, and caked into their little butt cracks. Mira changed Matty first because he'd cried the hardest when she got home. He was still hiccupping with it, looking up at her with wide, glassy eyes. She sang the "five little duckies" song to distract him on the changing table, but he whimpered when she had to work too hard with the baby wipes to get the caked-on shit off his tender bottom. It looked red and sore when she was done, but it was clean, and he wasn't crying. She dusted it with baby powder and tickled his belly before lifting him off the table and placing him back on the floor.

Andy was easier. He'd never much minded a dirty diaper, and as long as she was singing the duckies song, he didn't seem to mind if she was being a bit rough with his behind. She looked into his eyes as she sang, and he never blinked, as if he were afraid she'd disappear again if he did. As she changed his brother, Matty held on to one of her ankles from his spot on the floor, humming wetly into her shin.

After Andy's diaper was changed, Mira got back down on the floor and pulled them both to her, and unbuttoned her stained blouse, unclasped her bra, and let her breasts fall out into their mouths.

("Good Lord, Mira, how long are you going to keep nursing those boys?" Clark's sister had asked six months earlier, when she'd come to visit from Atlanta. The twins had only just turned two then, but Mira had felt chastised, and stammered something about the boys only nursing once or twice a day. It was more of a habit, she tried to explain, than anything else. A way to calm them, or to get them to sleep on hectic nights. They were eating solid foods, of course. Pretty much anything she and Clark ate, the twins ate, and they ate a lot of it, and since Mira was gone a good part of every day, they certainly did not depend on breast milk for *food*.

"Jesus," Rebecca had said, "I quit nursing Ricky at six months when he got his front teeth. I thought he was going to bite my nipple off."

But Rebecca was married to a packaging engineer. She'd stayed home with Ricky until he went to kindergarten, and even after that she worked only two mornings a week, at a children's bookstore. She'd never, Mira felt certain, come home and found Ricky wearing a diaper stiff with shit while her husband slept like a dead man in another room.)

As the boys sucked harder, tears sprang into Mira's eyes. She'd wasted a precious forty-five minutes in her office with Perry Edwards when she should have been home with her babies—and afterward she'd stopped in the doorway of Dean Fleming's office just to smile and wave, and ended up wasting another half hour. She'd stopped there on purpose, knowing he would ask her how her "work" was going, and for the first time in a long time, she actually had something to say because she was working on something quite promising: a book-length consideration of the folklore of death on the American college campus.

Dean Fleming had raised his eyebrows as if he, too, saw the huge potential in her project. "Interesting," he said, nodding, clearly pleased and impressed. "I knew you'd zero in on something great in time." He wished her luck, offered his support. He said, "If you need travel funds or a book allowance, let me know. We'll see what we can find."

She left Godwin Hall feeling lighter than she had in a long time. She had a project. Because there'd been a rainstorm that morning, and Clark had grudgingly let her drive the car to campus, she decided to drive by the location of the accident, Nicole Werner's accident, which she'd begun to think of as *material*.

Mira had driven by it hundreds of times since the accident because it was on the way to half the places she needed to be (grocery store, drugstore, gas station). Like everyone else in town, she had watched the accumulating expressions of sentimental grief, the mounding of more and more debris at the site. Girlish, and ghoulish.

It had begun with a white cross with the victim's name on it, and then a few stuffed animals were added, along with some wreaths of pink and white flowers—and then, within a few weeks, it had grown to a full-scale folk monument: A wisteria was planted. A banner was wound around the branches of the tree at the site. Some ornaments were hung in the branches. (Angels? Fairies? Mira couldn't tell from the road.) More stuffed animals and some baby dolls accumulated around the tree's trunk, and a laminated blowup of that senior portrait of Nicole Werner leaned against it, staring at the place where she'd lost her life. There were mounds of fresh flowers, and an unfathomable number of silk and plastic bouquets, ever replenishing, although Mira had never actually seen anyone tending to these items or dropping them off. (Did they come under cover of darkness?) Floral wreaths stretched from the side of the road across the drainage ditch to the electric fence, beyond which there were always a few sheep looking dazed and doomed.

Mira slowed down as she drove past. The next sunny morning, she thought, she would bring her best camera out here, and take photos.

The twins had fallen asleep as they sucked, and when Clark came out of the bedroom, he looked down at Mira for a moment, at the two flushed and dreaming twins still clinging to her nipples by their teeth. He must have realized that she was crying—there were tears running down her neck and onto her bare chest—but the expression on his face was unreadable, and far above her.

"I'm going for a run," he said, and was gone.

23

I t was the second week of January. She was lying on Craig's bed when Perry got back to the dorm room after the first winter semester meeting of his International Human Rights seminar. She was on top of Craig's comforter (Craig had started making his bed since he'd started dating Nicole) in a T-shirt. Her legs were bare. Perry thought, with a jolt that felt a bit like panic, that he'd caught a glimpse of pale blue underpants when she crossed her ankles. She was wearing a silver ankle bracelet. It had what looked like a bell, or an anchor, or a crucifix, hanging from it. She had a book in her hands.

Perry looked away. He strode purposefully to his desk, sat down with his back to her, and said, "What are you doing here, Nicole? Craig's not going to be back until after dinner."

"I'm just reading," she said. "It's quieter here than in my room. Josie's always got Norah Jones playing. Drives me nuts. Whine-whine-whine."

Perry could hear the springs on Craig's bed squeak. She must have shifted her weight, rolled onto her side. He wasn't going to give her the satisfaction of looking over. He turned his computer on, and there was the usual sound of an angelic choir starting up—one discordant but celestial note, which hung in the air.

"No offense, Nicole," Perry finally managed to say, "but when my roommate's not here, I actually enjoy my solitude."

"Well, Craig said you wouldn't mind," Nicole said casually. "He gave me his key."

Perry's screen saver came up then (comets shooting through a blue-black sky) and, at the same time, something hit his shoulder, sharp and surprising, and it took him only a second or two to realize that it was Craig's room key clattering on the floor behind him. Before he could stop himself, he was turned around in his chair, glaring at Nicole.

She was, as he'd thought, lying on her side. One leg was slung over the other. One of her bare feet (toenails painted shell pink) was pointed, swinging like a pendulum over the side of Craig's bed.

"Come on, Nicole," Perry said. "Why are you here?" He rubbed his hand across his eyes, trying to seem more exhausted than agitated. He didn't want to give her the satisfaction of seeming as unnerved by her presence as he was. Since she and Craig had taken up full time, she was, like Craig himself, a constant irritation, mainly because Craig never shut up about her, was in an endless cycle of manic ecstasy and despair about her. When he wasn't frantically trying to call her, or find her, he was on the phone with her, or in their room with her. They couldn't hang out in Nicole's room because Josie hated Craig's guts, so they were here, or in the hallway waiting for Perry to get dressed so they could get in. Whenever Perry said something to Craig about it, Craig just said, "You're jealous, man. You're in love with my girlfriend. The sooner you face it, the better off we'll all be." It seemed like a joke now, with Craig, but it was still exasperating.

"I think you know why I'm here," Nicole said before she stood up and crossed the room—those bare feet, and the toenails, he tried only to look at those—and knelt down at his feet, looked up at him, directly in his line of vision, so he had to look back, and then she reached up for his face, pulled it gently toward her, and before he really understood what she was going to do, and what was happening, kissed him with her mouth open, her tongue slipping warmly, mintily, over his.

24

Shelly typed *Josie Reilly* into Google.

It was Monday, and Josie hadn't made it into work at all. Shelly had come into the office to a raspy message on her machine in the morning:

"Hey, this is Josie (cough, cough) and I'm really sick. I can't come in. I'm really sorry. I'm going to Health Services now. I'll be in on Wednesday I'm sure."

There were an astonishing number of Google hits.

Of course, *Josie Reilly* wasn't a completely unique name. One Josefina/Josie Reilly seemed to have been involved somehow in the Salem witch trials. Another Josie Reilly was a CEO of a large, bankrupt corporation. There was also a long list of genealogical connections—Reillys and Rileys and Reileys going back several centuries, traversing the Atlantic, claiming to be related to one another, as if it mattered. (What, Shelly always wondered, did people feel they gained by claiming kinship with strangers, alive or dead?)

But then her Josie Reilly rose to the surface, incontrovertibly the coed sorority sister from Grosse Isle, the one Shelly had hired as a work-study student for the Chamber Music Society:

DEAD FRESHMAN'S ROOMMATE SPEAKS OUT AGAINST DRUNK DRIVER.

There she was—Josie, in all her sloe-eyed Black Irish beauty, holding a microphone on the steps of the Llewellyn Roper Library. The sun shone down on her inky hair, which matched the black halter-top dress she wore. Behind her, the familiar apple tree that seemed to grow out of the foundation of the library (the one they were always threatening to rip out because it was fucking up the plumbing) wasn't yet in bloom.

The Dead Freshman's Roommate?

Shelly clearly remembered asking Josie of Nicole Werner, "Did you know her?" And the shrug. *We all knew her. She and I rushed and pledged at the same time, so . . .*

Josie had said nothing about being her roommate. Nothing whatsoever. Nothing about standing outside the Llewellyn Roper Library in May, speaking out against drunk driving and about her dead roommate. Why?

That night, after a distracted glass of Cabernet Sauvignon and a cursory page-through of the *New York Times*, Shelly called Rosemary.

For over two decades she had spoken to Rosemary on the phone every few days, and a bit more lately, since Rosemary's eldest son had become a teenager and there was so much to say about this terrifying passage. For the first half of the conversation, Shelly listened to Rosemary rail against the public schools and the fact that they allowed fourteen-year-old children to neck on the benches outside the building during lunch period.

"Can you *imagine* if we'd tried to get away with that in middle school?" Rosemary asked.

She wasn't expecting an answer, so Shelly didn't say that, actually, she *could*, and that she remembered, herself, the spring of eighth grade, meeting Tony Lipking (ironically named, since he was her first kiss) out in the parking lot every lunch hour it wasn't raining, and the warm feeling of Tony's Ford's grille against her thighs as he held her between himself and that grille with his face locked onto hers for the entire hour, when she should have been eating her mother's turkey sandwich and carrot sticks.

When Rosemary was done railing, Shelly told her the story of Josie, and how she'd Googled her on the Internet and discovered her as Nicole Werner's grieving roommate.

"Why wouldn't she have told me that, when I asked? Why would it be a secret, especially after I told her that I was at the accident?"

Rosemary seemed to consider this for quite a while, although Shelly could also hear a sink running in the background. (Often it seemed that Rosemary was multitasking while they talked.) "Traumatized?" Rosemary finally offered. "Or maybe she thinks it's controversial? Maybe she doesn't want to get into it? Trying to get past all that?"

"No," Shelly said. She didn't even have to think about it. "That's not this girl. This girl would be *thrilled* to get controversial. Believe me."

Shelly went on to tell Rosemary everything she knew about Josie Reilly—the boys waiting in the office, the early departures, late arrivals, the excuses. She described the spaghetti-strap tops she wore. The little silver sandals and the black flats with frilly bows. Jeremy, Shelly's cat, was licking his catnip mouse on the braided rug at her feet as Shelly detailed the habits of her work-study student and this odd mystery surrounding her.

"Shelly?" Rosemary asked when Shelly was done. "Can I ask you a question?"

"Of course," Shelly said.

Rosemary lowered her voice, hesitated, and then asked, "Are you, you know, in *love* with this girl?"

"*What?*" Shelly was surprised to find her pulse racing, her cheeks and chest prickling with heat. "Why would you ask that?"

"Oh, I'm sorry, hon. I'm not accusing you of anything! I don't know," Rosemary said. She laughed nervously. "There's just something in your voice. You seem so—*intrigued.*"

"I can be *intrigued* and not be *in love,*" Shelly said.

"Well, of course you can," Rosemary said. "Forget I said anything, okay? Just forget it. But, you know, if you decide you *are* in love with her, you call me before—"

"Rosemary, Jesus. She's not even twenty years old. I—"

"Like I said," Rosemary said, "just forget it. I never said it. You're right. Ridiculous Rosemary. Tell me a joke or something, okay? Or, like, what did you have for dinner tonight? See any good movies lately?"

25

D r. Truby asked Craig, solemnly, as if speaking in his lowest voice and leaning forward might seduce it out of Craig's subconscious, "And that evening—earlier—you don't even remember how you ended up in the car, how Nicole got there with you, where you were going when the accident occurred?"

Craig bit his bottom lip and looked at the ceiling. Swallowed. Closed his eyes. He *wanted* to remember. He wanted to deliver some tidbit to Dr. Truby, something for all the man's hard work. But what? He'd already gone over what he could remember with the guy, and it wasn't much:

By now he remembered well enough that he'd been driving Lucas's old Taurus. He hazily remembered Lucas, stoned in his dorm room, handing him the keys, and saying, "Good luck, man." But he had no recollection of what it was he might have needed luck for. Craig had been told by his lawyer that, questioned later by detectives, Lucas had said, "I didn't know what was going on. He came into my room saying, 'I gotta borrow your car,' so I tossed him the keys, told him where it was parked, and said, 'Good luck, man.' He was in way too much of a hurry to ask him what the problem was. Frankly, I thought it might be, you know, Nicole—some female thing. Like, she was having a hemorrhage, you know. I knew a girl that happened to once, and she almost died. It was like a coptic pregnancy or something like that—I don't know what you call it."

The police also reported Lucas as saying that Craig had seemed stone-cold sober when he came to get the keys. But, coming from Lucas, that might not have meant much, both because of Lucas's own substance abuse track record and because he was the one who'd loaned someone a car in which a fatal accident had taken place.

Craig looked from the ceiling to his lap to Dr. Truby and said, "Well, I remember a cell phone call. She needed me. I was pissed off about the party. There was someone there I didn't want her to be with, but I can't remember who." He closed his eyes. He saw a blue shirt. Some flash of an insignia. Not a Boy Scout, surely. Not a cop. "A paramedic?" Craig asked, looking up at Dr. Truby, as if *he* might remember. "You know, some kind of ambulance driver?"

Dr. Truby nodded, motioned in the air between them, coaxing. "You were jealous?"

"I . . . guess so. Even though she never gave me any reason to be. Nicole was really specific about monogamy. She told me that if she ever, even for a second, thought she was going to be attracted to someone else, she would tell me, and she asked me to do the same. We were really clear on that. Really honest. There was no reason not to be. Nicole was a big believer in *courting*. She only wanted to date in order to find someone to marry. She wore this ring her dad had given her, on her left hand, like a wedding ring—this promise ring."

Dr. Truby shrugged a little with one shoulder, still nodding, not seeming surprised. Maybe he'd heard of promise rings before. But it had been a real eye-opener for Craig, finding out that there were girls whose fathers got involved in their sex lives to the degree that they gave them rings and had them take pledges that they wouldn't have sex until they were married. Nicole's ring looked just like an engagement ring: a gold band with a little diamond.

"She took that stuff seriously, but I knew there were a lot of guys interested in her, and I'd been totally banned from parties at her sorority because of that incident I told you about. I was always afraid, you know, that something might happen when I wasn't there. I mean, I didn't think she'd cheat on me, but I thought she might meet somebody, get interested in some other guy."

Dr. Truby was still nodding (Jesus, Craig thought, he could get a job as one of those dogs on a dashboard), but then he looked at his watch, so Craig knew it was time for him to go. The therapist cleared his throat and said in his "conclusion" voice, "You've come a long way, Craig, for someone with the kind of brain damage you sustained. Just a bit more, a bit longer, and we'll have this sorted out."

"Right," Craig said, trying to make it not sound as sarcastic as he meant it, as if there would ever be anything that would *sort out* his having killed Nicole.

His dad was there in the Subaru, waiting outside Dr. Truby's office, which was in a sort of segregated part of the hospital campus, as if the shrinks and their patients really shouldn't be glimpsed by people who were genuinely sick—cancer, heart problems, diabetes.

"Hey, pal," his father said when Craig sat down and pulled the car door closed. He reached over and patted his son's knee hard enough that Craig probably would have flinched if he were feeling more energetic— but, as it was, he just looked over and nodded. "How'd it go, son?"

"Okay," Craig said. "I guess."

"Well, you don't have to tell me anything," his dad said, holding his hands up over the steering wheel. (How many times had he said this by now? Was he getting so used to Craig being a zombie that he was just going to keep saying it forever?) "But if you *want* to, I want you to know I'm happy to listen, and I won't say a word if you'd rather I didn't."

"Thanks, Dad," Craig said, and then he turned to the window to let his father know that he wasn't going to be able to talk about anything at that particular moment, and that they could just drive home.

"Home," now, was Craig's father's apartment in a complex called the Alpines, on the outskirts of Fredonia. Scar and his mother had stayed in the house. Having been at college while the finer details of his parents' separation were being worked out, Craig wasn't sure how it had happened that Scar had stayed with his mother in the house—except that it was no secret to anyone that Scar and their mother were far closer to each other than either of them was with Craig or his father—and since, after the accident, when he found himself back in New Hampshire, Craig was in a kind of coma, he also didn't know how it had been decided that *he* would move in to the Alpines with his father.

Not that he minded.

He didn't even mind, anymore, that his parents were getting divorced. It was like whatever happened that made him lose his memory of the accident had also wiped out all the rage and despair he'd felt about that, too.

His parents' separation had been in the works for months before the accident, taking place all through the most beautiful early months of his relationship with Nicole, like a bad and blurry backdrop.

"What the hell is going on there?!" Craig had shouted over the phone to Scar one Saturday afternoon in January. He'd called home to demand more answers from anyone who would give them. He had actually been calling for days by then, nonstop, but no one answered the fucking land line or any one of their cell phones since his father had called to give him the news:

"Your mom's leaving me, son. She thinks life's too short to spend it with me."

A few hours after that, his mother had called, either to try to soften it ("We'll just take things a day at a time, and see what happens") or to deny responsibility ("I know your father says this was my decision, but I'm sure it's no surprise to you, or any one else, that this has been coming for a long time, and it's no one's *decision*").

Well, it *had* come as a Big Fucking Surprise to Craig, who'd been planning to spend the weekend in a blissful state of sleepy love with Nicole in his room, since Perry was going back to Bad Axe for somebody's baptism. The last thing in the world Craig had considered was that he'd get news like this from home. Home was supposed to just stay *home*.

"How the fucking hell did this happen?!" Craig screamed at his little brother over the phone.

"I don't know," Scar said, sounding stoned—although, before Craig had left for college in the fall, at least, Scar had been vehemently opposed to smoking weed. ("Why would anyone want to get *stupider*?") But Craig also knew that their mother was pretty excited about all the new psychopharmaceutical miracles taking place in the world, and she was always suggesting to her friends some cure for malaise, or annoyance, or mild anxiety. Maybe now she had Scar on something for *his* mild anxieties, which Craig thought were pretty normal for a kid that age and would go away on their own in time, like his scar, which, in its fading, had begun to look like only the vaguest shadow of a crucifix dug into the skin on his back.

He'd been in sixth grade when he'd gotten that. It was after school, and he was walking home along Mill Creek, probably listening to Nirvana on his iPod, when a kid a year older jumped out of the bushes, wrestled Scar to the ground, pinning his face into the grass between the sidewalk, and, without saying a word about anything, let alone *why*, lifted up the back of Scar's SKI PURPLE MOUNTAIN T-shirt, and cut a crucifix into his back. Then the kid jumped off Scar, ran into the road, and flagged down a passing motorist—a hippie lady in a van, lost off the freeway, looking for a coffee shop.

The kid (Remco Nolens) had pointed over to Scar and said to the woman, "He needs help!" before sprinting back to his house, where the cops came and picked him up an hour later.

Apparently, Remco had been tripping on bad acid when he did it, and couldn't tell anyone why he'd been hiding in the bushes, or why he'd jumped out with the knife, why he'd cut a crucifix into Scar's back. Remco was sent to live with his grandparents in Florida after that, and part of his punishment was that he had to send Scar an apologetic letter every year.

These letters were cause for general hilarity at the Clements-Rabbitt household, as they were so stiff, and so clearly unapologetic: "I wish to tell you again that I am sorry for scratching your back with my pocket knife."

In the end, the wound wasn't life threatening—although it was also more than a "scratch." The nickname had been an attempt to make the kind of light of it Remco had made—as if by calling him *Scar* they could pretend that what had happened wasn't much worse than having a tooth knocked out by a Frisbee.

But to Craig, it had seemed much worse; for months afterward he'd woken from dreams in which he was wrestling his little brother's limp body away from some winged black thing he recognized as Remco. Still, if it bothered Scar, he never said so.

You better talk to Mom or Dad about that," Scar said on the phone. "It's not really any of my business if they're splitting up."

"Not any of your *business*? Huh? Last time I checked, they were your parents too, pal."

"Don't call me *pal* when you're yelling at me. It's just like Dad."

"*What*? What are you talking about? Since when does Dad yell at you?"

There was a silence on the other end of the line. Craig couldn't figure out whether that was a validation of his point that their father never yelled at Scar (never yelled at any of them), or something else—some hint that there was a new family dynamic now, that their father was yelling, that their father had something to yell about.

"Just don't ask me about Mom and Dad," Scar finally said. "Ask *them* if you have to—but personally I think you should just forget it."

"Forget it? Just, like, forget that my parents are getting divorced?"

"Come on, Craig," Scar said, still sounding dopey, far away. "You're a big boy now, get—"

Craig hung up on his brother then, and didn't speak to him again until he was brought back to New Hampshire in March, with only a vague idea of who the boy with the shaggy hair in his eyes was. And then it was weeks before Craig could spontaneously remember the kid's name, and another week before he really understood what it meant that Scar was his brother.

26

L ucas!"

Perry recognized the ponytail and the long lopsided gait from a block away, and he jogged up behind Lucas on the sidewalk, and then next to him. "Hey."

Lucas jumped and spun around. He had apparently not heard Perry calling his name until he was right next to him. "Jesus Christ, Perry," he said. "You scared the shit out of me."

"Sorry. I thought you heard me."

"I didn't," Lucas said. He was panting. His face, in the bright autumn sunlight, looked strangely haggard, much paler than it had even the week before, when Perry had last seen him. He looked like he'd been stoned for days, and maybe like he hadn't slept more than a few hours the night before, and maybe like he was losing weight, rapidly.

"I wanted to tell you something," Perry said.

Lucas stopped. He turned to Perry, although he was glancing to his left and right at the same time, as if looking for someone, or wondering who might be nearby to overhear them. But there was no one on their side of the street. All the students were flooding in the direction of Main Campus, hurrying to make their morning classes on time.

Lucas was carrying a bag. It looked like maybe he'd just come out to go to the store and buy a six-pack, and was headed back to his apartment.

"Is it about *her*?" he asked.

"Not exactly," Perry said. "It's about my professor. Professor Polson. I'm taking her seminar."

"The Death one?"

"Yes."

"I thought that was for freshmen."

"Yeah, well, she let me in."

"Why?" Lucas asked. He looked expressionless and suspicious at the same time.

"Because I asked her to make an exception. I wanted—"

"Because of *her*?"

"Partly," Perry said. Lucas had made it sound like some kind of accusation, and Perry felt defensive. "Also, Professor Polson is working on a book about—"

"Why are you talking to me about this?" Lucas asked, suddenly animated, waving his free hand as if to shoo Perry away. "I don't want to hear about this."

"Because she wants to talk to you, Lucas. Professor Polson wants to ask you some questions. About Nicole. I told her what you told me. And about Patrick, too. And what I've seen. She'll believe you. She needs to interview you, though."

"You talked to a *professor* about this? Are you out of your fucking *mind*?"

"Lucas, it's important. She can help."

"Help? What's she going to do to *help*?"

Perry opened his mouth to answer, but could think of nothing to say.

It was raining when Perry and Professor Polson had met, after class, at Espresso Royale. They sat at a table near the back, far from the windows that faced the street, but Perry could hear rain on the roof—hard, fast rain, like a lot of small feet running furiously overhead—and Professor Polson's dark hair was curled in damp ringlets that clung to her neck and the sides of her face. She looked cold, wearing only a silk dress and a cardigan, and she'd gotten soaked, it seemed, on her walk over from Godwin Honors Hall. Perry had gone ahead when she'd told him she had to stop by the library and drop off a book before meeting him. Now, looking across the table at her, he felt bad. *He'd* had an umbrella. If he'd known she didn't, he would have given her his own, or walked with her to the library and then to the café. She wrapped her hands around the white paper cup and brought it to her mouth to breathe in the steam before she sipped from it. It was the kind of thing Perry had seen women do in movies—drink a cup of coffee like this, with both hands, sipping and peering up over the rims of their cups at the same time, but he wasn't sure he'd ever seen anyone do it in real life. Professor Polson's hands were very white and thin, with a few pale blue veins crisscrossing them.

"I'd like to interview Lucas," she said. "Have you told him that you shared his information with me?"

"No," Perry said. "But he never told me I couldn't tell anyone. I'll find him. I'll bring him to your office. I think he'd be willing."

"Maybe not the office," Professor Polson said. "I'd like to record it. I don't want him to be inhibited by the office. Let's meet off campus. Perhaps you could bring him to my apartment."

"Sure," Perry said.

"After that, we'll see. Maybe Patrick Wright, too. What do you think?"

Patrick had been, it seemed, avoiding Perry since the night he'd spoken about Nicole. He'd been drinking when he called Perry. They barely knew each other—Patrick had been a sophomore on Perry's and Craig's hall at Godwin the year before—but he knew that Perry had gone to high school with Nicole, and he knew that Perry's roommate had been the one who'd had the accident that had killed her. ("I just wondered," Patrick had slurred, "you know. Have *you* seen her? Am I losing my mind, Perry? Whass happening here?") Perry'd had no idea what to say to Patrick, so he had stammered something about sobering up and call- ing back in the morning, but Patrick never called, and Perry didn't run into him. He'd heard the details from Lucas.

"But, let's see how it goes with Lucas first. And, Perry?" She put the cup down on the table between them and tucked her hands somewhere inside her sweater. "Have you told anyone else—for instance, anyone else on the faculty—about any of this?"

Perry had no idea why he was unable to hold her gaze. He hadn't told anyone, and he had no reason to lie to Professor Polson, but he glanced down at her cup instead of at her. There was something about her eyes. She had crow's feet—something he knew women worried about, because his mother had about a hundred different potions to combat those and was always complaining that they didn't do a thing— but around Professor Polson's eyes, they were crinkly and intriguing. They made her look both sexy and wise.

"Perry?" she asked again.

"No," he said. "No, ma'am. I haven't said anything to anyone. Not even Craig. Not even my parents. You're the only one I've talked to about any of this."

Professor Polson removed a hand from the place she'd had it tucked between her sweater and her dress, and raised it over her cup, and said, "I'm not asking you *not* to. I'm just curious what the rumors might be, if any."

"I understand," Perry said, nodding.

"And I don't want to mislead you, Perry. My angle on this might not be exactly what you're hoping for. I believe what you're telling me, that *you* believe it, and that what you're hearing from others, like Lucas—I believe you're each telling the truth as you see it. But I also know that death is a deep, potent, incomprehensible force on the psyche—especially for the young. In other words, I'm not necessarily on a hunt with you for Nicole Werner, Perry."

"I understand that," Perry said.

"But I also *believe* you. I believe in your sincerity, and also in your intelligence," she said. "I have no reason *not* to. Based on what I've seen so far, you're an impressive person, Perry. I'm proud to take on this project with you."

W hy would she believe me?" Lucas asked. He lifted one shoulder, let it fall again, and it seemed to Perry that his shirt shifted oddly on his back, as if he might be even thinner under his clothes than he appeared to be.

"She believes *me*," Perry said. "She's open-minded. I mean, I don't think you have anything to lose, Lucas. She's not going to have us both committed, or—"

Lucas shrugged again, and said, shaking his head and starting to walk away, as if the conversation were over, "*I've* definitely got nothing to lose."

27

W ho is that guy?" Craig asked. Nicole was wrapping and wrapping a long red scarf around her face. Only her eyes were showing by the time she was done.

Hard little bits of snow flew at their faces as they walked across campus. Craig held onto her hand, but between his insulated ski glove and her fat wool mitten, he might as well have been holding anything—the university mascot's paw, a tree branch swathed in bandages. She said something into the scarf, but he couldn't hear it.

"What?"

Nicole shook her head. She looked over at him. There were little heartbreaking flecks of snow on her black eyelashes. He couldn't see her mouth, but he could tell by her eyes that she was smiling, and he decided to drop the subject.

But, a few days later, Craig saw the guy again: thick-shouldered, blond buzz-cut, slushing in black boots through the snow across the yard of the Omega Theta Tau house only seconds before Nicole appeared on the front porch, wrapping the scarf around and around her face again, raising a mittened hand to Craig.

"That was him again," Craig said.

"Who?"

"That guy, Nicole. Don't play dumb. He had to have just left the house. *Again.* That's the third time this week I've seen that guy coming or going from the house. He leaves just before you do. Those are his footprints." Craig pointed to the melting impressions on the lawn.

Nicole squinted at the footprints, and then looked in the direction of the blue-jacketed man on the other side of the street. She shrugged her shoulders, shook her head, looked up at Craig, and raised her eyebrows as if the mystery intrigued her as much as it did him.

"That's not a frat guy," Craig said. "That's not some sorority sister's boyfriend. That's a man."

"Well," Nicole said. "Some of the sisters date *men*, you know. We're not all strictly into boys."

"You know what I mean," Craig said. He took her trigonometry text out of her hands and tucked it under his arm. He'd lost his gloves by then, maybe left them in the cafeteria, and the tips of his fingers were completely numb, but he knew enough from watching sitcoms that you didn't let your girlfriend haul a book this heavy around without helping.

"What I mean is," he went on, "that guy doesn't look like he belongs around here."

Nicole slipped her hand through his free arm and leaned against him. Even through the layers of nylon and down feathers between them he thought he could feel the little thrill of her heart beating against his side. It was a Thursday afternoon, the time of the week they usually headed straight to Starbucks to linger, holding hands, with their cappuccinos and their unopened textbooks between them. He'd looked forward to it since going to bed the night before. But when they got to the corner of State and Campus Boulevard, Nicole stopped and said, "Craig, I can't do Starbucks this afternoon. I told Josie I'd meet her back at our room. We have to start making tissue roses for the formal. We—"

"You have to start *today*?" (Whining. He wished he weren't, but he was whining.) "I thought the formal was in, like, three weeks."

"No, it's in *four* weeks, but you have no idea how many of these things we have to make. And Josie and I are *it*. We're the only ones assigned to the roses, and there have to be at least *five thousand*."

"What?" Craig literally stopped in his tracks at the absurdity of this. "Five thousand tissue roses?"

Nicole laughed and nodded. They'd gotten to the edge of campus, and the arm Craig was using to carry her textbook was cramped. He shifted the book to the other, and then stepped around Nicole, put his stiff arm around her shoulders, exposing his bare hand to the cold again—but who cared, since it was already completely numb?

"Five *thousand*?"

"Yeah!" Nicole said, seeming to share his astonishment. "And it takes us like an hour to make a hundred. So far, we've only got, like, a hundred and ten."

"What the hell is this?" Craig asked. "Some kind of indentured servitude? I mean, it's not like *they're* paying *you* to be in this sorority. Don't they think you have a life?"

He was sincerely outraged, but Nicole laughed pleasantly, and Craig heard the sound of it echo off the brick wall of the Engineering Building a few feet ahead of them, like a lot of little bells.

"Craig, they think Omega Theta Tau should *be* my life!"

"Well, is that what you want, Nicole? I mean, do you want to be locked in a room making paper roses with Josie for the next four years?"

"Well, it's always the new pledges who make the roses, actually, so next year—"

"Okay, not roses. Next year you'll be baking crumpets or something. It'll always be something."

"Sorry, Craig." He looked at the side of her face. The scarf was down around her chin now, and she was doing that pouty thing with her lips. At the bridge of her nose was the faintest bump—an adorable little glitch there that made it possible, Craig thought, to tell her apart from the two or three other completely perfect girls in the world. He was about to apologize for getting all worked up, but she brightened suddenly and turned to him. "You could help!" she said. "Josie would be fine with that. She suggested it anyway—getting some guys to come and work on it, if, like, we got some beer to pay them with or something. You could bring, like, Lucas."

Craig felt the familiar sensation of sweat breaking out in a fine film under his arms, which happened each time Nicole brought up the subject of Josie, of his doing anything that might involve Josie—Josie joining them for a pizza, for instance. Or even when Nicole just said something like "Josie says to say hi." Or the one time he almost lost his dinner as he and Nicole were stepping out of the cafeteria and there was Josie with her arm hooked through Lucas's, both of them clearly stoned out of their minds:

"Hey, big boy," Josie had said, waving at Craig with all her fingers up near her mouth.

"Josie," Nicole had blurted out, laughing. "You're totally stoned!"

"Yup," Josie said. "Be careful, or I'll jump your boyfriend's bones."

Nicole had playfully slapped Josie's arm, while Craig started walking away as fast as he could. Nicole followed him, still laughing, and Josie called something else in their direction, but it was slurred, and Craig couldn't hear it over his pounding heart, and after they'd rounded the corner, Nicole had stopped him, turned him to face her, and looked at him carefully.

Outside, the sun was setting behind the glittering lead-paned windows that looked out onto the Godwin Hall courtyard, and her eyes in that light seemed nearly fluorescent in their blueness—like the ocean in Belize, like the sky from the top of Mount Washington. "What's with you, Craig?" she asked, suddenly terrifyingly serious. "And Josie?"

For a second, Craig couldn't breathe, but he worked hard to hold her eyes as if he had nothing to hide. All these weeks he'd held on to some glimmer of hope (false, he could see now) that maybe Josie had told Nicole all about it, and Nicole didn't care—or, at least, that she *understood*. He'd never had any evidence of that, he realized, and he had no reason whatsoever to believe that if and when Nicole heard about what had happened between him and Josie she wouldn't dump him in a heartbeat. Especially now that they'd been seeing each other for two months and he hadn't said a word.

"Nothing," Craig said. It sounded ridiculous. His voice actually squeaked when he said it.

"Then why does she hate you?"

"What?" Craig tried to make his expression look like one of surprise.

"Why does Josie hate you?"

He tried to open his eyes even wider. "She *hates* me?"

Nicole burst out laughing. "Uh, yeah. You haven't noticed?"

Craig shrugged.

"Well, you avoid her like the plague, so you know *something*. You quit coming to the study group even though you seemed so into it for a while. You never even walk by our room if she might be in there. Practically every time I even say her name you change the subject as quick as you can."

His mind was blank. His mouth was open. Over the weeks, Craig had tried to think of a few things he might possibly be able say if this subject came up. Excuses. Lies. Or at least some kind of spin-doctoring. He'd tried to come up with some way to make it sound like Josie had been so drunk and insistent that night that Craig felt he had to do *something* or it would have hurt her feelings, which was pretty much true, except that he'd been completely happy to fuck her; it had nothing to do with being polite. But maybe if he could find the right words? Nicole, Craig knew, was pretty naive when it came to people and their secret sex lives. She was always astonished to find out that some unmarried celebrity was pregnant, or that Craig had seen some girl from her hall slip out of the room of some boy on his hall in the morning. ("They were probably studying," she'd say in total seriousness, and then punch him hard in the bicep when he laughed.) It was possible, wasn't it, that she'd believe whatever he said?

But here, now, actually confronted this way in the hallway near the cafeteria with Nicole's beautiful eyes lit up in the sunset—all that pink and mauve pouring through the window panes, and her little half-smile, her head cocked like a chickadee, waiting—not only his mind but his *soul* went completely blank. She waited another long second or two, and then she shook her head. "O-kay," she said. "Uh, just forget I asked."

He tried as hard as he could to read her face as it was closing down before him. Did she know? Did she know and not care? Did she not know, and if she did know, would she slap him as hard as she could and never speak to him again?

He had no idea, he realized, and remembered fifth grade. Map reading. He couldn't do it. He tried to fake it ("Mongolia?"), which resulted in gales of laughter. This was what it would be like in Limbo, he realized. It could go either way—everything that mattered.

"Nicole, I—" he blurted with no idea what he was going to say. Luckily, she held up a hand to stop him.

"You're probably right," she said. "I probably don't want to know. Or, actually, I think I probably *do* know."

Craig took a step back. He was afraid to look at anything but the place directly between Nicole's eyes. He was wearing an army green T-shirt, and he was sure there must be spreading triangles of sweat at his pits. Nicole wrapped her arms around herself, holding on to her own arms hard. Her knuckles went white.

"You liked her first, didn't you?" she asked, a little sob in her voice. "*She's* why you were in the study group, and then you found out that she's got that boyfriend from Grosse Isle. That Princeton guy."

Craig took a trembling breath, trying not to explode with relief. It was like watching in the rearview mirror as the tanker that had been barreling down on you flipped straight into a ditch. "No!" he said, finding that he could blink again because now he was actually telling the truth. "No! My God! Nicole, I was knocked out by you the first time I saw you. *You* were the only reason I joined that group. I hadn't even *seen* your roommate. I've never felt this way about *any* girl. Josie? Jesus. No . . ."

"Craig," Nicole said. "I know you love me *now*. But I also know that there are other girls, girls who are prettier, and—"

This time Craig did explode, with laughter. He put his hands in his hair, as if to keep his head on his neck, and then he rushed at her, lifted her off her feet, laughing and kissing her and twirling her around in his arms as the after-dinner crowd started pouring out of the cafeteria, which had just closed—all those faceless others splitting around him and Nicole, not even glancing at them, and Craig thought he could just hold her and kiss her there forever. She was laughing, too, and he hoped she thought he was so sweaty and his heart was beating so hard because it was so warm in the hallway, and because he was so in love.

That afternoon he didn't say anything more about the paper roses, or the amount of her time they were going to take away from him between now and her formal (which she couldn't even invite him to because he wasn't in a frat: "I'm just going to go with a sister," she'd assured him when he'd asked).

They kept walking, past their Starbucks, back to the dorm so she could start on the roses. They'd changed the topic to how crazy it was that someone had spray-painted a different word under every Stop sign in town, so the signs read, STOP WAR, STOP SHRUBBERY, STOP STOP-PING, STOP UP, STOP OVER, STOP DIAPER RASH, etc. They speculated about which campus group would have done it, or if it was just one weird guy, or maybe high school students—who knew? Craig had his arms wrapped around her, and his mouth and nose were full of the smell and taste of her red wool scarf. His hands were so numb he had to look at them every few feet to make sure the trig book was still in them.

Then Craig saw *him* again: up ahead, that same guy who'd come out of the Omega Theta Tau house just before Nicole. He was walking out of the bank in his blue jacket, stuffing his wallet into the back pocket of his khaki pants.

"There he is again," Craig said, pointing.

"Who?" Nicole asked absently. She wasn't even looking in the direction he was pointing.

"That guy who was in your house. That man."

Nicole looked around this time, seeming to scan the horizon, not finding anything of interest. "So?"

"I just want to know who he is," Craig said. "Who is he, Nicole?"

"I wouldn't know," she said. "I can't even see who you're pointing at." She was looking in the exact opposite direction. The guy turned around then, and Craig was sure he looked right at them, as if he'd known they were there, as if *he* were looking for *them*.

There was a patch on the guy's jacket pocket. Craig could see it clearly now: "EMT."

"He's an ambulance driver or something," Craig said, more to himself than Nicole.

"So?" she said.

"Why does he hang out at your sorority? Why is he always there?"

Nicole held a hand up to her forehead and looked in the wrong direction again, and then said, "I have no idea what you're talking about Craig. There's no EMT hanging out at the sorority."

Craig looked at her and said, "How did you know he was an EMT?"

"You just said it," she said, and seemed to stomp her foot a little in frustration. "Sheesh!"

"No, I didn't," Craig said. "I said 'ambulance driver,' after I saw there was an EMT patch on his pocket."

"Same thing," she said.

"It's not," he said.

She continued looking around, exactly where the guy was not standing, and then the guy turned his back and stepped into the street, and a white truck pulled into the intersection, blocking Craig's view, and by the time it had passed, the man was gone and Craig was staring at nothing but a brick wall.

Nicole got on her tiptoes and kissed his cheeks. "Okay, I guess this is where we say good-bye," she said. "You're going back to Starbucks?"

"Without you?"

"Why not?" she asked. "You'll study better without me there anyway. I'll see you at dinner, okay?"

"Okay," Craig said, feeling a little bit like he'd been duped in some kind of card trick—not an unpleasant one, just confusing—and then she was half-walking, half-skipping away from him in the direction of Godwin Hall.

28

Professor Polson's lecture that day concerned the soul.

"In some cultures, you can never speak the name of the deceased person again because the soul might hear its name and come looking for its body. Or, worse, the body might come looking for its soul.

"In fact, the tradition of cremation, which seems to us one of the most modern means for dealing with human remains, has its origins in this impulse. If the body is burned to ashes, there can be no reinhabiting, no return.

"Some anthropologists believe that many mourning customs originally served the purpose of keeping the dead at bay. Schneerweiss—you read the translation of the article, right?—hypothesized that the reason widows were instructed to wear black for at least a year and to change their hairstyle was so as to be unrecognizable when their dead husbands came looking for them.

"Why," Professor Polson asked, "might this be? Why would any self-respecting widow not be thrilled to have her dead husband return to her?"

Most of the class responded in unison, "Putrefaction!"

"Exactly. The fear, the *aversion*, that we think of as superstitious or religious is, in fact, based on physical reality. It's based on experience. *Difficult* experience. So, primitive people, we see, cannot be so easily dismissed as the sort of fools we tend to think of them as. In actuality, they had a much closer, much more intimate experience with the dead than most of us will ever have—unless we go to war or into the mortuary arts. They knew what they were trying to avoid."

She turned to the chalkboard, on which she'd written a quote from Thomas Mann, *The Magic Mountain*:

> What we call mourning for our dead is perhaps not so
> much grief at not being able to call them back as it is
> grief at not being able to want to do so.

Perry tapped his pencil over a sentence from that day's reading:

> H. Guntert: *Larve (Ger. Mask)* is etymologically con-
> nected with the hidden spirits of the Kingdom of the
> Dead, the *Lares* (Lat.), and their name is cognate with
> *latere* (to be hidden or to keep oneself hidden) and
> Latona, the goddess of death (*Leto* in Greek), and gives
> expression to human's immediate feeling about the
> corpse—the visible presence of the body, and the deepest
> concealment of the person.

He wanted to ask Professor Polson there in class, instead of in her office (where she often seemed too preoccupied about childcare to talk about the subject at any length), if she had any thoughts on this, if she thought that this idea of seeing the dead one's body, and recognizing that his or her soul was no longer animating it, was the basis of even more superstition and folklore. He had, himself, some ideas about this.

But she was answering some bland question presented to her by Elwood Campbell about why, given the horrors of putrefaction, so many people were *not* repulsed by the dead, but fascinated by them, *wanted* to see pictures of them. "What about people who love to look at gore?" he asked, and snickered. Perry suspected Elwood was speaking for himself. He'd been one of the students who hadn't lunged forward to get a closer look at Marilyn Monroe's morgue photograph, and Perry had the impression it was because Elwood was already familiar with it, that he was probably one of those guys trolling the gore.com-type websites, or posting things on them.

"How about necrophilia types? Right?" Elwood prompted. "You know, people who want to have sex with corpses?"

A few of the girls shook their heads and glanced at one another uncomfortably, but Professor Polson didn't bat an eye.

"'And so all the night-tide I lie down by the side / Of my darling—my darling—my life and my bride / In the sepulchre there by the sea . . .' Poe," she said, "was only one of many poets and philosophers who has described the death of a young woman as one of the most beautiful sights one could behold."

"Yeah," Elwood said, seeming to take this as affirmation of his opinion.

"Kind of puts the 'fun' back into *funeral*," Brett Barber said, and almost everyone burst out laughing, but none laughed as hard as Elwood.

"On that note," Professor Polson said, shaking her head, "we're done for today. See you Tuesday."

She didn't wait for the students to leave before she herself left, and she wasn't in her office when Perry passed by it a little later.

Sweetheart," Perry's mother said when he talked to her on the phone that evening. "Is everything all right?"

"Of course, Mom. Everything's fine. Don't worry so much, okay?"

"Is Craig okay?"

"Craig's okay. Not *great*. But he's definitely okay."

"You're a good friend, Perry. I'm proud of you for sticking by him. That poor boy. Tell him we said hello, okay? Bring him to visit, if—"

"That wouldn't be a good idea," Perry said.

"No, of course not. I don't know what I was thinking. I just wish we could do something to—"

Despite the outpouring of animosity toward Craig in Bad Axe (someone had actually put up a Wanted poster in Leazenby Park with Craig's photograph and "For Murder" scrawled in red Magic Marker underneath, and this had made the papers all over the state), Perry's mother believed absolutely that the accident that had killed Nicole had not been Craig's fault. Even before the blood tests came back and showed conclusively that Craig hadn't been drinking, hadn't been smoking dope, she'd believed Perry that driving drunk wasn't something Craig would have done.

"How are things there?" Perry asked. "With you guys? Is business good?"

"Oh," his mother said. "You know your dad. He wouldn't tell me one way or another. We could be billionaires or in debt to our eyeballs for all I know. But he's making enough money to pay for that boat of his. And I got a new winter coat." (It was a game his mother always played, and they both knew it was a game. She was, after all, the one who kept the books for Edwards and Son. She probably made 90 percent of their business decisions without bothering to let Perry's father in on them.) "Yesterday," she said, her tone becoming lower, more somber. "I saw the Werner sisters."

"Oh," Perry said. "Where?"

"At the cemetery."

"Why were you at the cemetery, Mom?"

"I was just driving by. I could see them from the road. They were putting flowers on Nicole's grave. So I pulled over. It was her birthday, Perry. Her nineteenth."

"Jesus," Perry said.

His mother didn't bother to scold him for taking the Lord's name in vain. She said, "I know."

It surprised him that he hadn't realized, hadn't remembered, that it was Nicole's birthday. Now, he recalled all those early-October cupcakes in elementary school and, during middle school, all the girls getting excited about some slumber party Nicole was having. There was a lot of

hoopla every year surrounding her birthday. Her locker decorated, singing in the cafeteria, that sort of thing. (She'd always been the most popular girl in every class.)

Now her sisters were gathering in the cemetery to decorate her grave.

"How did they seem?" Perry asked. "Her sisters?"

"Well, about like you'd imagine," his mother said, and then said no
more, as if he *could* imagine. But he couldn't. He really could not imagine them in a cemetery. Those perky blondes, and all that laughter. He
couldn't imagine them bent over any grave at all, let alone their little sister's. "They didn't have anything good to say about Craig," she said, "as
you'd imagine. I didn't tell them he was your roommate again. I don't
think they know you even know him, and I think that's just as well."

"Yeah," Perry said, and then thought, Shit.

Had *Craig* known it was Nicole's birthday?

Surely, he had.

Was that why he'd hurried out of the apartment so early that morning and Perry hadn't seen him all day?

Who knew how many anniversaries of this or that thing—her birthday, their first date, their first kiss, the day he'd given her that amber
ring—Craig was living through, and would live through? He wasn't
going to tell Perry about them, Perry was pretty sure, but he still felt like
a bad friend for not knowing.

"They told me that their parents aren't doing so well, Perry," his
mother said. He waited for her to go on, but she said nothing more
about Mr. and Mrs. Werner. They talked, instead, about the Bad Axe
football team—the worst season in a decade, although they never had
been very good.

As his mother spoke, Perry walked over to his desk, pulled open a
drawer, and took out a folder. He slid the photograph out, laid it on his
desk, pulled the chain on his desk lamp, and bent over it, looking
straight down into the glossy image, where, in the corner, blurred but
familiar, he saw the fleeing form of the girl he knew—he *knew*—was
Nicole Werner.

He stared until his eyes went dry, and he had to blink as his mother told him more of the details of the family business, of her days, of how much she loved and missed him.

"I love you, too," Perry said.

"You be good. Stay safe. Eat vegetables. Get enough sleep. Don't—"

He closed his eyes and flipped the photograph over on his desk so he could focus.

"I'm fine," he said. "Everything's fine. Tell Dad I love him. I'll see you soon."

29

"What *is* this?" Mira asked. She was trying to control the alarm in her voice, so the question came out breathy, hoarse, as if she were doing an imitation of Marilyn Monroe.

"Obviously, it's a duffel bag full of clothes," Clark said. "I'm sure you won't remember my having told you I'm taking the twins to visit my mother."

"What?"

"Twins? You know, those two kids who run around here? I think you gave birth to them?"

"Clark, can you quit with the sarcasm? What are you talking about?"

"I told you weeks ago, Mira. It's my mother's birthday. I'm taking the twins to visit her for two days. What do you care? It'll give you time to work."

Mira stared at Clark. She'd been preoccupied, she knew, but she would never have forgotten something like this. Clark had *never* taken the twins anywhere without her, certainly not to visit his mother. Mira herself was the one who had to plan and organize every visit to Clark's mother, for whom Clark seemed to have nothing but a terrible cocktail of pity and contempt that made it nearly impossible for him to carry on a conversation with the poor old woman without it ending in an argument.

Visiting? With the twins? "No," Mira said, and shook her head.

Clark let his jaw drop theatrically. For a flash of a second, Mira saw his molars—a little mountain range of bone in the dark. He shut his mouth before she could look more closely, but it had seemed possible to her in that quick glimpse that his teeth looked unhealthy.

A dark spot in the back?

Maybe, she thought, it was why his breath had begun to smell strangely—not bad, exactly, but *organic*. On the rare occasions they kissed, she thought she could taste clover on him, or the paper of an old book.

"Uh, *no*?" Clark asked. "Did you just say *no*, I can't take my sons to visit my mother for two days? I'm sorry, Mira, but I'm not sure you have the right to grant or deny that permission, especially since if I go without them there will be no one here to take care of them."

"I could have made arrangements to go to if you'd told me," Mira said. "I *would* have." Even as she said it, she wondered how she could have, whether she actually would have.

"And cancel your classes? Postpone your research? God forbid, Mira! I mean, the way you go on and on about the importance of those classes, and how the whole world hinges on your student evaluations, and how if you lose a research day, the fall of Rome is sure to follow, it certainly never crossed my mind that you 'would have made arrangements' to go with us."

Mira stepped away from him. She tried to imagine herself as the director of this scene. Or as its literary critic. Clark, the main character here, was far too agitated for this to be about his mother's birthday, or even his bitterness about his wife's work schedule.

"Why now?" she asked, attempting the dispassionate tone she took with students, with colleagues, although every nerve ending in her was vibrating with emotion. "Why are you going now? In all the years I've known you, you've never once—"

"Because my fucking mother is turning *seventy*, for God's sake. I don't want to be like you, Mira, and just show up finally for the fucking funeral."

Mira looked at her stinging hand to find that she had just slapped Clark hard on the side of his face without realizing it, without realizing that she was even capable of it.

Then she looked to up to see that he was reeling backward, swearing.

It took a few more heartbeats before she could focus enough on her surroundings again to understand that the twins, awakened from their nap in the other room by Clark's shouting, had begun to scream and cry. And a few more heartbeats passed before Mira realized that there were tears streaking down her own face, that she was sobbing.

Clark had been the only person to whom she'd ever spoken of it, and it had been the hardest confession she'd ever made, and she remembered him cradling her head in his lap as she wept, years ago, when finally she'd told someone, and the relief that someone knew: "I didn't go home when my father told me that my mother was dying because I was afraid I would flunk my exam . . ."

And the way he'd kissed and consoled her, and stroked her hair, and how he had kissed her tears—how she'd known then that she would marry him, that he was answer to all the prayers she'd never even said, the prayer for forgiveness.

The prayer for self-forgiveness.

"You were just a kid, Mira, really," Clark had said. "How could you have known? You loved your mother. She knew that. She understood . . ."

Now Clark was holding a hand to his cheek, staring at her with narrowed eyes.

"Fuck you, Mira," he said. "Fuck you."

30

Who's there? Perry?"

Craig sat up in bed. He was still sleeping, wasn't he? That was it. That was why someone was standing just outside his door, which was open a crack—a bare leg in the dark hallway, the fluttering of some airy material. A girl. *This was a dream.*

A girl.

She nudged the door open with her foot. A silver sandal. Toenails painted red.

It was going to be a sex dream.

How long since he'd had one of those?

Since long before—

She wrapped the fingers of one hand around the door. The fingers were elegant, long, unfamiliar. Her fingernails were also painted red.

"Who's there?" he asked again, this time in a whisper.

A bit of the dress or gown or sheet she was wearing wafted in, and then back out, as if in answer, and then she stepped farther into the room, and Craig could feel his heart pounding in every pulse point—his chest, his wrists, his throat, his temples.

Her long dark hair was swept to one side and her eyes were closed. The lids were painted dark blue. Her lips were pale, but they glistened. He could see straight through the thing—the gown, yes, or drape. Her breasts were perfect globes with wide pink nipples, and he could see the dark triangle of pubic hair between her legs. She opened her eyes.

They were gray, or they were hidden in the shadows of her voluminous, shining hair.

She parted her lips and took a slow step, closer to him.

He would have moved—whether to approach her or to flee, he wasn't sure—except that he couldn't. He was in that paralysis part of a nightmare where you want to scream but have no voice, want to run but can't move your limbs.

He managed, however, to whisper again: "What's your name?"

Her voice was like air when she spoke. He was surprised he could even hear it. Or he'd read her lips, which formed the word *I'm* and then *Alice*.

"Alice," he repeated.

She nodded as if there were a great weight on her back, as if the sound of her own name reminded her of it.

"Alice who?"

She rolled her eyes to the ceiling then, and he could see them better in the overhead light. They were a blazing blue. Turquoise. Extraordinary. Especially against her white skin, her black hair.

"Meyers," she said in that husky-nothing that was her voice. "Alice Meyers."

"Alice Meyers?" Craig said. He knew the name, but had no idea where he knew it from. He said it again: "Alice Meyers."

"Can I come in?"

At first he could say nothing, but then, knowing that it would be the best answer in a nightmare like this, Craig managed, "No."

Suddenly she was screaming at the top of her lungs, a scream that sounded like a horse being beaten, or something worse, and he squeezed his eyes shut, and when he opened them again she was gone, and he heard the front door of the apartment slam shut, and the sound of someone running down the hallway, and he was sitting up, screaming in the pitch black room, only a bit of moonlight slipping through the crack in the window shade. *Help! Help! Help!* Finally he managed to silence himself, put his face in the crook of his arm, squeezed his eyes shut, bit his lip until the silence became his own heartbeat, slowing, maybe, slowing down. *Shit. Shit. Fuck.* "Perry?" he finally managed to whimper into the darkness.

As Craig stumbled out of his room and crossed the hallway to Perry's room, he was still in a state of panic, but also shame, turning on the lights as he went, trying not to whimper. (*God, like going to find your Mommy in the middle of the night: I had a bad dream . . .*)

But surely Perry had heard him, and would be wondering what the fuck—

He opened the door to Perry's room and could see in the light from the hallway that there was no one in Perry's bed.

"Perry?" he called toward the kitchen, the living room. But it was a tiny apartment —if Perry had been there, of course he would have heard him before this.

Hell, probably everybody in the apartment house had heard him.

Perry wasn't there. Definitely not there.

So, where the hell was he? Sleeping over at some girl's he hadn't mentioned to Craig? (Maybe the Mystery Chick from freshman year—the one whose panties Craig had found on the floor at the foot of Perry's bed? Perry had refused to acknowledge those, no matter how much Craig made fun of him.) Just because Perry didn't *seem* to have a sex life didn't mean he didn't.

He was starting to calm down, to feel more pissed and jilted than terrified. He went to the front door and locked it, even hooked the chain. If fucking Perry came home that night, he could knock his ass off, and if Craig didn't hear him, he could sleep in the hall.

And then he unhooked the chain, because that was stupid. Hell, Perry was entitled to a night out. Still, he thought, he'd have liked to have had Perry there—to laugh with, if nothing else, about the ridiculous dream.

I'm Alice Meyers. It would have been funny if—well, if it hadn't scared the shit out of him. Craig was back in bed with the lights out and the blankets pulled up over his ear when he realized where he knew that name from.

Of course.

Fuck.

Godwin Hall.

The Alice Meyers Memorial Student Study Room.

His heart was beating hard again, but he wasn't going to freak out. It had only been a dream. He turned the bedside lamp on, picked up the crappy novel written by his father's best friend and rival, Dave Cain—*The Boiling Point*—and decided he'd stay up reading until morning.

It could only be a few more hours until it was light outside.

Right?

31

It was the second week of October. Until now, the weather had been unseasonably warm—like summer all through September, and like early September at the beginning of October. Then the weather changed, literally, overnight.

Shelly went to bed with the windows wide open because the house was stuffy from having been shut up all day (the morning weather report had predicted rain, so she'd closed everything, although rain never came), and had woken up in the fetal position in one corner of the bed with a sheet and a thin comforter twisted around her. Jeremy was purring, pushed up against her hip as if huddling there for protection from the elements, and the curtains were whipping around in the window frame. The temperature in the room could not have been above fifty degrees.

"Shit," she said, jumping out of bed, sending Jeremy tearing out of the room as she hurried to the windows to close them. How had she slept through this complete scene change? The clock on her nightstand said 7:02, but it was pitch black outside—huge rolling dark clouds in the sky seemed to be preparing for a battle of epic proportions. Shelly grabbed her robe and wrapped it around her, and followed Jeremy out to the kitchen. Passing the thermostat on the way, she twisted the dial to seventy degrees—five degrees higher than she usually kept it even in the dead of winter, and eight degrees higher than her ex-husband had ever allowed her to turn it.

The weather change was going to be a problem. She'd need to find her down jacket and waterproof boots before she walked to work, and she was already running late, and the cat needed feeding, and she needed a shower—and the disconcerting darkness, accompanied as it was by inky rain, and the unappealing prospect of trekking across town, gave her the idea that she might, this being Tuesday and Josie's early-morning day, call in sick.

What could it hurt? She was caught up with all the work she had to do for the next four concerts, and she had no new projects that couldn't wait until tomorrow. She could just call the cell phone Josie kept permanently attached to her ear, say she wasn't feeling well, and then call Security to unlock the doors so Josie could get in and answer the phones. Surely Josie could handle the one or two phone calls she might get while filing her nails in the office and playing around online.

The plan coursed through Shelly like fresh blood.

She'd had no idea, she realized, until this moment, how badly she wanted a weekday away from that place. Had she become one of those people who hated their jobs? Only once before in nineteen years had she consciously, brazenly, called in sick when she was certifiably in the pink of health, and that was the morning she woke up for the first time beside Paula and realized that it would take a lot more than the Chamber Music Society to pull her out of that bed if Paula was going to be in it.

Even given all that had happened, that snatched day had been a good decision: a stolen, sensuous morning, the details of which (coffee spilled on the pillows, eggs grown cold, the sheets twisted around their legs) were seared onto Shelly's memory forever. The memory of that day still filled her with pleasure and contentment, even knowing now, as she did, that Paula would, a few months later, go back to her husband when he was diagnosed with clinical depression and when her grown children told her their father might die if she didn't go back to him and that they would never speak to her again if he did.

True, it had broken Shelly's heart. But even that seemed somehow beautiful, being proof as it was that she'd been capable of that kind of love at least once in her life. She'd walked through the world like a zombie for an entire season—like the beast in the Stephen Crane poem, eating of her heart and enjoying it, because it was so bitter, and because it was her heart. But she carried within her the deep satisfaction that she had thrown everything she had into that love, had done everything humanly possible to persuade Paula to stay with her.

That, Shelly had learned, was the difference between heartbreak and regret:

Heartbreak could be lived with if it weren't accompanied by regret.

She watched the storm from the kitchen window and sipped her coffee calmly, even when Jeremy, unnerved by the storm, abandoned his cat food prematurely (usually he licked the bowl until it was shining) and ran back into the bedroom, where, she knew, he would hide under the bed.

It was 8:45, and Shelly decided it was time to call Josie on her cell phone, so she wouldn't arrive at the Chamber Music Society to locked doors—although, with this weather, it seemed unlikely to Shelly that the girl was dutifully making her way to the office.

"Shelly?"

Josie answered on the first ring—or at the first note of some pop star's latest single, whatever Josie's personalized ring tone might be— and Shelly was surprised to think that Josie either knew her phone number by heart, or had her number programmed into her phone. She didn't remember Josie ever calling her at home.

"Josie? Hello?"

"Yeah! I'm at Fourth and South U. I'll be there in five minutes."

"Oh," Shelly said, "that's not why I called. You're not late—" (for a change, she thought). "I'm calling because—because I'm not feeling very well, and I—"

"Are you *okay*?"

The alarm in the girl's voice was, frankly, touching. Shelly could imagine Josie holding the phone to her ear inside the hood of one of her black or gray cashmere hoodies, bent over, wind in her face, black ballet flats exposing the pale tops of her feet to the elements, stopping to hear Shelly more clearly.

"Oh, sure, I'm okay," Shelly said. "I'm perfectly fine. Just under the weather, I guess. I was going to see if you could take calls in the office this morning without—"

"Oh, no problem," Josie said. "I can stay all day if you need me to. I only have one class, and it's—"

"That's not necessary. You can leave when you were supposed to, at noon, but if, when you do, you could leave a note on the door and . . . ?"

Shelly went on with the instructions, including Security, who would need to come and let Josie in and lock up when she left, and Josie enthusiastically agreed to everything Shelly said, and by the end of the phone call Shelly felt both relieved and confident about choosing that day to call in. Maybe Josie was starting to settle into the semester, and into the routine of the job, and her attitude was changing accordingly. Maybe Shelly wouldn't need to fire her after all.

She put the phone back in its cradle and looked around the dark kitchenette for a minute, and then turned and peered into the living room (coffee table, overstuffed couch, braided mat for Jeremy next to Shelly's reading lamp), feeling a little confused about what she was supposed to do next (shower? get dressed? check email?) until she realized it was okay, it was perfectly fine, to go back to bed, and she did.

The pillowcases smelled fresh, and like lavender. The sheets had cooled pleasantly, and the staticky pummeling of the rain on the roof was both calming and deafening, and Jeremy came out from under the bed and found his place at her hip, and Shelly was asleep within seconds.

It must have been about two hours later, in Shelly's dreams, that the doorbell rang—a pale blue bird opening and closing its mouth in a cage at a mall she used to shop at with her mother as a child. That dream bird was making the muffled chiming noise of a doorbell instead of a whistle. It sounded maybe three or four times before Shelly realized that she was sleeping, and that the doorbell actually was ringing outside of her dream as well as in it, and she swung her legs off the side of the bed. Jeremy, sensing her alarm, jumped off and raced under it, his claws making a desperate scratching noise on the wooden floorboards as he did.

Shelly wasn't yet sure what time it was, or when the rain had stopped, or even what she was wearing, or why she was in bed instead of at work—and was only slightly less confused by the time she got to the door, got on her tiptoes, pressed her eye to the peephole, and looked out to see Josie Reilly standing there, outside her door.

Josie was wearing one of her skimpy tank tops with a pink hoodie halfway zipped up over it, holding two large Starbucks cups with white lids, and she was looking up at the peephole with a faint little smile on her lip-glossed lips, as if she could see Shelly's eye peering out at her through it.

32

Professor Polson's apartment house looked like a place a student would live, Perry thought, not a professor with a family. In fact, last winter he'd met a guy from his International Human Rights seminar who'd lived in this same building. Around midterms the guy had asked Perry to come over to study with him, but when Perry had shown up the guy had been drunk and didn't seem to remember that he'd wanted to study, or even who Perry was.

Then, and now, the building's stairwell smelled like old beer soaked into carpet. Lucas climbed the stairs ahead of him, taking each step as if it were much higher than it was. Perry had to slow down so he wouldn't charge over him. Lucas looked like an old man, holding tightly to the railing, shoulders hunched and bony in his threadbare T-shirt. There was stenciling on the back of the shirt, but it was so faded Perry couldn't tell if it read, THE FINAL TOUR or SHE FINDS OUT.

"What's the number?" Lucas asked for the second or third time when they stepped out into the hallway.

"Two thirty-three," Perry said, and gave Lucas a gentle push in the direction of the door with 233 on it.

Professor Polson opened it before they knocked (she'd had to buzz them in, so she knew they were in the building, coming up the stairs, and then she must have heard them in the hallway) wearing a ruffly purple blouse, long-sleeved and flowered, and faded jeans with a patch on one knee. This outfit was, Perry realized, exactly what he'd imagined she might wear when she wasn't wearing professor clothes. To class, Professor Polson always wore black—black dresses, black skirts, black jackets—but it looked to him as if she were playing a role that required these costumes, and that in fact she'd be a lot more comfortable in some kind of hippie dress or skirt, some T-shirt with a Monet painting on it. He could easily picture her in a floppy hat and strappy sandals, some kind of bright silk skirt.

She opened the door wide and motioned for them to come in, and then said, "Sit down, boys. I'll get some tea."

Perry wandered in behind Lucas, not sure where to go. Lucas was moving toward a chair in one room, and Professor Polson had disappeared into what must have been a kitchen. He could smell that the tea was already brewing—either that or she'd had a candle burning before they'd gotten there, and had just blown it out. The apartment was what his mother would have called a mess. There were books on the floor, some of them open, and a little pile of what looked like sweaters and dishrags next to the couch. The rug was a bright, Oriental embroidered thing, all blazing reds and yellows where it wasn't worn away in thready gray patches.

Lucas sat down heavily on a green velvet recliner, and it squeaked when he did, and he made a little face, like maybe something had jabbed him in the back. Perry sat on the couch, which looked old and tired, too, but was comfortable, and had a fancy lamp beside it shedding a warm golden light through a lacy lampshade. It seemed to Perry that everything in the apartment could have been either bought at a garage sale for fifty cents or an expensive heirloom—or both. It was, he thought, about the most interesting place he'd ever seen outside of a movie. He had never been able to picture Professor Polson in her apartment, but now that he was here, he knew this is what he would have imagined. When she came in carrying three mugs, he said, "I like your apartment."

Professor Polson rolled her eyes a little, handed him a mug. "Be careful," she said, "it's hot." Lucas looked up at the cup as she held it down to him as if he had never seen a mug of tea before. Eventually, he reached up and took it.

Since Perry had gone by his place to pick him up, Lucas had been doing everything this way, in slow motion, and Perry had finally just come out and asked him, after Lucas spent about twenty minutes trying to zip up his jacket, seeming unable to fit the two ends of the zipping apparatus together to save his life, "Are you stoned, man?"

"No," Lucas said, struggling, albeit languidly, with the zipper. "I'm not doing that anymore. I quit. Bad sleep."

Perry had been about to offer to zip Lucas's jacket for him when he'd finally managed to do it himself.

"Thanks for coming over, guys," Professor Polson said. She sat down beside Perry on the couch and rested her mug of tea on the flowered patch on the knee of her jeans. "How are you, Lucas? I haven't seen you yet this year, have I? Was your summer okay?"

"It was okay," Lucas said. He was staring into the swirling steam over his cup with some apprehension. "Yeah."

"Perry told you we wanted to talk to you about—?"

"Yeah," Lucas said again, and looked up. "He told me."

"That's okay with you?"

"Sure," Lucas said.

For the first time Perry noticed that there was what looked like a perfectly round quarter-size circle of hair missing just over Lucas's temple. It looked like someone (Lucas himself?) had grabbed a handful of the hair there and yanked.

"Lucas?" Professor Polson said, leaning forward so that, from the angle at which he observed her, Perry could see a silver charm dangling in the neckline of her blouse, there in the dark shadows between her breasts. He looked away, looked over at Lucas, who was now staring at one of the worn-away patches on the Oriental rug.

"Is everything okay?" Professor Polson asked. She was studying him. "You look tired. Are you sleeping? Are you smoking dope, or taking something harder?"

Lucas shook his head, and told her the same thing he'd told Perry, that he'd quit smoking dope "and everything else," hoping it would help with the sleep. "But I don't sleep. Not since this thing with—"

There was a long pause as Professor Polson waited for him to finish the sentence, before she finally finished it for him.

"Nicole?"

Lucas brought his hands to his temples and began to rub with his index and forefingers, and Perry saw that he was rubbing in a circular motion at the exact spot where the quarter-size circle of hair was missing.

"Are you really ready to talk about this?" Professor Polson asked.

"You know, you don't have to. I'm not acting with the university in any way. I'm only inquiring into this as a scholar, and my interest in these kinds of things relates to the *tradition* of these kinds of things. I don't want to mislead you into thinking I'm a supernaturalist—you understand that? I'm a folklorist.

"I mean, I'll listen to what you have to say," she went on. "And I'll believe you, that you're telling the truth as you've experienced it. But I have some ideas of my own about how these things happen—and eventually, maybe, those ideas might help you, but I don't know." She hesitated for a moment, shrugging her shoulders, which Perry thought looked fragile, thin, like the shoulders of a little girl.

When he didn't say anything, she said, "They *might* help you feel better, make sense of things, but you might also want to get some professional help, and I'll give you some references for that. For the sleep problems, if nothing else?"

Lucas took his hands away from his temples, put them in his lap, and looked up at Professor Polson. He nodded.

"So, then, do you mind, Lucas, if I tape-record our conversation? Do you trust me when I say I'll share this with *no one* without your written permission? And, in fact, I'd like to give you this, to ask you to read and sign." She stood and went over to the bookshelf, where a piece of paper lay on top of a row of hardback books. "It states for the record that I won't share what you've shared here with anyone without first obtaining your written permission."

Lucas took the piece of paper, which fluttered loosely in his hand, and looked at it for a few seconds, nodding again, and when Professor Polson handed him a pen, he signed what seemed to be his name across the bottom of it.

"Okay," she said, taking the paper from him and putting it back on the shelf. "I'll make a copy of this and give you the original. So, is it all right if I record what you have to say?"

Lucas said, "Sure, whatever," and inhaled.

He did not, to Perry, look or sound like someone who would have the ability to speak loud or long enough to tell any kind of story, lucid or otherwise, truth or fiction, but when Professor Polson took out her little recorder—a shining, silver thing, sleek and glinting like the charm between her breasts—pressed a button, and set it on the table, Lucas began, as if he'd been waiting a long time, holding his breath, to speak:

So, okay. Like. Jesus. (long sigh) You know, I didn't even know her very well. I was friends with Craig, and I didn't think she liked me. Right from the beginning he told me she told him she didn't approve of the smoking, that it was, you know, against her religion, and also that she thought it turned Craig into an asshole. Which, I guess, you know, it did. Craig got really weirded out sometimes on weed. He'd start talking to himself, sort of muttering. He'd want to pick a fight, or he'd start crying about his parents getting a divorce or something. Or he wanted to steal things. I don't know. She had a point. And she thought I was his supplier, even though Craig was getting dope from other dealers. It wasn't just me. But she didn't like me, I guess, I thought. Or, he said she didn't like me. We hardly spoke two words. Except one time. Well, the one time before the other time. I was in my room, and I was smoking, and listening to music, and she knocked on my door, and as soon as I saw her I was like, Sorry, he's not here. I don't know where he is. And she was like, I didn't come to find Craig. So I just held the door open, and I was like, Okay, so, how can I help you? (Except I was stoned, so maybe I didn't say it like that, maybe I said, okay so what the fuck or something, because I remember she made a little disapproving thing out of the corners of her mouth.) And she just walked on past me into my room, which was a single, you know, because I was the resident advisor, and she walked over to my bed and sat at the edge of it. She was wearing a short skirt, and flip-flops, even though it was, like, the beginning of February, and she leaned forward and put her hands on her knees and just sort of looked at me, and I was standing there, and maybe because I was stoned and also her hair being so blond, so she was sort of covered with this light, like smoke light, and the light was sort of pulsing, like—I don't know. So, anyway, I'm not sure, but I think she unbuttoned the top two buttons of her blouse, and then she kind of pressed her boobs together, and she said something like, Don't you like me? Which I did, I guess, but I was friends with Craig, you know, and they'd been going out already for like four months and he was totally in love with her, so I said something like, Sure. Did you and Craig break up? And she just burst out laughing, and she said, Haven't you ever fucked your friend's girlfriend before? And then I guess I was so stoned I didn't know what to say, because I swear she had these little flames, like flickers, like horns, coming out of the sides of her head. I mean, sometimes when I'm really stoned, I see this stuff. It's a hallucination or whatever. I saw a halo once over my grandmother's head. And I thought my ex-girlfriend had a tail one night, when she got up to go to the bathroom, and it was swishing around (laughs, coughs). But Nicole's little horns freaked me out, and I was like, Okay, Nicole, time for you to go, and I went over to the door and opened it, and stood there, and she got up really slow and walked past me with her blouse still undone, and then she put her arms around my neck and pushed up against me, and kissed me, and it was just a reflex, I mean, she was a very hot girl, maybe the hottest girl I'd ever even seen, really, so I was kissing her, and it went on a long time, and she sort of tried to pull me back into the room, but I said, No, you better go, and she started laughing, and buttoned back up, and then she said, I'll be back, Lucas. You're going to sleep with me, and you know it, because I know you want to, and I want to. After that, I just tried to avoid her when she was with Craig because I felt guilty, and because she made me really nervous. She only came to my room one more time without Craig, but Murph was with me, and we were cutting up this bag of (clears throat)—and she came in and lay down on my bed, and she was sort of reaching over and playing with my hair, and Murph was looking at me like what the fuck, so I told her she better leave, that if the cops or the administrators came by she'd be an accessory or something, and she was such a goody-goody on the surface that I knew she'd leave when I said that, and she did; she left. And then I was gone for a week, in Mexico at the break, and I barely saw her and Craig before that night, when he—I-I know it wasn't my fault, you know, but the whole thing. Her. Me. All the drugs I was selling, and doing, and it was *my* fucking car. She died in *my* fucking car. Because of my car.

(Here Professor Polson can be heard in the background, her speech muffled, too far from the tape recorder to be distinguished clearly.)

Yeah. Well I tell myself that every day. But, you know, you can't get around the fact that if I'd just said, No, man, you seem too freaked out, and I don't want you driving my car, or whatever. If I said I couldn't find the keys, or I'm taking the car someplace myself, they wouldn't have had the accident and Nicole wouldn't be dead. Nobody else around here had a car to loan him. Well, whatever. It doesn't matter now, but basically I thought about that all spring. And the memorial service, and the posters, and . . . And I wasn't sleeping then either. And I was still smoking a lot. And I probably should have gone home or taken the job in Montana I was supposed to take for the summer, but I decided to stay here, I don't know. I didn't even really finish the semester, even though my profs gave me B's and let me slide on my finals and all that. So, I was here all summer, and it was like the whole town was empty except for me and Murph, and Murph was not doing that well either, for different reasons.

His girlfriend. And also he got into speed, which was having this effect on him, so I wasn't even hanging out with him. I was subletting this apartment in a building over there on Coolidge, and the building had like forty apartments in it, and they were all empty, I think, except for one where there was this Meth Lady, and she was walking around the halls at night with black eyes and shit, talking about how she was looking for a baby and all this crazy stuff, and it was really creeping me out, so I started staying out of the apartment most of the time, walking around town listening to Coldplay on my iPod. That last CD, it's all about death. And that's when I started seeing her.

(There's a pause. In the background, Professor Polson: "Nicole?")

Yeah.

(Another pause. A question is asked that can't be heard on the tape.)

Okay. Sure. I *knew*. I mean, it wasn't a matter of wondering if it was her. It was her. I recognized her. She'd dyed her hair, but it was Nicole. She knew it was me, too. The first time, she pretended she didn't see me, and she turned around and started walking fast in the opposite direction. It was over by Barnes and Noble. It looked like she'd just bought a book. I totally froze. It was like, I don't know. Not like seeing a ghost. It was like seeing . . . into a crack.

(Pause. Another question.)

Exactly.

(Professor Polson: "I'm sorry to ask, Lucas, but were you stoned?")

No. I wish I had been. That would have explained it. I was taking a break because I was applying for this seasonal job with the Road Commission, after I realized it would take me at least another year to graduate, and for the application there was going to be a drug test, but I ended up

not going for the test anyway. And then that afternoon, I
went back and got stoned—I knew I wouldn't pass it anyway,
with all the shit I'd been smoking a couple weeks before—
and then I started seeing her everywhere. She was sitting with
some guy at the bar at Clancy's. They were doing something,
like, looking at the screen of a laptop, typing things in. I
knew it was her again. I mean, the hair was different, but
that was it. And then I saw her a couple days later, crossing
the street by the Law Quad, and she saw me. She was like, I
don't know, fifty feet away, and I know she saw me because
she smiled and gave me this little wave, and then, the last
time, it was late, and I was coming back from Murph's, and
I'll admit it, I was stoned, weed, and there were some other
drugs involved, but I know what happened, I know—

(Clears throat. Pause.)

She was a block behind me, following me, and I kept
looking behind me, and I could see that it was her.

(Professor Polson: "Wasn't it dark?")

Street lights. It was bright out. I knew it was her, and I
was trying to hurry, and then I guess I just thought, what am
I doing, and I stopped, and I turned around, right outside the
door to my apartment building, and I said, I know it's you.

She laughed, and she kept walking toward me, and I
said, I'm going inside, and I kept walking, and went to my
apartment and unlocked it, and went inside, but I didn't
lock the door behind me—I guess I wanted her to come in.
So I just sat on the couch and never even turned the lights
on because, I don't know, it seemed worse to look at her in
the light, and that's when she came in, and she just kind of
hovered in the threshold for a minute, and I could really see
her in the light from the hallway, and she was smiling, and
she said, "Can I come in?" and I was like, "Yeah. You can
come in," and then she shut the door behind her, and it was
just like the first time, she unbuttoned her shirt, which was

sort of filmy and white, and took it off, and unzipped her shorts, and then she slid down next to me on the couch and we were kissing, and I think I was even crying, and when we were done she said, Told you, didn't I?

And then she put all her clothes on and left.

(Question. Pause.)

I don't know. I don't remember what I said, or if I even asked her. I—It was like we were somewhere else. I was scared. Excited, too, but really scared, and I was shaking. I remember she laughed about that. My teeth were chattering. She thought it was funny. She was like, I'm the one who's supposed to be cold.

And now I haven't seen her since, but it's like I see her all the time. Every time I turn a corner, but then it turns out not to be her. I sleep with the light on, or I just don't sleep. I . . .

(Here the interview ends.)

"Lucas," Professor Polson said. "I don't want to hurt your feelings, but I really have to do something now. I'm going to pick up the phone now and call Mental Health Services, and make an appointment for you."

Lucas nodded, as if he'd seen this coming.

Professor Polson was in the kitchen, on her phone, for what seemed to Perry like a long time, and finally came out with a scrap of paper and the name of a therapist and an appointment time for Lucas in the morning. Lucas looked at Perry, as if questioning whether he should take the scrap, and Perry nodded at him, feeling sad and relieved at the same time.

33

Mira put a tiny drop of dishwashing liquid into the dead center of each of the three mugs and then let the hot water pour into them, watching as they overflowed with suds.

It was 3:00 a.m.

After the boys had left, she'd walked around the apartment for half an hour—paced, really, a kind of back-and-forth followed by intervals of standing in place, wondering if she was standing in the middle of a particular room for a reason and, if so, what that reason could be. Finally, she'd noticed the three mugs—two on an end table, and one (hers) on the floor in front of the sofa, and was relieved to have a chore, a reason not to be in bed yet.

When the bubbles in the mugs stopped flowing, Mira turned the water off, tipped the cups over, poured the clear water out, and set them upside down on the dish drainer. She turned the lights off and then stood staring toward the sink for quite a while before she leaned against the wall and slid down it until she was sitting on the floor.

When was the last night she'd been at home alone?

Certainly it had been before the twins. But going back even further, it had been, she supposed, only a few times in the early days of her marriage—only in hotel rooms (conferences, job interviews). This was different. This was the place the twins were supposed to be, asleep with their blankets pulled up to their chins (they both did this, rosy fingers grasping the satin edges, lying on their backs, pink-cheeked, eyes moving around in their dreams beneath their vaguely light blue lids).

And Clark.

Mira was supposed to go into the bedroom now and find him asleep on his side, the bed torn to pieces by his shifting and rolling, shirtless. The silver St. Christopher medal she'd given him would catch the light from the hallway.

She'd brought that medal back with her from Romania when Clark was only a fantasy—after having spent only about a week in bed with him before she'd left for her fellowship year—just an intriguing and sexy guy she hoped very much she might be seeing more of. Back then, it had been a gesture that surprised her even as she made it, sliding the paper-wrapped medal into her bag. She could not have called what she had with Clark when she'd left for Eastern Europe a "relationship." (And what *were* "relationships" during those graduate school years when the most important virtue was negative capability, when you knew better than to even dare ask—such anxious grasping—"Will I be seeing you again?") She'd bought the St. Christopher at a little wooden stall outside of a church near the shore of the Black Sea, knowing as she bought it that it was for Clark. When the old man who'd sold it to her put it in the palm of her hand, he wrapped her fingers around it for her and then he kissed her fist.

If Clark were there, in bed, in their apartment, he'd grumble when she came in and lay down beside him, and Mira wouldn't know if he was asleep and annoyed to have been awakened, or awake and simply annoyed that she had entered the room. It had been a long time (a year? two?) since he'd rolled over and put his arms around her waist and buried his face in her hair.

Was this what it was like when you found yourself sliding, impossibly and inevitably, toward a divorce?

And what then?

Would she and Clark and the beautiful miracle of the twins be turned, as seemed the custom now, into one of those joint-custody arrangements? An elaborate plan sketched out, and signed by a judge? Thursday through Monday with Mira. Monday through Thursday with Clark. Or every other week? Or every two weeks? Vacations numbered, accounted for? Holidays divided up like so many shiny pennies?

Back in the days of Mira's childhood, when there was a divorce, the fathers generally just slipped away to California and were replaced by the mothers' new husbands. But Clark was not the kind of father who would slip away. He might very well be, in fact, the kind of father who would fight her for full custody. He might very well be the kind of father who would be *granted* full custody by a left-leaning judge who wanted to show that she valued the role of the stay-at-home father as dearly as that of a housewife.

Mira was, she realized, crying.

There were tears running down her neck. There were tears pooling around her lips. She wiped them away. She held her breath to try to make the hiccupping sobs subside. She was being ridiculous, getting way ahead of herself. Clark had said nothing about divorce, had he? He'd only taken the twins to visit his mother. It was his mother's birthday. His mother's *seventieth*. He would be back. He'd been right—she couldn't have come along in the middle of the week.

Mira took her hands away from her face and forced herself to think of something else.

The interview.

She would think about that. Lucas. Her research. Her book. When the boys had first arrived, Mira had been certain that she'd know what to make of Lucas and his account of events. He'd slouched into the apartment looking quite a bit worse for wear than she remembered him—but drugs tended to do that, even to the very young. Jeff Blackhawk had told her that Lucas was in his poetry workshop that semester, and was an interesting writer but seemed unable to speak. Mira remembered him as a *terrible* writer—all adjectives and unsubstantiated opinions—who could not be dissuaded from dominating every class discussion with his opinions. Halfway through the term with her he'd had that trouble with a drug bust, and after that he had gotten quieter, although his papers became even more opinionated and full of purple prose. She remembered one essay he'd written that had nothing whatsoever to do with whatever assignment he'd been given, and had become, instead, a rant against oppressive drug laws:

Why does the United States, perhaps the earth's most variegated garden, feel it must oppress the very youth it purports to wish to nurture into blossom?

And she also remembered reading this first line to Clark while grading papers at the kitchen table. It was supposed to make Clark laugh, give him an idea of the mind-numbing work she was doing at the kitchen table as he bounced the newborn twins to sleep in the chair across from her, but Clark had just snorted and said, "*Really,*" in agreement with Lucas's sentiment.

But the Lucas in her apartment that evening had appeared drained of his saccharine passions. There was a strange quarter-size patch of hair missing just above his left temple, and repeatedly during the interview he'd pressed his fingers to that spot and rubbed it as if he were experiencing sharp pain there. He must have managed to rub the hair away, and then continued to rub enough to prevent it from growing back.

His monologue had been chilling, baffling, incredible. Unless he was a future Academy Award winner, this could not have been an act. Mira had the impression he'd not told a soul the story until then, and that perhaps he'd even managed not to think about it in detail until he'd opened his mouth to speak to her.

But what had actually happened?

Mira knew what she *wanted* to believe—the thing that would fit the thesis she knew she shouldn't have already developed, but had.

There were *thousands* of accounts of ghosts reported on college campuses. Murdered coeds thumbing rides to the cemeteries where they were buried. Suicides still weeping in dormitory shower stalls, drunken fraternity brothers still prowling around under the balconies they'd drunkenly fallen from. The youthful dead were particularly inspiring when it came to such stories, and the living youth seemed particularly inspired by their dead peers. And Nicole Werner was the perfect campus ghost. The beautiful virgin with that already ghostly senior portrait. The evil boyfriend. The grieving sorority sisters. The dark, cold night of her violent death. Her roommate had to identify her by the jewelry she was wearing because the gorgeous sorority girl had been *unrecognizable.*

In a graduate seminar Mira had been invited to take her senior year in college (because Professor Niro had said he thought she was the most serious undergraduate student of anthropology he'd ever encountered), they'd read Charles Mackay's classic, *Extraordinary Popular Delusions and the Madness of Crowds.* The book had impressed Mira deeply—probably more than it impressed the other students, because she was so young. The professor had expressed some contempt for the shoddy research, the slapdash psychoanalysis, the exaggerations in the book, but Mira had carried the impressions of that text with her through all the years of her education that had followed, and she still felt them. There had been no chapter on ghost sightings on college campuses, but Mira remembered very well Mackay's chapter on haunted houses, and his conclusion that the weak and credulous people who were drawn to them would be the very sort of people who would see ghosts in them.

Lucas might certainly be one of Mackay's weak and credulous. Lucas was easy. But what about Perry? Could *both* boys be suffering from the same overstimulation of the imagination?

Mira looked down at the watch glowing green on her wrist: 4:02. She had to teach her class in five hours. And somehow it didn't even startle her (a movie camera would have captured her only casually looking up from her wristwatch as if she'd been expecting the sound all along) when there was a tentative-sounding knock on the door and a whisper she'd never have heard if she had been in bed: "Professor Polson? It's just Perry Edwards again, if you're there."

34

Nicole was down to her bra, her panties. They matched. Pink. He hadn't been able to look closely, but Craig thought he'd glimpsed a little heart, or maybe a bird, sewn onto the right-hand corner of the panties. And he was pretty sure he'd glimpsed the palest bit of downy hair between the panties and the high bikini spot of her inner thigh. Her cheeks had gone from a pink that matched the underwear to a deeper shade of pink in the course of their two hours in his bed. God only knew what color his own cheeks were. He was bathed in sweat. His hair was matted against his forehead. His heart had been beating so hard for so long in every part of his body that at least he knew for certain that he had no undetected heart defects. He'd never have lived through this if he did.

Perry was at home in Bad Axe for the weekend, so Nicole had spent the weekend rising from and returning to Craig's bed in their dorm room.

"No, Craig, not yet. But it feels so good. Oh my God. No, stop. O—"

It was like a refrain now to the loveliest song he'd ever heard. He would have done anything she'd said. He felt certain that if she'd have let him, he could have levitated with her in his arms and they could have made love on the ceiling. He could have unzipped his body and wrapped her in his skin. He could have buried himself in her neck and slipped into the place between her shoulder and her throat, and been soldered by passion to her forever.

But she wouldn't let him.

"No, oh, Craig, it's so hard to say no. I want. But, no. Please. I'm not ready. If I were, it would be you, and it would be now. But—"

"It's okay. It's okay. I know." He breathed the words into her mouth. "I just want to press against you. Just let me hold you. Can I touch you—"

"There. Yes. Oh my God. O—"

35

It was one of those October days during which it seemed like the middle of the night all day, and that, Shelly supposed, was why she was waking up so disoriented. That, and the bottle of wine.

Where was she? What time was it? Who was sleeping beside her?

Two bottles of wine?

They'd started drinking after lunch—some tuna filets in olive oil, some tomato slices. First, they'd split the expensive bottle of white, and then the cheap red stuff Shelly kept on hand for cooking. Had they finished both of them?

Truly, Shelly had no idea how much they'd had to drink, but she could still feel the wonderful muscle exhaustion of the sex. Of the *hours* of sex. Her lips were swollen with it, and she licked them, and there was the taste of it on her lips and tongue—salty, sweet. Her breasts felt heavy. Her nipples were still hard as little nails. Between her legs she felt bruised and wet.

How, exactly, had *she* come to be sleeping in this bed beside Shelly? How, exactly, had they gotten from *there* to *here*?

A full moon was shining through the window (Shelly hadn't bothered to pull the shades), and after she finally managed to open her eyes fully and to rub them into focus, she could see clearly and deliciously that Josie Reilly was asleep on her side, the sheet pulled up only to her naked hip, pale and white, her black hair spilling over Shelly's rosebud pillowcases. In the corner something with green eyes blinked, and it took Shelly a breathless second to realize that it was Jeremy, standing stockstill, as if on high alert or turned to stone. Confused. Disapproving. Displaced. She remembered Josie saying in the sweetest, most apologetic voice, "Can you please get the cat off the bed? I really don't like cats."

Now, Josie Reilly sighed and opened her eyes, and smiled when she saw Shelly looking down at her. She reached up one elegant arm—the one with the silver vein of a bracelet around it—and placed her fingertips against Shelly's throat before propping herself up slowly on one elbow and kissing the place she'd touched as she slid her hand from Shelly's neck to her breast, and her lips moved up from Shelly's neck to her lips.

It had been just past noon when Josie had stepped into Shelly's house bearing two Starbucks cups, shivering in her soaked cashmere hoodie.

"Can I come in?" she'd asked, and Shelly had said, of course, of course, although she was incredibly annoyed to find Josie there, when she was supposed to be minding the office, and to have been woken up from her nap.

Josie's cheeks were crimson, mottled, and there were tiny raindrops on her forehead. Shelly must not have been able to hide the annoyance on her face, because Josie had bitten her lip and then said, "Oops. Should I not have come over? I thought you might need some cheering up."

"No," Shelly said. "It's fine. It's . . . nice. Thank you, Josie. How thoughtful." She took the cup Josie was holding out to her with one hand, and pulled her bathrobe closed around her chest with the other. "Come in. Sit down, and give me your hoodie. I'll toss it in the dryer— on the delicate cycle."

Josie blinked, looking pleased, and the raindrops fell from her eyelashes onto her cheeks. She handed her own Starbucks cup to Shelly so that she could unzip her hoodie.

"Thank you. I'm *soaked*."

The zipper made a sound that made Shelly think of a comet—something traveling at an incredible speed, very far away—and then Josie Reilly was standing before her wearing what she knew girls now called "camis," or "tanks," but which, when Shelly was this girl's age, had been lingerie. The kind of thing you might wear on your wedding night.

It was pale green, raw silk, hemmed with a paler green lace. It was also wet, and it clung to Josie's breasts, making the perfect outline of them visible, no imagination needed. Her nipples were hard. There were goose bumps on her arms.

"Is it okay, I mean, if I hang out for a bit? I can't go out like this." She opened her arms as if to display herself fully in her camisole to Shelly, as if to invite her, *incite* her, to look at her body, and Shelly did—she couldn't help but look—and then she looked at Josie's face, and it was impossible not to interpret the expression on it as flirtation.

Flirtation verging on seductive invitation:

Her lips were pressed together. She was batting her eyelashes. A small smirk played at the corners of her lips. Her weight rested on one leg, and the hipbone of the other was bare, a blinding inch of pale exposed flesh.

Shelly's breath felt ragged when she inhaled, and she raised her eyebrows, opening her mouth before exhaling and saying, holding up the hoodie, trying to sound casual, "I'll take this downstairs."

"Thanks, Shelly," Josie said, and then, "Is it okay if I sit down? I don't think I'm so wet I'll ruin your couch or anything."

"Of course," Shelly said, and even to herself she sounded like someone in a trance, under a spell, like someone who had just stepped off a treadmill onto unshifting ground. She was almost surprised, when she got to the basement, to find the washer and dryer where they had always been. She pulled out the limp previous load of her own socks and panties, tossed them into the plastic basket waiting in the corner, and then ran her hand through the lint trap before putting Josie's hoodie on the delicate cycle and turning back toward the stairs.

"I *love* your house," Josie said.

She'd taken off her shoes and left them by the front door. Her feet were bare. Her toenails were painted silver, like her fingernails. She had one leg crossed over and under the other in a position that was impossibly dexterous and casual at the same time. Her elbow was propped up on the back of the couch, and her fingers were playing through her hair, lifting and pulling and twirling the black strands as, with her other hand, she lifted the Starbucks cup to her lips, sipped, licked them, and then said, looking around, "It's *so* cool. Do you live alone?"

"Yes," Shelly said. "Except for my cat."

"Oh," Josie said. "What's its name?" She looked around, as though worried that Jeremy would show himself.

"Jeremy," Shelly said.

"Why Jeremy?" Josie asked. "Isn't that a little odd for a cat name?"

"I guess," Shelly said.

She had, she realized, no clever story to tell about Jeremy's name. She'd simply wanted to avoid giving the cat the kind of name all of her single, academic, lesbian friends had given theirs: Plato. Sexton. Amadeus. Sappho.

She'd pulled the name Jeremy out of thin air, thinking it had no baggage whatsoever, that she'd never known a single person named Jeremy. It was only months later that she remembered the one Jeremy she'd forgotten: a retarded boy who'd lived in her neighborhood, who'd fallen down a flight of stairs in his house and been killed.

"I'm not wild for cats," Josie said. "I'm a dog person. Cats seem a little creepy. No offense."

Shelly sat down in the chair across from Josie, pulling her robe over her knees as she did. She'd forgotten her Starbucks cup on the kitchen table, and by now it was probably cold. She thought she'd just leave it. She had no idea what treacly beverage Josie might have brought her today.

"Wow," Josie said, looking around again. "I'm so used to living with a ton of other people—it would be weird, but really awesome, to have a whole house to yourself." There was a dreamy look in her eyes, as if she were actually imagining herself in the rooms of Shelly's house, ambling between them on her own, considering what it would be like if they were hers.

"Well," Shelly said. "It's definitely better than—"

"A fucking sorority," Josie said, and took another sip of her drink, looking demurely away from Shelly. She'd never said the word *fucking* in front of Shelly before—although, once, when the printer made three times the number of a long document than it was supposed to, Shelly had heard Josie shout, "Shit!"

Shelly cleared her throat. "Well, do you have to live at the sorority?" She hated the sound of her own voice, and the frumpy way she was holding her robe around her.

At the gym, lifting weights, looking at herself in the mirror, Shelly felt physical, powerful, beautiful. She flushed easily, and knew that men were looking at her. But in the presence of Josie Reilly—in the presence of a girl whose body had been through only nineteen, twenty years— she knew that the kind of admiration she got from men at the gym meant nothing. Here before her, in the form of Josie Reilly, was the embodiment of beauty and youth. This girl had just barely emerged from the cocoon of childhood. In fact, Shelly thought she could see a film of something like dew on Josie's neck, on her chest, and she even thought she could smell something wafting off of her limbs like pond water— rank and sweet at the same time, so potent.

Why, Shelly thought soberly then, was she letting this happen?

Was this happening?

Never once had she thought of herself as the kind of old dyke who would sleep with a student, a *girl*. The only women she'd ever found herself attracted to in the past had been her own age, or older. She'd disliked the lesbians she knew who kept women half their ages, and paid their rent. It was so obviously nothing but physical—and wasn't part of the point, the point of being a woman who'd chosen women over men, to reject that kind of objectification? To reject that abuse of power?

She was, after all, Josie Reilly's *boss*. And the girl was *less* than half her age. But she was also radiating, indisputably, on Shelly's couch, her own inalienable power:

She'd stretched out. One leg was extended luxuriously on the couch. Her fingers continued to move through her silky black hair. Her short top had made its way higher, and two lovely inches of white, flat stomach had been exposed. Under her arms was the downiest bit of unshaven hair. One of the straps of her tank top had slipped over her shoulder bone, and now the top of her right breast was exposed. It was painful to look at, and impossible not to stare. Josie rested her coffee cup on her crotch, and looked at Shelly and asked, "Do you have anything to eat? Like, a sandwich or something?"

36

It was impossible not to stare at Professor Polson as she cooked. Like Perry's mother, she cracked the eggs with one hand, and then tossed the shells into the sink. She didn't measure anything. Two burners were glowing blue on the stove at the same time. She grated cheese straight into the pan of scrambled eggs.

Professor Polson reminded him of his mother, but she was also like a girl Perry's own age—hair uncombed, falling around her face in a mass of curls and tangles. Her hands were full, so she used her shoulder to push the hair out of the way as she leaned over the stove. In her jeans and Indian-print shirt, she could easily have passed for a college girl. She was thin. Even a little bony. You would not have known she'd given birth to twins. He imagined that she didn't eat a lot, because she also didn't look athletic. In Bad Axe the only women he knew who were mothers and weren't overweight were the athletes: the hikers and bikers and swimmers. Or the smokers. The alcoholics. Professor Polson looked healthy, but she did not look like someone who worked out at a gym or who spent much time outdoors. She looked, Perry supposed, exactly like what she was: a reader, a writer, a teacher. Someone who'd spent her life studying something very particular and obscure, and who'd become an expert on it because she was more interested in it than anyone else had ever been or might ever be again.

And at the same time that Professor Polson reminded him of women like his mother, his aunts, the mothers of his friends—and also girls like Mary, Nicole, Josie Reilly, even Karess Flanagan—she was also nothing like them.

She was neither young nor old, fashionable nor out of touch. Professor Polson existed somewhere in between the worlds of the mothers he knew and the girls he knew, and he could not take his eyes off of her as she peeled slices of ham out of a plastic package and dropped them onto a skillet, where they shriveled up quickly and filled the kitchen with the smell of meat and maple. He was, he realized, ravenous.

They'd talked for hours since he'd come back to the apartment, he guessed. He'd lost track of time. But it was pitch-black night when he'd returned, and now the sun was shining through her apartment windows. Hours had to have passed.

After the interview, when they'd left Professor Polson's apartment, Perry had walked Lucas back to his place, and then he'd turned around, intending to go back to his own apartment. But he'd found himself instead walking directly toward the Omega Theta Tau house.

The rain had stopped at some point during Lucas's interview, and now the streets were shining with dampness in the moonlight. The sky was completely clear, looking as if some kind of blue-black satin had been rolled in enormous bolts all through the town. The moon was somewhere close to full, but not quite, and it turned the branches of the trees to a kind of parody of October—spooky, damp. Leaves had blown out of the trees during the storm and lay in tatters in the streets, and on the sidewalk, on the lawns. They caught at the toes of Perry's shoes.

He couldn't help himself.

He had to go there.

He had to stand outside the house.

He had a feeling, and when he'd had that feeling before, she had appeared, or *seemed* to appear.

Perry had already known, more or less, the story Lucas was going to tell Professor Polson, but it had terrified him anyway. The matter-of-factness of the account. The mundane details. Lucas's plainspoken, shamed recounting of events. It had required self-restraint for Perry to keep himself seated, listening. More than once, he'd had the urge to flee. He'd seen himself in his dark suit again, pictured himself in Bad Axe at the funeral, walking with the coffin on his shoulder, the terrible, solid, indisputable shifting of weight inside the coffin when Nicole's cousin stumbled as they carried her out of the church and into the hearse.

And there were other things he remembered.

Back in his dorm room, in Godwin Hall, just those few weeks before the accident.

Told you, didn't I?

Nicole had kissed him afterward, and stood up, and, as she was buttoning her shirt, had said, "Told you, didn't I? I knew you wanted to fuck me, and that you would." Then, she put on her clothes, closed the door behind her—somehow managing to leave her panties at the foot of the bed for Craig to find (although Craig didn't recognize them, and instead teased Perry mercilessly, pitifully, about his "mystery slut"). Why had she done that? It could not have been a mistake. He'd known Nicole most of his life. She wasn't ever sloppy. Even in kindergarten she'd been the first one to throw her empty milk carton away, or fold up her nap mat.

At first, Perry had thought she might have been sending a message for Craig—but, later, he wondered if it had been something else, a way to discredit Perry, cast suspicion on him. Surely she could tell that he and Craig were starting to become friends.

He could see the light on the porch of the Omega Theta Tau house, but Perry couldn't tell, from where he stood on the sidewalk looking up at it, whether anyone was on the porch.

It was a flat town, a flat *state*, so it was that much stranger, eerier, that the sorority house was perched on a hill above the rest of the block.

Behind it, the memorial orchard sloped down to the wall between the sorority property and the smaller yard of the frat house next door. There were no leaves at all left on those cherry trees as far as Perry could tell—two skeletal rows of shiny, wet black branches and moonlight. From inside the house, there seemed to be only one light: a dim flickering in one of the upstairs windows. Perry couldn't tell if it was a candle doing the flickering or some shadowy figure pacing around by the window. There seemed to be lacy curtains, and they seemed to be closed. He supposed it wasn't so odd that all the lights were out at this time of night—or morning—in the middle of the week before exams. Omega Theta Tau was supposed to be one of the studious sororities.

Perry stood staring up at the house until he was sure there was no one on the porch, and then he stepped off the sidewalk and onto the grass. He wanted to get closer, but he thought it was a bad idea to go straight up the front walk, which was bathed in porch light. He didn't know why. He had no idea yet what he thought. Did he think Nicole was *in there*? And, if so, how? And if she wasn't, what was he afraid of? And if she was, what then?

He stayed in the shadows, and made his way up the side of the lawn. The ground was soggy, slippery, carpeted with fallen leaves. He walked slowly, with no idea what he planned to do when he reached the porch. (Knock on the back door and ask to see Nicole? Peer in the windows to try to catch a glimpse of her?)

He stopped. Looked behind him. Looked in front of him. He looked toward the porch, and just before he saw what he thought was a man in some kind of dark suit or uniform, the light switched off and Perry was left standing on the lawn in the dark, and then he heard what sounded to him (so out of place here that it took him more than a few seconds to recall it from duck hunting with his dad at Lake Durand, or deer hunting in the national forest with his grandfather, from the hundred or so Boy Scout rifle competitions he'd attended at the Bad Axe Rod and Gun Club) like the slide of a shotgun being racked, and he crouched down and, holding his breath, made his way back across the lawn, away from the house, as quickly and as quietly as humanly possible.

It was blocks later that he realized that he'd run all the way back to Professor Polson's apartment, the outside entrance of which had been propped open so that he didn't have to buzz her, and that he'd run up to the stairs to her door, and he was knocking on it.

She opened the door as if she'd been expecting him.

Clearly, he hadn't woken her. She was still in the same top and jeans she'd been wearing during Lucas's interview. Her eyes looked watery, as if she had been either crying or coughing. Her hair was a little more mussed. (Perhaps she'd been lying down?) But when she saw that Perry was nearly doubled over, out of breath, standing in her doorway, Professor Polson pulled him into the apartment without asking any questions, and led him to the couch.

"I'll get you some water," she said. "Try square breathing. You know what square breathing is?"

He knew what square breathing was only because she'd told them about it in class, in preparation for their trip to the morgue—had told them that if they began to feel faint during the visit, or to feel as if they might be sick, or hyperventilate, they should close their eyes and do square breathing.

("Breathe in through your nose to the count of four. Hold the breath to the count of four. Exhale to the count of four." She'd had the whole class practice. "I used to lose at least three students to the linoleum every field trip until I taught square breathing.")

As Perry sat panting on her couch, and Professor Polson went into the kitchen, he tried it:

One. Two.

The apartment looked different in the dark.

Three. Four.

She came back to the living room with a sweater draped over her shoulders and a glass of water for him, three ice cubes bobbing in it. She turned on the light beside the couch and handed him the glass, and then sat down on the chair across from him, perching on the edge of it, leaning forward with her elbows on her knees, and asked in a soft, concerned voice, "What is it, Perry? Can you tell me?"

The square breathing, or *something*, had worked. He was calm now. He didn't even feel winded. He told her what had happened. The darkness. The candle. The man he thought he saw in the shadows, and the sound of a shotgun being racked up, and how he'd run, not realizing he was here again until he was.

Professor Polson had seemed to think for a long time about what she was going to say before she spoke, and then said, "Perry, I think maybe we've already taken this too far. I think I've encouraged you in some—" she pulled the sweater off her shoulders and onto her lap, and then gathered it in her hands, brought it to her face, seemed to breathe it in for a minute before she continued, "unproductive thinking. When the imagination—and I'm not talking here about *your* imagination per se. I'm talking the collective imagination, the occult imagination—when it's stimulated, many things that aren't real can come to seem to be real. Perfectly sane people, people who—"

"No," Perry said.

Professor Polson nodded as if she'd expected him to object, but she went on:

"Let me tell you something," she said, and she told him, then, a story about her childhood. Her mother. A kind of transformation in a pantry. A white coffin, and her own realization, staring into it, of what the unconscious was capable of. The imagery that informed this life, this culture.

"You can pretend you aren't superstitious," Professor Polson said. "You can imagine that you are not religious. You can be certain that you don't believe in life after death, if that's what you want. But, Perry, it doesn't stop the fact that we are in a very strange position here. We humans. With such a clear knowledge of how it will end, and no idea what will happen afterward—just some symbols, some music, some stories to show us the way.

"Of course you believe your friend is alive. That she lurks around every corner. That her death could be something as alive as her sexuality was, as your own. You're nineteen years old. Who *dies*, Perry? Who believes in *death* at your age? People with a lot more life experience than you have believed stranger things. Have seen stranger things. Folklore is full of—"

"I'm sorry, Professor Polson, I know what you're saying. But it isn't folklore. This. It—it isn't."

There was a kind of sad understanding in her eyes, but she was shaking her head at the same time.

"Perry, folklore doesn't mean something doesn't make sense. Or doesn't seem real. Truly, it's the opposite. Beliefs—traditional and superstitious beliefs—arise and are passed down for coherent, substantial reasons. They're based on psychological and physical data, real or not. Shared experiences. In the field we call this *elegant rationale*. There's often an elegant rationality to even the strangest beliefs. But it doesn't make them real. Being based on fear, inspired by hope, they can be dangerous, Perry, and I think we're headed in that direction, and that we need to stop what we're doing now, before it leads to something—"

"Please," Perry said. "No. Please. I'll talk about it any way you want me to. We can call it *elegant rationale* and *campus folklore* if you want to. But, please. Don't stop . . . listening to me. Professor Polson—"

She reached across the coffee table and took his hand. She held it in her own for a few seconds, and he could feel for himself how cold his own hand was. She squeezed it before she let go, and said, "I know. I know. Okay."

"Thank you. I—"

But she held up a hand to stop him from saying anything more. She stood up then and gestured for him to follow her into the kitchen, where he leaned against the wall as she made him a cup of tea, and they talked about class, about the article on apotropaic magic they had been assigned for the next week and which Perry had already read. She told him about her travels during her Fulbright year, the village in which she'd stayed a few nights, where every house and every inn, every restaurant and church, kept nailed to its door a piece of a broken mirror that had once hung in the ladies' room of the local cathedral, until the cathedral had been bombed.

There had been only one woman in the cathedral at the time—an old deaf lady who hadn't heard the air raid sirens. She'd been blown into too many pieces to gather and properly bury. The mirrors were nailed to the doors to keep her from stopping by.

They discussed the section of the essay on the *motif of harmful sensations*. The Sirens. The Lorelei. The Harp of Dagda. The Hungarian Suicide Song—a song, it was believed, that to hear would cause the person who heard it to commit suicide.

He told her that when he was in high school, a rumor had gone around that there was a YouTube video posted on the Internet—a body swinging from a rope tied to a tree—that, if you watched it, would cause you to hang yourself within three days. Girls had gone around Bad Axe High School frantically whispering about who had been reckless enough to watch it at the last slumber party. He'd even witnessed some tears in the hallways, and the principal eventually wrote a note home to parents letting them know about the rumor, urging them to talk to their children about it.

"Yes," Professor Polson said, smiling, excited. "This is exactly the kind of thing we want for our study, Perry. Exactly."

Perry was still hearing her words *our study* in his head, and the little thrill of that, when she said, "I think it's time for breakfast. I don't know about you, but I've got to get to the class your parents are paying me to teach, and teach it." They both looked at their watches at the same time, and then they sat down to eat the eggs that had grown cold on the table as they'd talked, but which were still delicious.

Part Three

37

Josie was wearing flip-flops even though the temperature outside could not have been over forty-five degrees. It was one of those deep-pewter late October days during which morning lasted until it finally bled without a whimper into twilight. Shelly had, herself, pulled her suede boots out of the back of her closet for the first time that year. Not only was it too cold for flip-flops, but flip-flops had been the one item of clothing Shelly had asked Josie, when she'd first hired her, not to wear to the office.

And she was over an hour late.

"Hey," Josie said breathlessly, pushing open the door to Shelly's office with her hip. "Sorry I'm late!"

Shelly tried to look away as nonchalantly as possible, returning to her computer on which she'd managed to call up a blank Word document as soon as she heard what she'd assumed was Josie coming up the stairs.

"You're not mad, are you?" Josie asked, but she was out of the door's threshold before Shelly could turn around and say anything, her flip-flops making a husky whisper as they slapped against the heels of her small white feet as she sauntered down the hallway toward the restroom.

It had been two weeks since they'd first slept together, and there'd been two dinners (both at Shelly's house, cooked by Shelly) since then. Three other times, they'd left the office together, gone back to Shelly's for drinks, and ended up in bed. These assignations had been initiated casually enough by Josie ("Hey, Shelly, are you up for a glass of wine after work?") and, after each time, Shelly swore to herself that she wouldn't let it happen again.

Too risky. Too risqué. Too unseemly.

But simply saying no seemed impossible. At least once or twice a day now, Shelly found herself nearly doubled over with longing for the girl:

The small hard nipples under her hands. The soft palpitating at the base of her throat. The way Josie (who required sometimes a steady, blissful hour of tongue and fingers to reach an orgasm) would throw her head back in the final seconds, and Shelly could glimpse just the bottom of her bright white front teeth between her parted lips, and a hissing sound would escape from Josie that sent what felt like a shockwave ripping through Shelly's body, bringing her to her own climax without even needing to be touched.

It was only when they were in bed that they discussed the fact that they had ever slept together before or that they ever would again, so each "date" was like some kind of extreme sport—the rush of not knowing what would happen next.

In the meantime, Josie's work ethic had dwindled down to nothing. She'd stopped bothering even to apologize for leaving early. She simply announced that she was leaving. Twice, she called in sick, depositing scratchy-voiced messages on the voice mail, having clearly timed her calls so that Shelly wouldn't be in the office to actually answer the phone.

This morning, the flip-flops. Late again.

It didn't surprise Shelly. (Why would it? Josie had been a bad work-study student from the start.) But it frightened her. She knew that the sexual relationship meant she was no longer in a position to reprimand Josie, or even gently critique her. That first morning, after that first night, Josie had shimmied her jeans on, zipped up her hoodie, and said, before sliding out Shelly's front door, "Shelly, I'm going to have to make up tomorrow for missing my Chem Lab yesterday afternoon, 'kay? So, I won't be in. But I'll see you soon?"

Shelly had found herself unable to remind Josie that she had responsibilities related to the St. Crispin Quintet concert the next day. Someone needed to walk them from their hotel to Beech Auditorium (because it was written into their contract that the St. Crispin Quintet did nothing without an escort), and it was the work-study's job to attend to these details. It was, in fact, the whole reason Shelly had been given a work-study student in the first place, because the experience of rubbing elbows with these professionals was supposed to be so beneficial to the student's education.

But that morning Shelly had stood in the doorway holding her robe closed around her and said, "Okay," to Josie, while any last shred of denial about the new dynamic between them dissolved as Josie cocked her head and blew a kiss in Shelly's direction. Shelly could feel herself flushing, but also could not stop herself from reaching out the door (in full view of the mailwoman across the street) and taking hold of one of the dangling pompoms on Josie's pink hoodie, and gently urging her back inside.

Josie had smiled sleepily, dreamily, allowed herself to be lured back through the screen door and into the foyer, where she kept her eyes open as Shelly pulled her to her and put her hands in the silky black hair and kissed Josie's lips with as much restraint as she could (and still found herself trembling, making little noises in her throat, her tongue running over those perfect little teeth, her hands, as if they belonged to someone else, traveling up to Josie's waist to her breasts again, running clumsily over them as Josie sagged passively, pliantly, against the screen door and let it all happen). When Shelly had finally managed to step back, there was what could almost have been a look of triumph on Josie's face.

She'd narrowed her eyes and licked her lips, sighed, and reached out to touch Shelly's throat, and then said, "See you next time," before turning and leaving (for real this time), swaying down the walk, surely aware that she was being watched, without turning around once to look at Shelly in the doorway.

In the other office, Shelly could hear her talking on the phone. Every sentence ended with the sound of a question.

"And then we went to the bar? And Crystal and Stephanie were there? And so anyway I guess tonight we're supposed meet back at the house and take away their privileges, you know? And after that, we'll vote? So, like, tell them not to wear any shoes, okay? Everybody else can wear shoes?"

Jesus, Shelly thought. What could Josie be talking about, or did she even want to know? Was this some sort of hazing? No "privileges"? No shoes?

Maybe a punishment for having been at the bar when they were supposed to be home making doilies for the Founders' Tea?

It was, Shelly thought, possibly Trials Week—which had been re-named Spirit Week by the Pan-Hellenic Association after the scandal a few years ago when a drunken sorority sister had been driven forty miles out of town and left on the side of a rural highway.

It was, apparently, a common prepledge trial these days. You were taken to a party, where you were prompted to get drunker than you had ever been before in your life, and then your sympathetic older "sisters" pretended to insist on driving you home because of their great concern for you—but, instead, they dropped you off in the middle of nowhere and told you, as their car sped away, to find your way back to the house.

Maybe most of the girls *did* make it back to the house, and lived long enough to inflict this trial the next year on a new generation of sisters. But one year, a victim panicked and tried to chase the car that had dropped her off, managing to run fast enough to toss herself against the bumper and hit her head and die.

The administrators and the parents and the Pan-Hellenic Association swooped in screeching, as if they hadn't known perfectly well that this kind of thing was taking place on a regular basis. There was a great deal of "shock" and "outrage" among the university community—especially since this was a sorority. "Girls Hazing Girls!" was the headline, as if it were news.

Not a single woman Shelly knew was surprised by the ruthlessness of girls toward one another—and certainly no one Shelly knew who'd ever been in a sorority could manage much more than the raising of an eyebrow, if not a stifled yawn, at the news that sorority sisters were dropping each other off in the dark, drunk, and laughing as they sped away. Shelly herself had never been dropped off drunk on a highway, but she'd had to go two weeks without brushing her teeth, and was required to arrive every evening on the front porch of the Eta Lambda house to have the scum on her enamel approved.

Over a cup of tea after their third time in bed together, Shelly had asked Josie if sororities still did things like that, and Josie had laughed pretty hard while recounting how, as a newbie, she'd had to wear the same underpants every day for four weeks—period to period—and take them off in the living room, standing there bottomless in front of the Pledge Board, while they passed her panties around and either sniffed them or screamed about them and threw them from one sister to the next until they were given back, and Josie had to put them back on.

"I cheated," Josie said. "I washed my panties out in the sink a few times, and then I put toothpaste on the crotch to make it look really yeasty, so they just freaked when they saw it, and didn't smell it—luckily, since it smelled like mint!"

"Jesus," Shelly had said, rubbing her eyes.

Although, as a hazing practice, this sort of thing happened only during the prepledge part of sorority life, the spirit of it was part of the very air they had breathed in the Eta Lambda house. Every few weeks some sister would find your hairbrush matted with hair on the bathroom sink, or some clump of something crusty in the shower after you'd just gotten out, and she would scream Ee-w-w-w! for everyone to hear.

And these little humiliations called up everything:

The filth of being human, of being female, of being alive, of living in a body, of having the shame of that exposed to prettier, cleaner, better girls.

•••••••———

Shelly looked up, and was startled to find Josie standing in the threshold, leaning against the doorjamb. One thin strap of her little tank top had slid down her shoulder. Her hips looked so thin that the denim skirt she was wearing seemed to be held up over her pelvic bone by some sort of antigravitational force. Shelly tried to keep her eyes on a spot just over Josie's shoulder as she said, "Oh, hi, Josie. Did you call the School of Music yet, about Jewett Smith?" Shelly could hear the thinness of her own voice as she spoke, and it made her want to crawl away somewhere to die.

"No," Josie said. "But I will."

"Thank you," Shelly said, and turned back to her computer, stared at the blank document on which she'd only managed to type, "Funds Request."

"Um, Shelly?"

Shelly turned and saw that Josie was chewing on the shiny pinkie fingernail of her left hand. What Shelly felt, seeing that pinkie between the girl's teeth, could only have been described as a sharp pain in her chest—a kind of sexual agony. If she'd been standing up, her knees might have buckled. When she tried to form the word *yes*, nothing came out of her mouth.

Was she losing her mind?

Was this what happened to old dykes? Was this some sort of perimenopausal insanity? She hadn't even blinked, but there before her eyes was a flash of Josie on her back, hips propped up on one of Shelly's flowered pillows, sleek thighs open, and Shelly parting the pink shell between her legs with her fingertips, leaning in with her own lips parted as Josie writhed beneath her—and Shelly felt a kind of terror that was so much like ecstasy that, sitting there at her desk in front of her computer, she had to bite her lip to keep from crying out.

"Shelly, I have to tell you something, and I'm *really* sorry."

38

Jeff Blackhawk lingered in Mira's office, touching a few of the little things she kept on her bookshelf, turning them over in his hands—a paperweight that had been a gift from a student (velvety red rose petal floating, without weight or age, inside a glass globe), a Petoskey stone Mira had picked up on the beach during a trip to Lake Michigan the year before, a couple of paperclips. A few minutes earlier he'd stood up as if he were leaving, so Mira had stood as well, but now he seemed reluctant to go, and genuinely charged up about their conversation, which seemed like a strange and not unpleasant turn of events, as Mira couldn't remember the last time she'd had a conversation about anything other than the weather with any of her colleagues.

She'd always thought that becoming an academic (especially if she was lucky enough to land a place, as she had, at a major research university, and then in a niche noted for its encouragement of free intellectual exploration like Godwin Honors College) would mean endless conversations in hallways, in offices. Graduate school had been rich with such talk among students, and although Mira had to admit now that she couldn't remember, looking back, ever having actually seen two or more professors speaking to each other about anything more interesting than whether or not the copier was out of paper—still, somehow, she'd expected that when she became a professor herself she would find herself engaged in passionate daily debates in the lunchroom over the finer points of the most obscure topics.

But she could not have been more wrong.

Nightshift factory workers probably spent more time philosophizing with one another than she did with her colleagues at Godwin Honors Hall. In three years, the most passionate discussions she'd had in the lunch room pertained to the best temperature at which to keep the minifridge and who kept stealing the secretary's Diet Cokes.

But today Jeff Blackhawk had stopped by to speak with Mira specifically about her new research. Dean Fleming had mentioned it to him in passing one afternoon, and it seemed to have genuinely seized Jeff's interest.

Last fall, he'd had Nicole Werner in his first-year seminar, and although he claimed not to have gotten to know her very well, he had clearly been affected by her death. Like everyone else, he blamed the boyfriend. He said, "The guy used to wait for her outside our classroom, like he thought maybe she'd run off with somebody else if he didn't walk her to and from class."

Given Jeff's reputation for romancing the most beautiful of his undergraduates, Mira ungenerously considered that he might have resented Craig Clements-Rabbitt's hanging around because that would have made it hard for him to snag Nicole Werner alone. Still, Mira was flattered by his interest in her research. He had a variety of suggestions for her, and although Mira had been trained to pay the least amount of attention to the creative writers in any department (their educations were always lacking), she thought that his ideas were genuinely good ones, his anecdotes interesting.

Did she know, for instance, that for many years, until the administrators managed to squelch it, there'd been a kind of hysteria in Godwin Honors Hall among groups of students who thought it was haunted?

"There was an article in the student newspaper. You could look it up. All these reports that a girl was coming around to the rooms, looking for somebody. I mean, the story changes with the teller, but it was more or less reported that this girl was frantic, and half-dressed, and looked like she was from another era, and when they asked her who she was, she'd tell them she was *Alice Meyers*."

He emphasized the name, and paused afterward, as if Mira should recognize it.

She didn't.

"You know. The study room? In the south end of the basement?"

Mira'd had no idea that there was a study room in the south end of the basement. Despite teaching a fair number of her classes in basement classrooms (an honor given mostly to assistant professors), she'd been on the south side, where there were no classrooms, only once, in search of a student she'd been told was in the ceramics workshop and who'd left her backpack in Mira's classroom. That side of the basement of Godwin Hall seemed to be just arts and crafts workshops, knocking pipes, and laundry facilities, although there was, she knew, a little student hangout over there somewhere called the Half-Ass, where they sometimes held poetry readings and bad student rock band concerts.

"Yeah. There's a study room down there. They've quit using it, I think. It was paid for by the parents of Alice Meyers. She was a Godwin Honors College student who disappeared in 1968. She posted her name on a board at the Union for a ride home to some small town in Ohio. The last anyone saw of her she was walking around the Union, looking for her ride."

"Jesus," Mira said. She was used to such stories, but they still gave her goose bumps.

"Well. Anyway. There's that. And, you know, the brass isn't letting it out, but there was another death on campus recently. A girl over in Bryson. A freshman. They just found her dead after somebody noticed the stench outside her room. I think they can't say for sure it was a suicide, so they're not saying much at all. This was three weeks ago, and it hasn't even made the papers. Luckily, I guess, her parents are nobodies from some rural town pretty far from here."

Mira nodded. She hadn't heard about it, but it didn't surprise her. There was always a student who killed herself, or himself, every year in a single, in a dorm. (An excellent argument for doubles.) Always a stench. Always the possibility left open that it had been an undetected heart defect or an accidental overdose, not a suicide or, God forbid, a murder, so the university could pretend it wasn't neglecting its young people—their mental health, their safety—although everyone knew that there wasn't the slightest bit of attention paid in a place this big to any individual's mental health or safety. The only people on campus with any responsibility for that at all were kids like Lucas, resident advisors, who got free room and board to pretend to be taking responsibility.

Jeff Blackhawk picked up a paperclip Mira had on the bookshelf and put it in his mouth. He held it for a second, first, between his front teeth, but then it disappeared. Being the mother of two toddlers, Mira had to check her alarm—her first instinct being to pry Jeff's mouth open and fish it out. But Jeff managed to keep talking with the paperclip in there.

"And you know there's that other girl from Nicole Werner's sorority."

"What?"

"Yeah. See?" He gestured at Mira as if he'd already proven his point. "Nobody's getting this information. State secrets. Cover-ups all over the place. This place is full of 'em."

"What happened? Who?"

"Denise Something. They're trying to pass it off as a runaway situation. Supposedly she was dating some older guy, and her parents disapproved, so she disappeared off the face of the earth. It was right around the time Nicole got killed, and her sorority sisters are all saying the last time they saw Denise What's-Her-Name was at that ghastly cherry tree thing, and then she got in a car with some guy, took her stuff with her, and that was that. The parents can't even get the cops in this town to investigate—which of course gives the brass around here a great excuse to just toss up their hands and say, 'Sorry your kid got lost! Not our problem! Even the cops can't help you!'"

"What year was she?"

"Sophomore, I think. Music school. She lived in the OTT house, but the year before, she lived in Fairwell—ironically enough."

He opened his mouth to laugh, and Mira was relieved to see the paperclip still on his tongue.

Fairwell was an all-girls dorm, and the campus folklore was that the girls who lived there as freshmen never got to be sophomores, that they all flunked out. Statistically, it wasn't true. Fairwell girls were no more likely than any other group of freshmen to fail their first years. But it was still a struggle to fill the beds in that dorm. The university allowed students to rank their top choices, and because Fairwell was so unpopular, the dorm was mostly filled with foreign students or girls from such small towns they'd never met anyone from the university to tell them this story. (Of course, with the Internet, it was getting harder and harder to capture the ignorant.) Mira had asked the dean once, at a stiff cocktail party for junior faculty, why they didn't just change the dorm's name. Wouldn't that solve the problem? Clearly, she pointed out, the rumor had started because the dorm's name, Fairwell, was *Farewell*.

"Never thought of that," he'd said. "But, nope. Marjorie Fairwell was the wife of the university's first major donor. She's got scads of descendants still pouring money into the place. They'd rather let it sit empty than change the name. Eventually they'll make it a charity dorm, I suppose. All the girls there will be on financial aid or academic probation, and just grateful to have a place to sleep, period."

Jeff leaned against her office wall, looking down at Mira's legs. He always got there eventually, it seemed to Mira. She was surprised it had taken him so long. It must have been an indication of his sincere interest in the topic they were discussing. She asked him, "How do you know about it, this runaway, if it's been kept so quiet?"

"A friend of mine works in the provost's office," Jeff said. "She's sworn to secrecy about everything that goes on there, but a couple glasses of wine and she's all tongue."

Mira tried not to picture the scene inspired by the choice of words, his female friend's tongue. Jeff was, himself, an exceptionally sexy man—tall, olive green eyes, a head of shaggy brown hair. But Mira found him as attractive as a catalog model of men's underwear. Sure, you looked twice, but there was that problem of *you* existing in the three-dimensional world, and his being just a flat, glossy surface. Plus, there was Jeff's absolute lack of discernment, it seemed. ("If she's breathing, he'll sleep with it," one of the part-time language teachers had told Mira once in passing. "It's pretty sad, really. If he were a woman, we'd all feel sorry for him and be worried about his self-esteem.")

Mira looked at her watch (where was Clark? she needed to call) and thanked Jeff, who took the paperclip out of his mouth before he said good-bye, and put it back on her bookshelf.

39

So many years in an academic environment: that had to be the reason that Shelly's first thought was, It's not a dead metaphor.

Her blood really had *run cold*. It dropped twenty degrees in her veins as she looked up at Josie in the doorway, realizing that, because Josie never apologized for anything she did wrong in the office, this was something else. This was something bad.

Josie swallowed. Shelly could see it in the muscles on her neck, hear the little wash of spit in the girl's mouth, as her own mouth went completely dry.

"What?" Shelly asked, curling her toes inside her suede boots. "What is it?"

"Oh, God, Shelly. You're going to be so mad at me." The girl was whining, but she also sounded strangely as if she were reading from a script. Without realizing it, Shelly found that she had stood up, and that she was stepping backward, as if to put some space between the two of them. "And I don't blame you. But. Well. You know those pictures I took? With my cell phone? You know, when we—?"

Shelly raised an alarmed hand to stop Josie from going on.

No, the hand said. Don't say it. No need to remind me. *Of course* she knew:

They'd been lying together in Shelly's bed. Skin to skin. The top sheet and blanket were crumpled on the floor at the foot of it. Josie had been kissing Shelly's neck, and her Cover Girl lipstick was smeared all over Shelly's throat (something she'd noticed only later, at the bathroom mirror, with alarm, thinking at first that she was bleeding) and they'd been drinking red wine, and a splash of it had landed in a violent-looking slash across the bottom sheet. Shelly was a little drunk, and Josie had seemed more so. She'd giggled hard enough at a very stupid joke Shelly had told her (while licking the girl's hip: "What do the hippies do?" "They hold the leggies on") that she'd finally jumped out of bed squealing, "Oh, my God, stop it, Shelly, or I'm going to pee in the bed!" (Shelly had noticed that the more Josie drank the more her speech became less and less of the Valley Girl and more harder-voweled Midwestern.) After the bathroom, Josie had stumbled back to the bed with her cell phone and snuggled next to Shelly, and held the phone an arm's length away from them, and then scooted down and sunk her sharp little front teeth pleasantly into Shelly's nipple, and snapped the cell phone at the same time.

A giggle.

Shelly said, "What did you do?"

She knew, of course, about camera phones, knew her own cell phone had such an application, although she'd never bothered to learn how to use it, but it still took a few seconds for her to process that Josie was snapping photos, and in those seconds Josie had managed to snap another, and another, and then she climbed on top of Shelly, straddled her pelvis—the incredible warm-moist sensation of Josie's crotch pressed onto hers—and held the phone at arm's length again, and managed to get them both together, smiling and naked and, surely, from a distance, completely obscene.

Then Josie had snuggled back down to show Shelly the photo:

It took her breath away.

This miniaturized image of herself as a fit, creamy-skinned middle-aged woman holding a dark-haired sylph in her arms. She was lost, completely lost, and knew it, even as she took the phone from Josie herself and snapped a photo of Josie reclining, sloe-eyed, one hand cupped under her breast, and another of Josie's dark hair floating around Shelly's hips as she flicked Shelly's clitoris with her tongue. After that, Josie took a photo of Shelly propped up against the headboard, legs spread, and Josie's hand—thrillingly recognizable by the little gold and ruby ring she wore—between them. A single bright index finger disappearing inside her, and Shelly's face registering the pleasure of it, her mouth a subtle O, eyes half-closed, the bliss of the moment, and the bliss of capturing it, perfectly and suddenly, like something snatched out of the air still buzzing and humming and coming and pinned to time forever with a tack.

If anything in this world had ever excited Shelly more, brought her more fully into this world, she could not have said what it was.

Now, as Josie stood before her in the Chamber Music Society offices, one half-naked shoulder raised in a tiny apology, Shelly recognized it, all of it, for what it was: insanity.

The undoing of her small, carefully constructed life.

Oh, how they would love it, too. After so many male professors had been taken apart, witch-hunted down for their dalliances with under-graduates, how satisfying and self-affirming it would be to chase a les-bian out the door.

"I was, you know," Josie said, "going to email them to you, you know. I thought . . ." Shelly groaned a little, closed her eyes tightly. "They were on my computer. And my roommate saw them, and I guess she turned them in to the Omega Theta Tau Board."

"Oh, Josie. Oh, my God. How could—"

Josie lifted her chin defensively, and shook her head so that the dan-gling pearl earrings she was wearing began to swing around in her hair.

"Well, Shelly," she said, sounding petulant. "I'm really scared, too. I mean, I won't tell them who, in the pictures, you know, I'm *with*. But I think there might be something about this in the by-laws. Like, maybe if I won't tell them, and they think you're a professor, or my boss, or some-thing—"

Shelly put her head in her hands and went back to her desk chair, sank down in it. After a few seconds she said into her hands, "Please. Just let me have a few minutes to think. Alone. Please. Go."

"Sure."

It was said so brightly that Shelly looked up, and it was a shock to find that Josie hadn't moved an inch, was still leaning against the door-jamb, was smiling down at Shelly, quite happily, it seemed, from a very great height.

40

M om?"
    "Perry. *Honey.* I've been trying to get a hold of you for days. Is everything okay there?"

"I've just been busy, Mom. I'm sorry. I started a work-study job for one of my professors, and I've been researching and interviewing. I lost track of how long it had been since I called."

"Oh, Perry. Don't let a job get in the way of your school work. That's why you've got that scholarship, sweetheart, so you have time for study-ing, not—"

"This is like studying, Mom. It'll be good. My professor's writing a book. I'm getting academic credit for it, too. Really, it'll be—"

"Okay. I believe you. I just worry when I don't hear from you. I don't want you to overload yourself. You don't sound right, sweetheart. Are you sleeping? Are you okay? Is Craig okay?"

"Craig's okay. I'm fine. I sleep."

There was a silence and, in it, Perry thought he could hear the sec-ond hand on the clock on the kitchen wall in Bad Axe make its little snapping sound, traveling between the black dashes between numbers. He closed his eyes, saw that clock over his mother's shoulder, and in that moment he considered, briefly, telling her everything.

Nicole. The photo. Lucas.

He imagined asking her—what? To pray for him?

To come and pick him up?

To tell him he'd lost his mind, or that, yes, this sort of thing, it hap-pened all the time.

Girls died, and they rose from the dead.

Did he think his mother would tell him, *Don't worry about it, sweet-heart. You'll figure it all out in good time.*

No, she would be stunned into silence. She would panic. She would cry. He cleared his throat, instead, in the silence, and his mother said, "Good, sweetheart. That's good. You just be sure to get plenty of sleep and eat right, okay? And tell Craig we said hi. I sent some cookies for both of you. They should get there in another day or two."

Perry rubbed his eyes. He said, trying to sound rested, well fed, sane, "Thanks, Mom. How's Dad?"

"Dad's fine. We're both fine. Can you come home for a few days before Thanksgiving, or won't we see you until then?"

"I'll work on a ride," he said. "I'll let you know. I have to check my calendar, and with my professor."

"Sure. We just miss you. That black bear is back."

"Really?" Perry asked.

"Really."

"Wow."

The summer before, there'd been a male cub wandering around in the backyard. They'd decided it must have been orphaned. There'd been an article in the Bad Axe newspaper about a black bear found shot in a cornfield outside of town. (Someone had taken the bear's head, and left the body, and the farmer who'd found it had called the Department of Natural Resources.) Everyone knew there were bears in the area, but there were not so many that it didn't make the news when one was found shot and beheaded.

"You're sure it's the same one?" Perry asked.

"Well, it's a lot bigger this year, and it's got a chewed-off ear, but it has to be the same one, don't you think?"

"Sounds like it. Is it causing trouble?"

"It figured out how to take the lid off the trash can without making any noise—but, no, otherwise, no trouble. Dad got a chain for the lid. Tiger doesn't want to go outside much, though."

They laughed. Tiger was the world's most timid tom. He'd sit outside on the back steps for a few seconds every day, and if a squirrel or a bird landed in the yard, he'd start scratching at the screen door frantically to get back in.

"I saw Nicole's parents at church last Sunday, honey."

"Oh. How are they?"

"Not well at all, Perry. Mrs. Werner's ill. They don't know what's wrong with her, but Mr. Werner talked to your dad, and told him it's a 'wasting disease,' which means, I guess, that she's losing weight and they don't know why. I thought he looked as weak as she did. His hair's all fallen out."

"Oh, man." Mr. Werner hadn't even been balding when Perry last saw him. "Is it cancer? I mean, Mrs. Werner?"

"Well, of course that's what we all think, but I guess the doctors say no. They've even been down there, to the university hospital, for some tests, and they wanted Jenny to come back in six weeks, but Mr. Werner said they couldn't go back. They just can't be in that town, because of—"

"Of course."

"And I saw the baby. Mary's baby."

It took Perry several seconds to realize who his mother was talking about. For a startled second he thought—when she said, "baby," "Mary"— of his imaginary friend, and the sister who'd died as a baby before him. "Baby Edwards." But then he remembered, both with relief and a stab of bitter pain: *Mary.*

"How is she?"

"Well, she's living with her sister now. The father, you heard what happened?"

It occurred to Perry then that his mother thought Bad Axe news made the news all over the state. "No. What?"

"Oh, he was injured. Brain damaged. He was in a hospital in Germany until last week, and now he's in North Carolina. One of those crazy bomber people."

"God," Perry said, and could think of nothing more to say.

"Perry, you still don't sound right."

"I'm fine, Mom." He rubbed his eyes with the hand that wasn't holding the phone, trying hard to sound "right." "Look, I'll call you in a few days about when I can come home. I just have to check on some things, okay?"

"That's fine, darling. You just keep up with your studies. That's what matters. You're keeping up?"

"Yeah, Mom. I'm doing well."

"I knew you would be. I knew you would. I love you, Perry."

"I love you, too, Mom."

"Bye, baby. Talk to you later."

Perry had put the phone in the cradle and was headed to the fridge (peanut butter? crackers and cheese?) when the apartment door slammed open, and Craig burst in, hair wild around his face and his eyes wide with—what? Horror? Awe? Joy?

"Read it. *Read* it," he said, holding a small square of paper out to Perry in a trembling hand.

41

The dean of the music school and his administrative assistant were waiting for Shelly in his office when she arrived.

Shelly hadn't slept that night but she'd run enough scalding hot water, followed by freezing cold water, over herself in the morning, and then consumed enough caffeine, that she thought she might at least look like someone with a heartbeat. She'd worn her gray suit, which hadn't been out of the dry-cleaning sheath in the closet for two years, and some pastel makeup, brown mascara, eyeliner. She was trying to look sexless, she supposed, but not like a sexless *lesbian*. Low-heeled pumps. Pantyhose. Some lace along the collar of her blouse. She'd painted her fingernails peach. She reached out and put her hand on the threshold of the dean's doorway before stepping in, and tried to breathe slowly—in through her nose, out through her mouth, counting to four, although she forgot to stop at four, and found that she had been exhaling a long time before she realized she was still counting, and that the dean and the administrative assistant were looking up at her gravely.

The dean seemed to be choking with embarrassment in his necktie. The administrative assistant, who was very young and very pretty and new enough in her position that Shelly hadn't met her in person yet, looked up, but not at Shelly. Her blue eyes traveled across the wall and fixed on the ceiling. She folded her cool little hands on a yellow legal pad in her lap.

Looking at those lily-white hands, Shelly reminded herself, inhaling, that she must not faint. And she must not cry. And she must not let her voice shake. And she must not put her own hands over her face and stifle a terrible little sobbing scream—although she'd done this at least once each hour since getting the news that a formal grievance had been filed against her, and that she should probably consult with a lawyer.

"Hello," the dean said, rising from his chair just long enough to get his butt a few inches off the seat before setting it back down, tightening his tie as if to hang himself, and then gesturing with a flat open hand to his administrative assistant. "This is Allison. She'll be taking notes. Have a seat, Ms. Lockes."

The dean hadn't called Shelly "Ms. Lockes" since he'd hired her. Although she would not have called him a personal friend, they had known each other a long time now. She'd watched him go gray. She'd sent cards to his children when they graduated from this or that, and a bouquet to his house when his sister died. He'd always liked her, and she him. They had, she thought, seen one another as occupying together an island of good taste in a sea of philistinism. Early on, he'd complained bitterly to her about the new Jazz Department, but that turned out to be nothing compared to the folk/rock, and then the pop/rock, course offerings that followed with the years. Their only disagreement when it came to music was about Mozart, whom Dean Spindler saw as superior to Handel. Shelly had insisted on her own assessment: that Mozart was a youthful machine, brilliant but soulless, and that Handel was a mortal who'd gotten a glimpse of eternity and put notes to it. Dean Spindler had charmingly pretended to be offended, but for Christmas she'd given him a recording of *Giulio Cesare*, and during Christmas break he'd emailed her telling her he'd been listening to it nonstop:

You've nearly convinced me, Shelly. I am surprised, and grateful, for this late-life awakening. I hope we have many years as colleagues ahead.

"Did you bring your lawyer?" he asked.

Shelly shook her head. She sat down in the empty chair across from him. "I don't have a lawyer," she said.

"But you *were* advised to seek legal counsel?"

Shelly nodded, but he seemed to be waiting for her to speak. "Yes," she said, and the administrative assistant scratched lightly across her pad without looking either at Shelly or at the words she was writing, as if she were trying to take notes without being accused of taking notes.

"We need to have that for the record—that you were advised to bring a lawyer, and chose not to do so," the dean said.

Shelly nodded.

"Also, we need to have it on record that you understand what this disciplinary action is about." He cleared his throat then, but he seemed less embarrassed now, emboldened by the high moral ground on which he safely stood. "So, do I need to show you the photographs, or can I simply describe them, and you can tell me whether or not you're one of the subjects in them?"

"You don't need to do that," Shelly said. There was no way to keep her voice from cracking. It was as if it belonged to someone else.

"Actually, I'm required to do that. Believe me, I'd rather not. But if you don't confirm that the photographic evidence we're using is the same evidence you're familiar with, later you could claim confusion, and this could go on forever."

Now he sounded bitter. Put out. She was, she knew, probably adding all sorts of tedious tasks to his day, not to mention the discomfort, the unsavory nature of this.

"It won't go on forever," Shelly said, "believe me," and then she put her face in her hands and began to weep, exactly in the manner she had vowed not to. With hysterical abandon. With deep wrenching sobs. With bottomless grief and self-pity and self-loathing. She had no idea what the dean and his assistant were doing as she wept, but no one said a word, or seemed to move, stand, leave the room, sneeze. It was as if they were frozen in time, and in horror, somewhere beyond her weeping. She wept and wept, and it was only when she realized that she had no choice—that she was going to drown right there in her own palms, her accumulated tears, if she didn't ask for a tissue—that Shelly finally looked up and saw that the administrative assistant was gone.

The dean, it seemed, had been paralyzed into silence. He managed to hand her a tissue, but the expression on his face as he did so was that of someone who'd been staring into an abyss of shame so long that its reflection was permanently etched on his face. She took the tissue from him, and then he handed her the whole box. He was squinting, as if Shelly were very far away from him, or incomprehensible in every detail, and then he said, like an actor stepping off a stage, "Shelly. Jesus. What the hell happened here? How did this *happen*?"

She opened and closed her mouth, but finally quit trying to speak. There were tears running off her lips. She could only imagine what her face looked like.

"You do understand," he asked her, "don't you, that this means the end of your employment with the university? And that's the best-case scenario. Who knows what other complications could follow? Lawsuits? Investigations?"

Shelly nodded, and he rubbed his eyes, leaned back in his chair, addressed the ceiling:

"You can have a day or two to clean out your office, and until the final paperwork, all of that, and the various committees, et cetera, you'll officially be on leave, with your salary. Again, you can get yourself a lawyer, but I have to tell you in all honesty, especially with our new policies regarding inappropriate use of power in student/faculty and employer/employee relationships, it's—"

"I know," Shelly said. "I know. I know."

He looked at her again, and then he nodded gently toward the door, and Shelly stood.

He said good-bye as she stepped out the door, but she couldn't turn around.

42

Even with the distraction of Lucas and Perry and teaching and meetings, Mira had been bereft without the twins. She found herself lingering in the doorway of their room, staring into it, feeling the kind of grief that would have been more suited, she thought, to their deaths than to their being gone for two days to visit their grandmother. When she found the UPS package with their Halloween costumes in it, she'd ripped it open, and her eyes had welled with tears.

She had ordered them off the Internet:

Little cow hoods with little cow horns, little hoofed hands, black and white spots.

The boys had been going through a cow phase for months. At the petting zoo they'd stood enraptured before one particular enormous bovine mass of weight and skepticism, humid nose pulsing, as if recognizing something from their previous lives.

The cow chewed her cud with such pensive blankness, looking from Matty to Andy, Andy to Matty (both were struck dumb in her presence), for so long that Mira finally felt the need to pull them back, fearing that this cow was either as in love with them as they were with her or was about to let loose her many years of petting zoo resentment and frustration on them.

But as Mira tried to take the twins' arms and guide them over to the llama, they began to shriek with the kind of outrage she'd seen on documentaries about parents trying to kidnap their children from cults.

And, after that day, everything was *cows*.

Cows in books. Cows in magazines. Cows in pastures glimpsed in passing from the freeway.

Mira had delighted the twins with two stuffed Beanie Baby cows one afternoon. She'd stopped and bought them at the bookstore on her way home from the office. Each of them had snatched one of the cows up and now guarded it jealously from the other. She had no idea how they could tell the cows apart, but they could. Once, she accidentally tried to tuck

Matty's cow into bed with Andy, and he'd sneered at it in disgust and tossed it over to his brother, exclaiming what sounded to Mira like, "Buckholtz!" or "Bullshit!" She was hoping it was *bullshit*, which would mean that the "imitative stage" of their language development, as the books she was reading called it, was getting on schedule. She had no doubt that they'd heard both her and Clark utter that word on numerous occasions.

They slept with the cows. They carried the cows with them everywhere. And, unlike every other toy they'd had so far in their short lives, they never lost the cows. The cows were never dropped and forgotten at the supermarket. They were never left behind in the backseat of the car overnight.

So, after that success, Mira had brought home a couple of plastic cows one night after teaching, and Matty and Andy had gone crazy with delight. A few days later, she bought a couple of cow-decorated cookies at a specialty bakery that she passed on her way to the parking ramp. They loved the cookies, licked the cookies, but they shrank from Mira when she pointed to her own teeth, her own open mouth, suggesting that they eat the cookies.

"You're overcompensating," Clark had said.

"What?"

"Overcompensating," Clark said. "Trying to buy them off."

"Buy them off?" Mira had tried to follow him down the hallway, to ask him what exactly she'd be overcompensating *for*, but he'd gone into the bathroom and shut the door and stayed in there until she had to leave for work.

In the nursery, Mira tacked up a poster of a cow grazing on a grassy hillside in Vermont, and every morning before they were taken out of their cribs the twins would stand and gaze at the poster, babble to each other in their language about the cow:

"Descher neigelein harva stora."

"Gott swieten mant brounardfel."

Mira imagined they were speculating. Was the cow happy? Did she have a family? Would her future be as peaceful as her present seemed to be? But when Mira herself pointed at the cow and said, "Cow!" and then waited for them to say the word, they looked at her blankly. "Haller," one or the other would say. "Haller," one or the other would reinforce. Then, they mirrored her own expectancy, waiting, it seemed, for her to say the word. To confirm it. To show that she understood what a *haller* was—that it was black and white and grazing on a grassy hillside in Vermont right in front of her face—and it was all Mira could do to keep from saying it (clearly they were talking about the same thing here, trying to give it a name), but she said, "Cow," again, more desperately this time, and with less assurance, and they looked, she thought, disappointed in her.

When Clark had finally walked in the door with the twins that afternoon, Mira got on her knees and embraced them so tightly for so long that Matty, who could never get enough, finally pulled away, looking alarmed.

"Mommy just really, really missed you," she said, and Matty gave her a reassuring kiss on the crown of her head and patted her shoulder as if she were an old woman in a nursing home. She'd looked up then and caught Clark's eye, and they'd both laughed. She stood and embraced him, and he seemed to take her in his arms with genuine warmth. "I missed you," Mira said, and they kissed—not a lingering kiss, but she'd felt the goodwill in it. He must have missed her, too.

Now she was hoping they'd have a good, peaceful evening. She'd bought two tuna steaks from the expensive gourmet market near campus. The woman behind the fish counter had wrapped them in several layers of white paper, and Mira had carried them hopefully home. Clark used to like to cook tuna steaks in sesame oil—pink in the middle, seared white on the outside. It had been at least a year since he'd done that, but she recalled that they were always delicious, and Mira fantasized that he'd make the fish that night after the boys went to bed, while she tossed a salad and boiled rice.

Maybe, after dinner and a last glass of wine, they would make love.

Clark seemed refreshed, in a better mood than he'd been in for a while. The only jab he'd made when she mentioned his good mood was, "It was nice to have some help."

Maybe, then, he'd seen the look on her face and was as eager as she was to avoid a fight, because he'd qualified it right away:

"My mother really takes over, you know. She'd have spoon-fed *me* for two days if I'd let her. She had the boys up and dressed and playing with an old set of my blocks before I woke up both mornings."

Since then they'd had only one stiff exchange—he couldn't find his running shoes, which he'd left under the bed, but which, before finding them, he accused Mira of having put "in the toybox or something" while he was gone—and one argument that had ensued when she found, after Clark had left to go running, a note in his handwriting on the kitchen counter:

2:20—Your boyfriend called again. I told him you were in your office, to try your number there.

Mira had held the torn piece of notebook paper in her hand for quite a while, staring at it, trying to discern its meaning. For a crazy second she imagined he was referring to Jeff Blackhawk, but never once had she spoken to Jeff Blackhawk on the phone. Still, Jeff was honestly the only man who'd even *looked* at her, as far as she could tell, since before the twins were born.

Surely, she thought, Clark couldn't be referring to any of the boyfriends she'd had before they were married?

When he came back in the door, Mira held the piece of paper up, and said, "What is this?"

Panting, red-faced, sweat trickling in zigzagging rivulets down his cheeks, Clark didn't meet her eyes. He brushed past her to the bedroom.

"Clark?" she asked, following him.

"You know perfectly well, Mira. Your Eagle Scout. Your 'work-study' student," he said, making air quotation marks around the word, and sat on the edge of the bed and began unlacing his shoes.

"Perry Edwards? Perry's my *boyfriend* now?" Mira laughed. "Perry's *nineteen."* Relieved, Mira thought, It's a joke, that's it, and reached out to ruffle Clark's sweaty hair, but when he felt her hand on his head, he flinched away from her.

"Clark?" Mira said. "You're joking, right?"

"Yeah," Clark said. "That's right. I'm a big joker. Or, I'm a big *joke.*"

He took his shirt off, soaked with sweat, tossed it on the bedroom floor, and walked past her. He was, Mira saw for the first time, losing a bit of weight. He didn't have the chiseled look of a few years before, but he was getting there. The extra ten (fifteen?) pounds he'd put on was coming off.

"What's this about?"

Mira whispered it, following Clark past the twins' room. They were blessedly asleep an hour earlier than usual.

"Clark?"

He'd continued to the bathroom and gotten in the shower. She stood outside, staring at the bathroom door until, finally, she went into the living room and tried to read the newspaper. When he came back out, he seemed to have forgotten the argument.

"Glass of wine? A little QT?" he'd asked.

She told him about the fish, and that she'd ordered Halloween costumes for the boys that she wanted to show him. She put two glasses of wine on the coffee table, and when he came into the living room—face still flushed, hair damp—Mira held up the cow costumes, and said, "Can you even believe how cute these are?"

Clark looked at them as if he didn't recognize them as children's costumes at first, and then he blinked, and he said with so little emotion that he might as easily have been expressing hatred or contempt as complete apathy, "Are those for the boys?"

"Yeah," Mira said, and couldn't help adding, although as soon as she did she wished she hadn't, "Who else?"

"I'm just asking," Clark said, "because cows aren't *boys.*"

It took Mira a few seconds to compose any kind of response at all, and then she said, "I'm aware of that, Clark," and let the costumes drop to her lap.

"Well, the twins *are*. Boys, that is. Males."

"Thanks for that penetrating insight," Mira said, and began to put the costumes back in the box.

"Well, it seems to me like, I don't know, Mira—*bulls*, Superman, something like that might be more appropriate for two little boys for Halloween? I mean, I'm sorry if this offends you, or it's too burdensome to come up with something gender-appropriate. It's not like I suggested that you sew a thousand sequins onto a handmade serpent costume or something."

Oh, yes.

The handmade serpent costume with the thousand sequins was something Clark's mother had made for him when he was a kid. It was something he'd told Mira about his mother when they'd first started dating, to give her a sense of the woman who'd raised him—her fanatical dedication to her son, how seriously she'd taken her role as Homemaker. ("I wore the thing once," he'd said. "The woman would have been perfectly happy to go blind making my Halloween costume.")

They'd been driving in the dark together, Clark at the wheel. Mira couldn't see his face, but there was no mistaking the grief, maybe even the shame, in his voice. She'd reached across to him, taken his hand, and her own eyes had filled with tears. She'd wanted, then, completely, to love Clark with that kind of devotion herself. She wanted to be, someday, the kind of mother to his child who would sew a thousand green sequins to a felt suit simply because the child had a passing fancy for sea serpents. She *would* be that kind of mother, she vowed to herself then, even if, someday, it pained her children to consider those pointless sacrifices. She wanted those she loved to be that certain of her love.

Now, looking up at Clark, Mira said, "Well, I wish I had time to stay home and sew the boys' costumes myself, but I have to pay the fucking rent. *Somebody* around here has to work to pay the fucking rent."

Mira hadn't even noticed that Clark had the newspaper in his hand until he'd thrown it at her, and it had fallen in a wrinkled rasping disorder around her, and she was grabbing it up by the fistfuls and ripping it to pieces, throwing it back at him as he headed for the door.

43

Hell Week? Is this, like, hazing? You've got to be kidding. I mean, why would you join a 'club' that tortured you for a week?"

"It helps you bond," Nicole said, and Craig choked a little on his milkshake. The way she said it was so sweet, so utterly naïve. "It makes it so you're really sisters," she went on.

"Nicole, I thought you already did this during 'Challenge' Month. I mean, if having to wear the same pair of panties for four weeks didn't cement your bond, what good will Hell Week do?"

"Come on, Craig. You promised not to joke about that."

He nodded. He had. He'd promised up and down as a way of getting her to tell him what she was so self-conscious about in November. He'd assumed she was planning on dumping him, since every time he kissed her she found some reason to squirm away, and even in the cafeteria she sat as far from him as you could get and still be technically eating a meal with someone. He'd showed up outside the Omega Theta Tau house after one of her "secret meetings" on a Tuesday night, holding a bouquet of red roses, and she'd burst into tears and started to run away from him. By the time he finally caught up with her, half a block away, he was crying, too. He grabbed her arm, but she yanked it away and she started to beg, "Please, *please*, just stay away from me for a few more days."

"Why? Nicole, I *love* you. What's wrong?"

She ran a little farther, but weakly, seeming to be losing her will to run from him, until he managed to pull her into an alleyway between a liquor store and a sushi place. By this time, he'd already tossed the roses onto a park bench. He grabbed her arms in both of his and pulled her to him, and she sobbed, but she also went limp when he wouldn't let go, and he muttered into her hair, "Please. Nicole. I'm dying here. I love you. Just tell me."

"You'll *hate* me," she said. She sobbed. "You'll think I'm so stupid. You'll think I'm so, so—gross. You'll laugh at me, or you'll tell people. You'll—"

"Don't tell me what I'll do, Nicole! There's nothing that would make me hate you. And I'd never betray you. You're the most precious, the most—"

"Okay! Okay! My underpants!" she shouted. Some guy walking by the alley did a double-take then, and Nicole cringed, buried her head in her hands, and said it again in a ragged whisper. "My *underpants*." And again. "My *underpants*."

"What?" A slideshow of brief, crazy images flashed through his mind. He saw a football team throwing Nicole's panties around on a field, panties flown from a flagpole, panties for sale on eBay, photographs of panties tacked to bulletin boards, and then she said, "They're *dirty*. You'll just tell me how *stupid* I am."

It took a long time in the alley, and a lot of tears soaked into his corduroy jacket, to get the story out. She had three more days to wear them. On Saturday she had to hand over the filthy things to the Omega Theta Tau president in some sort of ritual celebration of sisterhood. Then she could wear new ones.

Nicole sobbed, "I can *smell them*."

It was hard not to laugh, but even harder not to lecture:

"This is absurd, Nicole. You're not joining the armed forces here. You shouldn't have to do this kind of shit just to live in a big house with a bunch of prom queens."

"I knew you'd—!"

"Okay, okay," Craig said, and closed his mouth by pressing his lips to her forehead.

That was back in November. Now, the first week of March, she was informing him that for Hell Week she wasn't going to be able to leave the basement of the Omega Theta Tau house except to attend classes.

"What the hell—no pun intended—are you going to be doing down there?"

"They don't tell you. But the girls from last year said it was mostly different projects. Stuff for events. And tests on Pan-Hellenic things, facts. The Founders." She shrugged.

"That's total, unadulterated bullshit," Craig said. "Why would you need to be in the basement?"

"It's a trial." Nicole lifted her chin, and he could see that it was quivering. "It's a tradition." She lifted a shoulder, let it fall. "I actually think it sounds fun."

"Fun?"

"You're not in a fraternity, Craig. I don't think you can relate to . . . to . . ."

"You got that right," Craig said. The waitress came over to their table then and started to take Nicole's plate away even though she'd never touched her grilled cheese. Craig put his hand out and waved the waitress away. "She's still eating that," he said.

"I'm so sorry," the waitress said without a shred of sarcasm, and held her hands up as if he'd tried to slap her. She was one of those infuriating middle-aged Midwestern women who used her friendliness like a weapon. Already she'd complimented everything about the two of them before she'd bothered to take their orders—I *love* your coat, I *love* your sweater, I *love* your hair thing, I *love* your ring, I *love* your boots. Craig had stared at the menu, imagining his mother shooing this woman away: *Thanks, we love you, too* . . .

But Nicole engaged the waitress exuberantly, told her that the sweater was from the Gap, that Craig's coat was from the Salvation Army (!), that the hair thing was just a scrunchie of her sister's, that the boots were Uggs, and the ring—Craig had given her the ring.

Here, at least, Craig quit grimacing at his menu and looked up at the waitress looking at the ring on Nicole's right hand. Nicole held it up to her like a queen waiting for it to be kissed.

"Wow," the waitress said, taking Nicole's little fingertips in her own, twisting her hand so she could see the ring in better light. "Wow. It's *sap*, isn't it? There's . . . something in it." She bent down to look at it closely.

"A little fruit fly," Nicole said proudly. "It could be forty million years old."

Craig had told her this.

His science teacher in sixth grade at Fredonia Middle had kept a little collection of things stuck in amber—a spider, a frog, some mosquitoes.

He'd even had a piece of amber with what looked like a long black hair floating in it, and another with two sad little ants scrambling over each other to get out before they were trapped in the stuff forever. Craig had been horrified and thrilled by the idea that, as Mr. Barfield had explained it, they'd probably stumbled in there in the first place because they were attracted to the whole sticky mess. Imagine, he'd thought, having the evidence of your fuck-up preserved for millions of years in amber.

"It's not sap," Craig told the waitress. "It's resin."

The waitress nodded then as if that were the most interesting thing she'd ever heard in her life, left their table finally, tossed the piece of paper with their order at the cook, and then disappeared, later leaving their sandwiches under the red lamps on the counter between the kitchen and the restaurant for a good ten minutes. When she finally brought them over to the table, they were stone-cold.

Why do you have to be so negative?" Nicole asked after the waitress was gone. "What difference does it make? If you were a Greek, you'd be doing something like this, and I'd understand."

"Look, Nicole. Hell Week, whatever. Do what you have to do—but, like, don't expect me not to be unhappy that I'm not going to see you for a week. I mean, if you were going to Spain or something, I'd get it, but sewing doilies in a basement?"

The tears that had been pricking at the inner corners of Nicole's eyes ever since he'd waved the waitress away turned into the real thing. When they started to run pathetically down the side of her nose, one of them even spilling over her upper lip, Craig jumped up from his seat and came around to her side of the booth, and put his arms around her, and kissed it away.

"Never mind, never mind. I'm an asshole, I'm sorry," he said, kissing and kissing. "Do your damn doilies. Just come back to me. I can't survive without you." He took her face in his hands and looked at it.

Nicole inhaled a wavering, aborted laugh before she put her head on his shoulder and started to cry even harder:

"But you're never going to understand. It'll always be this *thing* between us. You'll always be laughing at me. I just—"

"Are you saying you want to break up?" Craig asked, stiffening, trying not to shout it. He was painfully aware of the waitress hovering around behind him now, and knew she wasn't going to go anywhere until she'd caught enough of this conversation to figure out what the problem was. He lowered his voice, and said, "So, you want to dump me for some frat asshole? Is that what this is about?" He started to pull away, and then Nicole reached out and grabbed the lapel of his corduroy jacket, bunched it up in her fist, the way a baby would, and it made him want to start sobbing, too, looking at her small soft hand clutching at his Salvation Army jacket. (She'd bought it for him. She and her sorority sisters had gone to the thrift shop to buy costumes for some carnival they were planning, and she'd seen it there. "I knew you'd look so cute in it! And it was your size!")

"No, Craig. No. I want *you*, but I just wish—"

"I told you, Nicole, I'll think about it. I can't join this year anyway. Next year, okay? I'll think about next year, okay?" She didn't nod or say anything, just continued to clutch the jacket with her face against his shoulder. "Okay?"

She whimpered a little, and then she said, "No. You won't. You'd hate it."

Craig was about to try to deny it, but then she looked up at him and she had a little smile on her face—a wistful, regretful little smile like nothing he'd ever seen on her face before, maybe never before seen on anyone's face.

She said it again, "You'd hate it," and started to laugh. "I can just see you." She was laughing really hard now, and he started to laugh, too, looking at her, looking at him, regarding him, and he realized what it was, that expression—that she was recognizing him, that she knew him for exactly what he was, and it amused her:

Despite herself, she liked what she saw.

She maybe *loved* what she saw.

He could see it in her eyes.

Had anyone ever looked at him that way?

Craig felt as if he were made of glass, that a note played now on a violin or a flute could shatter him into a thousand pieces. He was trembling, he realized, and he had her hair in his hands, and he was trying to keep himself from sobbing out loud, and he vowed in that moment, not for the first time, that whatever she wanted, whatever it took to keep her, for the rest of his life, for the rest of her life, he would do it.

A bitterly cold wind blew through their booth at that moment, and he instinctively turned to look at the door of the diner. Someone had come in—a silhouetted figure in the doorway, blurred in Craig's teary eyes—and the figure stood in the threshold for a second or two before Craig, blinking, looking more closely, recognized him just as he turned quickly and walked back out the door.

Craig pulled away from Nicole, and nodded toward the door. "That was him," he said.

"Who?"

"That guy. The EMT guy, Nicole. The fucking ambulance driver. He saw us, and he left."

"What EMT guy?" Nicole asked, bringing her napkin to her eyes to wipe them. "What are you talking about?"

"I've seen him, that guy, like five times at your sorority. I told you already. Remember? I told you that I keep seeing him around there. Who is he?"

"I have no idea what you're talking about, Craig. I don't even know what EMT stands for."

Craig didn't bother to argue with her, or to tell her what EMT stood for. He watched the plate glass window to see if the guy would walk past it, but he must have gone the other way: To avoid the window? To avoid being seen by Craig?

Craig stood up, as if to follow, although he had no idea what he'd do if he caught up with the guy—and, anyway, Nicole took the sleeve of his jacket in her hand and tugged him back down to her, wrapped her arms around his neck, and kissed him so sweetly, and for so long, that even the waitress, who'd been watching them, must have felt embarrassed, and went away.

44

L et me get the mail," Perry said, trying to grab Craig's elbow as he turned from the window to the door, but Craig was already gone before Perry could stop him.

They'd been watching from the window together, waiting. Below, the mailman was finally crossing the street, his face down against what must have been a pretty stiff wind (a bright end-of-October day, not a cloud in the sky, but the bare branches of the trees were being whipped around mercilessly, and the wind blowing through the gaps between the window frames and the glass panes felt frigid to Perry). The mailman disappeared from view for a few minutes, presumably standing in the foyer of their apartment house, sorting and distributing. Then they saw him emerge and start to walk across the grass to the apartment house next door, a bright red leaf stuck to his blue cap, scores of other leaves catching to his black boots as he trampled through them.

Perry stayed behind in the apartment and listened to the stairs make their familiar groaning and rattling sounds as Craig slammed down them in his sneakers on his way to the mailbox. He could even hear the missed beat of Craig skipping over the seventh step.

A week earlier, someone's foot had punched through that one, and there was a hole in it now that you had to avoid if you didn't want to end up knee-deep in the stairwell on your way up or down. No one in the building seemed to know who it was who'd gone through it first, but since then, one of the girls next door had twisted her ankle, and she was on crutches, so Perry had left the landlord a message about the problem. When there was no response to that, he left a note at the top and bottom of the stairs himself ("CAUTION, HOLE IN SEVENTH STEP"), and when the girl on crutches found out that Perry was the one who'd put up the sign, she hobbled over with some cookies she'd baked, to thank him for his concern.

The cookies had tasted like cardboard, but she was a pretty girl— bright red cheeks and dyed black hair cut in a kind of bowl shape around her head. If she'd told him her name, Perry had forgotten it. A couple days after Perry taped up the warning, someone had written on the bottom of it, "Signed, Rumpelstiltskin."

Craig must have fished the mail out of their little metal box by now. Perry could hear him coming back up, taking the stairs two at a time. Maybe three at a time. He could hear what sounded like panting, and then Craig shoved the door open and stood there in the threshold holding another fluttering white postcard out to Perry in one hand, a handful of glossy pizza and sub sandwich flyers in the other.

"It's her. It's really her," Craig said. "It's another postcard from her."

Perry took a step carefully toward him and took the postcard from Craig's hand. It looked the same as the last one—one of those prestamped post office cards made of thin, pulpy paper. Perry looked at the address, reading Craig's name there, and then he flipped it over.

He had to rub his eyes, and look again, and then rub his eyes again: The *handwriting*.

Perry had been seeing that handwriting for years. Soft fat pencil on lined paper. Crayon signatures at the bottom of art projects. Invitations, exclamations pinned to lockers, notes he'd had to borrow, to copy, in Global Studies, in AP English, for classes he'd missed, and poems written out in this handwriting in a poetry workshop he'd taken with her in eleventh grade.

He rubbed his eyes again, but Perry would have recognized those loopy lowercase consonants anywhere, even if he didn't know exactly the kind of poem she would have written to Craig on a postcard. Mr. Brenner had taught them about slant rhyme. He'd been especially harsh with Nicole (whose poems always rhymed: "What's the point otherwise?!" she'd said) regarding her "moon/June predilections."

She'd been a good student. She'd absorbed the lesson completely by the end of the quarter, and gone on to critique her classmates' poems for exactly the same thing Mr. Brenner had said about hers.

I cannot tell you who I am now
I cannot say how sorry
You did not kill me, Craig, please know
My soul they cannot bury

"Jesus Christ," Perry said, "Jesus Christ," as he sank onto the couch, the postcard still in his hand. His heart was slamming against his ribs. He hadn't been sure before, despite what he himself believed about Nicole and despite all Craig's insistence. The last postcard had only said, *I miss you. N.* It could have been from anyone. It could have been a sick prank. Perry had said this to Craig, who'd seemed to take it in, but for the past two days, the way he'd been waiting for the mail, it was obvious he'd only been humoring Perry while waiting for another postcard from Nicole.

"Fuck," Perry said, and he handed it back to Craig, and then he turned around, heart still slamming, and hands shaking. "Fuck. Fuck. Fuck."

Until now, he hadn't believed anything, had he? He'd been unable to believe anything. He'd been on a search for something, but he hadn't expected to find it.

Now, Perry's hands were trembling, and he felt his throat all but close in a kind of panicked voicelessness when Craig said, as soberly as Craig had ever said anything, "She's not dead, Perry. Or. She's—she's *something.*"

Perry looked up at him, and found himself both shocked and not even surprised to see what he saw:

Craig was happy.

Craig didn't even seem confused.

Craig had a bright look on his face that Perry hadn't seen there since before the accident. He looked, Perry thought, like the girls at Confirmation Camp right after the Final Acceptance of Christ into Our Hearts ceremony: shiny-eyed, full of faith, seeing beyond this world and its flimsy trappings. Ecstasy. That look was ecstasy.

He had to tell him. He had to show him the photograph. He had to tell Craig about Lucas, and Patrick Wright, and Professor Polson. Until this, it had seemed too crazy, too cruel. But now—now Craig had to know.

But first, Perry had to call Professor Polson. He had to ask her advice. He had to tell her about this.

"I have to go for a walk," he said. "I have to clear my head. And I need to call someone. Give me your cell phone."

"Sure," Craig said. "Sure. Sure." Nodding like a lunatic. Smiling like a little kid. He'd have given Perry anything at that moment. If they'd been standing on a rooftop, Craig could have flown right off of it. Not only had he been expiated from the worst crime imaginable—killing the person you love the most in the world—he'd also learned that the dead could come back to life. He handed his cell phone to Perry as he continued to cradle the flimsy postcard in his hands, the way he might an injured bird. He wandered out of the living room with it like a zombie, back to his room, seeming to be laughing and crying at the same time.

Perry didn't bother to put on his coat. He just turned up the collar of his shirt against the wind and dialed Professor Polson's phone number as soon as he was out of the apartment house.

Her office phone rang and rang, and finally he hung up before her voice mail clicked in. He'd have to call her at home. He didn't want to, but he had to know what to do next. Whom else could he ask? Still, he hesitated. The last time he'd called, a couple of days before, Professor Polson's husband had answered and said she was in the shower, and then hung up without saying good-bye, as if he were pissed that Perry had called.

"Hello?"

It was the husband again.

"Hello. This is Perry Edwards, Professor Polson's—"

"Work-study," the husband said. "As usual, she's not available. I'll tell her you called again, pal."

He hung up with what sounded like the receiver slamming against a wall.

45

Mira hadn't slept or eaten for a day and a half. For the first half hour, she tried to fake it for her class, but that eventually proved impossible. Every time she stood up from the desk with a piece of chalk and headed for the blackboard, the blackboard telescoped away from her. She wrote the same thing on it twice without realizing that she had:

Bachlabend Perchtennacht
Bachlebend Perchtennacht

She only noticed it when Karess Flanagan pointed out that she'd spelled it differently the second time. Then, Mira had turned around, and, indeed, there it was, misspelled the second time. She had no memory of having written it on the board the first time.

She was trying to conduct a class on the subject of Frau Holle-Percht, the German Death Demon, the "Hidden One." It was usually one of her favorite classes to teach. The students had been assigned to read the translation of a fifteenth-century Latin manuscript from Tegemsee condemning the pagan practice of decorating houses in December to appease the Death Demon and the leaving of little cakes on the hearth for "Frau Holle and her seven lads."

It was an epiphany for eighteen-year olds, making the connection between Santa Claus and the fear of death. There was always at least one student in every class who'd been afraid of Santa Claus as a child, and told a story of lying awake on Christmas Eve terrified.

But that day Mira got only as far as the custom of tossing little swaddled dolls into the darkness on December 24 (still practiced in a village in the Harz Mountains that Mira had visited her Fulbright year) to try to trick Frau Holle into believing she was being given the families' actual "dead" babies, and she began to tear up. *Where were her own fucking babies right now?*

She'd come home from an Honors College curriculum committee

meeting later than she'd said she would Tuesday night because there'd been an unexpected challenge to the syllabus for her proposed upper-level seminar on Death and the Cultural Landscape. The chair of the committee wanted to know why Mira had chosen to substitute "field study" for one of the two required theses, and Mira had found herself having to explain that the field study was a precursor to the thesis, that the field study would be the foundation upon which a thesis would be written, and that it would be impossible to accomplish both in a mean-ingful way in fifteen weeks if she had to assign two papers.

Even Dean Fleming, who'd urged her to propose the course in the first place, had seemed skeptical, and the meeting ended with nothing more than an agreement to revisit the proposal at the next meeting, al-though it also managed to run an hour over.

It was raining when Mira finally got out of Godwin Hall, and she had no umbrella. She was ruining her shoes, she knew—nice Italian leather pumps she'd bought on sale a few years before—but she couldn't risk calling Clark for a ride. He'd have had to bring the twins out with him in the rain, and all the car seat stuff, and he'd specifically asked Mira to get home as early as she could because he wanted to go to a meeting of the Armchair Philosophers, a book group recommended by one of the mothers from the regular Espresso Royale play dates. This mother, too, had been on her way to a degree in philosophy ("The real thing," Clark had said of her, "studying with Kurdak at Princeton"), which had been derailed by a baby. The group she'd talked Clark into joining sounded to Mira like exactly the kind of thing Clark would de-spise, but he seemed to want to go.

"I don't know," he'd said noncommittally, "probably a waste of time, but she said these were serious people, and that the group might save my life."

Clark snorted then at his own words, but Mira could tell that he'd con-fided in this coffee klatsch companion that his life needed saving, and that her advice meant something to him. Mira might have been suspi-cious of Clark's relationship with this female philosopher, except that a few weeks earlier, on the street outside the hardware store, Clark had introduced Mira to her (Deirdre), and Mira had seen that not only was Deirdre pregnant again—seven months—but that the rolling enormity of that pregnancy was on top of what appeared to be already a lot of excess weight. His interest really was, it seemed, solely in the club, and the idea that Clark might rekindle his passion for philosophy filled Mira with a kind of hope that also felt like panic. She hadn't realized how much she'd missed that Clark—the one with the books piled up beside the bed, the one with the pencil tucked behind his ear.

So, now she was filled with grief for the lost opportunity of the Armchair Philosophers as she ran for their apartment, her shoes filling with water (she could literally feel the fine stitches and the glue that held them together melting around her feet), knowing that it was too late. Even if she'd gotten home ten minutes earlier, Clark could not have made it across town to the meeting in time, and he was not the kind of person who showed up at something like this late. He would be furious, probably. Relieved, too, but he would be angry at her for that relief. He hadn't spoken to her since their fight the night before, except to remind her to get home on time so he could make it to the "book club for would-have-beens," and she'd assured him that she would do her best.

Mira ran through the parking area outside their apartment house so quickly that she didn't notice that their car wasn't parked in its usual space, and when she found that the door to their apartment was locked, she assumed he'd done it to frustrate her, to make her have to fish through her bag to find her keys. She felt so guilty about being gone that it didn't occur to her to be furious. He was probably on the couch with the newspaper, listening to her struggle with the lock.

Then, when she'd finally gotten herself into the apartment, thrown her bag on the floor, and called out, "Clark?" and he hadn't answered, she figured he was in the bedroom, fuming, that she'd find him on his back in their bed, staring at the ceiling, an angry little lecture all prepared—or, he'd simply put on his shoes, walk past her without a word, wearing his running shorts, heading out into the rain, refusing to turn around when she spoke to him.

But when Mira went in the bedroom and he wasn't there, she put a hand to her mouth, her first thought being, Jesus Christ, he's gone to his fucking meeting and left the twins alone in the apartment.

"Andy? Matty?"

They weren't in their room. The Thomas the Tank Engine sheets were on the floor, and the dresser drawers were open:

Clark had taken them with him to the meeting, she thought, and she almost laughed out loud with relief. She went into the kitchen, looked on the counter.

No note.

Typical.

He wanted to punish her. But that would be nothing compared to the guilt he'd pile on her when he got back, and told her how the twins had ruined the meeting for everyone.

Or, maybe not. Maybe Deirdre's husband was watching the kids? What was her last name? Had Clark ever mentioned it?

Mira opened the phone book, but soon realized there was no point combing it for a Deirdre. She'd simply have to wait for her punishment. She'd make it up to him with a loaf of Irish soda bread. It was her specialty. Clark loved it. Or, he used to love it.

Mira poured herself a glass of wine from a bottle they'd opened a week before, wrestled off her ruined shoes, and tossed them in the closet. She mopped up the floor with a paper towel where she'd tracked in water, and then opened the cupboards and took out the canister of flour, the little yellow box of baking soda.

The wine tasted like vinegar and rainwater and reminded her of a train station in which she'd once had to spend the night. (Was it Albania?) The station was in a small village with no hotels, no restaurants, and no one to tell her why the last train of the night hadn't arrived, or when it would. Luckily, there'd been an old man selling loaves of bread and bottles of wine to the few passengers who, like Mira, had shown up for the train but who, unlike Mira, did not seem surprised when it didn't arrive. So, she'd drunk the entire bottle of wine, which was sour and warm, and eaten the bread, and listened to the rain until she fell asleep, and in the morning, the train blew its whistle outside the station, and the passengers who'd waited all night for it simply handed over their tickets, and got on.

She mixed the flour and water and baking soda, and listened to Mozart. She drank a second glass of wine. The bread came out of the oven looking perfect, but, Mira thought, she wouldn't slice it until Clark got home. It would be her peace offering. She'd pour him a glass of wine, ask about the meeting. It was late, and the twins would go right to sleep if they weren't already asleep in his arms when he walked in.

It wasn't until midnight that her own stupidity began to dawn on her, the time she'd wasted baking bread, the short-sighted relaxation of the wine (how had she allowed herself the evening to relax? Who had she thought she was?) and went back into the twins' room and realized that the dresser drawers were open because Clark had packed the twins' clothes when he left with them, and that the sheets were on the floor because he'd taken their blankies with him, too. She stood staring at the room while her heart caught up with her mind, beating wildly, and then she turned to the doorway with her hands held out, empty.

What was she going to do now?

Stupidly, she thought of the cell phone plan she'd intended to sign them up for but hadn't gotten around to, getting two phones for the price of one. They had only one cell phone, and it was in her purse.

Mira stumbled into the living room and, after some frantic searching through scraps of paper in the junk drawer, found Clark's mother's phone number, and punched the digits in as quickly as she could with her trembling hands.

Her mother-in-law sounded startled out of a drug-enhanced sleep when she answered—panicked, confused, panting. "Kay," Mira said, "it's just me. Please, is Clark there? Are the twins with him?" After much stammering, Mira finally managed to explain, in the mildest terms and tone she could muster, that she and Clark had argued, that Clark had left with the twins, that Mira supposed they were on their way to Kay's. "Has he called you?" she asked.

"No," Kay said, but managed, even in her half sleep, to muster the maternal energy and clarity to comfort Mira. "But he'll call in the morning, honey, if he's not home before then. He's probably bringing the boys here, but it got too late, so he stopped at a motel. You two will make it up. Believe me, sweetie, if I had a dollar for every time Clark's daddy and I had a fight like this—"

The tone of her voice, quaveringly compassionate, and the image in Mira's mind of Clark's mother, her thin hair a mess on a flowered pillow, her slack cheeks creased with sleep, lying on her side talking into a telephone in the dark, wearing a ratty polyester nightie, trying to make *her* feel better, caused Mira to whimper, audibly, into the phone, and then Kay sounded alarmed, suddenly fully awake.

"Honey? Honey? Don't worry. Clark's not going to do anything. Clark's not like that. Clark loves you, and he loves the babies, and tomorrow you two will talk this out. Now, you get in your bed, okay, and you call me the second you hear anything, and I'll call you, too, and in a year we'll be laughing about this. I'm a lot older than you. I know about this stuff. Okay? You're listening to me?"

"Yes," Mira said. She held the receiver away from her mouth so Kay couldn't hear her voice trembling. "Thank you."

"Yes, of course. Now, you call me if you need me, but you try to sleep, okay?"

"Okay."

"Everything's going to be fine."

"Thank you, Kay."

"Good night, sweetheart."

But Mira hadn't slept, and by the time she had to leave to teach in the morning, she hadn't heard from Clark, and Clark's mother hadn't answered her telephone when Mira called. She considered calling the dean, explaining that she was having a crisis and couldn't teach her class, but what would she do instead? Drive? Where? In what? Clark had the car. At what point did you call the police to tell them that your completely sane husband, a loving father, a house husband who spent more time with your children on a daily basis than you did, had gone somewhere with the kids without leaving a note?

And what did the police do then?

She brushed her teeth and ran a washcloth across her face, set her cell phone to vibrate mode in a little pocket in her blouse, over her breast, where she would feel it no matter what she was doing, and left a large note on the kitchen counter.

CALL ME. PLEASE. CLARK. I LOVE YOU.

Mira turned from the blackboard shakily to face the class, and then had to steady herself to sit down, and then just told them the truth:

"I had a bad night. I'm sorry. I'd like to start this lecture again another day. In the meantime, can we have a class discussion?"

The look on her students' faces—profound surprise and concern—made Mira's heart feel actually heavy. (How many clichés were more accurate in describing the eternal verities than anything poets could come up with? It never ceased to amaze her.) Her heart sank in her like bait at the end of a line, buoyed up only by reverse gravity again, and those expressions on her students' faces.

"Please, tell me what attracted you to this class. Why are kids your age so interested in death?"

Mira wasn't even really expecting an answer, just trying to think of a way to manage the rest of the hour without completely dropping it. She knew that Dean Fleming was in his office. He'd certainly notice if she went back to hers before her class could possibly have been over.

Jim Enright spoke first. He was a quiet guy from a small town up north. Mira had already pegged him as the Savior. He was the student who couldn't stand to see any of the other students stammer, or lose their train of thought. Once, another student had been trying to think of the word *cremation*, and Jim Enright had offered about ten possible words that he might have been searching for until the student landed on it.

Now Jim Enright said in a tentative tone, "Because we're not afraid of it yet?"

Mira managed to nod.

Ben Hood said, "Yeah. Or, like, we—"

Melanie Herzog jumped in:

"*I'm* afraid. I think it's just so scary, you know, thinking of *never existing*—so everybody wants to know about what might happen afterward. I mean, I think the class isn't about death. I think it's about the afterlife."

Mira couldn't help but feel revived then. These were interesting thoughts. They'd come up with nothing new, but they were earnest, and expressing themselves fairly well. She nodded, and then Karess (who had her long, smooth legs wrapped around each other a couple of times) scooted to the edge of her seat and said, "You know, I think maybe we're still young enough that we might have it right. Like, we haven't given up hope. I mean, old people think it's scary to die because they've seen other people die, but we haven't, so we don't have all this baggage, so we still know you can, like, maybe, *live* after you die."

There was a bit of laughter—mostly inspired by her California accent, Mira thought. Karess couldn't say anything without sounding like a character in a Disney sitcom.

"Well, okay," Mira said, and folded her shaky hands on her desk. "I guess I haven't asked this question yet, and maybe now's a good time to ask it. How many of you think you will live beyond your deaths?"

It took a little time (some people always took a bit longer to search their souls before answering such a question) but, eventually, every hand was in the air.

Mira looked at her class.

The room was full of hands held above heads, acknowledging the saddest, most personal hope of all the sad, hopeless, personal hopes in this hopeless world, and this caused Mira to put her own hand over her mouth to keep herself from sobbing, or crying out, or even laughing. She shook her head a little, took her hand away, and said, "That's all. Class is dismissed. We'll meet here Tuesday to walk together to the morgue."

46

Karess Flanagan followed Perry out of class, down the hall, and around the corner. He'd turned right when Professor Polson hurried out of the room, following at what he hoped was a considerate distance. He didn't want to annoy Professor Polson, but he also needed to speak with her. Often she stuck around until all the students were gone—erasing the board, packing up her things, turning off the lights, and closing the door behind her. But today there was something wrong. She'd said it to the class, although she hadn't needed to. They could all see it in her expression when she'd walked in. Her eyes were puffy.

Perry thought of her husband and that angry slamming of the phone.

Something had happened—and besides wanting to talk to her about the postcard, about Craig (he had to ask her what he should do: was it okay to tell Craig about the photograph, about Lucas, about Patrick Wright?), Perry also didn't feel right not going up to her office, asking her if there was something he could do. He knew they weren't friends exactly, but he was not, any longer, just her student either.

And the look on her face: her hand over her mouth, staring back at the class. He'd wanted to stand up right then and go to her. He'd imagined, so easily, putting his arms around her, maybe kneeling in front of her, taking her heart-shaped face in his hands.

He hadn't, of course, but he'd followed her out of class. After all the other students had turned left out of the classroom, Perry headed to the nearest stairwell, the one that led to the hall where Professor Polson's office was (she was still close enough that he could hear her heels clicking on the stairs), and because the others were leaving from the other direction, Perry couldn't help being aware of Karess behind him, her pointy black boots striking the linoleum sharply, in quick succession. She was hurrying after him, it seemed. Perry began to walk faster himself, and it occurred to him that if he turned around he might find that Karess was actually running to catch up with him. He hoped not. He had absolutely no interest whatsoever in having any kind of conversation with Karess Flanagan at the moment.

"Hey!" she called out just as he reached the foot of stairwell. The heavy fire door was propped open. "Hey. Perry! Can I talk to you a sec?"

Reluctantly, he stopped and turned around.

There she was, the whole glittering thing of her, only a few feet behind him: Karess Flanagan in some kind of purple leggings and thigh-high boots, some kind of blousey top that was half shirt, half dress. Her hair was floating around her shoulders in luxurious curls, ablaze with expensive highlights and lowlights and whatever else brunettes like Karess got done to their hair to make it too dazzling for mere mortals to behold. She had tiny silver half-moons dangling from her ears, and was wearing a sheer red lip gloss that made it look as if, recently, she'd been kissing a raspberry patch so deeply that her lips had begun to bleed. "Okay?" she asked, stopping, taking a step toward him. "Can we talk?"

Perry didn't answer. He tried to look at her as if he didn't understand her, as if that might make her go away, but it didn't. She stepped closer.

"Like, can I ask you what's going on?"

She said it in the same tone in which she said everything: "Do we need, like, a blue book?" "Are we supposed to, you know, have a title page?" "Is there, like, a special font or something we're supposed to type in?" "Is the universe, like, expanding?" No matter what she said in class, she always sounded half-exasperated, half-confused, and pretty stupid. Apparently she sounded that way outside of class, too.

"What?" Perry asked.

"Well?" Karess said, holding up her palms. They were pale, and for a crazy second Perry considered looking into them, and felt pretty sure that if he did they would be completely unlined. "What's going on with you, and this class?"

"I have no idea what you're talking about," Perry said, although he was afraid he might.

"First, like, why are you *in* this class? It's a freshman seminar. You're not a freshman."

Perry just stared at her.

"I mean, maybe it's none of my business, but—"

"*Maybe* it's none of your business?"

She laughed good-naturedly about this, maybe even blushed a little. She was wearing so much blush already that it was hard to tell, but he gave her credit for it. He'd sounded hostile, even to himself, and she seemed unfazed. Or maybe a little genuinely embarrassed by herself.

"Okay," she said, "it's *definitely* none of my business. I'm just, I guess, really curious. I don't expect you to tell me, since, like, why would you, since we don't even know each other, but something really weird seems to be going on here. I mean, I don't necessarily believe it, but a lot of people in the class think you're sleeping with Professor Polson."

Spontaneously, Perry choked out a wild little laugh, and then he could feel *himself* blushing, a rising burn from his chest to his scalp. Karess shrugged and made a wistful little smirk, as if she'd caught him at something and felt a little bad about it. She crossed her arms, waiting, it seemed, for him to speak, but Perry couldn't even take a breath. Finally, she cleared her throat, and said, "Well, *that* was awkward."

Tucking a dark ringlet behind her ear, Karess licked her lips and went on, "Well, I'm not saying anyone cares. You're a big boy, and she's obviously got some domestic issues, but between that and all this shit in the dorm about *Nicole Werner* and *Alice Meyers* and that girl who *ran away*"— she emphasized every few words with both her intonation and a rolling motion of her hands, as if to churn the air around each new item on the list—"and all the *Internet photos* of Nicole Werner's roommate having metro-sex with the music prof, and then this weird-as-fuck class, going to the morgue next time, and Professor Polson having, like, a nervous breakdown in front of us today. I for one am starting to wonder what the hell kind of college this is. I mean, I got into *Columbia*. I came *here* because I thought it would be *calmer*."

"Josie?" Perry managed to ask after moving backward through her monologue, searching it for meaning.

"What?" Karess asked.

"Nicole's roommate. Josie?"

"I guess so. That sorority chick. It's been all over the Internet. I got it forwarded to me from like four hundred different people. I don't think her name is there, just all these disgusting pictures, but people have been saying she was Nicole Werner's roommate."

"That's Josie," Perry said.

"Well, whatever," Karess said. "So, like, my parents hear about this, and they want to know what the hell is going on down here? I was in a parochial school before this. I mean, we might be from Hollywood, but we're Catholic."

"Who's Alice Meyers?" The name was familiar to Perry, but he couldn't attach a face to it.

"Oh, God, you don't know? *Everybody* knows. She's the ghost of Godwin Hall." Karess opened her eyes wide and made a fluttering gesture in the air with her hand, which Perry supposed was meant to indicate ironic spookiness.

"What are you talking about?" Perry asked.

Karess tossed her book bag onto the floor against the wall, as if she intended to stand there in the basement of Godwin Hall talking to Perry for a very long time. She jerked her thumb behind her.

"The study room," she said. "You know. Alice Meyers? She disappeared in, like, the sixties or something? No one'll go near that study room because they say she's still in there."

The Alice Meyers Memorial Student Study Room. Of course.

"We used to study in there," Perry said. "Last year."

"Well, whatever," Karess said, batting her eyes and raising her eyebrows at the same time, as if to say, *"That* figures." *"Most* people don't. I guess they'd finally gotten a grip on the whole ghost rumor thing in the last few years, before Nicole Werner. So, maybe you missed it last year, and didn't know. You're not living in the dorm this year, are you?"

"No."

"Well, Alice Meyers is showing up all over the place—but mostly, you know, it's this group of girls. These cutters. They have this club.

They've done all this research on Alice Meyers, and they go down there to the study room, supposedly, and do voodoo and Ouija board and shit. I mean, I don't know. I just know there's a girl across from me in the hall walking around with all these razor scratches on her arms, and somebody told me she was part of this club. It's sick."

Karess made a face that portrayed genuine horror, but Perry wasn't too surprised by any of this. Even in Bad Axe there'd been some Goth girls who were into Wicca and cutting. There were always rumors that they'd go to the cemetery and lie naked on the graves of dead teenage girls. Perry had never taken as much interest in those rumors as some of his classmates had, but now he thought of Professor Polson, and her book. This would be exactly the kind of thing she'd want to hear about. Something else he needed to talk to her about. Perry nodded, hoping it might conclude the conversation, and turned back toward the stairwell, but Karess reached out and grabbed his arm. She said, "Hey, I'm not done talking to you."

It was so preposterously demanding that Perry actually guffawed, and Karess, who at least seemed to understand, again, how ridiculous she was being, stammered, "I'm sorry. I just—you know, I'm curious about you. I'll buy you some coffee, or breakfast, or whatever. I just want to talk. Do you have an appointment or something? I mean—"

She nodded to the stairwell, and was clearly indicating Professor Polson's office.

"I mean, Professor Polson didn't seem like she was in much shape to talk about whatever it is the two of you are always in there talking about. Why don't you come talk to me instead?"

She lowered her eyes then, still looking up at him, and batted her heavy eyelids in a parody of flirtation. Perry opened his mouth at the outrageousness of it, and tried to speak, but he couldn't manage even to shake his head. Karess waited, and when it became clear that no response from Perry would be forthcoming, she pretended to pout, and then she said, "I'll let you carry my ten-thousand-pound book bag," gesturing toward it on the floor.

47

The girl with the sprained ankle was standing near the mailboxes when Craig hurried down to check the box. He'd been watching from the front window for the mailman to leave ever since he'd heard his boots stomp across the front porch.

The girl, whom he and Perry now called the Cookie Girl, apparently hadn't heard Craig come down the stairs—he was in his socks—and she jumped, stifling a little yelp, and whirled around as fast as a person can on crutches.

"Jesus," she said, "you scared me."

"I'm sorry," Craig said. He tried to smile politely, but he was hoping she'd hurry up and get out of his way so he could get the mail, and she wasn't budging, just sort of sagging there with her armpits pressed hard into the crutches' rubber rests, letting her left foot dangle loosely over the floor.

"You never leave the apartment," she said, not to him, exactly, but to a spot over his shoulder, "except to get your mail."

Craig shook his head, feeling the smile freeze on his face. "Sure I do," he said. "I go to classes."

"Do you?" she asked. "I mean, I guess you must, but not much."

Craig shrugged, his discomfort growing as she continued to regard him. She hadn't even gotten her own mail out of the box yet. It would be a long time before he could get to his unless he pushed her out of the way, which he obviously couldn't do.

"Are you okay?" she asked.

At this, Craig consciously tried to turn the smile into a straight line. He never had been that clear on what the expression on his face revealed about him, and had been accused by his mother a million times of smirking or grimacing, accused by girlfriends of rolling his eyes. Once, in middle school, one of his teachers (Ms. Follain, Language Arts) had actually stopped in the middle of a little lecture she was giving on phonemes and asked Craig what was so funny.

Craig had looked up at Ms. Follain, completely taken by surprise. *Nothing* had been funny. And he wasn't even stoned. He hadn't even been *thinking* about anything funny.

"What are you laughing about?" Ms. Follain asked.

"I'm not laughing," Craig said—but then, of course, he couldn't't help starting to laugh. The irony—and the absurdity of it: that he hadn't been laughing when she accused him of laughing, and now he was going to start laughing his ass off. He'd put his face in the crook of his elbow, but was helpless to stop, and the rest of the class started in then, snickering at first, followed by outright hysterical laughter, until finally Ms. Follain, hollow cheeks blazing, tossed him out of class and into the hallway, where he managed to get hold of himself only after about twenty minutes of gasping. Luckily, the bell had rung before he had to either go in and get a hall pass from Ms. Follain or go down to the office. When his friend Teddy got out of class, he'd said, "Jesus, man. What the hell was so funny? We could all hear you still laughing in the hallway. I thought Follain was going to shit her pants."

"Nothing," Craig said. "I was laughing because I *wasn't* laughing."

Of course, that started him laughing again.

"You are so fucked up," Teddy had said.

The Cookie Girl seemed disinclined to say more, but she was looking at him as if maybe the expression on his face was very strange, or a little threatening, and when Craig tried even harder to straighten it out, she opened her eyes in alarm, and then she looked away, hopped around with her back to him, and managed, after a lot of struggle with her keys, finally to open her mailbox and take out a flyer for the Hungry Hippo ("Buy One Hungry Hippo Sub and Get One 1/2 Off!"). When she was able to turn back around, Craig was already trying to inch around her to get to his and Perry's mailbox, and she froze in front of him and blurted out, "I know who you are, and I just want you to know that I don't believe you killed that girl."

Hand poised with the key at the mailbox, Craig felt what could only have been his blood running cold. Literally, there was the sensation inside him that some faucet connected to a frozen river had been turned on, and icy stuff had been let to flow. He did not move.

"What happened to you—something like that happened to me," she said under her breath. She wasn't looking at him, but he could feel her presence burning into him nonetheless. "Ran a stop sign," she muttered. "Didn't even see it. I killed a guy on a bike. I was sixteen. Got my driver's license the week before. His sister still sends me hate mail. I think about it every, fucking, minute, of every, fucking, day."

Her voice was a deep, wild, awful sob with the last sentence—and although she was on crutches and it had to have taken her at least five minutes to make it up the stairs, Craig had the sense that she had been blown away in gust of wind, taken off in a cloud of dust, far too quickly for him to say anything in response or to reach out to touch her shoulder. And by the time he'd turned around with his mail trembling in his hands, he was beginning to wonder if the Cookie Girl had been there at all—had he hallucinated her?—and also to hope that if she actually existed she hadn't paused at the top of the stairs, turned, and seen how he'd dropped to his knees after he'd flipped through his mail. The Hungry Hippo flyer, a piece of first-class mail for Perry, and a postcard from some tourist spot:

The Frankenmuth Glockenspiel.

And on the back, Nicole's unmistakable handwriting.

*Visited this place, know you would laugh, I miss who you were,
I am what they say.*

48

Shelly didn't bother to get out of her robe and slippers for four days except when she had to take them off to get into bed. Eventually she'd have to go to the store, she knew, mostly for cat food and litter, but today she thought she might be able to get away with one more twenty-four-hour robe-and-slipper stint. She turned on the bedside lamp and picked up the book she hadn't been able to read one page of in all the hours she'd spent with it open in front of her face since the afternoon she'd been fired.

That afternoon she'd come home and unplugged the phone, and she hadn't turned on the computer even once. A few times there'd been knocks on the door, and once it had sounded as if someone had thrown a brick or a dead body onto her porch, but still she hadn't stepped outside to look, or even parted the curtains. The mail came through a slot in the door, so she didn't have to worry about it piling up outside and the neighbors wondering if she'd slipped in the bathtub. She didn't subscribe to a newspaper. She just let the bills and flyers and whatever else came through the slot pile up on the floor where it fell.

Jeremy thought he'd died and gone to heaven. Finally, he had a companion all day and all night—a companion who slept even more hours than he did.

Still, Shelly wasn't so foolish as to think she would stop living. Sooner or later she was going to have to pay the bills lying scattered on her floor. Sooner or later she would have to put the house up for sale, pack all of her things, and move somewhere she could get a job.

But not today.

Today would be another stare-blankly-into-*Cold Mountain*-day.

Back in the last months of her marriage to Tim, Shelly had lived for the few days a month when he'd go away for work or on one of his fishing weekends and she could pull on the robe (it was, actually, the same robe she wore now) and pull down the shades, and crawl into their bed.

She'd never thought of herself as depressed back then. She had not yet seen the now-ubiquitous list of the symptoms of depression in magazines, at the top of which was always something like "can't drag your ass out of bed." She'd ask Tim to call her when he was about an hour from home, and told him it was so she could have something on the stove for him—when, in truth, it was so she could get herself up, and shower, and dress, and be ready to face the world in the guise of Tim again when he stomped through the door.

Now there was no one to drag herself out of bed for, to impress or appease—although Shelly knew that if this went on much longer (the phone unplugged, the cell phone off, not even checking her email), Rosemary would become alarmed, and come by.

But Shelly had gone longer than a week in the past without talking to Rosemary. Rosemary would assume for a while that Shelly was just busy with work. Rosemary had no idea that Shelly had been fired. Shelly had not mentioned Josie to Rosemary again after the phone conversation during which Rosemary had asked, "Are you *in love* with this girl?" She'd planned to tell her, eventually, but hadn't gotten around to that yet. Let alone the sex. Let alone the photographs. Let alone the disciplinary meeting with the dean. There would be, as they said, a lot of catching up to do.

Shelly rolled onto her side, and Jeremy growled a little, dreamily, and rolled onto his side as well.

Jesus.

And to add to the horror, the shame, Shelly found herself, each time she closed her eyes, to her own shock and amazement, instead of thinking about the public humiliation, instead of grieving the loss of her livelihood and her identity and her job and her *life*—thinking instead about Josie Reilly.

About her clavicle. About the shadows gathered there in the moonlight in Shelly's bed. About those white teeth locked onto her lower lip, damp and shining in the morning light.

Like her cat, Shelly growled a little, and put her face in her hands, and remembered the last phone call she'd answered from the university administration. "We want to be certain you understand that there is to be *no communication* between you and the student in question. Any attempts to contact her may result in legal action on her part or on ours."

Shelly had held the phone away from her ear then, and muttered, "Of course," thinking, Oh my God, as she hung up. I've become the kind of lecherous vermin they fear will call and stalk a student.

But even as she was thinking it, Shelly was flipping her cell phone open to the address book, scrolling down to Josie's number, uttering a little cry before she snapped it closed.

Never again even to speak with the stupid little bitch, the most beautiful creature in this whole exhausted world?

Shit.

Now she shoved off the blankets, put her feet on the floor.

What did she really have to lose?

They'd told her she could not attempt to contact the "student in question," but they had not told her she could not sit in the Starbucks that she happened to know for a fact the student in question visited ten times a day.

49

"Where *are* you?"

"What do you care, Mira? The boys are fine. I've just dropped them off at my mother's. They were ecstatic to see her."

"Why didn't you tell where you were going? Why didn't you *call last night* to tell me where you were?"

Mira was trying to keep her voice down. She was in her office and had just passed Jeff Blackhawk in the hallway. A few days before, they'd made plans to talk in her office after their Tuesday classes, and now he was waiting for her. She should have told him that something had come up, that they'd have to meet another time, but he was talking to Ramona Cherry out there, Godwin's only fiction writer and its worst gossip, and Mira couldn't bring herself to speak as she passed. She *knew* the expression Ramona would be wearing: that looking-on-the-misfortunes-of-others-from-a-distance-with-amusement look.

Schadenfreude, but Mira's Serbian grandmother had called it, so much more beautifully, *zloradost*—"eviljoy."

Mira couldn't have stood it. She'd simply held up a hand in greeting and hurried past them, and then the phone rang as soon as she closed the door behind her.

"How was I supposed to know you were home?" Clark asked.

"What are you talking about?"

"Well, I waited for you. You said you'd be early, or at least *on time*, and then you didn't show up. For all I knew *you* were the one who'd taken off."

"I didn't *take off*. I was late. I was in a meeting. I'm trying to make a living here, Clark."

"Yeah, yeah, I know all about that Mira, and I'm sorry I've been such dead weight, you know, dragging you down the toilet along with your glorious career. In the meantime, everything's fine, and you can just go about your business, your *important* business. The twins are being taken good care of by their grandmother. I'll pick them up in a few days, and then—"

"What? What do you mean you'll *pick them up*? Where are you going?"

"I'm taking a little R-and-R. I've earned it, Mira. I've spent the last two years trapped in a nine-hundred square-foot apartment with two toddlers while you were pursuing your Big Career. Now I'm going to rent a little cottage on the lake, and maybe a boat. Maybe fish for a few days. I'll let you know—"

"Fish? It's almost winter."

"Yeah, well, there are still fish in the lake, Mira. They don't migrate."

"For God's sake, Clark, why did you take the twins with you? Why didn't you leave them home with—"

"Are you kidding, Mira? Because there's no one to take care of them at home! They need a mother. I left them with the only mother they have—mine."

"Fuck you, Clark. Fuck you. Fuck—"

But he'd hung up already, and Mira was holding the receiver in her hand, staring straight ahead at her bulletin board, on which a snapshot of the twins—red Kool-Aid smiles shadowing their real smiles, wearing Chicago Cubs caps and bathing trunks with sharks on them, Lake Michigan frothing in the background—was thumbtacked at a terrible slant so that they appeared to be slipping sideways into a pile of ungraded student papers on her desk.

Mira dropped the receiver and lunged at the photo, tore it off the bulletin board and pressed it to her breasts. She was clinging to it when Jeff Blackhawk pushed open her door, which she'd left unlocked in her hurry to answer the phone, and said, registering the expression on her face, "Mira? Is everything okay?"

50

Perry followed Karess Flanagan up the stairs to her dorm room. He hadn't been on the residence floors of Godwin Hall since he'd moved out last May, and the scent of it (old carpeting and something else that smelled inexplicably of wet straw) brought the whole previous year back to him. Karess's midthigh boots had clunky heels, and each step she took rang through the stairwell. She talked loudly over the sound of her own footsteps.

"You never answered my question about why you're in the class. Did you flunk your own first-year seminar or something?"

"No," Perry said, sounding more defensive than he'd intended. "I'm taking it because I find it interesting."

"Really?" Karess made no attempt not to sound skeptical. She got to the door at the top of the stairwell first, and held it open for Perry, who hesitated, trying to engineer some way to walk behind her, hold the door open for her, or at least for himself. He wasn't used to girls holding doors for him, and was not, in fact, sure that a girl ever had. But he couldn't avoid it without elbowing her out of the way, so he walked through the door as she held it.

"Why's death so interesting to you?"

Perry didn't answer. He waited in the hallway for Karess to pass over the threshold herself.

The residence floors of Godwin Honors Hall were divided into halls named after alumni long forgotten except for their associations now with the better bathrooms or the direction the windows faced. Perry and Karess were in Hull House, where Nicole and Josie had lived the year before. All along the hallway, doors were open, and Perry could see girls sitting at desks, staring into computer screens, lying on beds, holding cell phones to their ears. One girl had a towel wrapped in a turban on her head and was standing in front of a wall mirror, holding a pair of tweezers to an eyebrow, seeming to be trying to muster up the courage to pluck. Perry looked away after that, and tried to watch his feet as he walked instead of looking through the open doors.

"You can wait here, if you want," Karess said. "Our room's a pigsty. I just need to grab my wallet and change my shoes." She nodded down at her boots. They looked like medieval torture devices. Perry felt relieved that she wasn't going to try to walk across campus to Starbucks in them. He leaned up against the wall and folded his arms.

Across from him, a bulletin board hung on a closed door. A pink plastic flower was tacked to it, and underneath that, a blurry photograph of a kitten. The kitten appeared to be running—either that or the photographer had been running while snapping the photograph. It was a bad photo, but he could imagine girls crowding around it, oohing over the cute haze of that cat.

He consciously chose not to look down the hallway in the direction of Nicole and Josie's old room, but he couldn't help but wonder who occupied it this year, and if whoever it was knew that it was the room in which the Dead Girl had lived.

Or, maybe no one lived there. Maybe the college administration did something in these circumstances. Or maybe they scrambled the room numbers so it would be impossible for the incoming class to figure out which room could be the haunted one. Godwin was the oldest dorm on campus. Probably quite a few students had died while living here. Likely, there was a procedure for handling the assigning of their rooms. Even if the residents themselves didn't mind living in a dead student's dorm room, parents might object, Perry supposed, to having their kid sleeping on the mattress that had been slept on by the previous year's Unthinkable Tragedy.

Then, Perry caught himself wondering if Nicole had come back to this hallway since her death. Had she wanted to get a look at her old room, to see if—

He was startled by Karess when she stepped out of the door and said, brightly, electrically, "Ready?!"

She wearing different shoes (an even higher heel, as it happened) and a different top—pale purple, lower cut, a little mesh of lace across her cleavage, which Perry looked away from even as he was noticing it.

"So," Karess said, "you were about to tell me what you find so fascinating about the death class. And if you can't come up with something convincing, I'm going to have to conclude, as most of our classmates have, that it's actually Professor Polson you find so fascinating."

Perry found himself opening and closing his mouth, issuing nothing but exasperated breaths, feeling what he thought must be a kind of hatred for Karess Flanagan.

Who the hell did she think she was?

She looked over her shoulder, batted her eyes, and said, "Cat got your tongue?" and Perry put his hands in his pockets so she wouldn't see that he'd balled them into fists.

"No," he said, finally, and continued down the stairs behind her.

Why? Why was he continuing to walk behind her, follow after her? Was it the same reason any guy might?

Because of those dark curls, and the way her waist tapered into her hips, and the way her ass looked like two solid handfuls of ripe flesh packed into that little miniskirt? Perry had noticed within hours of first laying eyes on her in class that she had such high-arched eyebrows that she always looked surprised—or as if she were flirting, or as if she were experiencing some kind of physical pleasure.

Sexual pleasure.

He'd made a conscious effort not to glance over at her. It had always seemed undignified, disrespectful, maybe even dangerous, letting a girl like that know you noticed her—although now, looking down onto her soft shampoo-commercial hair (a few strands lifted away from the rest, shining and amber in the sun that was coming through the little panes of the windows), another possibility occurred to him:

That Karess Flanagan was actually harmless. That she was just having fun. She wanted him, too, to have harmless fun.

He felt better, thinking this. She'd simply been *teasing* him. That was something Mary had always said ("I'm just *teasing* you, Perry") and that he'd never understood. The little jabs, the sarcasm. ("Don't be such an *Eagle Scout.*") He'd taken them all wrong, he thought now, hearing Karess Flanagan's throaty, casual humming under her breath. She was enjoying his company. She wanted him to like her.

Was this what girls did?

Long silver earrings twirled down from her lobes, nearly grazing her shoulders, glinting, and he could smell something citrusy, slightly bitter but also spicy and appealing, wafting off of her. She had some kind of leather thong around her neck, some kind of charm dangling from the end of it, but also a gold chain, and a silver chain, and something else that was beaded. She had about twenty bracelets on each wrist.

Jesus, Perry thought, it must take this girl four hours to get dressed every morning.

She chatted on and on brightly about what a drag it was to live on the third floor, and how, when her parents moved her in they'd had to lug all her stuff up the stairs because the elevator was broken.

"The elevator's always broken," Perry said.

"What floor did you live on?" Karess asked him.

"Fourth," he said.

"What house?"

"Mack."

"So, you knew him? Craig Clements-Rabbitt?"

They'd reached the bottom of the stairs, and she was waiting for Perry at the door. There was a sign on it that read, FIRE EXIT, ALARM WILL

SOUND, but everyone knew there was no alarm. Karess pushed her way through it, and out into the brisk late-morning air.

He considered lying, or saying nothing, but what would be the point? Karess was obviously curious enough about everything that she was going to find out one way or another. Perry's name, Googled along with *Craig Clements-Rabbitt*, told that whole story. Except for a few things about his making Eagle rank, which had been in the Bad Axe paper, Perry's Internet claim to fame was that he'd been Craig's roommate and had said to a reporter for the local paper, "He's not a murderer."

"He was my roommate," he now said to Karess.

She whirled around. "*What?* You *lived* with him?" Her eyes were so wide he could see the little pinpricks of her pupils pulsing in the startling blue of her irises.

"Yeah," Perry said.

"Well," she said. She smiled. Her teeth were so white they seemed, like her incredibly blue eyes, more like fashion accessories than body parts. "The plot thickens."

"What do you mean?"

"Well, it must have been pretty fucked up, your freshman year, living with a killer—"

"What?" Perry asked.

"A fucking murderer."

"He's not a murderer," Perry said.

"Jesus," Karess said. "You're not still friends with him, are you? I mean, he killed his girlfriend."

"He didn't kill his girlfriend," Perry said. "He had an accident, and his girlfriend got killed."

"That's not what *I* heard," Karess said.

"Then you heard wrong."

"I heard he was stoned and drunk, and he picked her up at her sorority because he was jealous of some older guy there, and even though she was screaming and pleading for him not to take her, he forced her into the car, and then he drove off the road at like a hundred miles an hour, to try to kill them both together. It was like some kind of sick love bond he thought they had. He wanted to die with her—and, so, like, she had no choice. And now she's dead and he's back here. Unbe*lie*vable."

Perry had to hold a hand to his forehead because, now that they were outside, the sun was shining blindingly over Karess's shining head. They were in the courtyard, and students were passing them, talking on cell phones, stuffing protein bars into their mouths, ears plugged into their iPods. Some pink-cheeked girl squealed when she saw Karess and was about to hug her, but must have seen the serious expression on her face, so just wiggled her fingers, made a face, and kept walking.

With no leaves on the trees, no clouds, and the sun so distant in the autumn sky, there was nothing to absorb the light, and Perry felt his eyes filling up with tears. He turned around and started to walk away from Karess. "Are you crying?" she called after him, and grabbed his elbow. "God, I'm, like, *so sorry.*"

"I'm not *crying,*" Perry said, but kept walking because he wasn't so sure he wasn't crying, and if he was crying, he had no idea why he was. He tried to walk fast under the archway to Godwin Avenue. It was always forty degrees colder under that arch than anywhere around it. Even when the temperature was ninety degrees outside, under that archway it was cool and damp. Someone had spray-painted the name Jean at the top of the arch, and Perry found himself stopping, putting his hand flat against the bricks, trying to catch his breath. "I'm not crying," he said again, although he was even more blind now, having stepped from the sun into this darkness. He rubbed his eyes and said, "But you shouldn't talk about things you don't know anything about. Where did you hear all this crap, about him forcing her into the car, and the death bond or whatever?"

"It's true," Karess said. She was standing so close to him that he could smell her breath. Cinnamon. "There was this, like, assembly for first-year women our second day in the dorm, and these sorority types came from Omega Theta Tau, and it was supposedly supposed to be this meeting about how to avoid getting into abusive relationships with guys, but mostly it just scared the shit out of us about living in the dorm where the dead girl had lived. They did this slideshow? Of Nicole? And told us how guilty they all felt because they all knew she was dating this stalker dude, Craig Clements-Rabbitt, who was always waiting for her outside the house and wouldn't let her have her own life, and then he killed her, and they were all crying, and by then *we* were all crying, and then we went back to our rooms, and I heard later that these girls who were living in her old room did the Ouija board in there, and then I don't know what happened, but I guess it scared the shit out of them, and they got a room change.

"Nobody's living in that room now. It's all locked up. And those Goth girls with the Alice Meyers Club thing are always lighting candles outside of it and burning these smudge stick things, and it sets off the fire alarms, and they make little shrines that the housekeeping people throw away. It's fucked up. And *you* were that guy's *roommate?*"

"Jesus Christ," Perry said. A kind of vertigo took over him—the archway seemed to shift, and suddenly he was feeling the weight in that white coffin again. The dead weight of a body sliding around inside.

Karess looked alarmed. She said, "Are you okay?" She took a step even closer to him, looking carefully at his face, and slid her arm through his. "Come on," she said. "I'll buy you a hot chocolate. I promise not to talk about this. Don't cry."

He looked at her.

"I'm not crying," he said, and having to say it again actually made him laugh.

She laughed, too.

"I think you're a really cool guy," Karess said, pulling him out of the archway by the arm that she had locked into his. "I thought so the first day I saw you."

51

The walk from her house to Starbucks seemed to take hours, but when Shelly looked at her watch, she saw that only fifteen minutes had gone by since leaving home and, now, passing the building that housed the Chamber Music Society. She willed herself not to look up at the window to her office, but she could feel the window looking down at her. She could feel her former self watching this present self walking by.

What might she have thought, say, six months before, if she'd been told of a woman who had a secure well-paying job at the university and had thrown it all away to have a sleazy affair with an undergraduate work-study student?

What would she have thought if she'd been told the way the woman had been caught red-handed in this affair—that she'd allowed a series of cell phone photographs to be taken of herself in bed with a nineteen-year-old sorority girl?

What would she have thought if she'd looked down now and seen this woman walking by, moving inexorably, but also as if there were heavy weights tied around her ankles and wrists, toward the place she thought she might be able to find this girl—this girl that university officials had warned her not to harass?

She'd have thought, perhaps, no fool like an old fool?

Or would it have been something harsher? Much harsher.

Now, she thought, imagining looking down at herself from the lofty heights she'd once occupied, she was one of them. The fallen.

She was so lost to these thoughts that, as she approached Starbucks and glimpsed herself in the plate glass window, she was surprised to see her own reflection. She'd expected, she realized, to see herself as a warted hag, a specter, a *creature*—lecherous and leering, and that much more repulsive because, although she looked sexless, she wasn't.

But that's not how she looked.

In the window, she looked frantic, even to herself. And pitiable. Harmless. Maybe sad. Her hair was messed but shining in the dim November sunlight. A man in a black suit and red tie looked her over appreciatively as he held the door for her. She did not, it seemed, appear to be a monster to him. To him, she looked like the reflection in the plate glass window. But there was no mistaking the horror on Josie Reilly's face as she turned at the counter, holding her white cup, and saw Shelly walking through the door.

52

Mira had never shared anything about her personal problems with a colleague before. Even in graduate school when her fellow students regularly wept late into the night in one another's arms over their breakups and their breakdowns, Mira had kept a close check on what she told others about herself.

One of her best friends, Tessa, another doctoral candidate in anthropology, had told Mira about the years of incest abuse she'd endured as a child by a much older half-brother, and then had reacted with bitterness that seemed to border on rage when Mira told her, many years into their friendship, about her mother's death.

"You never told me your mother was dead."

"She died years ago," Mira tried to explain. "I was an undergraduate. You and I hadn't met."

"But we've discussed your mother on about five hundred occasions," Tessa had said as Mira recognized in her friend's eyes a dawning apprehension, a withdrawal, a dismissal that heralded the end of their friendship, "and you never once indicated that your parents weren't both still happy and healthy and living in Ohio. I told you all about *my* father's death. It seems like that might have been a good time to mention that you, too, had a parent who'd died."

Mira hadn't intended to shrug. She knew that a shrug indicated that either it didn't matter or she couldn't comprehend the big fuss. But she'd felt herself doing it anyway—and, as she shrugged, she felt as if something shawl-like (her friendship with Tessa?) was slipping off her shoulders, discarded behind her.

⋯⋯⋯⋯⋯—

So it was that much more surprising to find herself now weeping into her hands as Jeff Blackhawk sat across from her, watching, rubbing his knees with his palms. She could not suppress the sobs.

Truly, Mira had meant to tell him only that she was in a hurry because she had to rent a car, that her husband had theirs, that she was going to drive up north to get her children from their grandmother. But the second she uttered their names (*Andy, Matty*) her lungs had seemed to fill instantly with tears, and she'd found herself choking, gasping, spluttering. Finally, after what must have seemed to him to be an alarming amount of time, Jeff said, "Mira," the way you might call a dog that was running toward the road, and she looked up, and the expression of doomed embarrassment on his face snapped her back.

Mira turned around quickly in her chair and grabbed a handful of tissues from the box on her desk, and hurriedly began to wipe her eyes and nose, her cheeks, her lips. God only knew what she must look like, she thought, or what the condition of her eye makeup might be, but she finally managed to take a deep, trembling breath, and speak.

"Jeff," she said. "I'm so, so sorry. I haven't slept and—"

He waved his hand as if to clear the air of smoke or tear gas. "No," he said. "You don't have to apologize, but I'd like to know what I can do to help. Certainly you're not in any shape to drive up north, are you? Let me call someone for you. Or, I don't really have anything to do until I teach on Thursday, except read bad student poetry. I could take you in my car. I like kids. I'd like to meet yours."

"Oh, that's so—" Mira felt the shame of her relief in that moment like an implosion. "But I—"

"Just *let* me, okay, Mira. They're predicting the first snowfall of the year today. Or tonight. It might even be a big one. The roads'll be slippery, and in your condition?" He held up his hands at the obviousness. "You owe it to your kids not to get killed on the road. Let me—"

"Okay," she said.

53

Who is this?" Craig asked. His hand was shaking, but he was managing to hold the phone to his ear. The clock on his dresser said 12:00. Was it midnight? No: The sun was shining weakly outside. It had to be noon. He'd set his alarm for 9:00 a.m., and he remembered it bleating for him to wake up, remembered hearing Perry close the front door behind him as he left for his early class, but then he must have turned it off, gone back to sleep.

There was no answer on the other end of the line.

"Who is this?" Craig asked again. He could hear breathing. He listened. He sat up. He put his free hand to his temple and rubbed it. He was trying not to say anything else, just listen, but then, despite himself, under his breath, he asked, "Nicole? Is it you?"

There was a high crazy scream of laughter then:

"No, you idiot! This is *Alice*. Did you forget about *Alice*?"

And then the phone went dead in his hand, and Craig, heart pounding, was out of bed, bolting through the apartment, into the hallway, and the door was slamming, locked, behind him.

54

The look on Josie's face, standing in front of the Starbucks counter (slender fingers wrapped around a white paper cup, just turning around) froze Shelly in the threshold, holding the door open with one hand, clutching her shoulder bag to her hip with the other. There was a rush of cold air around her ankles, and it seemed that, in addition to Josie, everyone in the café had turned at that moment to look at her, to see where the draft had come from, to scowl at her for holding the door open. (When had it gotten so cold? Shelly had walked all the way here from her house in a thin dress. Was the dampness she felt on her neck that of melting snow?)

A woman with a stroller pushed past, and after she'd managed to squeeze by Shelly with her baby and her contraption and her diaper bag, she turned back around and nodded at the door. "Better shut that," she said. There was such gentleness in her tone that Shelly looked at the woman, trying to comprehend not what she'd said but the way she'd said it. "The door," the woman said, nodding at it again. "It's gotten cold out."

Shelly stepped all the way into the coffee shop and let the door swing shut behind her. By then, Josie was on the other side of the room, putting a lid on her cup, glancing furtively around her, and Shelly, despite the warnings of the university bureaucrat, was approaching her, moving her mouth, saying the girl's name loudly enough that other people were turning at their tables to look.

Josie started to back away, but Shelly was ready for it, and reached out, took hold of the slender arm (bare, despite the cold: Josie was wearing a pair of faded jeans with holes in the knees and a little silky black top, a cashmere sweater wrapped casually around her waist, like an afterthought)—and held on.

"Please," Shelly said.

Josie yanked her arm away, looked around, exasperated, and, under her breath, said, "What do you want?"

"I have to talk to you."

"You're not supposed to harass me."

"I'm not harassing you. Josie. Please. I'll leave you alone, I swear, I won't"—Josie took a step back as if in anticipation of the word *touch*— "but I have to talk to you. Please."

"No." Josie was shaking her head emphatically, but then she stopped, seemed to think briefly, but seriously, about something, and then, to Shelly's great relief and surprise, she was nodding her head. "Okay," she said, sounding more annoyed than reluctant or frightened. "Okay, *okay*," she repeated, as if in defeat, and then she lifted her chin and pointed it toward an empty table in the back corner, and Shelly followed her to it.

Josie slid behind the table and leaned back, tossing one leg over the other and crossing her arms over her chest. Shelly sat down hard in the stiff wooden chair across from her, doing everything she could not to slump. (That was something her ex-husband had accused her of: "You don't *sit* in a chair, Shelly. You *slump* in it.") Josie didn't hesitate to look her straight in the eyes when she was seated, or to lean forward with her hands folded on the table between them. Shelly had expected an awkward silence, but right away, Josie was talking:

"Look, I know you're probably pissed as hell at me, but I have to tell you this is really not my fault. I can't help it if we had this . . . *involvement*, and maybe I should have, yeah, kept my pictures where no one else could see them, but you're the older one here, you're the *authority figure*. You were supposed to—" Here, Josie seemed to search for some word she'd memorized and couldn't find. Instead, she went on with some thoughts about the nature of the student/employer relationship, which seemed both scripted and poorly delivered, and for the first time Shelly began to wonder if it had *all* been an act.

She reached across the table, put a hand on Josie's wrist to quiet her, and said, "Why?"

"Why *what*?" Josie said, looking startled to have her monologue interrupted.

"Why any of it?"

"I was just explaining that," Josie said. "There are certain perimeters in student/employer relations at the university—"

"Parameters?" Shelly asked.

"Whatever," Josie said. "But, being your work-study—"

"Why me?" Shelly interrupted. "Is this some kind of hazing thing?"

Josie didn't laugh.

She didn't even blink.

She held Shelly's gaze long and hard enough that Shelly didn't need an answer to the question, and then she finally said, "I told you, Omega Theta Tau doesn't participate in hazing."

"What about the underwear?" Shelly asked.

"What are you talking about?"

"You told me. You said you had to wear the same panties for a month, and—"

"Oh, *that*." Josie swatted her hand through the air as if to clear it of an annoying insect. "That's not hazing."

"Well if that's not hazing, maybe this isn't either."

"What's 'this,' " Josie said, making quotation marks in the air around her own face.

"You know," Shelly said, her voice sounding automated even to her, "an affair. With a woman. Photographs. To prove it. Maybe getting someone in trouble, getting someone fired."

"No way. We'd get kicked out of the National Pan-Hellenic Council if—"

"No," Shelly said. She realized that she was shaking, but her words came out of her passionlessly, as if she were reading them, and what she was reading was already familiar to her, had been read and reread a hundred times. "I was in a sorority, too, Josie. We did all the same stuff, knowing full well we'd never get kicked out of the National Pan-Hellenic Council. We knew, just like you do, that if the National Pan-Hellenic Council ever heard about it, they'd just help cover it up. People who've never pledged might be fooled by that, but not me."

"You can't prove anything," Josie said, and the way she crossed her arms and leaned back in her chair made it clear to Shelly that Josie was right.

55

Jeff chewed on hard cinnamon candies as he drove, and the sound coming from his closed mouth was so loud and chaotic it occurred to Mira that he was splintering his teeth, but when she looked over at him, and he looked back at her and smiled, she was relieved to see that his teeth were intact. "Would you like some?" he asked, pointing to the bag of candies between them. "Help yourself."

"No, thanks," Mira said.

After they'd left Godwin Hall, and before they'd gone to get Jeff's car from the university parking garage, they'd gone back to Mira's apartment so she could get her credit card. (Despite Clark's protests that she was treating him like a two-year-old, Mira had insisted on keeping their joint card at home, in a box at the bottom of their bureau, since they were already so deeply in debt that it could only, in her opinion, be used in emergencies.) But when she'd gotten to the bureau, to the bottom of the drawer, and then to the bottom of the box, it wasn't there.

Clark had taken that, too?

She'd called to Jeff in the other room, "I'll be right out!" as she pawed through a few other drawers, and even looked under the bed, and went to the closet to check the pockets of Clark's jackets.

Not there.

She could hear Jeff in the living room humming to himself as he paged through some of the books on her shelf.

Now what?

It was two hundred miles, at least a couple of tanks of gas there and back. She'd had the ATM withdrawal maximum lowered to fifty dollars a day (again, so there would be no temptations), and she certainly didn't want to make Jeff stand around in line at the credit union as she tried to get money out of hers and Clark's savings account.

"I'm sorry this is taking so long!" she called, mostly to buy herself some time to think about what to do.

"It's not a problem, Mira," Jeff called back. "I've got forty hours before anyone will notice I'm missing, and that'll just be a dozen relieved undergrads. That's the great thing about being a bachelor. Nobody files a Missing Person's report for at least a week. Hey, I see you've got a whole shelf of Camille Paglia. Are you a fan?"

Later, Mira thought, she would tell him about her interest in Paglia's popularization of literary criticism, and how she hoped, herself, to emulate something of it in her own anthropological studies—but at the moment she was back on her hands and knees feeling the carpet under the bureau for the credit card. She sat for a few minutes on the floor before she stood, went into the living room, and said to Jeff, because she had to, "I don't have any money. Except what I can get out of the bank. My husband took the credit card."

Jeff was holding *Sexual Personae* in his hands as if it he'd never held an actual book before, as if he had no idea how to open it, both hands wrapped around the edges like a plateful of potluck food. He looked over at Mira, shrugged, and said, "I've got cash and a full tank of gas. And now I know where you live. I have people who can help me get the loan repaid if I have to." He raised and lowered his eyebrows ridiculously, without bothering to smile, and Mira understood instantly, physically (although she couldn't muster the energy to *feel* it) why, if the rumors were true, so many girls and women allowed themselves to be used by him.

"Thank you," she said to him for the tenth or fifteenth time that morning, and he acknowledged it with another shrug, turning back to the book. She offered him a cup of tea, or a sandwich, but he said he'd rather hit the Wendy's on the freeway if she didn't mind.

"I have a man-size hunger," he said. "I'd like to wait for a Baconator if you don't mind."

They'd headed together to the parking garage closest to Godwin Hall then. It was a short walk, but the sky was spitting a damp snow, and they had to keep their heads down. It would have been impossible to carry on an easy conversation, even if Mira had been in a state of mind that allowed for small talk.

Jeff was parked on the first floor, under a sign that read, NO PARKING. He pulled the ticket off his windshield and tossed it into the backseat without saying a word about it.

His car was a mess.

Mira had, she supposed, expected a Porsche. Although she knew Jeff couldn't make much more money than she did, she also found herself so continually surprised by the opulent houses and the exotic vacations of her colleagues (who had the same salaries that, for Mira and Clark, barely covered the rent) that she'd grown used to assuming that most academics had secret sources of income—trust funds, inheritances, law suit settlements. If Jeff were one of those, with that kind of money, Mira had imagined he would spend it on something flashy, something women would be impressed by, like a sports car.

But not only wasn't this a sports car, it was even rustier and more exhausted-looking than Mira and Clark's car:

The door of the glove compartment had been torn off somehow, and Jeff had stuffed it with candy wrappers, many of which had fallen on the floor. The backseat was a pond of memos and flyers and Wendy's bags. (Where, Mira wondered, looking back there, would she put the twins? Clark had their car seats, too, she realized. But she'd have to worry about that later.) It took Jeff several tries to start the car—and once he did, the motor made a sound like a spaceship taking off, only to grow disconcertingly silent as he started to drive. It crossed Mira's mind that they were actually coasting out of the parking ramp, with no engine at all, but Jeff seemed in control of things, and the confidence he exuded— popping candies into his mouth, fiddling with the ancient-looking radio dial—was reassuring. He said, "I know she doesn't look like much, but she's as reliable as they get. We'll be the fastest thing on the freeway, sweetheart."

The little endearment did not seem to Mira to be a come-on, or even overly familiar. It seemed, instead, to be an attempt to comfort her— and, again, for the hundredth time that day, tears sprang to her eyes, and she vowed to herself that she would buy that slim collection of his poems she'd seen at the bookstore on the shelf of Local Authors as soon as they got back: *The Blind Horizon*. She would read them carefully, and ask him about his influences, his inspirations and aspirations. She would treat him with more respect. She was sorry, *so* sorry, that she hadn't done so before now.

Jeff flashed his U-Parking pass at the attendant in the booth. Then they were winding their way through campus.

The day was getting colder. The sky, darker. It would be a matter of minutes, Mira felt certain, before the first blizzard of the year began in earnest—and, still, there were boys crossing the street in short sleeves, girls in mini-dresses and tank tops. Was this vanity, ill-preparedness, or did their youth give them some sort of metabolic advantage in the cold?

Mira herself was shivering as Jeff's car's heating system blew cool air smelling of dust through the vents and into her face.

Jeff slowed down at an intersection full of pedestrians and bicyclists, and at the corner of State and Seymour, Mira saw Dean Fleming standing under the crosswalk sign, waiting for the signal to change. His red tie had blown over his shoulder, and he had his tweed cap pulled down low on his head of bushy gray hair. He looked, it seemed, right at Mira as they passed—but if he registered who she was and that she was a passenger in Jeff Blackhawk's junker, it didn't show on his face. An enormous snowflake landed on the windshield right in front of Mira, and made no sign of melting.

"Freeway? Wendy's?" Jeff asked.

"Sure, yes," Mira said. "And, Jeff, I'm so, *so* grateful for this."

"I know," he said, and ground his molars down on the piece of candy in his mouth, turned to her, and winked without smiling.

56

Craig was in his boxer shorts and an old, soft SKI FREDONIA! T-shirt, no shoes. He knew he'd locked himself out as soon as he heard the inner workings of the knob and the doorjamb click into position, but he was too freaked out to care.

He was bathed in sweat, and the sweat was cold, but instead of shivering (it was always a lot colder in the hallway than in the apartment because people were always propping the front door open so their friends could come in without having to be buzzed in) he was burning. He felt the way he used to when he was running track in middle school, before he started smoking dope instead of running track: that feeling, after a long run, that somebody was giving you a bear hug from behind, and it was crushing your lungs, and you were desperate for air, but that the temperature of the air was seven hundred degrees, and breathing it in short little gasps was going to set your insides on fire.

He leaned over in the hallway, trying to stop the gasping, the way the coach had showed them back in Fredonia, and then he put his hands on his knees and tried to count to four as he inhaled through his mouth, hold it for four, exhale to four, but he was panting about ten times faster than that.

He'd thought it was Nicole. He'd been sure of it. That Nicole was calling him from . . .

He didn't hear the Cookie Girl come out of her room, and didn't know she was there until she cleared her throat beside him, and then he jumped back about a foot, standing up straight, clutching his chest. Her eyes sprang wide open in alarm, and she said, "What's the *matter?*"

It didn't even occur to Craig, yet, that he was half-naked, crazed looking, and that he didn't know this girl. He said, "I don't know. Someone's fucking with me. Someone's *haunting* me."

A sad look crossed the Cookie Girl's face, as if he'd told her something she'd dreaded hearing but had fully expected to hear. Her small, pale face in the dim hallway light looked, he thought, anguished. It was the same expression she'd had on her face just before she'd told him, at the mailbox, in a monotone, "Killed a guy on a bike. I was sixteen." Now, in a sad, calm voice, she asked, "Is your roommate home?"

Craig shook his head.

"Did you lock yourself out?" She looked toward his closed door. All Craig could do was nod.

"Look," she said. "Come in here." She gestured for him to follow her to her apartment. "My roommates are out. You can sit on the couch and cover up with a blanket, and I'll call the landlord to let you back in."

The Cookie Girl hopped, then, on her one good foot, to the door, and turned to look behind her to make sure he was following. She pointed at the couch for him to sit on, and hopped around a corner, out of sight. "I'll get the phone," she said as she hopped.

The air inside the Cookie Girl's apartment smelled closed and flowery to Craig. It reminded him—painfully, suddenly, completely—of Josie and Nicole's dorm room: that smell of girls' foreign products, perfumes, toilet waters, conditioners, clean clothes, floral soaps. And also chemicals, like nail polish and nail polish remover, and witch hazel, maybe—that's what his mother used to clean her face with, wasn't it? And creams and lotions with honey and buttermilk in them.

He sat on the Cookie Girl's couch and put his elbows on his knees and his head in his hands, and in a few seconds she'd hopped back out with the phone and a soft, pink blanket. She wrapped the blanket around his shoulders and held out the phone to him. When he just stared at it blankly, she said, "Okay. I'll call him."

But apparently the landlord didn't answer. The Cookie Girl had gone back into the other room, and Craig could hear her say to a machine, "This is Deb Richards? 326? Um, my neighbor is locked out? Can you call me back so I can let him know if you'll come and let him back in?"—followed by a string of numbers: land lines, cell phone numbers, Craig's apartment number, her apartment number. She came back into the living room, this time leaning on her crutch, and said, "I'm going to make you a cup of tea."

Craig nodded.

"Look," she said when she came back out of her kitchenette holding a microwaved mug from which a cloud of steam swirled, a string with a little Lipton flag hanging off the rim. "Look. I know you don't know me, but I have to talk to you. I think I know what's going on here—but first I have to ask you not to tell anyone that I talked to you about this. And that other thing? That I told you in the hallway? Nobody here knows about that, okay? I purposely came to a school two thousand miles away from where that happened, and I only told you because I've been listening to what people are saying about you, and I looked up this stuff about you on the Internet, and I feel like I can—relate, and now I have to tell you something else."

Craig nodded again. He sipped from the tea without bothering to take the bag out or even bounce it around in the water the way he knew he was supposed to. The tea tasted like very hot water, and burned his tongue, but it also seemed like the best thing he'd ever put to his lips. The mug said FIELD DAY on the side. There was a little hockey stick under the words.

"They're fucking with you," the Cookie Girl (Deb?) said. "I know some of these girls. My roommate from Woodson Hall freshman year is an Omega Theta Tau, and whenever she has more than a couple of margaritas she starts to blab. Those girls have a plan to get you off this campus."

Craig sipped from the mug again. He felt strangely and entirely at peace. Wrapped in this nice girl's pink blanket. Sipping her tea. Her voice reminded him of his mother's—his mother's voice back when he was a child, when she used to speak to him quietly, enunciating every syllable. Deb Richards didn't seem to understand that Craig already knew how much Nicole's sorority sisters hated him, how they wanted him off campus. She seemed to think she would shock him if she spoke too quickly—either that or this was simply the most natural way to speak to someone you'd just found panting in his boxer shorts in your hallway, doubled over, flipping out.

Deb went on about how she'd overheard this or that, and how the father of the boy she had killed had stopped in his tracks at her hometown supermarket and shouted, pointing, *"That fucking bitch, that fucking little bitch, that fucking little bitch killed my little boy,"* so loudly and frantically that she couldn't even leave the store because people were staring at her, and also screaming at her, and how a cashier even stood in front of her to block her way to the exit, turning all red, saying something about how she, Deb Richards, was the one who should be dead and, *"You're gonna rot in hell you negligent spoiled brat, you're gonna rot in hell every night of your rotten life and then for all of eternity in hell . . ."*

Craig felt awful for her.

And it was so kind of her to feel awful for him, which made him even sadder that he couldn't even pretend to be surprised at what she had to tell him. She seemed to think these were pretty big secrets. She told him that she felt pretty sure the Omega Theta Tau sisters had all kinds of plans to scare him, and torment him, and drive him out of here. Did he have any idea how vengeful girls could be? *Sorority* girls especially?

Briefly he considered telling her that, yes, he did know all about how much Nicole's sorority sisters hated him, but that, no, it wasn't Omega Theta Tau today. It was something else. *Someone.* It was Alice Meyers. She'd visited him, too. She was somewhere, and she knew Nicole. She and Nicole, it seemed, were together somewhere—sending postcards, making house calls, making phone calls. But he said nothing.

And then Deb Richards was tearing up, taking his hand, telling him everything would be all right, but he really should go to school somewhere else, that it was the only thing that had helped her, that it had saved her life to get away (although, to Craig, she looked as if she had that place with her, right there in the room and all around her, in her posture, in her face) and he had to at least consider it, because—

And then she said, "I know Lucas, too."

"Lucas?" Craig asked.

"I met Lucas last year. He used to sell me weed once in a while. They've got it out for him, too, you know. I don't know why. They think he sold you bad dope or something. Or, just that he let you borrow his car, and you were stoned, so—"

"I wasn't," Craig said, but he said it without force, having said it so many times he no longer thought anyone cared or believed him.

"They've got some bad thing going with Lucas, like you. My ex-roommate, she had this story she thought was hilarious about how he'd called the suicide hotline, and one of the Omega sisters who happened to be a volunteer on the hotline that night took the call and recognized the caller ID, and was really trying to talk him into killing himself. He was going on and on about how he'd been seeing ghosts and shit, and some girl who died like twenty years ago was haunting him, and this sorority bitch was just like, 'Oh that's so scary. I would just want to be dead if I were being haunted by a ghost. I mean, ghosts just choose people at random, but after that it's like your whole life they follow you around. Do you have, like, access to a gun or anything, because that would help a lot . . .'

"And they were all just cracking up, waiting to read in the Police Beat in the newspaper that some college senior had shot himself."

"Lucas?" Craig asked again.

He hadn't thought about Lucas for a little while, and it suddenly dawned on him what all of this must have done to Lucas, too—and then he put the mug down on the table next to the couch and started to feel really bad, looking around (for help? For an excuse?) like *Jesus, Craig, how many people's lives do you think you can ruin in the course of your own?* All he'd done for Lucas was one stupid phone call in the summer, from New Hampshire, when some of the pieces had fallen into place again. On the phone, Lucas had said nothing, really. He'd muttered, "Oh, man. Craig, Jesus," a few times, and then, "I have no hard feelings toward you. But I gotta go. I really can't talk about this, man. I hope everything works out, and I have to say, if I were you, I'd stay back there, you know. Go to school in Connecticut or something. Here, you know, it's not cool right now. But maybe someday we'll meet again. Peace, man," and he'd hung up.

Lucas, shit. He'd ruined Lucas's life, too.

Deb seemed moved to tears again, looking at the expression on Craig's face, and she got out of her seat and put her arms around his neck, pulled the pink blanket more tightly around his neck, and hugged him, and Craig felt himself sag into the hug just the way he remembered sagging against his mother as a little kid, even when he knew she was pissed at him, because at least she was pretending she wasn't.

And then he was back there, eyes closed, sobbing into his mother's shoulder, soaking it, and saying things in a language he wasn't even sure he spoke, and she was patting and patting him—Deb, not his mother, and crying, too. "Look," Deb said, "just get in my bed and go to sleep. The sheets are clean. If the slumlord ever shows up to unlock your door, I'll wake you up. In the meantime, just rest."

When Craig woke again, the Martian green hands of the clock beside the Deb's bed read 4:10 (a.m.?). The room was dark except for the glow of her iPod in its charging dock, and there wasn't a sound through the whole apartment. He wanted to pee, but not badly enough, he decided, to wake up an apartment full of girls and scare the hell out of them. He lay on his side between the Deb's crisp sheets, which smelled of Nicole and the starch his mother used to spray on his khaki pants, and watched the hands of the alarm clock move in little twitches around the dial until Deb came in and sat down beside him in a T-shirt and gym shorts and laid a cool hand on his forehead.

And then he fell asleep again.

57

Josie seemed to soften after it became clear that, although Shelly had uncovered a truth, she wasn't going to make threats, or a scene.

Maybe Josie even seemed excited.

She was sitting at the edge of her seat now, leaning toward Shelly, moving her hands lightly through the air between them, explaining the finer points of hazing in sorority life. She was bouncing her knee a little, and although she didn't look directly into Shelly's eyes, she grazed Shelly's face as she talked, letting her eyes linger on Shelly's shoulder or earring for a split second before scouting the room around them again.

"We never do anything physically dangerous," Josie said. "But you really can't feel like a *group*, you know, without some rituals and traditions. And secrets. If it's not at least a *little* dangerous, there's no point in keeping it a secret, so—"

Could Josie simply be relieved that the truth had come out, and that Shelly seemed to have accepted it?

Josie was thrilled, Shelly realized, to be able to spill the secrets, to have a captive audience in Shelly. Because what could Shelly possibly do with any information she received from Josie now?

"I mean, it's not hazing like they used to haze. We've heard all about that. The sisters used to cut their palms—I mean really slice them open until they were gushing blood—and stand naked in a circle around a candle and have these, like, mystical things happen or something that made them sisters. In the attic there are these black-and-white photos from the sixties or something, and there's blood all over the place, and some naked guy with long hair playing the flute. Freaky."

It seemed like the kind of thing that would have gone on in the sixties, Shelly thought. Josie was laughing.

"I wonder what happened if someone bled too much?" Shelly said, more to herself than to Josie. She was thinking of a story her ex-husband had told her about a girl he'd had to treat after something like that: some blood ritual between volleyball teammates. They'd sliced their inner arms, and the girl had managed to hit an artery. Shelly's ex-husband had described it in such a way that she could still, twenty years later, see the imagined girl (red, white, and blue, wearing nothing but her Wildcats Varsity jacket), who died in the ER waiting room.

"I suppose they'd get help," Josie said, seeming disinterested. What did she care? What were the sixties to her? "*We've* always got someone standing by, in case something goes wrong."

Josie checked behind her shoulder, but there was nothing there except the wall. Still, it was clear she knew she was now headed toward forbidden territory, about to tell Shelly something she wasn't supposed to tell.

"We've got this EMT. This paramedic guy. He *belongs* to us. He's like everybody's boyfriend or a mascot or something. We love him. We make him wear his uniform because it's so cute! He sleeps in a room at the back of the house, and the sorority pays him to be there for the events, and to be on call so . . ." Josie drifted off, eyes seeming to go unfocused, moving down to some place between her own knees and the floor.

"What 'events'?" Shelly asked.

"Well, there's this thing. There's a Spring Event and a Winter Event. You do it your second year—so, for me it's coming up." She giggled a little. "I'm scared shitless. Promise not to tell anyone?"

The absurdity of this seemed to occur to Josie even as she said it, and she continued before Shelly could have answered.

"We're *reborn*. As sisters. You won't *believe* this."

Shelly raised her eyebrows, as if to say, *Try me*, but the thing she was having a hard time, at the moment, believing was that she'd ruined her career, tossed off her entire life, to go to bed with this chatty, banal, empty person, who was sitting across from her at Starbucks talking about her sorority as if she were the only person who'd ever been in one, as if the things that took place in it were of some kind of import in the wider world. Only a week ago, Shelly marveled as she looked at Josie Reilly's pale, excited face, she had felt she would be willing to chop off a few digits if it meant another lazy afternoon in bed with this girl. She'd actually believed herself to be in love.

"It's called the Raising. We keep a coffin in the basement," Josie said, leaning forward, whispering so energetically that if anyone in Starbucks had the slightest interest, they could have heard her from four tables away. "And every second-year pledge gets *put into it*. They do this thing where—well, first everybody's drunk off their ass, and then the girl who's being raised sits on the floor, and you breathe in and out really fast for two minutes exactly, and another girl presses on your neck, your artery, and you're *out*.

"They put you in the coffin, and when you come to—there you are, reborn. And your sisters are all holding candles.

"The pledges all wait upstairs because they won't let you see the ceremony until you're either being reborn or have already *been* reborn.

"It's my turn in three weeks."

"Jesus Christ," Shelly said, but she was reacting not to the upcoming ordeal but to the wideness of Josie's pupils. Her eyeballs—had Shelly ever noticed before how large they were? Certain cartoon characters came to mind: Minnie Mouse. Betty Boop.

"Can you believe it?" Josie asked.

"Yes," Shelly said. "I mean, no."

But of course she could believe it. It seemed almost laughably believable. Par for the course. Shelly would have thought that by now sororities might have come up with some truly new, shocking, and innovative ritual. This one hardly merited the term *hazing*. She had herself, in fact, participated in such passing-out rituals in junior high, in Valerie Kolorik's rec room while her parents were at their country club. There'd been no coffin, of course, but only because they could never have located or afforded one. They'd have *loved* a coffin. Shelly could still remember the feeling of Valerie's clammy hands on her neck after the two minutes of hyperventilation. Those small clammy hands were the last physical sensation she'd had before slipping into oblivion. When she awoke, the other girls were all sitting around her, laughing.

"Yeah," Josie said, nodding at Shelly with such anxious energy that it occurred to her that the girl might actually be scared. "I mean," she said, "it's really just a game, but there have been times when sisters got hurt. So the EMT's there, in case."

She sincerely whispered this last part—no longer the stage whisper—and Shelly knew it was her own cue either to ask about the sisters who'd gotten hurt, or to express concern for Josie, but she couldn't bring herself to do either. This, she thought, was its own kind of falling into oblivion—but, this time, the little hands around her neck were Josie's, and Shelly knew she'd be feeling them there for the rest of her life.

"You're not going to tell anyone, are you?" Josie said, her eyes narrowed to slits. A statement, not a question. "About the Events. I mean, it's not really hazing, but if the Pan-Hellenic Council—"

"No," Shelly said. "Of course not."

"Thank you," Josie said, but it was pure formality. "Especially after Nicole got killed, and all this bullshit with fucking Denise disappearing . . ."

"Denise?"

Josie waved her had and smirked. "Ran away or something. She was creepy. But people keep snooping around like we buried her in the back yard or something."

It came back to Shelly from her research of the accident: the music school student who'd disappeared. "What happened to her?" Shelly asked.

"How would I know? But *we* can't be blamed for psycho sisters running off. She should never have gotten in to OTT in the first place. She was the kind of trash that belongs in—" She stopped herself before naming Shelly's sorority, and a ridiculous flush spread across Shelly's chest. She blinked, and swallowed, and stood (chair legs scraping loudly and obscenely against the bare Starbucks floor), and said, trying to sound composed, "I should go now."

Josie looked annoyed, and disappointed, as if she'd had more surprises in store, as if she were considering whether or not to *let* Shelly go—and they both knew that if Josie commanded her to sit back down, Shelly would have to, so she stayed where she was, standing before Josie Reilly, waiting to see if she would be dismissed, and Josie seemed to be considering this as she looked around the coffee shop, and then to the front door, where, it seemed, someone more interesting had just stepped in.

When Josie rose, Shelly saw her opportunity to say good-bye, and even found herself bowing a little, but Josie brushed past her, and said, "Sit down, would you? I have to say hello to someone, but I'll be right back."

What could Shelly do?

Slowly, but inexorably, she felt her weight, and the weight of Josie's words, pull her into the chair as she sat back down.

58

Jeff Blackhawk drove with one hand on the steering wheel. He ate his Baconator with the other hand, kept his gigantic Coke between his knees, and Mira held his carton of large fries within reach for him. As he ate and drove, Jeff also kept up both sides of the conversation for them. It seemed that the difficulty Mira was having holding up her end had become apparent to him after he'd asked her about her childhood (the simple stuff: where had she grown up, what had her parents done) and she'd spluttered something about her mother being a housewife before she'd had to stop talking in order to stifle the sob she knew would be coming if she allowed herself to utter even one more word.

"I fucking hate this state," Jeff said. "I grew up in West Texas, which everyone makes fun of, but I'll tell you what—" He chewed on that and his Baconator for quite a while before he continued. "People know how to live in West Texas. You get yourself some land, no trees, for one thing. A trailer. Flat. Flat! And there's the sky. It's *everywhere.*"

It occurred to Mira that Jeff Blackhawk's poetry might be of the super-minimalist variety. He seemed to need a long time to find the words for what he wanted to convey, but when he did, they were the right words.

She could see his West Texas, although she'd never been to it. The trailer. The flat land. A bush far out in the distance. *Blue. Blue.*

"Here," Jeff said, waving his Baconator at the windshield as if to erase the landscape. "Clutter. Junk. Nothing."

He was nothing like Clark, Mira was realizing. Clark would never have used the word *fucking* in casual conversation, only in anger—and if he'd found himself having to go to Wendy's for some reason, he would have ordered a chicken breast with lettuce and tomato. If he'd had to eat in his car, he would have eaten in the parking lot before driving off. He would never, *ever*, Mira felt entirely certain, have offered to drive a woman he knew distantly from work two hundred miles away to retrieve her children from her mother-in-law.

"How's your research going?" Jeff asked Mira, but he didn't wait for her to answer. "I've gotten even more interested in your subject, you know. So, sorry, but you might have some competition from me. Not that I can write prose, so you don't have any competition *there*. But this whole thing, with the girl. I probably shouldn't tell you this, but a couple of years ago I dated a girl. She wasn't *my* student"—he turned to look at Mira seriously here, and didn't look away until she'd looked him in the eyes—"but she *was* a student, and she was in that sorority, the one Nicole Werner was in. *Hoo*. Did she have some stories! She got out when they wanted to put her in a coffin and raise her from the dead, and then they ostracized her so badly she transferred to Penn State. Now, *there's* something for your sex and death book: sorority girls in coffins.

"She was an incredible girl, really. Hair like"—he swallowed the last bite of his Baconator, but it seemed to be going down with difficulty, as if crossing paths with the simile he was considering—"glass, sheet metal.

I don't date students usually, Mira. I'm well aware of my reputation, but it's just a lonely man's reputation, not a Casanova. I have a bad feeling, anyway, these days, that if I decided to cut a swathe through the female student population of Godwin Honors College, it would be more like a square inch than a swathe. But!" He held both hands above the steering wheel and said to the windshield, "There *was a time*! Yes, indeed, there was a day in the life of a lonely man named Jeff Blackhawk. Indeed."

Mira looked down at his knees. There was a grease stain on his jeans where he'd rested the burger between bites. She realized, then, that the scent that wafted around him in the hallways, the one she'd taken for some kind of masculine emission of heat, was the smell of this car, and Baconators. She resisted an urge to put her hand on the knee and pat it. It was not a sexual urge, and Mira felt certain that he would not have misconstrued it as a sexual gesture—but at that moment he did not have his hands on the steering wheel, and he seemed so excitable that Mira was a little worried they'd end up in the median if she made even the gentlest of sudden movements.

59

H i, Perry."
    "Josie."
    "Haven't seen you around for a while."
    Perry couldn't walk around her. She was standing directly in front of him and in front of Karess, who was standing beside him. The only place to go without knocking over one of the two of them was to crawl over a table at which two guys who looked like graduate students sat, passing a page full of calculations angrily back and forth between them, and he couldn't do that.
    "Yeah," he said to Josie, and looked around her showily in the direction of the Starbucks counter, trying to make it clear that he was on his way *past* her, that he didn't plan to linger here *with* her. But Josie had

never been one to take her cues from other people. "Are you living with Craig?" she asked him. "Because that's the rumor." She glanced at Karess, head to toe, and seemed to dismiss her before turning back to Craig again.

"Why do you want to know?" Perry asked.

"Because I want to know," Josie said.

"Look. Josie, I've—"

"Excuse me," Karess said, sounding meekly polite as she squeezed between Perry and Josie. When she reached the counter she turned and gestured for Perry to follow, but he couldn't, because Josie was still standing in front of him.

"Who's that?" Josie asked, jerking her head in Karess's direction. "You're dating a hippie chick?"

"Josie—"

"Look," Josie said. "I want you to tell Craig something for me."

Perry looked at the ceiling. He waited.

"I want you to tell Craig 'fuck you' for me."

Perry continued to stare at the ceiling—although, out of the corner of his eye he could see that Karess was still waving her pale hand at him, a bit more frantically now. Her bracelets seemed to catch the light, which danced around on the ceiling. He tried to concentrate on that even as he saw (as if, suddenly, he had panoramic vision and could take in all of Starbucks without taking his eyes off the ceiling) Josie's equally pale hand rise up and rush toward him, colliding with his face.

The smacking sound was oddly muffled to him because, along with his cheek, Josie had struck him in the ear, but it was clear to him, even in his shocked state, that everyone else in Starbucks had heard it, because they all turned to stare at him at once as Josie's little black shoes snapped away, back to the corner she'd come from, sounding like claws or talons tapping across the linoleum as she went.

"Oh, my God!" Karess cried out, and rushed toward him as if she thought he'd been shot. She grabbed his arm and body-slammed him toward the door, pushed him out into the street. "Oh, my God!" she screamed again. "That girl slapped you!"

60

Shelly turned at the sound of a slap to see Josie red-cheeked and openmouthed, heading back toward their table, the boy she'd apparently slapped and his girlfriend careening back out the door into what now seemed to be an actual blizzard.

The same feeling of surrender, defeat, with which she'd sat back down when Josie told her to came over Shelly when she realized she was going to have to walk home in that blizzard wearing only a dress and a thin sweater. Maybe Josie would slap her, too, before she had to go back out there.

Josie tossed herself down in the chair across from Shelly, and the whole room erupted in cheers and laughter, as if the home team had just scored a touchdown. Two scholarly-looking guys at a table near the door high-fived each other. There were a few whistles, and a girl alone at a table in the corner looked up from her laptop, pumped her fist in the air. "You go, girl!" the cashier behind the counter shouted. The guy who was making cappuccinos and lattes stabbed a thumbs-up into the air, and even the mother with the toddler in the stroller who'd followed Shelly in from the cold and spoken to her so kindly was smiling.

Had something been said that Shelly hadn't heard—something for which the boy deserved to be slapped? And if he *had* said something, could so many have heard it? Shelly herself hadn't heard a thing until she'd heard the sound of the slap, and the girlfriend's alarmed exclamations, and some of those hooting with approval had been sitting even farther from the scene than she was.

Of course, had that boy slapped Josie he would have been tackled by the very guys who were high-fiving one another now. The police would have been called. The boy would have been taken out of Starbucks in handcuffs.

Josie was pink-cheeked, her lips parted. She wasn't smiling, but neither did she look particularly upset.

"What happened?" Shelly asked, trying to sound more concerned than she felt, more alarmed. What she wanted was to get out of there.

"Fucking asshole," Josie said. "He lives with somebody I hate."

"Who?" Shelly asked, and Josie muttered a name. Shelly leaned forward and asked again. "Who?"

"Craig Clements-Rabbitt," Josie said, exasperated, as if Shelly had been badgering her about it for days. "He's this jerk who—"

"The boy who was in the car crash," Shelly said—and as she said it, her own voice sounded to her like someone else's. A narrator's voice. The distant voice of a storyteller. An omniscient narrator. A narrator who'd known all the facts all along but had chosen to reveal them slowly. "Craig Clements-Rabbitt," she repeated, not to Josie, but to herself. "You knew him."

Josie snorted, and rolled her eyes. "Yeah. I knew him," she said. "He's a liar and a womanizer and he deserves everything that's coming to him—and, believe me, it will be bad, what's coming to him."

"You think he killed your roommate," Shelly said. "Nicole. Your friend."

Josie didn't deny it, although she'd yet to tell Shelly that she'd been the dead girl's roommate. And in all that had passed between them since, Shelly had never asked.

But now, if there'd ever been a reason to deny it, there was no longer any reason, and no more denying it. Josie shrugged, and said, "Yeah. That's part of it."

It was a dismissal.

Yes, he might have killed her friend, but there was something even worse he'd done.

"What did he do, Josie?"

Josie waved her question away, and said, "It doesn't matter now. He's going to pay."

"He's already paid," Shelly said, trying to keep her voice from trembling. "I was at the scene of the accident. I saw what happened. And what *didn't* happen."

"Everybody pays in the end," Josie said, and then she laughed without the slightest hint of joy.

"Is that how you feel about me?" Shelly asked her.

Josie looked genuinely surprised at the question. Her eyebrows disappeared under her bangs.

"No," Josie said, after considering it for what seemed like an eternity. She then uttered one more sharp, strange laugh, and left her mouth hanging open afterward, still looking at Shelly in surprise. "Don't you get it by now? This has nothing to do with *us*. And it's not some stupid hazing thing like you think. I mean, I wouldn't degrade myself for something like that, and Omega Theta Tau would never ask me to! *God*. The thing with us has to do with that: You were at the scene. They want to get you out of here."

Josie leaned back against her chair and regarded Shelly as if from a very great distance. She had the expression of someone who had just dotted the last *i* on a writing assignment, stapled the pages, and handed it in:

There you have it, what do you think?

Shelly could do nothing but stare back.

Part Four

61

I wouldn't have offered if it was a problem," Jeff said. "I think your kids are cute, and you've got this library full of Camille Paglia. Who *wouldn't* want to babysit here?"

"They like you," Mira said, more out of surprise than as a compliment. Andy and Matty each sat on one of his loafers as he bounced his feet. Jeff was sprawled out on the couch as if the apartment were his, and he'd placed his coffee cup on the floor, where it was sure to be knocked over, but this carelessness somehow made his presence even more beneficent, more welcome. "Thank you," she said again. "I'll be back in time for you to get to your class. I swear."

"Hey, my students never expect me on time anyway, and you can't run out of the morgue without saying good-bye. Take your time. We'll just be reading feminist literary theory here and smearing graham crackers all over ourselves."

"I hope you don't have to change a diaper," Mira said. "But—"

"*Butt?!* Jesus, I hope not too. But, yeah, it's all fine. Little secret: I took a Red Cross babysitting course when I was in middle school, hoping to make some extra money for dope, and I did great in the class, but somehow no one would hire me to watch their kids. Until now! Still, I remember that whole thing about diaper changing. Not to worry."

Mira waved good-bye to the boys, who squealed, holding tightly to Jeff's pale, hairy ankles, exposed between his socks and the frayed cuffs of his khaki trousers.

It was unpleasantly cold out, and the clouds were sinister blue things skimming low over the buildings. The students hurrying past her on the sidewalk on the way to class had their heads buried in their parkas, although a few still mysteriously, or brazenly, wore flip-flops. A bicyclist tore through the damp street, tires making the sound of hissing snakes. A man stood in a front yard pounding a stake into the lawn.

A For Rent sign, Mira supposed.

She supposed, too, that soon she'd have to start reading the classifieds and looking at the posted For Rent signs, looking for an apartment, and the thought of this filled her eyes with tears before she even realized she'd thought it.

Clark.

Jesus Christ.

Up in Petoskey, his mother had actually, physically, tried to keep Mira from leaving the house with the twins.

"Mira, Clark left them with *me*. He'll be back tomorrow, I'm sure. What am I going to tell him?"

"You'll tell him that their mother, his wife, came to get them. That she's taken them home."

"But, Mira, you can't just—"

But by that point Mira already had the diaper bag packed. She'd buttoned the twins' jackets up over their sweaters, and was carrying one child on each hip like two sweet bags of groceries. They'd been so excited to see her that they'd begun to scream, and now, on either side of her, they were patting her cheeks as if to check that they were the real thing. It stung, the patting, but Mira loved it.

Clark's mother took hold of the sleeve of her sweater and said, "Don't go, Mira. I'll have to—"

"You'll have to what?" Mira asked. She was careful not to raise her voice, which would have alarmed the twins, who, after all, adored their grandmother. "What will you have to do, Kay? Call the police? Tell them the twins' mother came and picked them up? Or call Clark? I've tried that myself. A hundred times. He doesn't have the cell phone turned on, or he doesn't have it with him, and what good would that do, anyway?

We've all got to go home eventually, and the boys need to be with their mother."

In defeat, it seemed, Clark's mother let go of Mira's sleeve, and Mira felt sorry for her. Her hair was grayer than Mira remembered, and it was all combed to one side of her head, leaving a bare patch of scalp exposed. She was wearing a ratty KEY WEST sweatshirt, a place Mira was certain Kay had never been. It broke Mira's heart, really. Clark's mother had never been anything but kind to her, and loving to the twins. But she had to go. She had to have her children with her, and she had to work, so she had to take them home.

"I'm sorry, Kay," Mira said. "And so grateful to you for keeping them, for taking such good care of them."

Kay swallowed, nodded solemnly, and then kissed each boy, and then she kissed Mira, too, on the cheek, with the same silly smacking sound she'd used on Andy and Matty.

"I love you *all!*" she said loudly, voice cracking, chin quivering, and Mira found herself crying then, too, and the twins were looking at her tears, wiping at them, seeming sober and astonished, looking from Mira to their grandmother, who walked Mira to the door then and looked out.

Jeff had stayed in the car so as not to be in the way. He had the engine running, and it was making guttural noises, blowing blue smoke out of the tailpipe. He appeared to be, possibly, singing to himself, or reciting something, while staring at his lap.

"Who is that?" Kay asked Mira. "Who is that man?" She said it as if she'd seen a ghost.

"His name is Jeff Blackhawk," Mira explained. "He's my colleague at the college. He offered to drive me because, you know, I don't have the car. Because Clark has the car."

Clark's mother nodded slowly at this, as if that all made a peculiar kind of sense, and then she said under her breath, "Is he an Indian?" as if he might be able to hear her.

"I don't think so," Mira whispered back. "I haven't gotten that impression."

Clark's mother nodded as if, at least, there was this bit of good news, and then she grabbed Mira's sleeve again and said, "Bring the babies back as soon as you can. And be careful getting home. Work things out with Clark. I love you, darling."

"I love you, too," Mira said, and she looked at Clark's mother for a long time before she turned with the twins to the door, to the car.

Back at the apartment, after the long drive home, and after Jeff had helped her carry the twins up the stairs (leaving with the tip of an imaginary cap, and a little bow), Mira was feeling so solaced by their return that she hadn't even thought of Clark. The relief of having the boys in her arms, nursing them, kissing them, smelling their hair and the napes of their necks, was complete, as if she'd been held hostage those days without them, and had just been released. Tears ran down her cheeks and into their hair as she rocked back and forth on the couch and they sucked greedily until they finally fell asleep. Then, she lifted them, put them in the cribs (a difficult feat with two limp toddlers, but they were sound asleep) and then lingered a long time afterward in the nursery, looking down at them in their cribs. Home.

It wasn't until she was on her way up the stairs to Godwin Hall to meet her class for their field trip to the morgue that Mira realized, fully, that a new part of her life had started, and would continue to be starting, whether she wanted it to or not.

62

Perry stood in the middle of his apartment and spoke to Craig's voice mail, leaving him a message ("Where the hell are you, man?") when he realized that the cell phone he was trying to reach was lying on the coffee table about three feet away from him, turned off. It had been twenty-four hours since he'd seen Craig, and he was going to be late to the class field trip if he didn't leave that second. "Fuck," Perry said to the phone, hung it up, grabbed his backpack, and headed for the door.

He *was* late.

Professor Polson was standing in the foyer with the class already gathered around her. She was giving them some directives—telling them that the university morgue was actually a secured facility, and that it was a special privilege to be allowed to visit it, a privilege granted to them because her research gave her a faculty pass, which she'd managed to have extended to "visiting scholars." The fact that her "visiting scholars" were actually freshman in a first-year seminar had apparently not been brought to the attention of the morgue director or the hospital security. Yet. And the class needed to provoke no interest or suspicion so it would stay that way. "Okay?" she asked. There were nods all around.

It also happened, she explained, that she was personal friends with the *diener* (the class snickered at the word, so close to *diner*, although Professor Polson had defined it for them as "the person responsible for handling and washing bodies"). This morgue's diener, coincidentally, had worked at a mortuary she'd visited in Yugoslavia, and they'd stayed in touch over the years, and then he had come to the United States.

"If there's joking, disrespect, *theft*—God forbid—or any kind of un-dignified behavior, I will likely never be allowed back with another class. More important, for you, the student or students responsible will fail my course and receive whatever other punishments I can come up with." She said this lightheartedly, but it was clear from her expression that she wasn't kidding.

That morning Professor Polson was wearing a black sweater and a deep purple skirt. Her hair was shiny and smooth, and there was color in her cheeks. She looked, Perry thought, as if she'd slept well that night. For the last few weeks there'd been circles under her eyes, but today they looked clear and bright.

She was so lovely to look at. Perry had a hard time taking his eyes off her, although he didn't want to appear to be staring. Through the gauzy scarf around her neck, he glimpsed what looked like a gold cross dangling near her breast bone. Maybe the slightest hint of a lace-trimmed bra or camisole. He had to will himself to look away, and found his gaze caught by Karess's.

She held it without smiling.

Perry tried to smile himself, but it felt to him more like a grimace as he did it, and the look on Karess's face—surprise, annoyance—made it seem even more likely that his own face wasn't doing what he wanted it to do.

But she also didn't look away. She seemed to be *refusing* to look away, so Perry, unnerved, pretended suddenly to notice that he needed to tie his shoe. He crouched down behind Alexandra Robbins's enormous ass, where he could see no one and no one could see him, until he heard Professor Polson say, "Okay, follow me."

On the walk to the morgue, Perry kept well behind the rest of the other students, most of whom seemed to be trying as hard as they could to walk next to Professor Polson (an impossible task, since the sidewalk was wide enough for only two people at a time, and there were sixteen of them). Karess was, herself, off on the muddy grass, slogging through it in cowboy boots. She was wearing what looked like two miniskirts— one black lace and, over that one, a denim one with a torn patch at the hip. There were feathers braided into her hair, as well as a couple of beads. She glanced over her shoulder for only a second, and it seemed to Perry that her face sparkled. Not with pleasure, but with that glitter girls sometimes wore. He remembered Mary having some of that on her cheeks at the prom a couple years ago, and how, as they danced, every time he looked at her it appeared as though her cheeks were awash in tears.

Brett Barber was doing his best to keep his position beside Karess. It looked like he was trying to take baby steps so as not to get too far ahead of her. Karess had begun waving her hand around in the air in front of her as if she were trying to explain some important concept to him, and Brett was watching her lavender wool mitten as if it held the key to the universe and he was afraid she might drop it.

The guy must have thought he'd died and gone to heaven. Perry didn't remember ever seeing Karess so much as glance in Brett's direction even once. If Perry'd had more energy, if he hadn't been up half the night waiting to hear Craig knock (wherever it was he'd gone off to, he'd left his keys behind), he would have tried to hurry ahead and catch up, step between the two of them. But, first of all, his legs wouldn't move that fast. Second, he didn't know if he was up for whatever kind of response Karess might have to his approaching her. He was hoping they'd parted yesterday as friends, but he had his doubts.

After Starbucks, after Josie slapped him hard in the face, and he and Karess had stumbled out into a strangely heavy snowfall, Perry had made the mistake of going with her back to her room, where the roommate excused herself the second they arrived (to "go study in the lounge"), as if on cue.

"Let me see you," Karess had said, and turned to Perry. She approached him with her hands open as if she were carrying a bowl, and she took his face in them—but instead of inspecting him, she kissed him.

The kiss lasted a long time. Karess was about his height, and with her arms wrapped around him and her body pressed against his, he saw no way (or at least so he told himself) to disengage without giving her shoulders a shove. He let her bite his lower lip, and his tongue traveled over her teeth, which tasted both like clove and like mint, but he kept his hands firmly planted on her shoulder bones, and didn't move them, although her own hands traveled up his back, and down it, and then to his face again. With her index finger she traced a line from his temple to his lips, and then she put her finger to the corner of his mouth and dipped it in.

Perry opened his eyes then, and hers were open, too, looking into his, and she stepped back, shrugging off her jacket, letting it fall to the floor, and took his hand and pulled him toward the bed, which had what looked like some kind of Indian tablecloth on it, along with about a million decorative pillows and a stuffed black cat with creepy green eyes. Perry shook his head.

Karess looked at him, and shook her own head as if in imitation. "What?" she said. It wasn't exactly a question.

Perry said, trying to sound apologetic, "I've got to go."

"What?"

"I just," Perry said. "Can't. I have to go."

"O-*kay*," Karess said, and then glanced at his jeans. He couldn't hide the erection. She said, "It *looks* like you can."

"It's not. That." Perry was trying to think of a way to say what it was, without himself knowing.

She was so beautiful. He knew what any roomful of guys hearing this story would have called him.

But Nicole had been beautiful, too.

And it had been awful, being with Nicole.

Whereas with Mary—who was not, by any standard, beautiful like these girls—he had wanted her so badly for so long that he would have died for it. He'd woken up some nights groaning. Some days in the hallway at school, he would take circuitous routes to classes and the cafeteria in order to avoid her, because he couldn't stand it, seeing her. Seeing her in whatever pretty blouse or silky skirt she was wearing would make him ache all day.

"Well, then, what is it?" Karess asked. "I'm not your type or something? You're not gay, are you?"

"No," Perry said. "You're so beautiful, but I—"

"You have a girlfriend, don't you?" Karess said. She sighed. "I wondered what the deal was. You never even *look* at girls except for Professor Polson. I thought you were either a virgin, or a Christian, or you were sleeping with our professor, but you have some girl up there in whatever that town is you're from—Bad Ass?—waiting for you, wearing a yellow ribbon or something, don't you?"

Perry hesitated at first, but Karess continued to stare at him, and not knowing what else to do, Perry nodded.

"Is that why that sorority bitch slapped you?"

"Well," Perry said. "Not exactly. She—"

"Well, thanks for sparing me her fate, anyway. Now, would you get out of here, Mr. Bad Ass? I've had just about enough of you for one day."

It was mostly a joke, but Karess turned away from Perry and went to the window and looked out, and she made a motion with her hand for him to go, and Perry cleared his throat, trying and failing to think of something to say before he unlocked her door and stepped out into the hall, and closed it quietly behind him.

Now Brett Barber was trotting beside her, all but wagging his tail, and whatever Karess was talking to him about, it seemed to require no response on his part. He wasn't even nodding his head. Professor Polson was taking long strides, in knee-high, shiny black boots, across the parking lot, and the group continued to follow down through an alley, which grew narrower as they walked. Soon it was narrow enough that only one person could pass at a time, so they followed her in single file. A couple of people laughed nervously, looked at the people behind them, raised their eyebrows. "Where the hell are we going?" someone whispered.

It surprised Perry, too. He'd expected the morgue to be its own building, bright and goofy like Dientz Funeral Home back in Bad Axe. Every holiday they decorated the front lawn—ribbons, flowers, wreaths, Easter eggs, Valentine's hearts—except for Halloween.

But the university's hospital morgue seemed to be sequestered exactly where you'd expect a place where dead bodies were kept to be hidden away: in a dungeon. Out by the hospital Dumpsters. No sign out front welcoming them with a smiley face. No euphemistic directions to CARE CONCLUSION FACILITY, or MEDICAL OUTSTAY LABORATORY.

Professor Polson kept going, and they kept following, past Dumpsters and chain-link fencing and No Trespassing signs, and on to a point beyond which it seemed they would find no entrance to anything, and certainly past the point where anyone would wish to trespass, and then Professor Polson was descending a long flight of stairs to a dark alcove and a windowless brown fire door on which was stenciled, in large caution-yellow letters, MORGUE.

63

The dean of the music school was leaning back in his upholstered chair, twiddling his thumbs, when Shelly stepped in. He was the picture of calm self-possession, except that he was blushing. His secretary had announced Sherry's arrival, and then Shelly had been left to sit in the hallway outside his office for fifteen minutes. He'd had ample time to compose this reclining, twiddling façade, but he couldn't hide his heart rate, which had been raised either by fear of an impending conflict or by simple embarrassment.

"Ms. Lockes," he said.

Shelly shook her head. She saw no reason to continue to play this game. "You can call me Shelly," she said sadly, "as always, and if it's okay, I'm going to keep calling you Alex. I've known you for twenty years, Alex. I'm not here to talk about my job."

The dean's cheeks flushed an even deeper shade of hot pink. He was a pale, porcine man. Not having met him earlier in his life, Shelly had always assumed he'd reached his portly state with middle age, but, for the first time, she found herself able to picture him as a rotund seventh-grader being hounded by lanky boys on a playground. Panting. Fighting back tears. His cheeks would have been exactly this color.

Alex sighed, and sat up and put his hands under his desk where she could no longer see them.

"I'm sorry, but I'm here to ask you a favor, Alex," Shelly said. She could see his chin twitch then, nearly imperceptibly, and she raised her hand as if to ward off something he would never have been able to bring himself to say anyway. "Don't worry," she said. "Again, it's not about the job, and I'm certainly not planning to ask you for a reference, or anything that would put you in any kind of an uncomfortable position, ever, Alex. This has to do with something else. University business, you might say. Do you remember the accident last spring? Nicole Werner? The student from Bad Axe. The freshman."

The dean nodded slowly, without opening his mouth, eyebrows raised as if he feared it might be a trick question. Shelly waited, looking at him, until he finally said, "Yes. Of course."

"I probably never had any reason to tell you about this. I don't remember seeing you much last spring at all, and it didn't concern you—and, despite my efforts, my involvement never even made the newspaper, so you'd have had no way of knowing, but I was the first one on the scene. I was driving home from the gym. I was the woman who called nine-one-one."

"Oh," he said, "my." He seemed intrigued, but also as though he were trying to hide his interest, to make it clear that nothing Shelly said could draw him in, lest she be drawing him in to some legalistic or psychological or academic trap.

"The newspaper reported that I didn't give directions to the scene, and that I left the scene, and a hundred other erroneous details about the accident—all bogus. Until now, I didn't understand. I thought it was incompetence. I thought the local newspaper simply couldn't get their facts straight, that they were such hick reporters and such a slipshod operation that I couldn't even get a letter to the editor published. But now I understand that that was what they wanted me to believe. Now I know that it's really quite the opposite. They're a very well oiled machine, the slickest of the slick, and the university is controlling them. I don't know how, or why, but—"

Shelly found herself momentarily stalled by the dean's expression. It would have been an exaggeration to call it horror or *repugnance*, but the emotion it revealed sprang from the same source as those emotions:

He thought she was crazy.

He thought she was, perhaps, a paranoid schizophrenic.

He was going backward in his mind through all the years he'd known her, and what the early signs of this might have been. There must have been some: The insistence on the superiority of Handel to Mozart. Her lesbianism. The picture of the cat that she kept on her desk. He was no longer blushing. He no longer needed to feel embarrassed, she realized, because he no longer believed he was with a peer, a colleague, or even a former employee. He was in the presence of a lunatic.

Shelly sighed, fighting back tears. She swallowed, and said, "You don't believe me. But I'm not even asking you to believe me. I've been in your employ for a long time, and I'm asking something very simple from you, and it's something only you can do: I need, very much, for you to ask for an inquiry into the disappearance of a young woman from the university here. She was a student in the music school. A violinist. A member of the Omega Theta Tau sorority. She's been missing since last winter, and as far as I can tell, from what I've read on the Internet, there has been no investigation by either the local police or by the university.

"Surely, as dean of the music school, you must want to know what happened to this girl? We can't have sophomores from the music school simply disappearing, can we?"

From the look on his face, Shelly could tell that he'd never even heard about the missing violinist, and he didn't want to be hearing about her now. Still, he'd moved beyond his concerns regarding Shelly's sanity to far greater concerns regarding his accountability, his reputation, his exposure. He was, to Shelly's relief, taking a pen out of his pocket, pulling a legal pad from the corner of his desk to the center of it, nodding for her to go on.

"What's your concern about this girl? And how do you know about it?"

"She was a sorority sister of Nicole Werner's, and also of Josie Reilly's, and it just seems too much, to me—just so many coincidences. Where is this girl, and why hasn't anyone come forward with any information about her?"

"So," he put down the pen. "You don't even know if she's still missing. She might be back in school for all you know, or back home with her folks?"

Shelly nodded. "I don't know."

"Well, I'll look into it, but who knows. I don't see what this has to do with anything."

"Thank you. I'm just asking you to look into it. And, can I ask you"—she started before she realized she'd been planning, all along, to ask the question—"how was it that Josie Reilly was sent to me for the work-study position? She wasn't a financial aid student, was she? Those positions are for students in need."

The dean closed his eyes and cleared his throat. He winced then, as if something he'd seen with his closed eyes had given him physical pain. When he opened his eyes again, he sighed and said, "Well, that in itself, Shelly, is part of the whole unfortunate situation. The student wasn't even being paid. She simply wanted the experience, and was willing to work for free because she knew she couldn't get the job without the work-study scholarship. So, I saw to it that she was sent your way. First of all, because she was such a lovely, fine student, and also because her mother and my wife are friends from their own college days. Sorority sisters, as it happens."

64

You're kidding, right?" Craig said. He was holding her in his arms. She was wearing a bra with orange daisies on it, and matching cotton panties. It had been her idea to take off her T-shirt and jeans: "I want to feel as much of your skin against mine as I can, without—"

She hadn't needed to say more.

He knew what she meant.

He'd agreed he'd never press the issue again after a night after winter break when he'd begged and pleaded with her to let him kiss her breasts. Finally, she'd nodded in a manner that had seemed almost ceremonious—the crucifer on the altar nodding to the priest—and Craig's heart had nearly exploded in his chest.

But when he'd propped himself up on his elbows to unfasten her beautiful pink lace bra, he realized that she was crying, that there were matching tears sliding sideways down each of her cheeks, zigzagging into her golden hair, where they disappeared, and he pulled his trembling hands away from her bra as if they'd been burned. He let them hover in the air over her for a moment before he sagged beside her on the squeaking mattress of his bed, put his head in her neck, and said, "No, Nicole. I'm sorry."

She said nothing.

"I won't ask again," Craig said.

"I love you," she said—and, as every time she had said it since the first time, something seemed to catch between Craig's soft palate and his throat. He couldn't speak. He'd made a thousand declarations of love to her since October, but he could never say it in response to *her* declaration—because of this sharpness that caught him as quickly as a fishhook every time.

Nicole smiled, seeming to understand. He didn't have to say it. He loved Nicole. He loved her. Nicole knew how much he loved her.

That had been six weeks ago, and since then he'd held her in his arms in her bra and panties a dozen times, and kept his promise not to ask for more.

"Tell me this is a bad joke," he said. "Your sorority doesn't really do this shit, right?"

"It's not *that* weird," Nicole said. "Secret societies have rituals. This happens to be ours."

Craig couldn't stop himself from snorting, but then he muttered an apology. He said, "Sorry. I guess I just don't think of your sorority as a secret society. I mean, I thought it was about formals and decorating floats and making cookies and maybe helping each other clip in hair extensions. I never thought you'd have a coffin in the basement, and—"

"Shhh—be quiet," Nicole said, and she actually glanced around the room as if someone might have overheard, although they were half-naked and completely alone in his dorm room. Perry was at his afternoon Poli-Sci lecture. Even the curtains were closed.

"Nicole," Craig said, but didn't bother to continue. It was cute, really, he thought. It reminded him of the way girls back in elementary school would get all excited about their own meaningless secrets, passing notes to one another, freaking out if some boy grabbed a note out of some girl's hands, although those notes had never said anything more exciting than *Deena likes Bradley!!!* Like anyone cared.

"Well, the Pan-Hellenic Society could have our house closed if they found out. This is considered *hazing.*"

"How often does your sorority have these . . . raisings?" Craig asked, trying to make it sound like a serious question, trying not to make air quotations around the word.

"Twice a year," Nicole said. "They did it back in November, but we— the new pledges—had to wait upstairs. They don't let us attend until the Spring Event."

Then, Craig couldn't help it. He laughed out at her calling it the "Spring Event." Basically they were getting sorority sisters drunk on tequila, having them hyperventilate until they passed out, putting them in a coffin, and "bringing them back from the dead," all newly risen in the Omega Theta Tau sisterhood. It hardly fit, in Craig's opinion, under the kind of seasonal "event" classification the Rotary Club might give to an Easter egg hunt or a skating party for kids with Down syndrome.

"Craig," Nicole said, and punched him softly on the arm. "You said you wanted me to tell you *everything.* And you swore you wouldn't tell *anyone.*"

Craig held his hand over his heart and said, "I swear. I mean it. Your secret society's secret is safe with me. But don't go brain dead on me or something, okay? You're sure this shit is safe?"

"It's so safe," Nicole said. "Hundreds of girls have done it since the *fifties.* Nothing's ever gone wrong."

"Yeah, but what if it does? You read about this stuff all the time. People with heart conditions they didn't know they had, that kind of thing—"

"Well, we have a dozen founding sisters present at the event. And this year I'm just a celebrant. I don't get to be raised until next year."

"Well, that's good," Craig said, although it still vaguely alarmed him. (For one thing, who *were* these blue-haired old ladies from the fifties who showed up for this weirdness, and why? Jesus Christ, would Nicole still be doing this stuff when she was eighty years old?) "I love you," he said, "but the idea of wiping the drool off your bib for the rest of your life is less than sexy. Still, I'd do it."

"Well, you don't have to worry. Anyway, we have our own EMT. The sorority pays him to be at the events and—"

"That guy," Craig said, and propped himself up on his elbow. "That guy. You said you didn't know who he was."

"What guy?"

"The one who's always hanging around your sorority. I pointed him out. I said, 'He's got a patch on his pocket that says EMT,' and you were like, 'What's EMT stand for?'"

"Huh?" She pulled Craig back down to her and kissed his temple. "Your eyebrows are all furrowed, Craig. I hate that."

She'd said that a lot—that she couldn't stand to look at him when his eyebrows were "furrowed," and when he'd tried to explain to her that it would be his *forehead* that was furrowed, because furrows were lines and you couldn't have furrowed *eyebrows*, she'd said, "I don't care. I can't stand that face you make."

"You know perfectly well what EMT stands for," Craig said. "Do you play dumb with me a lot, Nicole?"

"So, like, are you asking if I'm playing dumb or just actually dumb?"

He laughed, and she kissed his forehead.

"Don't make fun of me," Nicole said, but she wasn't angry. She licked his forehead then and nuzzled into his neck, and he let his hands drift around the safe, soft, bare skin of her torso.

65

Kurt embraced Mira in front of the students with all that Eastern European physicality she remembered from her year in that part of the world—smelling strongly of cologne, literally lifting her off her feet.

"Mira!" he said, and set her back down.

When she turned back around to her class, they were staring at her with what could have been alarm, but mostly, she supposed, they were registering their surroundings (the starkness, the coldness) and smelling the lively, corporeal presence of Kurt against the antiseptic smell of the autopsy room on the other side of the sliding doors, from which he'd emerged wearing his white smock, red hair tucked up into a gauzy blue cap, big grin sans one front tooth.

"Mira," he said again, and then looked at her students looking at him. He raised a hand to them and said, "Welcome to the morgue."

There was a burst of laughter, followed by nervous silence. The students nodded back with more energy than usual. Mira could already tell which of the girls were hoping to faint—although these were rarely the ones who actually fainted. The actual fainters were usually the tough guys or the serious young women who'd always wanted to be surgeons.

"We'll be entering the 'Waiting Mortuary' in a moment," Mira said, and gestured for the class to follow her through the sliding glass doors. "This is the part of the morgue that was specifically designed for the purpose of confirming that a dead body was actually deceased. Until very recently, as we've already discussed, there were no trusted methods for verifying death, and people had sincere fears of being buried alive. The Waiting Mortuary was designed to house the dead for a period of time during which attendants would be on alert for any sign of life. Right, Kurt?"

Kurt nodded sincerely. He was nothing if not sincere. When Mira had first met him, they had been leaning over a grave full of Serbian dead together, peering down.

Skeletal remains. Some scraps of clothing. A couple of wristwatches. A ring.

Kurt had turned to her, looked at her for what seemed like a long time, and then he'd reached over and put his hand over her eyes.

Since his move to the States, Mira had seen Kurt only during these visits with her classes to the morgue. She'd asked him to have coffee with her once, but he'd said he was busy. She invited him over to dinner once, but he'd declined.

"Your husband wouldn't like it."

"No, he *would* like it," Mira insisted. "Clark would like to meet you. He's heard so much about you."

"No," Kurt said again. "I am a single man. He looks at me one time. He knows I feel for you. I am a shy man, Mira. Large, yes, but timid. I do not want to fight your husband."

"Fight?" Mira had exclaimed, and laughed out loud, but Kurt was serious, and she realized that because of this seriousness, there could be no dissuading him without insulting him, without implying that her husband would never have considered him a rival, that there would be no fight. So she hadn't argued—although, when Clark had laughed and laughed after she told him about Kurt's fears, so adamantly amused, she'd briefly considered telling him, that, actually, Kurt had been a figure for quite a while in her sexual imagination.

His large Eastern European presence with his scent of cologne and his experience of the world, and war, and hardship, and death.

Kurt bowed a little to Mira's students then and said, "You must be very quiet, although of course the dead cannot hear." (Again, excited and uneasy laughter.) "But because, you know, the word *morgue*, it is a French word. It means, at one and same, 'to look at solemnly,' and 'to defy.'" Kurt waited for this to sink in, and then said, "You see, the sameness? And the strangeness?"

They were all nodding by this time. Perhaps they did understand, or maybe they were starting to feel as if their lives depended upon the goodwill of this man, their diener.

They stopped at the sliding glass doors. Mira turned and said, "Here we are in what the Victorians quaintly referred to as the Rose Cottage. At children's morgues, they called it the Rainbow Room. And though these euphemisms might be charming, and funny, we have to remember that eventually most of us will find ourselves in a morgue, not *viewing*, but *viewed*."

"*Too*-day," Kurt said, "we have a man who has had a brain aneurysm. We have a woman of old age. We have a suicide. But I must warn you, because it is disturbing, there are a family, two children, father, grandmother, they were hit by a head-on. It is a busy day at the morgue."

One or two of the students took a step backward, and began to look around as if in a panic to find the exit.

"As I've said," Mira said (pointlessly, because no one ever left), "this is optional. You can wait for us here, or leave altogether if you need to. No penalties."

The shock turned to resignation then. In some, it looked like excited anticipation. They might insist that they did not want to see dead bodies, but they did. And each semester this viewing was a turning point in her class. For a while afterward, anyway, they would feel in a way they hadn't felt before that the living body was a temporary condition. Funereal black would no longer be a fashion statement. They would communicate with one another and with her more carefully.

The glass doors slid open, and Kurt stepped through them, and Mira and all of her students followed.

66

I love you," Nicole said again, and squeezed her eyes and kissed him. "I love you, and I love you, and I love you. But now I have to go."

He watched Nicole's small, tight, perfectly smooth body as she got out of his bed to slip into the black dress she'd bought to wear that night to her sorority's ridiculous ritual. Except for the girls who were being raised, who wore white dresses, the others were to wear funeral black. The ones who'd already been raised, and the ones who were yet to be raised, were "mourners."

It *was* ridiculous, he thought, even as he admired the dress as Nicole unfurled it from the hanger she'd so carefully put it on when she brought it to his room—and even more ridiculous that the sorority hadn't been imaginative enough to come up with a name for it that didn't rhyme with *hazing*.

Still, he vowed, he would say no more about it. It was the kind of absurdity you had to be outside of to see. Nicole, he knew, would have found absurd the painfully hard slaps on the ass his track teammates gave each other after a meet, and the writers' conferences he went to with his father (languid poets and novelists wandering around with glasses of wine and little leather-bound diaries), not to mention the tradition among teenage males in Fredonia every winter, just before the ski resort opened, of getting naked in the middle of the night on the slopes, dropping acid, and beating the living shit out of each other.

Briefly it crossed Craig's mind to call Lucas and ask him to crash the party with him, but he dismissed it instantly. He couldn't risk the wrath of Nicole's sisters again. He wasn't even allowed to step onto the porch to pick her up anymore. And Nicole would hate him for it.

Her black dress was made of something that seemed silkier than silk. Craig sat up with his feet on the floor, and had to will himself not to crawl to her on hands and knees and kiss the hem of it. She'd gotten her hair cut a few weeks before, and although it was still long, there were blunt little ends now that curled up a little around her shoulders. She'd started wearing it loose more often. Sometimes, when she was studying or thinking or standing in front of the mirror, she'd run her fingers through it and it would appear to pour through them like molten gold.

Now she pulled out Perry's desk chair and started rolling a sheer black stocking up her leg, and Craig stared at her ankle until she started to laugh.

"You're drooling, Craig," she said, and he snapped his mouth closed.

Her other foot was still bare.

The toenails were painted pale pink. In the light that shone through the crack in the curtains, those toenails seemed to glow—and then he *was* on his knees, crawling across the floor, taking the foot in his hands, cradling it, bringing it to his lips, kissing first the top of it, up near the ankle, and then moving down toward the toes, until she was squealing, "Stop! Stop! It tickles!" And then he heard a key flip the lock on the door, and Perry was standing there, looking down at Craig, in his underwear, on his knees in front of Nicole, holding her bare foot to his lips.

"Excuse me," Perry said, looking up to the ceiling. "But if you could open the door when you're done. I've got to get my food plan ID out of the desk to get some dinner." The door slammed shut behind him, but not before Craig and Nicole had burst out laughing. How could they not? What must the scene have looked like to Perry? Craig released the foot and took her face in his hands, and pulled her gently toward him for a kiss, and then sat back on his heels to look at her. All that gold hair. Her cheeks flushed.

He tried not to imagine her then, in a basement, in a black dress, a bunch of drunk and stoned sorority girls holding hands and chanting.

"We'd better hurry," Nicole said. "Perry will be mad."

"Screw Perry," Craig said, loudly, toward the dorm room door, as if for Perry's benefit, although he doubted Perry could hear him through the solid wood of the door, and he really had no great desire to hurt Perry's feelings or piss him off. Perry had been particularly nice lately, letting Craig go on and on about his parents' divorce, offering commiserating head shakes. He was gratifyingly appalled by the behavior of Craig's mother, leaving his father. Once, he'd been in the room when Craig had called home and his mother had said to him, wearily, "Craig, this has nothing to do with you. This is between me, and Dad, and Scar."

"Between you and Dad and *Scar*?" Craig had shouted, and then, without waiting for her answer, he'd slapped his phone shut and thrown it against the wall.

Perry had jumped up from his computer and taken Craig by the shoulders and said, in the voice of a really mature guy, "It's okay, man. It's okay. You gotta calm down, okay?"

He'd helped Craig duct-tape his cell phone together again. (Perry was great at fixing broken mechanical things, as Craig had learned when Perry'd accidentally stepped on his own calculator.) Afterward, he'd gone to Z's with Craig, and they'd gotten pretty shitfaced—Craig, albeit, much more shitfaced than Perry.

And Craig found that he had grown oddly fond of the way Perry bleached his socks and rolled them into obsessive little balls lined up in the top drawer of his dresser. When Nicole was off at some sorority function, they'd eat in the cafeteria together, and now and then they'd go down to Winger Lounge and sprawl all over the couch to watch some basketball game neither of them cared about.

"Don't be mean to Perry," Nicole said. "He's like family."

Craig turned back to Nicole. She wasn't joking. She was so sweet.

"You're right," Craig said. "I lucked out in the roommate department."

"Yeah, Perry's true blue." She was looking at the ceiling as she said this, and her eyes looked oddly blank to him. He stood up so he could see her better, and even from overhead, the expression on her face seemed strange to him. She looked pale, he thought. Even her irises.

"What?" she asked, without looking at him, as if she were blind.

"Are you okay?" he asked.

"Why wouldn't I be?"

"I . . . don't know."

"Then don't be silly." There was so little intonation in her voice, and her face still looked weird. Could he be having one of those dreaded acid trip flashbacks, even though he hadn't dropped acid for years?

"Nicole?"

She snapped out of it then, and looked at him. Pure Nicole. Little dimple near the right corner of her lip. He was so relieved, he put a hand on his chest and sighed.

"What's the matter, sweetheart?" she asked.

"Nothing," he said, but suddenly he had a very bad feeling about the Spring Event.

"Nicole," he said, kneeling down again at her feet, looking up at her. "Can't you blow this off? This is so fucking stupid, and—"

"Are you crazy, Craig?" She was serious. She looked sincerely shocked, as if he'd suggested they jump off the roof together. He shook his head, to let her know he wasn't going to push it. Instead, he straightened up, and she slid the stockings all the way on, and slipped her feet into lacy black heels, blew him a kiss, opened the door, and Craig heard her call bye-bye to Perry, musically, as she stepped out of the room, and he stepped in.

"Want to go to dinner?" Perry asked, grabbing his meal card off his desk, as if he hadn't just walked in while Craig was half-naked kissing

Nicole's little foot, as if it were just any of the other hundreds of times they'd headed down to the cafeteria together.

6 7

From the Waiting Mortuary, Professor Polson's friend Kurt took them into a hallway lined with doors.

There were numbers nailed to the doors, but the numbers seemed random. Room 3 was adjacent to 11. Room 1 seemed to be missing altogether. Tacked to the door of Room 4 was a photograph of a white cat standing beside a blue mailbox. Perry wondered about that photo, in a place where there were no others, what the significance of that could be, when someone in a pale green shower cap and matching scrubs opened the door and looked out, white light pouring on him (or her), before shutting it again.

Everything in the hallway was bright, and cold. It wasn't the outdoor, winter kind of cold, but a dry, artificial cold, as if freeze-dried air were being poured down from the ceiling by the fluorescent lights.

When they reached the end of the hallway, Kurt stopped, turned, and held up a hand.

"Thank you for being so quiet," he said. "We do not have them today, but this is where sometimes a parent or a wife or husband must come to identify a deceased person. It is not like in the TV show, exactly, because we do not bring them into a room and take off a sheet and show them their loved one's face. Instead they are shown the effects. Wallet, jewelry, et cetera, and then a Polaroid photograph of the deceased's face. They know, or do not know, and if they are not sure, they must see. If they are sure, but still wish to see the body, they may request. It is easier, the Polaroid. Luckily for us, today, any families have already been and gone."

Nicole. Nicole had been here, of course, and it had been Josie Reilly who'd come to identify her—and although it was utterly impossible to imagine Josie Reilly clipping down this hallway in some pair of cute little shoes, it was even harder to imagine Nicole in this cold brilliance, laid out in whatever manner they laid out the dead, which he was about to see, and suddenly did not want to.

But wasn't this one of the reasons he'd taken this class? To see for himself?

He felt exhausted, dizzy, as if a grave mistake had been made by someone he used to be and no longer was. He put a hand to his head.

Professor Polson, standing off to the side of the hallway, looked over and raised her eyebrows as if to ask him, *you okay?* But she seemed pre-occupied, too, looking at Perry as she also held her cell phone to her ear. After a few seconds, she looked at it in the palm of her hand, and then she seemed to be scrolling through her messages, or her address book. The fluorescent light turned her hair to a reddish gleaming that Perry had never quite noticed before. He watched her until he noticed out of the corner of his eye that Karess was staring at him, again, staring at Professor Polson.

"Today," Kurt said, "is an autopsy, but it is not yet to begin. I am tak-ing you to autopsy room, where there is one body, which you will see it. This is not someone who has been disfigured, but will look typical of a corpse who has died by strangulation, because it is believed he has hanged himself. If you will faint, or be disturbed, you might wish to not."

Kurt nodded solemnly then, as if they'd all understood what he meant, and then, whether they did or not, they followed him into Room 42—all except Professor Polson, who was again holding her cell phone to her ear, seeming to be trying to get a connection, which Perry thought pretty unlikely, deep in this basement, a place out of which he imagined very few cell phone calls were intended to be made or received.

"We shall proceed," Kurt said, "four people at a time. You will wear booties, cap, and gown." He pointed to a doorless locker where the mint green garb was hanging on hooks, and he shrugged. "We have only so many clothes." He made *clothes* a two-syllable word, and tapped four students—one of them Karess—on the shoulder, pointing toward the locker. "You must wear such cloth-es when there is a body."

Karess looked backward then, directly into Perry's eyes, seeming to be asking for some kind of guidance.

Stupidly, apologetically, Perry smiled frozenly, and she looked away. Her new friend Brett Barber was another one of the four included in the first group, and he leaned over and whispered something into Karess's hair. Perry guessed it was a bad joke when he saw Karess lift a shoulder as if to block Brett from saying anything else—a flinch—and then she was stripping off her coat and her ratty, lovely sweater, bearing her long, thin arms for the surgical scrubs, and sliding the pale green of them over her body.

68

Mira couldn't figure out how to turn up the volume on the cell phone she'd bought to replace the one Clark had taken with him when he left. It was a cheaper model, but it had even more buttons and games and gadgets than the older, more expensive one.

During Kurt's spiel about the autopsy room, and while the first group of students were putting on their surgical booties and gowns, Mira had noticed a new voice mail—the little cartoon envelope on her cell phone window—although she'd never heard the phone ring. She called for her messages immediately, worried it might be Jeff, that the twins needed something, or he needed to know something, or something worse. (Andy had taken to crawling on the back of the couch, and Mira had taken on terrors that he'd fall off and hit his head on the window behind it.)

At some point, Mira had stopped expecting Clark to call, and she figured that if he came home while Jeff was there, Jeff could handle it. Jeff was far too affable to pose any threat to Clark.

But the message wasn't from Jeff. The call was from the college (Mira recognized the first three numbers on the caller ID as the university's prefix), but she could barely hear the message, and couldn't figure out how to turn the volume up. It seemed miraculous that she was managing to get any reception at all, there in the morgue, deep in the basement of the hospital—all cinderblocks and heavy fire doors—but reception didn't do any good if she couldn't make out the message:

"Mira, this is . . ." (Dean Fleming?) ". . . after all . . . within the next couple of . . . absolutely imperative that . . ."

It surprised and alarmed her that he already had this new phone number. She'd left it with his secretary only two hours earlier. She didn't recall his ever dialing her cell or home number before, always casually leaving his messages on the voice mail in her office, or scrawled on sticky notes and left on her office door.

Mira hit Return Call, but as soon as she did, the phone went dead in her hand.

Perry Edwards walked past then, made eye contact with her, and Mira flipped her phone closed, held up a hand for him to stop.

"Perry," she said. "I've got a call I've got to return. I'm going out to the alley, or maybe up to street level if I have to, can you—?"

He was nodding before she'd had her request articulated. "Sure," he said. "I'll come get you if we need you."

"Yeah," Mira said. "If, God forbid, someone faints, or—?"

"We'll be fine," Perry said. "You go ahead."

"Thank you, thank you, thank you," she said, hurrying out. He was such a good kid. Mira had thought they'd stopped making his kind around 1962.

She'd had an urge to kiss his cheek before she hurried out with her phone, the way she might have kissed Andy or Matty's cheeks, but she didn't. She just said thank you again for a fourth time, long after he could have heard her.

69

Why are you playing games with him?"
"What games?" Nicole asked.

"What *games?*"

She was pulling on a green silk tank top, no bra, and let it linger over her breasts before she covered them, and then she turned her back on Perry.

It was exactly the cream white expanse he'd imagined with his eyes closed and his hands running down it, but he winced and turned his face away when he realized what it reminded him of: Mary. Her backless prom dress. Slow-dancing to some dumb song while she whispered to him about how in love with him she was. His hand on the bare expanse of soft skin between her shoulder blades.

Nicole came over, wearing the tank top and nothing else, and sat down on the bed beside him. She ran her hand up his chest, to his neck, let it linger there, and then lifted it to his cheek, and then up to his eyes, the lids of which she gently closed with her fingertips before leaning over him and kissing them.

Perry felt the staticky gossamer wisps of her blond hair around his face, her breath (licorice, Mountain Dew) near his ear. She ran her hand down his side, to his hip. She moved her mouth down to his Adam's apple, kissed it, licked it, and then bit it hard enough to make him flinch, and then she sat back and laughed.

He opened his eyes. "You didn't answer my question," he said.

"No," Nicole said. "You didn't answer *mine.*"

Perry put a hand over his eyes so he was no longer looking at the delicate curve of her breast beneath the silk top, or the cool shoulder bone, the startlingly perfect flesh of her upper arm. If he looked further, he could have found the perfect golden triangle between her legs. Who was he, to be doing this with her? Who was *she?*

With a hand over his eyes, he said, "Craig thinks you're a virgin, Nicole. He thinks you're a Christian, and some kind of white-bread Midwestern milkmaid."

"Well, he thinks you're a great roommate, and a true-blue Boy Scout. He thinks *you're* a virgin, too."

"Yeah. I'm a shithead, and I admit it. A shitty friend. A shitty room-mate. But he just tolerates me. He thinks he's going to *marry* you. He thinks you're the future mother of his children. Pure angel. He thinks it's his duty to preserve your innocence in this filthy world."

Nicole laughed again, and said, "Well, I'd say he's the one playing the game, in that case."

Perry waited for her to go on. She didn't, and eventually he asked, "What do you mean?"

"Well, why does he want to believe those things? And if that's what he wants to believe, why shouldn't he?"

"Because it's not true."

"But he doesn't want the truth. The kind of girl he thinks I am, he's never going to find anyway."

"So, you just figured out what kind of girl Craig wanted, and decided you'd pretend to be that?"

"Isn't that what everyone does?"

"What? No!"

"No? What was all that class-ring crap with you and Mary about? Seems to me like you had her game all figured out, and played it pretty well for a nice long time."

Perry sat up. He put his hand to his Adam's apple, where she'd bit him. It was damp, and when he looked at his fingers, he was surprised to see a drop of blood on them. "What the hell are you talking about?" he asked. "*Mary's* the one who had *me* figured out."

"No," Nicole said, shaking her head, still smiling. "You knew she wanted that whole Eagle Scout thing. Small-town boy. Good daddy some-day. Gonna work at the Edwards and Son Lawn Mower Shop in Bad Axe and tinker with the minivan on weekends. She thought all that ambi-tion—the scholarships and the grades and the SAT scores—was all about making sure you could buy her a nice little house on the outskirts of town and an engagement ring a year or two after you got your high school diploma, and started with the babies. And that game worked out really well for *you*, didn't it? You had the sweetest girl at Bad Axe High for three years, and then you ditched her. Did you ever once tell her the real story—that your actual plan was to go to a fancy university, maybe study something like philosophy? Go to school for about ten more years, and then maybe travel around Europe with a backpack for a few more? Jesus Christ. Poor Mary must still be lying awake at night wondering what the hell happened, who the hell she was actually dating all that time she was dating you."

Perry's heart was pounding—not just in his chest, but in his throat, throbbing against his Adam's apple. It was pounding in his wrists, his legs, his temples. He was out of the bed without knowing he'd stood up, looking down at Nicole, who was looking up at him, still with that fucking little smile—and he wanted to say something horrible to her, something that would change her life, something that would scare her, something—but he couldn't. He never would. Looking down on her smiling up at him, he couldn't even maintain the desire to say it.

Jesus.

No wonder Craig was such a dupe and he himself was such a chump, a backstabber, a lying asshole.

She was *so* beautiful. Plato's ideal, as he now knew from Philosophy 101. She always had been, but now he could see it for what it was, even knowing that it wasn't what it appeared to be:

Her face was tilted sweetly, like that of a sparrow or a kitten, and she wore that ludicrously girlish smile, and Perry was suddenly reminded of what must have been her second-grade school photograph. Pigtails. No front teeth. Frozen in black and white wearing a little bit of lace around her collar and a silver cross, and then he remembered with perfect clarity sitting behind her in fourth grade, Mr. Garrison's class. They were talking about sanitation, and Nicole had raised her hand and asked Mr. Garrison, "What *happens* to the poop after it's flushed down the toilet?" and all the other kids, especially the boys, were doubled over with laughter at the sound of the word *poop* coming out of the pretty little mouth of Nicole Werner, who turned around to Perry then, horrified, blushing two bright spots on her cheeks, looking straight at him, as if for help, and Perry was incredibly relieved that he'd reacted, himself, too slowly to laugh, and was able now to look her in the eyes, shrug his shoulders, as if to say, *Who knows what these idiots are laughing about? Who cares?*

Now he was looking at her, lying half-naked on his bed, the strap of her silky top slipping over her beautiful, womanly shoulder, and Perry couldn't open his mouth, but he knew by her expression that he was asking her with his eyes to tell him, *Is that who I was? Is that who Mary thought I was? Is that what I did? How did you know when even I didn't?*

Instead of answering, she stood, gathered her jeans off the floor, slid them up, and he watched, remembering only a few months before, when he'd found her standing on the front steps of Godwin Hall wearing that bulky sweatshirt—homesick and sad—and how she'd put her head on his shoulder and cried, and the helpless way his mouth had opened, and nothing had come out. Had she really been homesick and sad? Or had that, too, been some kind of test?

Now Nicole put her arms on either side of his face and kissed him (a quick, sweet, nonsexual parting kiss) and said, "Hey. It's okay. We come from the same place, Perry. I know who you are, and you know who I am. I'll see you around, okay?"

70

Shelly found them on the Internet with no trouble: the parents of Denise Graham, the Omega Theta Tau "runaway." As the desperate tended to do in a computer age, they'd created a website: BringBackDenise.com.

There she was on Shelly's computer screen—a blond beauty with big blue eyes. If it hadn't been for the coloring, she could have served as Josie Reilly's stunt double. The same straight, shiny, shoulder-length hair. The smoky eye makeup. The perfect gleaming teeth.

In this photograph, Denise Graham was wearing a lacy tank top. She was sitting in a plaid armchair that had the look of family room furniture. There was a longhaired cat in her lap. Denise Graham was petting it, smiling.

PLEASE! DENISE GRAHAM IS OUR BELOVED, BEAUTIFUL, BRIL-
LIANT DAUGHTER. SHE DISAPPEARED FROM HER SORORITY IN
MARCH, AND HAS NOT BEEN SEEN SINCE.
The bright red capital letters went on to scroll out the details. The
time and date of her last contact with her parents. Her height and weight
(5'5" and only 115 pounds). Also, her favorite foods (nachos, Dr.
Pepper) and various nicknames (Shiny, Sweeties, Neecey)—as if she, like the cat
in her lap, might need to be coaxed out from under a porch or a vehicle
with these pet names.

The Grahams' phone number was there, too—how many prank
phone calls, Shelly wondered, had this inspired?—along with their
address, their email addresses. They lived only thirty miles from the
university town where their daughter had disappeared.

Twice Shelly picked up the phone to call them, and twice she composed emails to them, and then she decided she would simply drive to
Pinckney and introduce herself, because, really, what did she have to
offer them, or to ask them? Better that they should see her standing
there humbled on the doorstep by their grief.

Or so she'd thought until she pulled up in front of their house.

It was one of those lavish new subdivision *homes*, the type built to
appeal to people who, Shelly imagined, wanted a kind of English country life without the country. It had a winding cobblestone path through
some bright green bushes bearing red ornamental berries. A light snow
had begun to fall, and everything about the place looked like an adver-
tisement for a lifestyle, the lifestyle being lived in nearly identical houses
all throughout the subdivision, except that here the lawn hadn't been
mown or the hedges trimmed, and the mailbox at the end of the driveway appeared to have been struck by a car (little black door hanging
open, side dented). And every window in the house had drawn shades
or curtains pulled across it. Although there were two cars parked at
crooked angles to each other outside the closed garage, it looked, from
the outside, as if no one had been home for many months.

Shelly was about to back up, turn around, when the front door flew open and a woman in a hot pink bathrobe hurried, barefoot, onto the front steps and began to wave her arms wildly in the air, as if flagging down an ambulance or trying to help land a plane.

There was no doubt who she was.

The resemblance was uncanny. Here was Denise Graham, the runaway sorority girl, aged thirty years. Frantic, exhausted, maybe medicated or a little drunk. Having spent the last eight months in the desperate hope that every time the phone rang, the mail came, or a car pulled into the driveway it would bring her lost daughter home to her. "Who *are* you?" Denise Graham's mother called out to Shelly, and Shelly had no choice now but to park the car and get out.

The living room was a gracious shambles. Newspapers were piled up on the leather sofa. Mail was scattered across the antique coffee table. There was a stain (coffee? Pepsi?) in the center of the plush white carpet. The cat Shelly recognized from the website was sitting in front of the cold fireplace, stone still. Only its eyes moved when Shelly sat down in the only chair that wasn't piled with papers.

"I want to tell you right away, Mrs. Graham," Shelly said, "that I don't—"

"Call me Ellen," the woman said, as if the interruption, the intimacy of a first name, might change the course of this conversation and lead her to her daughter. She took a place on the couch across from Shelly without bothering to clear a place for herself, sitting down on a newspaper, a few pieces of junk mail. Her robe spilled open over her chapped-looking knees, and she didn't bother to pull it back into place. Out of respect, Shelly looked away, but the only other thing to look at in the room besides Ellen Graham or a messy pile of something was the cat, unnerving in its calm return of Shelly's gaze.

"Okay, yes," Shelly said, "and you can call me Shelly. But I want you to know that I don't have any information about your daughter. I'm with the university, but I work—or, *worked*—at the Chamber Music Society.

The only connection I have here is to one of your daughter's sorority sisters, and I've been reading about your daughter, and about another incident at the sorority—"

"Nicole Werner," Ellen Graham said. "That accident happened the night my daughter disappeared."

Shelly nodded, although the accounts she'd read put the disappearance of Denise Graham at least a week before Nicole's death.

"I'm not a professional in any way," Shelly continued, "and I probably have no business—"

Ellen began shaking her head. "I don't care about that," she said. "I don't care about anything except finding Denise. Who cares about being professional or even polite? That's gotten us nothing. We don't care if you're just plain nosy, if it's morbid curiosity. We just want someone to *help* us."

Ellen Graham's hands went to her knees then. She began to scratch at them absently, rocking back and forth.

Shelly paused, trying to decide where to go from here. She took a breath and said, "I was the first person at the scene of the accident. Nicole Werner's accident. I saw what happened, and I know that what they're saying happened *didn't* happen. I'm trying to find out what actually did happen. I don't know if it had anything to do with your daughter—"

"Denise," the woman said, as if she'd been waiting for an excuse to say the name.

"Yes," Shelly continued, "with Denise. But I know, now, that either the university, or the police, or the newspaper, or the sorority, or all of them together are willing to lie. They're covering something up. They've got something to hide. They're—"

"Who is this girl, the one you know from the sorority? Is her name Josie Reilly?" There was no mistaking the tone of Ellen Graham's voice when she said the name: bitter hatred. Fury, and anger, and derision.

"Yes," Shelly said, astonished. "How did you know?"

"I'll show you how I know," Ellen Graham said.

Although she stood up, her body seemed to retain the shape of the sofa, the posture of someone who'd been sitting in it, slumped, so long that she had *become* it. Shelly followed her to the stairway, where there was more plush carpet and piled-up debris—magazines, paperbacks, unopened envelopes. Ellen Graham simply stepped over the piles and around them, so Shelly did as well, and then they were in a long hallway hung with photographs of a girl who had to be Denise: Denise in a bassinet, zipped into what looked like a lacy pink envelope. Denise with pigtails, riding a tricycle. Denise in a startlingly low-cut blue satin gown, hand tucked under the arm of a boy in a tuxedo. Denise squinting into sunlight, wearing a mortar board.

They stopped in front of an open door.

"This is Denise's room," Ellen Graham said, as if Shelly could have mistaken it for anything else.

There were piles of stuffed animals on the bed—the prized, expensive kind of stuffed animals (endangered species with personalized name tags and hand-painted glass eyes), not the dragged-through-the-mud-since-preschool kind. There was a complete set of the *World Book Encyclopedia* on the bookshelf, ceramic cats holding the volumes in place. The only mess in this room was on the bulletin board, which was three layers thick with snapshots of adolescents in bikinis, or on bicycles, or driving boats, or singing into microphones, and glossy pages torn out of magazines, greeting cards emblazoned with YOU'RE THE BEST and WAY TO GO, GIRL, and small, dried-up things that must have been mementos from parties and dances and dates.

The girl's violin was out of its case, lying on its side on top of her dresser.

"I haven't changed anything," Ellen Graham said. "Before the police came, I made a chart of everything, where everything had been, so that everything would be exactly the way she left it, for when she comes back." She looked with unnerving ferocity into Shelly's eyes, seeming to be making sure Shelly understood that Denise *would come back*. "The only difference is that I put her clothes and things from her room at the sorority away, in her closet, when those girls brought me her things. "See?"

Ellen Graham led Shelly to a closet and slid the door open. A row of white lights blazed on without any switch being flipped, and Ellen

Graham stepped into it—into that light, and into that closet—turned a corner, and seemed to disappear before Shelly's eyes.

Shelly followed, but hesitated, and then she realized that this closet was the size of most rooms. A closet the size of a small apartment, or a trailer. It could not have been called, even, really, a walk-in closet. It was a space that could have been *lived* in. The only thing closetlike about it was the row after row of garments crammed together along the walls, and the fact that there were no windows.

Ellen Graham turned to look at Shelly and then tossed her arms up in the air, as if either to reveal something miraculous or to try to express the total futility of some unending task, and then she stood up on her tiptoes and pulled down a small black-enameled box, opened it, and turned it toward Shelly, as if to present her with the contents.

Black satin, bearing jewelry.

A pair of earrings.

Two grapelike clusters of opals and rubies dangling from elaborate Victorian-scrolled gold settings. These were the kinds of jewels that were kept under glass at Holyrood or Buckingham Palace. When Denise had worn them, they must have hung down to her shoulders. They must have weighed a ton, cost a fortune.

Ellen Graham picked one of them up and said, "They were my grandmother's. She was Italian. A countess. You don't have to believe me. You can look it up on the Internet."

Shelly nodded, and immediately regretted it, thinking the nod might make it appear that checking out Ellen Graham's grandmother's pedigree on the Internet was something she planned to do.

"I let Denise borrow these for the Spring Event. She was wearing a white dress we bought together in Chicago. She was so excited. I'd never even let her *touch* these before.

"My daughter is an angel, Shelly, but no one could claim that, when it comes to material things, she's overly responsible. She lost four cell phones between her senior year in high school and when she disappeared.

"Still, she knew what these were worth, and what they meant."

The Spring Event. Josie's description of it. The tequila. The coffin. Shelly wondered if Denise disappeared before or after.

"And that *fucking little bitch*," Ellen Graham said, her voice cracking on the last word before she snapped the enameled box shut and tossed it back on the shelf above her daughter's sweaters and dresses. "Josie Reilly! That fucking little bitch who came here with one of those other little Omega Theta Tau brats with a trunk full of my beautiful daughter's things. But no earrings. No white dress. 'Where are those?' I asked. How stupid was I?"

Ellen Graham was acting out a scene now, reading from a script.

" 'Have you seen, by any chance,' I asked, 'a white dress and a pair of beautiful Italian earrings worth about twenty thousand dollars?'

" 'Oh, *no*, Mrs. Graham. Golly. We went all through Denise's stuff. We brought you everything! We never saw a white dress or any Italian earrings. Denise was long gone before the Spring Event. Maybe she was wearing them when she left?' "

Shelly watched, waited for the scene to play itself out.

"Well, that didn't make sense, did it, Shelly? Why would Denise be wearing her Spring Event outfit if that was still three nights away? But, you know, I was confused. I was desperate. The police and the university and the Pan-Hellenic Society—everyone was looking into this. Everyone was working so hard. Wearing ribbons. Making phone calls. I just felt grateful not to be Nicole Werner's mother by that time. *That* mother had it worse than I did, I thought. I felt lucky anyone cared at all about Denise's disappearance with *that* on top of it.

"And, of course, these girls were so sweet. And so beautiful. Josie, and this other girl, Amanda Something. They could have *been* Denise. Their hair, and their clothes, and their 'likes' and 'you knows' and the little mannerisms, their pretty manicures. I thought, Okay, my daughter wore her grandmother's earrings and her Winter Event dress and got on a bus, and—and what?

"And by the time these girls brought me her things, it had been six weeks already. Six unbearable, sleepless weeks. And then the summer was over and the police told me they were 'working' on the case.

"So I sat down at the computer and looked her up—Nicole Werner—mostly because her parents were the only parents on earth I could think of who had it worse than I did. Maybe there was some kind of perverse satisfaction in that. I read every word I could find about the accident, and the funeral, and the memorial service, and the sorority and their fucking cherry trees, and then I came across one very, very interesting item.

"I came upon a photograph of that pretty dark-haired girl who'd brought Denise's belongings home. She'd been, it seemed, Nicole Werner's roommate. And there she was in this photograph, standing at a lectern giving a little speech during the dedication of the cherry orchard, supposedly two weeks after my daughter disappeared, and that little fucking slut was wearing my *goddamned Italian countess grandmother's earrings.*"

Shelly saw it, herself, then—the Googled image—suddenly before her: Josie Reilly in a sweet, tiny, black dress, gripping the sides of a lectern with both hands, wearing sunglasses, a branch full of blossoms lit up behind her head, and the bright glinting blur of Ellen Graham's grandmother's earrings dangling from her ears.

Those earrings hadn't even registered on Shelly until now. If she'd noticed them at all she'd have assumed they were some kind of costume jewelry, something Josie had bought at the mall—at Claire's, or Daisy's, one of those places where sorority girls love to stock up on baubles.

"It was September by then," Ellen Graham went on, despite the shaking of not only her voice but her whole body, "and I called in my baby brother, who's a bouncer at a bar in Ypsilanti—six feet tall and two hundred pounds of solid muscle—and we went straight to the Omega Theta Tau house and sacked the place. When we found them in her room, Josie Reilly pretended to be astonished that the earrings were my grandmother's. She claimed Denise had given them to her, told her they were costume jewelry. When I pointed out that I hadn't let Denise borrow them until just before she disappeared—well, it didn't make any difference. Those girls have a story and they're sticking to it. But I know for a fact that my daughter wasn't gone before the Spring Event. She was there, and she wore her dress, and she wore those earrings. I just don't know what happened after that."

"What about her phone? Did the police check the cell phone records?" Shelly asked. "And her attendance in her classes?"

"She'd lost her cell phone the week before. One of the four. We were getting her another one. And the only class she had from Monday until Wednesday was a lecture with three hundred students in it. Her violin lesson had been canceled because the professor was sick. It's a huge place, as you know. No one was keeping a record of where she was or wasn't.

"And those sorority bitches. Those lying little bitches. Denise was a girl who was Twittering and Facebooking and texting all day, and so are those other girls. They've got messages flying from one end of town to the other twenty-four/seven. So if they had no idea where my daughter was, why wasn't there *one single message* left on her Facebook page after the day she disappeared? How come I can't find one single girl who posted a word on the Internet saying, *Gosh, I haven't see my sorority sister in six months, anyone know where she is?"*

The light in the closet was so bright that Shelly's eyes had begun to tear. She put a hand to her forehead, like a visor. She looked at Ellen Graham, whose own eyes were so red-rimmed it appeared as if she'd lined them with lipstick.

She swallowed, and then asked, "What do you think, Ellen? What happened to your daughter?"

"You think we didn't try to contact the newspaper? You think we didn't make about a hundred trips to the police, to university security, to the administrators? I know the layout of the University Administration building like the back of my own hand. We hired a private detective. We tried to involve the FBI. We aren't perfect, but our daughter had no reason to run away from us."

Shelly believed her. Completely. Implicitly. Maybe Shelly had spent the last three decades of her life in academia, where no one really believed that anyone outside of it could actually be intelligent, but she knew otherwise. There was the hard, glittering force of pure intelligence in Ellen Graham's eyes. She could be anywhere, doing anything. She was smarter than Shelly, smarter than all of them.

Ellen Graham put a hand to her own throat, and said, "I know what happened to Denise, but I don't know why, and I can know it without accepting it. I knew it that night, the night of that Spring *Event*." She spat the word *event*. "Somebody killed my daughter. Her dad and I were on a jet, on our way home from our vacation. It was the middle of the night. We were over the clouds. I was planning to call the sorority the second we touched down, to see how her special night had gone, but when I looked out the window, there she was, wearing her white dress and my grandmother's earrings. She was kind of peering in at me, like she wondered if I could see her, and there were tears running down her face, and when I put my hand to the window it was burning hot, and then she was gone, and now I'll never see my daughter alive again."

There was no self-pity in it. No whining. Just finality, factual clarity. Denise, Shelly realized, would have grown up to be just like her mother: The mother the slacker teachers in the public school would hate to see coming. The woman on the school board who actually made things change. The kind of person who lived the good, fulfilling life, who paid the taxes that made it possible for so many of Shelly's academic colleagues to spend their lives feeling superior. Denise Graham, like her mother, would have married intelligently, maybe stayed home with her children, seen to it that they ate a hearty breakfast every morning, been there to pick them up after school, to supervise their homework, to drive them to their music lessons. She'd have enjoyed her home, her town, her parents as they slid from vital presences into old age. She'd have been at their bedsides when they died.

Shelly had to will herself to hold Ellen Graham's gaze, and then the only thing she could think to say was, "But, you're still looking for her . . ."

Ellen Graham snorted, tossed her head like a horse with an uncomfortable bit in its mouth. "What else?" she said. "What else would you have me do now?"

71

Karess came out of the autopsy room looking bleached of color and flushed at the same time. She had her hair tucked up into the shower cap, and when she took the cap off her head, the hair came tumbling down around her shoulders.

She tossed the scrubs to Perry and then tossed the cap in his direction, too, although it landed at his feet. She kicked the booties off with some difficulty, stumbling backward and managing not to fall down only because Brett Barber was standing behind her. She slammed into him, and he caught her awkwardly under the arms. Karess shook her head and looked back at Brett, appearing more annoyed by his presence than grateful. She hurried past Perry, and he could smell her, both in the gown she'd tossed to him and in the breeze she left as she ran: Formaldehyde. Sweat. Shampoo. Powdered flowers.

She smelled, he thought for a horrible moment as he slipped the gown she'd tossed to him over his arms, like the church on the morning of Nicole Werner's funeral.

"It's fucked up in there," Brett said, leaning in to Perry. "I'm just warning you. This whole thing is fucked up. Professor Polson should get her ass fired for bringing us here."

Perry did not even dignify Brett Barber, who was sweating profusely and breathing hard, with a nod. After he got his scrubs on, Perry followed the other three students and Kurt through the doors to the autopsy room. The doors closed behind him with a pneumatic hush, and the effect was like being teletransported onto another planet, with an entirely different kind of atmosphere: thin, and dustless, and tinged with a terrible sweetness. The walls were white, but everything else was made of gleaming stainless steel, even the floor, at the center of which there was a drain hole. Perry found himself in the center of the room, following Kurt and the other students, with that drain hole at his feet.

In it, there was a nestlike tangle of tawny-colored hair.

Perry took a step back and felt a cold pulsing at his right temple, as if someone were tapping at it with an index finger inside a cold latex glove. He put his hand to the temple.

"Are you okay?" Kurt asked. "You are okay?"

It took Perry a moment to realize that Kurt was talking to him, and that the other three students were staring. He swallowed and said, "Yeah," and made a conscious effort not to look at the drain hole again, or speculate about its contents.

"Here we have the cabinet of the instruments needed for autopsy," Kurt said, pointing at a brilliantly shining silver cabinet. He reached into a metal bin and briefly held up what looked like a large, thick needle before tossing it back down.

"Here," Kurt said, "is chalkboard for recording data." Perry looked in the direction Kurt had pointed. It was the kind of blackboard Perry remembered from his first-grade classroom in Bad Axe, before the whiteboards and the Magic Markers. What looked like a crude drawing of a torso was on it. A few dots were drawn around the neck. *A–17–00 Wt NTD DB* was underlined several times beside the drawing. Beside that was a list, checkmarks next to each word:

> Liver X
>
> Rt. Lung X
>
> Lt. Lung X
>
> Rt. Kidney X
>
> Lt. Kidney X
>
> Spleen X
>
> Thyroid X
>
> Brain X

Apparently, the last autopsy had been completed.

"The word *autopsy*"—Kurt pronounced the word as if it were one long vowel—"means 'see for yourself.'"

The students giggled a little at the colloquial quality of this. The simplicity.

"So . . ." Kurt said. (There was no overlooking the showman in him now. He had been waiting for this part. Back in Yugoslavia, he'd probably been an amateur actor, or a magician.) "See for yourself."

He pulled out a drawer by a handle that Perry hadn't even noticed was in the wall. It made a slippery tinny sound, and suddenly it was rolling into the room so quickly that the little group of them had to part to make room for it. And then the smell was *exactly* as he remembered it from Nicole Werner's funeral—Karess's sweetness as he slipped the gown over his head—and it took Perry several seconds to realize that there was a sixth person in the room suddenly:

A person on a gurney.

A naked guy with bluish fingers and toes and a sheet thrown casually over his stomach, and what looked like some kind of crude embroidery over his throat, and Perry had to stop himself from saying anything, because the first thing that came to his mind to say was, "Lucas. What are *you* doing here?"

72

The cafeteria was steamy, a runny fog of it on the windows that looked out onto the Godwin Hall courtyard, a wavering cloud of it hovering above the stainless-steel bins of pasta and Mystery Meat and soggy broccoli.

As always, Perry went straight to the salad bar with a little brown plastic bowl on his tray.

("How do I know how much dinner I want until I have my salad?" he'd say when Craig asked him why he didn't just get everything at once.)

Craig got a pile of manicotti with a couple of slices of garlic bread tossed on top, a big cup of the broccoli, and a plastic glass of Coke without ice, and took it to the table he and Perry always occupied when they ate together.

"Sorry, again," Craig said when Perry sat down across from him with his pale lettuce and a little stack of baby carrots drizzled with something one shade of orange darker than the carrots. "I hope you didn't sustain any emotional damage, witnessing me kissing Nicole's sweet little feet."

Perry sighed and picked up his fork. He seemed to be purposely avoiding Craig's eyes. Even though they'd been getting along so much better since the start of the semester, it still seemed to piss Perry off royally when he found some article of Nicole's lying around the room. One time he'd whipped a pair of her pantyhose (admittedly, they'd been lying under his desk chair) at Craig so hard that, if they'd been made of anything other than that airy pantyhose stuff, Craig might have gotten hurt. He wouldn't have liked it any better, Craig knew, stumbling in on the half-naked foot-kissing scene.

"But you'll get over it, right? Okay, man?" Craig asked, stabbing his fork into the manicotti, which gave way like clay, some of it spilling off the plate and onto the table. "You hear me, Perry? I'm genuinely sorry about—"

"Drop it," Perry said.

Craig shrugged. "Whatever," he said. "But, you know, if you had a girlfriend, I think I'd—"

"Drop it," Perry said again.

Craig nodded, but he was trying to think of something else to say, something to change Perry's mind about being all pissy. He had a hard time dropping things, he knew. He used to overhear conversations like this between his mom and dad, and it was always his dad who was saying, "For God's sake, can you just let it go?" and Craig would be thinking to himself, Yeah, why the hell doesn't she just shut up?, as his mom went on and on and on with her grievance or apology or explanation. Now Craig realized how hard it was to just drop something when you had something left to explain.

He said, after a few moments of silence, "I wish you'd loosen up about Nicole, man. She's my life. I'm your roommate, so it's sort of like—"

Perry put his fork down loudly on the table. It startled Craig, but he couldn't stop.

"I'm going to marry her, man," Craig said, looking up from the fork to Perry's stony expression. "This isn't just any college fucking-around kind of thing. This is love, and I—"

Perry pushed his salad bowl away, and it slid toward Craig. It might have landed in his lap if Craig hadn't put a hand up to stop it.

"What the hell's the matter with you, Perry?"

Perry leaned across the table then. Maybe it was just the humidity in the cafeteria, but his cheeks looked strangely flushed, and there seemed to be a light film of sweat at his temples and on his forehead—and then, as if he'd been thinking about it for a long, long time, Perry said, "Look, Craig, if you're not going to drop it you're going to have to hear something you don't want to hear, okay? I've been keeping my mouth shut, but if every time we have dinner you're going to start in on me about how uptight I am, and how Nicole's this innocent virgin, and how you two are so madly in love, I'm *warning* you, man, I'm going to tell you something you do not want to hear."

73

D id you get my message?" Mira said, bursting into the apartment. "I'm so—"

Jeff raised a hand to silence her. He was sitting cross-legged on the shabby Oriental rug on the floor of the apartment. Andy was at one of his knees, Matty at the other. They glanced at Mira, and then back at Jeff. "*Listen*," Jeff said, and Mira could hear the intensity in his voice, so she stopped, although what she had to tell him hardly felt like something that could wait.

Slowly Jeff lifted one finger of the hand that was raised, and moved it in front of the twins' eyes.

"One," Andy said.

Matty nodded. "One."

Jeff didn't look up at her. If he had, he'd have seen her stagger backward, a hand to her mouth. Mira had *never* heard either twin speak a recognizable word. Not *Mama*, not *Papa*, not one single word.

Then, like a magician preparing for a trick, Jeff put the hand behind his back and brought it around again with two fingers raised.

"Two!" the twins shouted in unison.

"Oh, my God!" Mira cried, holding her face in both hands.

This time there was no goofing around. Jeff raised the third finger, and before they even saw it, they screamed out, "Three!" and he turned to Mira, laughing. "Mira, they can get up to ten, no problem. I don't know what language you guys have been teaching them, but they have no problem with *mine.*"

It took Mira a long time, a lot of hugging of the twins on her knees, and the repetition of the trick over and over, up to five, up to eight, up to ten, before she had the heart to set the blocks out for them and say, "Mama will be right back."

Jeff stood up, grunting a little as he did (clearly he'd been sitting crossed-legged on the living room floor for a long time) and followed her into the kitchen, where, as soon as she was sure the twins couldn't see, Mira turned and threw her arms around his remarkably large, soft torso (how was it she'd always thought he'd looked so solid? In her arms he felt plump and pliable) and hugged him with her face pressed into his over-warm chest as he patted her sweetly between her shoulder blades. Mira could have stayed like that forever, breathing in the tavern and car and fast-food cologne of him. She would have liked to stay like that, and maybe have wept, and maybe taken him afterward to her bed, where she would have slept for hours in his arms, but she had to tell him what had happened. Still with an arm around him, she led him to the table, sat down, and began:

First, the morgue.

She had been trying to reach the office of the dean, to return his call, in a panic about what his indecipherable voice mail message to her could possibly have been about. She'd been pacing in the alley, punching numbers, holding the fucking phone to her ear, and every time his secretary answered, either the secretary couldn't hear Mira or Mira couldn't hear the secretary, or they were simply, abruptly, cut off. Mira had been inching away from the building, closer to the street, hoping to get better reception, but also afraid to stray too far from her class, when she heard the morgue door open, and turned to see Perry running into the alley in his mint green booties and scrubs, ashen-faced.

"Professor Polson, Professor Polson, Lucas is in the—"

She'd been alarmed by his expression, although she didn't understand what he was trying to tell her. She'd dropped the phone into her bag and followed Perry back, and hadn't bothered with the booties and scrubs, just burst through the doors, passing Kurt, who said to her as she passed, "You knew of this student?"

And, indeed, there he was—poor, sad, scroungy, familiar Lucas laid out under a sheet up to his shoulders, with what might have been a rope burn around his neck, his eyes closed.

"You knew of him," Kurt repeated, and Mira, fighting the urge to bolt from the room, could not even manage to nod. She put a hand to her mouth, and stifled what might have turned into an actual scream if she hadn't. Except for Perry, the other students had already left the room, thank God, but they were still out there stripping off scrubs, putting scrubs on, some still waiting to get their chance to see the autopsy room.

"Jesus Christ," Jeff said. "Lucas?"

They talked for a while about Lucas and how, if there had been a most-likely-to-hang-himself award on campus, Lucas might have won it. The drugs. The posture. The delusions. The nihilistic books and music. All that world weariness carried around in his hemp backpack. Still, Mira couldn't help but ask, "Do you think it had to do with Nicole Werner, with—"

"*Shit* yes," Jeff said. "A kid thinks he's had sex with a dead girl? Either he was mentally ill beforehand or he would have been after."

Mira told him then about the cryptic, urgent call from the dean.

"I haven't called him back yet," she said. "It's something urgent. What do you think he wants?"

"Nothing," Jeff said. "Staples—you're missing a couple. Or he wants to know if you need more. I know you don't have tenure yet, Mira, and I'm familiar with all the fantasies a person without tenure has, but, believe me, Dean Fleming is just calling to ask you if you like his new tie or something. Go in and see him. The sooner you get it over with, the better."

Mira felt such a rush of warmth again she was afraid she'd melt into tears. She'd desperately missed—without even knowing it—having an adult male tell her that everything would be okay. How direly she'd needed a man who, despite the obvious flaws in his personality, seemed competent, and sane, and full of goodwill toward her. All Mira could manage was to stare at him in wonder, and gratitude, and then Jeff was standing up, handing Mira the purse she'd dropped on the table.

"Go," he said. "Get thee to the dean. I have two hours before your little urchins destroy me with the secret linguistic and mathematical knowledge I was so foolish as to impart to them."

"Oh, Jeff."

"'Oh, Jeff' nothing. Go."

He pulled her up from her chair by the arm and pointed her toward the door.

74

Well, go ahead and fucking tell me, man. You think I can't handle it? What? Are you having regular wet dreams about my girlfriend? You think I don't know you have a hard-on five miles long for Nicole?"

"Fuck you, Craig."

"No, fuck you, Perry. Just tell me. You know you've been just shitting your pants and swimming in your own piss since I started dating Nicole, so why don't you just get it over with, you jealous fuck? Spew your guts.

You and your fucking Boy Scouts back in Bad Ass—did you used to sit around in your tents and jerk off to her yearbook picture or something? Nicole told me all about how some other dude knocked up your hometown girlfriend, so maybe you couldn't get it up, or—"

Perry shoved the table into Craig, and the salad he'd been eating and the manicotti that had been congealing on Craig's plate splashed over the edge of the table, splattering onto the linoleum with a sick wet-crap sound, and then Perry was over the table, not knowing how he'd gotten there, and his left hand was full of Craig's T-shirt and the other one was a fist making contact with Craig's nose, and then they were down on the ground, Craig's back slapping onto the manicotti and salad, and then Perry was staring into his roommate's bloody nose and hearing himself shout, "I've fucked Nicole, you fucking fool. Half of fucking Godwin Hall has fucked your virgin girlfriend, you stupid, stupid, deaf, blind, fucking idiot."

With each of the last six words, Perry lifted Craig off the floor by his T-shirt and pushed him back down, and then they were panting and bleeding and staring into one another's eyes, and something so horrible and honest and intimate passed between them at that moment (even worse than Perry's sudden realization that they had become, somehow, at some point, friends) that, for a horrible moment Perry felt that he *was* Craig, looking up, seeing his own face looking down—that they had switched places, switched faces, and bodies, and selves, and *become* each other.

Then some beefy guy in a steamy white apron hauled Perry up by the back of his shirt and shoved him toward the cafeteria exit.

75

I think," Dean Fleming said, making a motion in the air in front of his face as if trying to coax the words out of his own mouth, "some of this is, at best, questionable. Or, I should say"—more coaxing—"it raises questions. Or, at least, one could see how *questions might be raised.*"

Mira nodded. She had no idea what he was trying to say.

She was having a hard time concentrating on his face, which seemed oddly distorted by the pale sun shining through his window, directly onto him, as if he were standing in headlights. She tried to appear as if she were carefully considering his words as she glanced around his office. For some reason, which she felt sure was not intended to be ironic and also had nothing to do with the Edgar Allan Poe poem, Dean Fleming kept a taxidermied raven on his bookshelf, just over his left shoulder. It had the beady eye of Poe's bird, and Mira could easily have imagined it squawking, "Nevermore!" except that part of its beak had crumbled away and one of its wings was mostly sawdust. Mira couldn't keep herself from staring at it. Dean Fleming had pulled a copy of her first-year seminar syllabus out of a file drawer and placed it on his desk between them. Now he was directing his comments to the syllabus, as if those six stapled pages could hear him.

"I've received a number of such questions from parents, which is, of course, of less concern to me than the concerns raised by the students themselves—"

Mira recognized instantly the reference, the *deference*, the dean was making to a recent Honors College meeting, during which numerous professors had excitedly, resentfully called for a moratorium on what was called "parental meddling." Implications had been made that the dean was passively encouraging this meddling by not actively putting a stop to it. It had been generally agreed upon by Honors College faculty that this generation of college students had parents who were over-involved. That the students were "adults," and that when it came to issues of curriculum, grading, et cetera, the faculty should not have to answer to parents, was the subject of several long monologues during that meeting, during which Mira had watched the clock with a rising sense of despair and panic because she had told Clark she'd be home a half hour ago.

Now she nodded to the raven, and Dean Fleming continued to speak to her syllabus on his desk.

"I think we need to reconsider," he said, "not only the direction your teaching is taking, but also your research."

This time Mira was surprised enough that she looked straight at him, hard enough that he had to look up and meet her eyes. The light was pouring down baptismally on his head, and she noticed that either he had a bald spot that was just sprouting new growth or the cold November light was somehow singeing away a round place in his full head of hair. She tried to think about how to say what she was about to say before she said it, but her heart had started to race, and she simply blurted out, trying to keep her voice from shaking, "I felt that you seemed quite supportive of my new project when we last—"

Dean Fleming waved his hand. Mira noticed, for the first time, a small dark ruby on his pinky. He seemed to notice her noticing it, and he tucked the hand away beneath his desk.

"I was laboring," the dean said, "under a false impression."

Mira leaned forward. "Which was . . . ?"

"I didn't realize it was so, so, so—*death-laden*, so *popularist*. Of course this sort of thing can work in some cases, but those cases are rare. We're a research institution, Professor Polson, one of the most formidable in the country" (how many times had Mira heard *this* since her first on-campus interview here?) "and the field of anthropology is not, it seems to me, particularly well suited to the, the, the . . ."

Mira wiped her sweating palms on her knees, feeling the heat through the black tights she was wearing, as if her hands could burn straight through her clothes, melt her flesh into her flesh.

"Anyway," he said, "it's beside the point. The point is we can't have you teaching Death Studies in our college, or doing 'exposés' concerning university tragedies of the magnitude of the Nicole Werner incident. I'm sure you see, yourself, how unseemly it is. How, how, how . . ."

"Dangerous?" Mira sputtered, unable to help herself.

"Yes," Dean Fleming said defensively. "Yes, well, dangerous. But also unseemly. As I said. It isn't done. For one thing, this fascination of yours is not material for a serious academic project. The sort of research you're doing, and the teaching is, is—"

"—is what I was hired to teach, and to research. You were on my hiring committee, sir. Except for some improvements, the class I'm teaching follows the exact syllabus I presented at my interview, the one I recall you praising for its rigor. You said, and I believe it's in my evaluation from last semester, that I brought something both to the college and to my research that was 'dynamically different.' "

"That was prior to the Nicole Werner work."

"The Nicole Werner work? What do you mean?"

"I'm talking about the suicide of one of our students, Professor Polson. You must certainly understand the seriousness of this, that—"

Suddenly, she understood:

Lucas.

He was already getting heat for Lucas. After every suicide, there was a witch hunt. Mira had been on college campuses long enough to understand that.

She swallowed. At least now she knew what she was dealing with. At least now she could address it head on. Blame had to be laid.

She looked from the bright spot on the dean's head to the raven, and then down to the syllabus on his desk, and then back into Dean Fleming's small, piercing eyes. She took a deep breath and said, "I certainly understand the seriousness of suicide, sir. It's one of the things I try to bring to full light for my students. My major purpose in teaching the courses I teach is to deromanticize death, and to effectively convince a disbelieving segment of the population, youth, as to its *permanence.* Believe me, there were no students at the morgue today who don't understand that now."

"I've been informed that he was working with you. Lucas. That he'd—"

"He wasn't working with me. I interviewed him about Nicole Werner, yes, and—"

"And he says as much in his goddamned suicide note, Professor Polson. Do you have any idea what this means?"

Mira shook her head. She could feel her blood beating at her temples and behind her knees. His suicide note. She said, nearly spluttering the words, "He didn't commit suicide because of me." Then she took a moment to think about it, and actually laughed out loud. "There were reasons that boy killed himself, and there was plenty the college could have done, but none of that had anything to do with me."

"Well, maybe that's true, but you were a faculty member aware of his problems, and—"

"And I informed Mental Health Services after the interview. I spoke with three therapists. I spoke with Lucas himself. I made an *appointment* for him. I did everything except walk him over there myself."

"Well, you didn't inform his parents, who, as you can imagine, are—"

Mira laughed again, involuntarily, in amazement. "Oh, my God," she said. "Dean Fleming, I have a statement in my contract specifying that, under the Confidentiality of Academic Information Act, I can *under no circumstances* contact my students' parents. The university is a *closed system*. Remember? I'm not to contact police, medical professionals, and surely not *parents*. Those were your exact words when I was hired. A *closed system*."

He cleared his throat. He licked his lips. He paused for what seemed like a long time, and then he said, "You misunderstood. And this course of yours, it's encouraging a death cult in our college."

This time it was so funny Mira couldn't even laugh. "I'm encouraging a death cult?" she asked.

"Yes. There are girls directly influenced by your class who have started a club devoted to trying to contact Nicole Werner and some other dead girl. They claim to be seeing ghosts. They've done some serious injury to themselves, and to the facility. Cutting. That sort of thing. Their candles caused a fire."

Mira felt all the breath inside her leave. She waited for the dean to go on, but neither of them spoke, and finally she shook her head and said to the silence between them, "There are always crazy college girls. Those aren't my students. You can't blame me for what crazy coeds do in a dorm."

Dean Fleming looked around him then, as if he'd lost his raven and was trying to locate it, and then he put his hands on his desk, folded, looked back at Mira, and said, "Believe it or not, there's more." He leaned a little closer, as if there were someone else in the room who might overhear. He said, "There's the question of your relationships, Mira, which have been called to my attention. Your husband has informed me that you're involved in a . . . situation. With a student. An *extracurricular* situation."

Mira had then the sensation of having been hit by a blunt object, a blow to the head, and she remembered, suddenly, once, in the dark, getting out of bed and stumbling into a bookshelf, jarring a solid brass bookend off of it, and the blank, dull feeling when it smacked her just above her left temple.

Such surprise, it wasn't even painful. The pain was somewhere so deep inside her it did not register on any physical scale. It took her several seconds to open her eyes again, blinking, and recover enough to say, "What? My husband? You heard from my husband?"

"Yes. But that's only part of this. A part of it. I have my own concerns, my own reservations, about your relationship with Professor Blackhawk."

"Jeff?"

"Yes."

Yes.

The drive out of town to get her twins, passing, on the way, Dean Fleming, who was standing at a crosswalk.

Now, Mira understood that the blank expression on the dean's face as they drove by had been his way of registering the two of them together, maybe adding it up with other things he'd suspected. Idle gossip in the faculty lounge. Hunches, glimpses. "Jeff?" she asked again. It was the only thing she could think to ask.

"In truth, it's none of my business," the dean said, "although it's another delicate matter, and relationships between colleagues in a program as intimate as ours have to be discouraged. But I'm less concerned about Jeff Blackhawk than I am about Perry Edwards, who is a student. I know you know how seriously this university takes the crossing of the line between a student and a teacher, and I have to warn you, Mira, these are puritanical times we're living in. You can't expect to remain employed here and behave in a manner that is, that is, that is . . ."

Mira put her hand to her temple, feeling it again—that dull ache in the dark at the back of her head—and managed to say, again, "My husband called you? *Clark* called?"

Was it possible? Was that why he'd left? Was that why he'd seemed not to feel any guilt about taking her children away from her, and then not even calling to tell her where they'd gone?

Dean Fleming lifted a shoulder as if he weren't sure what his answer should be.

"Where is he?" Mira asked. "Where did Clark call you from?"

"Mira, this was some time ago, and your marital problems, although regrettable, aren't the reason why—"

She stood up, although she could not feel her legs beneath her. She said, looking down on his bright spot, his bald spot, his *soft* spot, "What *is* the reason, then, Dean Fleming? Because all of this, whatever *this* is, has been—no offense, Dean Fleming—utter bullshit."

She felt the shock of her own words register in the look on his face, but didn't wait for him to react. She held up a hand, and said, "I'm sorry. Forgive me. But there's something else happening here. This has nothing to do with Jeff Blackhawk, and certainly nothing to do with Perry Edwards. This has to do with Nicole Werner, and the sorority, doesn't it? It has to do with Nicole Werner, and my research, and my class, and Lucas and Perry, yes—but it's not what you're saying it is."

But what was it? She found herself saying it before she'd even thought it:

"The runaway."

Jeff's story was coming back to her now.

A new sense was being made of everything.

She said, as if in a trance, "The girl from the music school. The other sorority girl. No one's looking for her. Why is that, Dean Fleming? Why would the university so quickly drop—?"

"Oh, for God's sake, Mira. Don't become a conspiracy theorist now on top of everything else. Frankly, and I'm sorry to be so blunt here, you were always a wild card. When we hired you we didn't know, really, what we were hiring. We had no way of knowing. I'll admit I, like your students, was intrigued by the material and your passion for it, but this simply can't be allowed to go on. I'm sure I don't have to remind you here that you don't have tenure, so if you're interested in keeping your position, Professor Polson, I suggest you take what I've had to say here very seriously, and, and, and . . ."

But Mira had left his office before finding out whether this time the word for which he was so desperately searching ever found its way to him.

76

People laughed as they passed him in the hallway, but when they saw the expression on his face and the blood smeared across it, they stopped. Only Megan Brenner spoke:

"You okay, Craig? Did someone punch you in the face or something? What's on the back of your shirt? That's not blood, too, is it?"

Craig said nothing to her. Megan was perhaps the most petite fully grown human being he'd ever known. He could have wrapped his arms around her waist twice. He could have carried her across the Sahara and not even gotten thirsty or winded. He and Perry had taken to calling her Mega, because it was so absurd. He looked at her—that face peering up at him, the size of a cat's—and all he could do was nod.

He went to the boys' bathroom. No one else was in there. Just the slick, bright, urine-colored tiles (Perry had suggested they'd once been white; Craig had said the tile people had simply been thinking ahead) vaguely reflecting him at the sink as he washed the blood off his face, careful to avoid the actual mirror and his actual reflection in it, and tossed the T-shirt with the manicotti on it into the garbage can, and headed to his room to put on a new one.

Perry was back from the cafeteria himself, sitting at his desk chair with his head in his hands. He didn't look up when Craig came in, but he cleared his throat. For a terrible second Craig thought maybe Perry was going to say something, that maybe he'd even try to apologize, or explain, and if that happened, there was no way Craig was going to be able to take it:

He would have to kill Perry, or die trying.

But that wasn't what he wanted to do, not at all.

Perry had been on top of him, straddling him, not that different, really, from the way what's-her-name, the girl in the hot tub (what *was* her name?) had straddled him in the MacGuirres' pool house back in Fredonia, looking down on him, staring him in the eyes, except that he'd been inside that girl, and she'd been looking into him, pretending that fucking was some big spiritual experience.

He doubted it was, since she had the same experience every Saturday night in Fredonia with a different guy. She'd been stoned as hell, and so was he, but Craig remembered her saying as she stared into his eyes, "I know what you're thinking. You and I are one . . ."

And how she'd slapped him hard when he started to laugh.

Even then, with his dick seven inches into her, Craig couldn't remember her name, and he'd told her that.

But Perry.

Craig had known something at that moment. Something transcendent. Truly, this time, as Perry was straddling him, staring down at him, slamming him into the floor, Craig had felt his whole life grabbed like his T-shirt in Perry's fist, and yanked, and shoved back down, and it *was* a spiritual experience.

"Fucker. Asshole. Listen. You stupid, stupid idiot."

Perry was his friend. His first real friend.

He didn't want to kill Perry. He wanted Perry to be Perry. Underlining shit in a book like his life depended on it, giving Craig advice on how to keep his side of the room a little bit tidier, piling up his salad bowl with things his mother must have threatened him for eighteen years to eat, and that he was still eating. He wanted Perry to be his roommate, his friend.

But what he *had to do* was see Nicole.

That had nothing to do with Perry.

Luckily, Perry didn't speak.

Craig grabbed his coat and closed the door more carefully than usual behind him—not slamming it, but not leaving any doubt that he was closing it, either.

He headed for Lucas's room.

He didn't have time to walk to the OTT house.

He needed a car.

77

Jeremy purred in her lap as Shelly sat at the computer and scrolled through the articles. There were a hundred of them, and she was familiar with all of them, but they were cast in a new light now.

The *lake of blood,* the *beyond recognition,* the *burned over ninety-percent of her body,* the driver of the car *fleeing the scene on foot,* and herself: the middle-aged woman who was the first to arrive on the scene, and who failed to give the emergency operator enough information about the location of the accident for the paramedics to locate it in time to save the victim.

According to the articles, by the time the EMTs had arrived, the victim had been abandoned, lying in a lake of her own blood, burned beyond recognition, in the backseat of the vehicle for over an hour.

No.

Not even close.

Shelly remembered one EMT hurrying out of the ambulance. He had a large black satchel in one hand and a fire extinguisher under his arm. Shelly had stood up from where she'd been kneeling beside the girl and the boy, on the other side of the ditch of water she'd had to wade through to get there.

She'd waved her arms to get his attention.

Naturally enough, he'd gone first to the car, and he was peering in the window. He had no way of knowing that the victim had been thrown from the vehicle, and how far.

"Over here," Shelly had called out, and he'd turned, looking confused. Where, she'd wondered then, were the others? Surely, there was someone with him—following, driving, on the way.

"Ma'am," the EMT had shouted. "Don't touch her! Step back! Please return to your own vehicle immediately."

Reluctantly, Shelly had followed his directions. She made her way back through the ditch of cold water, passing him as she did so. He didn't even look at her. He'd tossed the fire extinguisher onto the ground, and he seemed to be muttering under his breath.

When she stumbled up on the other side, she'd looked behind her again:

The couple in the moonlight.

The boy with his arms wrapped around the girl.

Shelly had seen the girl up close. She'd seen and touched both of them. They were warm. They were alive. She'd been grateful to feel that warmth. The girl was wearing a black dress, and it made her bright gold hair shine even more brightly in the moonlight. When Shelly put her hand on the girl's neck to feel for a pulse (and she had felt it, that little insistent throbbing of some artery beneath the skin), her eyelids had fluttered. The boy had kissed her forehead then, and then he'd sobbed with relief. He'd said her name. Nicole. And at the sound of her name, Nicole had opened her eyes and looked at him, smiling and wincing at the same time.

Fine, Shelly had thought. She's fine. Bruised and shocked and disoriented, but utterly alive.

Shelly opened the next, familiar Google result, and there was Josie in her black dress, black sunglasses, a wristful of black bracelets. The sun shone down on her black hair and those elaborate, exotic earrings she was wearing, which were Denise Graham's dead great-grandmother's. Beyond her, a fresh orchard was in bloom.

Shelly enlarged the photo.

She looked more closely.

They were all wearing the same black dress.

Every single sorority sister.

The same V neck, the ruffle at the hem. The sleevelessness and drape of the dresses identical. The small satin ribbon around the waist. Shelly remembered saying to Josie one afternoon in bed, "The thing I hated about being in a sorority was that we were all supposed to look and act alike." And how Josie had snorted. "Like that's not how it is with everybody? Like all the lesbians your age aren't all trying to look and act alike? Like all the counter-culture kids, or all the conservatives, or all the professors or librarians or bookstore clerks around here aren't, every one of them, completely interchangeable?"

Interchangeable.

The word, frankly, had surprised Shelly.

It had seemed beyond Josie, somehow, that word, as if she'd been thinking about sameness, about sororities, about the human condition or *something* for a long time, trying to find just the right word to describe it. Thumbing through the thesaurus. The effect of hearing Josie use this word, so perfect, was not unlike the way it might have felt if Jeremy had suddenly turned to her and expressed a dislike for a certain brand of cat food. (*I would prefer no more Fancy Feast, if you don't mind.*) It seemed somehow to change the rules of the game she thought they'd been playing, if only for a second or two.

In this photograph, there were at least thirty girls, and every one wore the exact same dress. Where had they gotten so many at once, especially since nearly every one of these girls would have been the same size? What store, what catalog, what warehouse, could possibly have held them all?

And the black sunglasses. The black bracelets. Some with straight blond hair, shoulder length, and the rest with straight black hair, shoulder length. Not one of them was smiling, but neither were any of them crying.

Shelly enlarged the image once more, and then again, and when she leaned farther forward, with more urgency this time, Jeremy jumped off her lap and went scrambling across the wood floors, sliding on his claws into the hallway.

"Jeremy? Baby?" Shelly called after him, still intent on her computer screen, but he didn't come back. She'd scared him.

One more double click, and the central thing in this image became something she had only peripherally registered until now:

A single blurred girl behind the scenes, moving with what looked like genuine swiftness through the parking lot behind them all. Her arms were swinging at her sides as if she were moving quickly. One foot was an inch above the ground. Her blond hair was blowing around behind her, either because of the swiftness with which she was traveling or because of a stiff breeze. There was a purposeful expression on her face. She was looking straight ahead. A few nice cars glinted in the sunlight around her.

There were still a couple of branches of blossoms framing the screen.

Shelly touched one of those without taking her eyes off the girl's face.

The multiple enlargements had obscured her features, but even through this veil of haze and distorted pixels, Shelly felt she knew exactly who this was, and where she'd seen her before.

With a trembling hand, she hit the left-hand arrow a few times until she was back at the article attached to the image, and the little box to the left of Josie's pretty feet.

"Craig Clements-Rabbitt has not yet been accused of a crime, inspiring outrage within the grief-stricken Omega Theta Tau community."

Shelly sat back, put a hand to her forehead, and then over her eyes. She had to find him. Why hadn't she done it already? What had she been waiting for? There were things this boy needed to know that only she could tell him. Her hand was still trembling as she typed in the Internet address of the university directory, and realized with some chagrin how incredibly easy he was to find. Like the Grahams, like all of them, he was captured there in the Web—his address and phone number and all the public and personal details of his life. Shelly jotted down the address and grabbed her purse, hurrying out the door.

78

Professor Polson's on her way over."

"Our professor is on her way to your *apartment*?" Karess asked. She was standing by the window with her arms crossed over her chest. Since they'd left the morgue and come back to the apartment, she'd never stopped shaking. She and Perry had walked so quickly they might as well have been running, and he was, himself, sweating in his jacket, but when they got to the front door and he saw how pale she was, and how much she was trembling, he took her in his arms and held her as she muttered, "Oh, God, Oh, my God, I remember that guy. Me and my roommate bought weed from him during Orientation. Oh, my God, Perry, that was his dead body."

Perry had pulled her into the hallway and pressed her up against the mailboxes, trying to warm her, hold her close enough to calm her—or maybe himself—but it hadn't worked at all. Hours and many cups of hot coffee later, Karess was still shaking, standing against the window with her legs pressed to the radiator. She'd barely spoken until now, except to say hello to Craig when Perry introduced them to each other, and to say no when he asked her if she wanted something to eat.

"Does Professor Polson spend a *lot* of time here?"

"We're working together on—"

"Yeah," Karess said.

"Look," Perry said. "She's never been here before, but this thing, with Lucas—I could tell on the phone, she's really upset."

"Fuck *her*," Karess said, suddenly completely animated. The jewels and feathers she was wearing started to swing and flutter around her. She stomped the heel of her boot hard enough that Perry felt pretty sure that if anyone had been sleeping in the apartment below them, they weren't anymore. "*She* was upset? She had us all set up, Perry. Couldn't you tell? That's why she left us all there, and went out in the alley. She knew there was a body in there, that it was a guy our age. I mean, that was her other boyfriend in there, that diener. You didn't notice the big hug and all that? You think he didn't bother to tell her there was a dead college kid in the morgue today? Professor Polson's been trying to scare the shit out of us since day one, and I for one plan to file a complaint about it. This class has been a freak show from the beginning. My parents are *not* going to be amused."

"She didn't know," Perry said. "I'm telling you, she had no way of knowing. She was as shocked as the rest of us. I was there when she recognized Lucas. I thought she was going to pass out."

"Yeah. Right," Karess said, and turned her back to him. He could see her shoulder blades under her sweater and the tank top and sheer blouse she was wearing. It crossed his mind that, undressed, she might be either impossibly beautiful or a skeleton. She was always decorated in so many layers of flowing clothes he could never have begun to guess how much she weighed, but it couldn't have been much.

From the bathroom, he could hear the shower running, and Craig in there bumping around in the tiny shower stall, and then the intercom buzzed through the apartment, and Perry hit the button to open the apartment house door. Karess snorted out of her nose, and Perry went to stand in the hallway, listening to the sound of what he thought were Professor Polson's black boots on the stairwell (solid, steady steps in sharp heels, as if she were tired or trying to figure out if she was in the right building, heading toward the right apartment), so he was surprised when the woman turned at the top of the stairwell, and she wasn't Professor Polson. At first he thought somehow that she was his aunt Rachel. Same coloring. Reddish-blond hair. Pale skin. Maybe forty years old. Pretty, but not trying to be. This woman was wearing a silk dress and a very large black down parka. "Are you Craig?" she asked.

79

"A re you Craig?" Shelly asked the boy who stood near the open door in the hallway, although he didn't look like the boy she remembered. He was handsome, in that buzz-cut, face-chiseled-from-marble kind of way—the kind of All-American boy she used to fantasize about when she was a teenager, but whom she never actually met. The closest she'd come was Chip Chase, who'd taken her to her senior prom, and he'd had longer hair than her own, which Shelly had pretended to like—running her fingers through the long, dark brown locks—when, in truth, she'd hated it.

This boy didn't look like the long-haired boy she'd seen at the accident. He looked, instead, like Shelly's brother. He could have *been* Shelly's brother, had Richie lived to be nineteen. If Richie had been a college student instead of a Marine. Josie's word *interchangeable* came to mind.

"No," the boy said. "Craig's in the shower."

"Oh. I was hoping to speak to him," Shelly said to this ghost of her brother, and he opened the door to let her in.

80

When Craig got out of the shower—dried and dressed—he was surprised to find Perry's professor already in the apartment. She was sitting on their couch. And a slender red-haired woman sat on a kitchen chair that Perry had pulled out for her. Perry and Karess stood next to each other at the window.

"I'm Shelly Lockes," the red-haired woman said. "I was at the accident. I was the first one there. I'm the one they said didn't give directions to nine-one-one. I saw you and Nicole the night—"

"The night she died," Craig said, sinking onto the couch beside the professor. It surprised him how easily he was able to say "she died." It had taken Dr. Truby four appointments to get those two words out of him, and that first time he'd said them aloud, when his memory had finally started to come back to him, he'd had to stand up fast, feeling as if his own words had somehow slugged him in the stomach. Then he'd collapsed again and wept into his hands until his session with Dr. Truby was over.

Now he could say the words over and over, as if they weren't the truth.

Shelly Lockes shook her head, as if to contradict him, but she didn't say anything else. It was like she was waiting for permission to speak again.

There was something familiar about her. She was beautiful. She looked the way he thought angels painted on Christmas cards would look if Christmas card makers had more imagination. She was feminine, but without makeup, and although she was petite and very pretty, she also looked incredibly strong. She looked like the kind of angel who could very easily pick you up from the hundredth story of a burning building and fly you back down to the ground.

He'd seen her before, he realized.

He'd seen her *everywhere*, he thought.

Again, she shook her head.

Beside him, Professor Polson was shivering. Perry's friend Karess had been shivering all along, as well. Perry looked cold, too. He had his hands shoved deep into the pockets of his jeans. But Craig felt, himself, like he was burning up. Maybe he was sick. He'd slept so solidly (twelve hours?) in the Cookie Girl Deb's bed, and still he felt sure that if he put his head down now for one second, he would fall straight back into that exhausted, dreamless state. If she hadn't woken him up to let him back into the apartment with the key the landlord had dropped off, Craig might still be there in her bed.

He might never have woken up at all.

Shelly Lockes looked flushed, too, he thought. Overwarm. A thin film of perspiration shone on her forehead, although she was wearing only a silky-looking dress, black tights, boots that looked more like fashion stuff than winter stuff. She was staring at him intently, as though either trying to read his mind or willing him to read hers

"You were there," he asked, "the night of the accident? You saw Nicole? The night she died?"

The woman looked around as if the question had been asked of someone else in the room, but everyone in the room was looking at her. She cleared her throat and then touched it, and then tucked a strand of hair behind her ear, and looked down at her boots.

How many millions of times had Craig seen Nicole tuck a strand of hair like that behind her ears, thinking before she spoke? This woman could have been Nicole, if Nicole had lived long enough to become her. Or Josie. Or any of the other sorority girls Craig had seen or known.

She licked her lips, and then bit them, and then she said, "She wasn't dead."

81

Shelly had begun to think that perhaps in the months since the accident she had reinvented the boy in her imagination. There'd been only that one night, and it had been dark except for the moon. Afterward, photographs of Nicole Werner had been everywhere, so she'd had an image of the girl to compare to her memory. But Craig Clements-Rabbitt had appeared again only in her dreams.

Now, looking at him sitting across from her on the low, sagging couch—his knees practically pressed against his chest—Shelly realized she would have recognized him anywhere.

The dark, shaggy hair. The pained expression she felt certain he'd spent all his adolescence attempting to turn into a rock star sneer. She'd known boys like him in high school, in college, and since. They were the ones who managed to turn into poets, or elementary school art teachers, if someone finally helped them shrug off that persona. If not, they just passed through this world with that sneer, drinking far too much, fucking things up.

The night of the accident, he'd looked at her and understood; she'd never doubted that. He couldn't have heard her, but he'd known what she was saying. He was looking at her that same way now, and Shelly felt sure, again, that something was rising up in him: memory, understanding.

Now, she understood, too:

He really didn't remember what had happened. That's why he'd never contacted anyone to set the record straight himself. *Amnesia*, she thought. *Confabulation. Fugue.* So many pretty words for forgetting, like names for gray flowers. Still, she felt sure that if she looked at him long enough, as deeply into his eyes as she could, he would see past her, and remember that night. Remember her. Finally, he seemed to, and said, "You were there."

"Yes," she said. "I was there. I was there, and it's not what they said happened."

He nodded. He understood. It was coming back to him, wasn't it? *She* was coming back to him.

"You were there," he said again. "You know what happened?"

Shelly nodded. "I was the first one there," she said again.

"What happened?" the boy asked.

Shelly felt a small sob start in her throat, and touched it. It was warm in the apartment, though everyone except Craig Clements-Rabbitt looked cold. The girl by the radiator was shivering, and the professor was blowing on her own hands, seeming to be trying to warm them up—but Shelly was either having another one of her hot flashes, or she had a fever, or it was a hundred degrees in here. She was sweating through her silk dress. She could feel that her feet were wet from the snow and slush she'd walked through to get here, but they weren't cold. She was thirsty. As if she'd walked through the desert as well as the snow. But none of that mattered. Finally, *finally*, she had this little gathered group of listeners to whom she could tell the story, and she was going to tell it. She cleared her throat and began at the beginning:

The tail lights on the two-lane road. How she'd been singing along to the radio, watching them up ahead in the distance, and how they'd disappeared.

The couple in the moonlight, and how she'd seen them from the other side of the ditch of cold water. She told Craig that she'd known she had to tell him not to move the girl, but that she was never sure whether or not she'd actually said the words. He'd been so far away, but—

"I heard you," he said.

She nodded.

But then he shook his head and said, "But Nicole was in the backseat. It would have been burning."

"No," Shelly said. "That's not what happened. She was thrown from the car. There was no fire. I called nine-one-one. I waded through the ditch, and I was right there. You had your arms around her. There was no blood. She was hurt; she'd been thrown. But you said her name, and she opened her eyes. She was going to be fine. I stayed until the ambulance came, and they told me I needed to get stitches for my hand."

Shelly held it up so he could see the scar. The professor leaned forward, too. She had hair as black and shining as Josie's, and a sharp, serious expression. She looked troubled, and very smart.

"So I left. I went to the university outpatient clinic when the ambulance left with you and Nicole. There was never any blood. There was never any fire. You never left the scene except with them. They don't want us to remember. They want us off this campus. They have something to hide."

"I told you," Craig said, looking over at his roommate. "The postcards. You convinced me, especially after they quit coming, that they weren't from her, that it was a hoax."

"You got postcards from *Nicole Werner?*" the girl by the window asked. She let her mouth hang open, looking at each of them in the room in turn.

"The Cookie Girl," Craig said. "She told me, too."

No one said anything until the girl near the radiator closed her mouth and then sputtered, as if she'd been listening so long to such a ludicrous story that she couldn't contain herself any longer, "Who's the *Cookie Girl?*"

"Our neighbor," Craig's roommate said.

Craig said, "She told me that, too. She said, 'They're trying to get rid of you. They don't want you here.' She told me there isn't a ghost."

He went silent then. Shelly waited for him to go on.

"Alice Meyers," he finally said. "I thought there was this girl. This dead girl. She calls. One night, she came here, into the apartment. She stood in the doorway and asked if she could come in."

The girl near the radiator huffed loudly this time, and swept a small, cold-looking hand through her tangled dark hair. "That's a bunch of crap," she said. "I live in the dorm. There's these 'Alice Meyers girls.' They're crazies. Cutters. They're obsessed with Nicole. They go around saying they've seen her—"

"Seen Nicole?" Craig asked, looking at the girl as if he hadn't noticed her until then. "They think they've seen Nicole?"

The girl shrugged elaborately, rolled her eyes, and said, "Her or Alice Meyers. Who cares? They're crazy."

Craig's roommate looked at the professor and said, "We have to tell him now."

The professor nodded, and Craig leapt to his feet, stepped toward his roommate and said, "Tell me what?"

"Craig," the professor said, also standing. She took a step toward him and touched his arm. "Other people have seen her, too. Or they *think* they've seen her."

"Jesus Christ," the girl by the radiator said. "I'm leaving here. This is crazy." She raised a hand as if she might slap the professor, but then put the hand into the pocket of her sweater. "You're crazy, Professor Polson. You're supposed to be teaching us, not fucking with us. I don't know what you think you're doing, but I'm done with it. I'm dropping your class, and I'm—" She shook her head, and then she looked from Shelly to Craig to Craig's roommate, as if trying to find the sane one, and, not finding it, walked quickly to the door, opened it, and slammed it shut behind her.

They all listened to the sound of her heels on the stairs until it was clear she was long gone, and then Shelly said, "I think someone died that night. But I don't think it was Nicole."

She reached into her bag and took out the little snapshot of Denise Graham that Denise's mother had given her earlier that day.

82

Craig parked the Taurus at the side of the street outside the sorority, but he stayed in the driver's seat for a few minutes, looking out.

The sky was clear, and the snow had melted into a wavering, wet carpet on the sidewalks and the street. From where he'd parked, the Omega Theta Tau House seemed to cast its own extra darkness onto the lawn around it. He couldn't see even a single candle flickering inside. It was as if the house had been abandoned, or never built. Craig shoved Lucas's car keys in his pocket, got out. Nicole was in there, and he had to see Nicole.

He crossed the lawn, purposely walking slowly, deliberately, upright, in full view of the house and anyone who might have been watching him from within it.

Why shouldn't he?

He wasn't a criminal. He was there to see his girlfriend. This was a sorority, not a secret society, not a high-security prison facility. Jesus Christ. He just wanted to see Nicole. Why should he have to crawl on his belly to do it?

Still, it made him nervous. He could feel his heart racing in his chest. Although the house was dark, and Craig heard nothing but silence emanating from it, he had the distinct feeling that he was being watched. He tried to maintain the slow, determined gait, but he was walking faster the closer he got. His hands were sweating, and when he reached the side of the house, he crouched down in the shadows, hiding.

He should have worn his jacket. It was that kind of late winter cold that was damp, not solid anymore. Back in Fredonia, you'd be able to feel the thaw in things. But this was a long way from thaw. This was going to be cold like soiled sheets or something. Like sleeping in your own wet laundry.

Suddenly, crouching in the dark at the side of the OTT house, he felt sadder than he'd ever felt in his life. On his knees. In the dirt. He found himself remembering, stupidly, his mother of all people:

Her ankles.

Traveling toward those ankles at high speed on his hands and knees because he couldn't walk. Because every time he tried to walk he fell on his fucking ass. Because he was a baby. Why wouldn't she pick him up? He was her *baby*.

He shook his head. How idiotic was that? Thinking about his mother? Right now?

("I've fucked Nicole," Perry had said. "Half of fucking Godwin Hall has fucked your virgin girlfriend, you stupid, stupid, deaf, blind, fucking idiot.")

He was behind familiar shrubbery, he realized—right where he'd been that other night, when he'd gotten tossed out of OTT. He put his face to the little window and looked down (blinking, blinking) at the whole tableau of the basement again.

This time, he hadn't really expected to see anyone.

There was no music. No strobe light. He'd convinced himself that he was right, that the whole house was either an illusion, or empty. There was no way a whole house full of girls all dressed up for their Spring Event could be so still, and silent.

It took a while for his eyes to adjust to the darkness well enough to make out the scene:

They were standing so motionless they'd blended into the atoms around them, it seemed. They were as gray as the air.

Sorority girls made of air, made of shadows. They were all in black, with their heads bowed, and the only bright thing Craig could see at all was the glinting silver handles on the coffin they were standing around. In the darkness.

But then he pressed his face closer to the window, and he could see that, in the coffin, there was girl. She must have been wearing white, because she was brighter than anything around her, but the darkness was so complete that she seemed to absorb it. She must have been the one they were raising from the dead. (Ridiculous. Pathetic.) He was about to stand up, just leave, when he heard what sounded like vague, dull, stupidly girlish chanting under him.

Girlish monks.

He snorted, hearing that.

Stupid game. Stupid hazing. Stupid him for being here, for caring so much, for crouching down behind a bush trying to catch a glimpse of his girlfriend, who was standing around a coffin in a basement pretending to raise some sorority sister from the dead.

And then, there *that* guy was:

The omnipresent EMT.

He was standing in a corner, in the shadows, the way he always was.

Craig remembered Nicole saying, "What's EMT stand for?" Denying she'd ever even seen the guy before. He heard Perry say it again: "You fucking idiot. You blind asshole."

He wanted to walk away, but it was mesmerizing, too—the sound of their voices. It was like music bubbling out of the ground. It was the coldness seeping through his jeans. It sounded ancient, and completely new. He could see it very clearly now, the whole thing in the basement. This was *no game*. The girl in that coffin was dead. The silky inner lining of the casket they'd placed her in was the same color as her blue-gray, blue-white skin. Yes, she was wearing white, but the white had turned to a deathly nothingness, a bluish absence. Craig stared, and stared, and held his breath. Shit. Had they killed her? Did they know she was dead? Was he the only one who could see clearly from where he looked down at her through the basement window that the girl was actually dead?

Did they have their eyes closed? Why was the fucking EMT just sitting there in the corner? Were they so caught up in their chanting that they couldn't see the girl was dead?

Before he even knew what he was doing, Craig was slamming his fists against the flimsy glass until he'd broken it, and was falling into it, and the girls were all screaming and running and shrieking, just like the time before when he'd run down the basement steps, except this time the screaming had nothing to do with him.

Part Five

83

"Something happened to him," Perry said, "after the accident. I know Craig. He can be an asshole, but he's one of the smartest people I've ever met. He remembers everything. He can tell you all the presidents in order, their terms of office. He won't admit it, but he can. He's not going to *forget* what happened on that night."

Jeff Blackhawk's car rattled around them disconcertingly, but Mira felt oddly comforted by the rattling, and the smell of it: the Krispy Kreme doughnuts and old French fries. When they'd left her apartment Jeff was watching *Sesame Street* with the twins, a show Clark insisted was the opiate of the masses. ("This shit's supposed to turn parents into asexual zombies," he'd said when Mira suggested that a minimal amount of PBS might help the boys with some language acquisition.) "Look!" Jeff was shouting at the television, pointing. "It's *Elmo!*"

"Elmo!" the twins shouted back, as if it were a name they'd known all their lives and had only been waiting until this moment to call out.

Jeff wouldn't even let Mira thank him—not for lending her his car, not for watching her children. "Just get some great material for your book," he'd said, "and thank me in the acknowledgments. It'll be my claim to fame."

Now Perry Edwards was sitting beside her, directing her to the lanes she needed to be in to get to the exits they needed to take to get to Bad Axe to find the mortician who'd accepted the mangled remains of Nicole

Werner, and who had slid them into the white coffin Perry had helped to carry down the aisle of the Bad Axe Trinity Lutheran Church on the day of her funeral.

Mira said, "Of course, there are head injuries that will cause selective amnesia—"

"But there were no head injuries," Perry said. "They did a CT scan. They did ten CT scans."

Mira stared out Jeff's cracked windshield. It was a small crack on the left side, making its way across the glass slowly but perceptibly enough that she could gauge the progress it had made since the last time she'd been in the car. Two inches. In four weeks, at this rate, it would traverse the windshield.

She tried to think.

Mira had seen skulls.

Plenty of them. Skulls in Romania. Skulls in morgues. Skulls in long, chaotic piles and heaps in the Paris catacombs:

Walking through that underground full of bones, Mira had been amazed. So many dead. She'd let her hand drift over the hundreds and thousands of skulls, breathing in the smell she knew was theirs (must, dust) while the dank ceiling dripped ancient water onto her head, and she'd let it sink in how truly flimsy that helmet that protected everything was. That fragile container of dreams and memories and longings and desire. Of *everything*. One well-placed blow with a tree branch could shatter it all.

The impression had never left her. When she was seven months pregnant with the twins, she'd told Clark (who'd rolled his eyes), "I want them to wear helmets when they're old enough to ride bikes. And they won't ever be playing soccer."

But, if there'd been no head injury?

There was nothing, Mira knew, that a CT scan couldn't show. If there was no head injury, no brain damage, how was it that Craig Clements-Rabbitt remembered nothing of the accident that had killed Nicole?

"Well," Mira finally said, "there are substances. Drugs. Injectables. There's something called the 'zombie drug.' Scopolamine. At high doses it kills you, but at lower doses it induces amnesia. Prostitutes have been known to use it to drug and rob their customers. In some countries they claim it's used to drug mothers and take their babies, traffic them to adoption agencies. They say it makes people so docile they'll help you burglarize their own houses—and long after the drug is out of their systems, they still have no recollection of the events at all."

Perry was running his hand over his head. Mira had noticed the buzz cut was growing out. It was as dark as she'd thought it would be.

"They used to give Scopolamine to women during childbirth," she went on. "Probably your grandmother was given it—just woke up, and they told her she'd had a baby. It completely blocks the formation of memory. You can't even hypnotize the person to help them remember what happened, the way you can with date rape drugs, because the memory is simply never recorded.

"They think it's been used for voodoo for centuries in Haiti. It's given to victims who are then buried alive and then dug up and told they've died and been exhumed as zombies—and they believe it. They're willing to live the rest of their lives as slaves or prostitutes or servants because they're convinced they died and were brought back to life."

Perry had stopped rubbing his head. Now he was drumming his fingertips on his knee. The jeans he was wearing were creased so nicely Mira thought maybe he'd never worn them before. It was hard to imagine a boy his age ironing his own jeans, but if any boy would, Perry Edwards would be the boy. He said, "Before he left that night, in Lucas's car, we had an argument. No," he interrupted himself, "we had an actual fight. A fight that ended up with him with a bloody nose and us on the floor. He never said a word about it again, either like it never happened or, like after everything else that happened, it didn't matter. I've never known if he just doesn't remember. How do you know about this drug?"

The good students, they always questioned you in the end. They would accept your word for it only so far.

"Well," Mira said. She went on to tell Perry how, while working on her master's thesis, she'd traveled to Haiti with the help of a small summer grant that she and another graduate student had received together for a proposal they'd made to meet with a woman the Haitian newspapers had tried unsuccessfully to debunk as the "Zombie of Port au Prince."

The woman's family had claimed she'd been kidnapped by neighbors who tried to extort money from them, and that when they were unable to produce the money, the kidnappers strangled the young woman and left her dead body at the side of a road. Passersby put the body in the trunk of their car and drove it to the police station. When the trunk was opened, the young woman's eyes were open, so she was returned to her family. But her family refused to take her back. When they saw her they said it was clear that she was missing her soul.

When word got out that this zombie was being moved from her hometown, where they'd have nothing to do with her, to an institution in Port au Prince, the institution employees resigned, and mayhem ensued among the other patients. By the time Mira and her fellow student learned about her and applied for the grant, the zombie was living in foster care—the fourth foster care she'd been placed in. It didn't help matters that she herself had insisted that she was a zombie.

It seemed like such a promising research opportunity, and Mira's advisors had been excited and supportive, but Mira and her research partner, Alexandra Durer, got only as far as the airport in Port au Prince, where they were refused entry into Haiti because riots had broken out. Americans had been killed. Armed rebels were said to have taken over the capital. Mira and Alex were boarded right back onto the plane they'd arrived on—and, after a lot of fruitless imploring and phone calls, they just gave up and got drunk on a bottle of duty-free rum they bought at the airport.

That winter, the Zombie of Port au Prince died of pneumonia.

Before they left for Haiti, Alex and Mira had done extensive research on the zombie drug, and their loose hypothesis had been that the woman had been drugged by her kidnappers, and that her 'rescuers' had mistaken her drugged state for death, and that the reaction to her return from the dead had been so influenced by the Haitian zombie culture that the victim herself, having no recollection of what had actually happened to her, had been willing to believe that she was a zombie.

"It's not unheard of," Mira said, "to find Scopolamine on college campuses—date rape, of course, but other uses, too. Hazing?" She shrugged. She'd never heard of this, but it seemed far from outside the realm of possibility. "Nicole might have known Greeks with access to the drug. Were she and Craig experimenters?"

Perry shook his head. "He smoked dope. A lot of dope. Probably other stuff, back in New Hampshire. I don't know about her. I always thought she was against all that, but there were other things I thought about her that turned out to be wrong."

He seemed disinclined to go on. He turned his face to the slushy scenery outside the passenger window, and put a hand against the dashboard, the heat vent. It couldn't have been more than forty degrees in Jeff Blackhawk's car, and Perry's fingers were very white, the fingernails tinged with blue. Mira would have offered him the gloves she was wearing, but she was afraid that without them she'd be unable to drive.

"Zombie drugs," Perry said after a long pause. He tucked his hands between his knees, paused again, and finally said, "All Craig can remember about the accident is what they told him, and what was in the reports: that Nicole was so badly injured and burned they could identify her only by the things she'd been wearing, and that he'd left the scene of the accident without bothering to try to help. That's our exit." He pointed to a green-and-white sign up ahead that read, BAD AXE.

84

Shelly's answering machine was blinking so rapidly and chaotically that she didn't bother to count the number of messages it must have recorded. She hit Play, and then she pulled a kitchen chair up next to the phone table, sat down, and began to unlace her boots.

"We know about you," the first message said, followed by a beep. A young feminine voice. Not familiar, but not a total stranger's, either. Shelly stopped unlacing the boot and put both feet next to each other on the floor.

"We know about you. You don't know about us. We're smarter than you think we are. You can't trace these calls."

An amused-sounding laugh, followed by a beep, and then:

"We've got a surprise for you. A *whole bunch* of surprises."

Beep.

"Shelly? This is Rosemary. Are you okay there, honey? I felt so worried after our last talk. Things will get back to normal, I promise you, but how about, until things settle down, you come stay with us for a while? I told the kids I was inviting you, and they're excited. Please?"

Beep.

"Surprise!"

But it was a different female voice this time. Lower. Sexier. Quieter.

Beep.

"Maybe you should have a look around your house. There's a present for you. It's in the bedroom. We know that's where you like to get your presents."

Shelly stood up.

Beep.

"That's right. Go on. Go see for yourself."

Beep.

"Hey, Shelly. Keep going." *Josie.* Shelly couldn't have proved it—too few words—but something about the cadence, the consonants pronounced at the very tip of the tongue against the teeth, seemed nauseatingly familiar.

Beep.

"Mee-*owwww*." And then there was laughter, hysterical laughter, but Shelly was heading into the bedroom now, hurrying, that laughter pouring down on her like glassy rain.

Beep.

"Here kitty-kitty-kitty."

Beep.

"You're next, you bitch, if you don't look out. I'd say it's time you got out of town. And don't think you can trace these calls, because the cops won't be able to figure it out, and there's no—"

But Shelly was screaming now, yanking on the rope that was strung from the light fixture over her bed and wrapped around her cat's neck, pulling his limp body down, cradling him in her arms, screaming his stupid, silly name into his blank face with his black lolling tongue and his glass eyes staring intently at nothing at all.

85

Mr. Dientz remembered Perry from Cub Scouts. His own son was many years older than Perry, so they'd overlapped for only a year, but he gave Perry a hearty handshake and said, "Lord. What did your parents feed you, boy?"

Perry asked after Paul Dientz, who was in mortuary school in North Carolina, and then introduced Professor Polson. Mr. Dientz was obviously surprised, and not necessarily pleasantly so (a quick raising and lowering and raising of his very bushy gray eyebrows) to find that the professor was a woman. A young woman.

On the phone, he'd said, "Perry, since I know you, and since you say you're doing this 'research' "—the word had come out of his mouth like something from a foreign language—"I'm willing to indulge you and your professor, of course, and have I mentioned how impressed I am that you're attending our state's finest institution?"

Perry had assured him that he had.

"But it's a part of my job I don't relish. The reopening of old wounds, so to speak. Perry, it would amaze you to learn how many family members and friends in the weeks, months, *years* after a funeral—especially in the case of cremations and closed coffins—become convinced that there has been some case of mistaken identity. They think they've glimpsed a deceased brother or son or daughter on the street, or in a magazine, or they've gotten a hang-up call in the middle of the night— and, if they weren't at the scene of the accident or the one to identify the body or if there were issues of identification, because many untimely deaths, Perry, let me be frank, leave behind corpses that do not resemble the living person—well, they can become fixated.

"Again, in the interest of 'science,' I am willing to meet with you and your professor and go over the record, but I must admit I can't recall all the details, except of course the terrible tragedy of it, and, as I recall, the Werners did not take our recommendation to view the body. In the case of their lovely daughter, it would certainly have been horrific, but there's really nothing better for a sense of finality, if you know what I mean, than to see the deceased with your own eyes."

Well, welcome," Mr. Dientz said, sweeping his arm toward two plush red velvet armchairs across from his desk. "I've gone through my files, and as soon as you're settled, I'd be happy to show you the reconstructive photographs."

Perry had no idea what *reconstructive photographs* would be, but he did know, because Mr. Dientz had told him on the phone, that the funeral home kept a digital library of photos and information about their 'clients.' He would be showing them photographs of Nicole? Now? Perry looked toward the door, wondering if he could excuse himself for a moment, but Mr. Dientz wasted no time booting up his Mac, and turning the screen toward Perry and Professor Polson, so they could see.

"You may well ask yourself," Mr. Dientz said, his voice shifting into the tone of a man on a radio commercial, clearly getting ready to say something he'd said a million times before but that still held meaning for him, "why it is we would spend the many hours we spend here at Dientz Funeral Parlor reconstructing the likenesses of decedents who have been disfigured by accidents or illness when, in fact, most funerals at Dientz Funeral Parlor are now closed-casket, and, in especially the most extreme cases, even family members will not be viewing the bodies?"

He looked at Perry and Professor Polson with rehearsed animation, as if gauging to what degree they had each been asking themselves this question.

"*Well*, I answer you with an anecdote from my earliest years as a mortician," Mr. Dientz went on. "A young man had been killed in a motorcycle accident. I won't go into the details, but like your friend Nicole, identification was difficult. Injuries, burns, even dismemberment. Everyone in the family insisted, as so many so often do, that they only wished to remember their loved one 'as he had been.' Of course, someone had identified him at the morgue, but it was a distant relative, and the identification was done mostly from clothing and a ring. The family insisted that they didn't want any kind of reconstruction, no embalming. They didn't even care what the deceased would be wearing in his coffin.

"Still, this was a very traditional family, and after ascertaining that they would not *object* to reconstruction and embalming, I went ahead with my usual practice of preparing a body for viewing—although, I will tell you, I did not charge the family for these services, or even inform them that I was going ahead with them.

"As I'd imagined might happen, at the funeral there was a great emotional outpouring. The mother was beside herself. The father had become almost violently inconsolable. One of the brothers threw himself against the casket weeping, and one of the sisters became hysterical, insisting it was impossible—insisting that her brother wasn't in the casket, that this was a terrible dream or a mistake, and this got the whole family and even some of the young man's motorcycle gang friends making similar outcries. A fight nearly broke out before the father pushed his other son away and flung open the coffin.

"Perry, Professor, let me tell you that if I'd had that coffin locked or sealed—or, if I *hadn't* and that young man had been in there in the condition the county morgue had delivered him to me—well, this is the reason I always insist on reconstruction if I am going to have a body in a casket at Dientz Funeral Parlor.

"Because of the reconstruction, the family and the young man's friends were able to gather around his casket and grieve properly. He was the young man they remembered. He was dressed in a decent suit. His hair was combed, and I'd remodeled what I could of his face based on the photograph they'd run in the newspaper.

"Nothing, *nothing,* makes a death as believable as being able to see, to *touch,* the loved one's body. We are physical creatures, Perry, Professor." He nodded at Professor Polson. "And although much has been done to ridicule and malign the 'death industry' in America, I can tell you from experience that there is tremendous comfort taken in being able to view a body, in repose, nicely dressed, tastefully remodeled, eyes closed, clearly at peace. And I make it my job to be able to offer that comfort to those who may not know, until the very last moments, that they will need it."

"But Nicole's family?" Professor Polson asked.

Mr. Dientz shook his head. "No," he said. "Nicole's family couldn't bear it." He shrugged, as if to say, *you win some, you lose some.* "Now," he said. "The photos!"

Mr. Dientz whirled around in his chair with a flourish fit for the unveiling of the *Mona Lisa.* He waved his hand over his keyboard, took up his mouse, and then clicked a file in the center that read, *NWERNER,* and then *JPEG10,* and in less than half a second an image opened and filled the screen, and before Perry even realized that he had seen it, he was scrambling out of his velvet chair and across the room with a hand over his mouth, and then out of the office and into the men's room near the entrance of the funeral home.

86

"Craig," Perry had said when he left for Bad Axe with Professor Polson. "Just stay here, okay? We'll be back late. Don't do anything stupid."

"Like what?" Craig had asked, forcing Perry to say it:

"Like going out looking for Nicole."

Craig had tried not to. He'd paced around the apartment. Turned the TV on and off. He'd eaten a salami sandwich. Taken his second shower of the day. Gotten in bed. Gotten out of bed, combed his hair and gone next door to knock on Deb's door, but there'd been no answer. Finally, he'd sat down next to the phone and willed it to ring, and, incredibly, it had:

"Hello?"

On the other end of the line, there was no sound.

Craig held the receiver closer to his ear, and said hello again.

Now he could hear something. It was very distant, maybe the sound of a car on a freeway. Maybe, very faintly, there was music playing on the car radio. Or maybe he was just hearing his own heartbeat.

"Hello?" he asked again. And then: "Nicole?"

Then the line went dead, and Craig stood up, grabbed his coat, and headed out to do the stupid thing Perry had told him not to do.

It was colder out than Craig had expected it to be. The snow fell in fat flakes that stuck to the sidewalks and to the roofs and windshields of the cars parked beside the curbs, although the traffic was churning it into a slick, wet shadow in the road.

It seemed to Craig that the streets and sidewalks were oddly thronged with students. Had he simply not been outside enough this fall to notice them, or were they out, for some reason, en masse?

As they passed him—walking two or three abreast on the sidewalk and in the streets and at the corners, it felt to Craig as if he knew all of these kids, or had at least seen them all before. They were whooping, slapping each other's backs, pretending to be arguing, telling jokes. Couples were holding hands. Girls had their arms slung around each other's shoulders. Everyone seemed happy. No one was dressed for the cold or even seemed to be noticing it, and Craig was painfully, completely, aware of how separated he was from the lives of his peers. He was like a ghost come back to haunt the scene of his last days. No one seemed to notice him at all.

He remembered that life, and what it had been like to be a part of it. He remembered Lucas with a flask in his back pocket, stumbling off to the fourth bar of the night, and Perry, disapproving, walking a few steps ahead of them. He remembered how they'd stopped to shout something stupid up to the Omega Theta Tau house. Something about fucking virgins.

He remembered loving it.

How dumb and wonderful he had felt.

He remembered that a girl had come out on the porch, and that she was all lit up from behind. Even from that distance he could see how beautiful she was.

He had loved being a stupid, drunk college kid. An asshole shouting up at a sorority house. He loved the girl standing there, looking down at them, and the house, and the sense that, inside the house and behind that girl, some solemn ceremony was taking place in candlelight. Chanting. Holding hands. He'd loved that there would *be* such a house, such a secret society of beautiful girls, and that he was outside of it, shouting obscenities at it, being a real jerk—an oaf—while a big equally stupid moon was hung over it all, and he was fumbling for the flask in Lucas's back pocket as Perry walked off without them.

But this was all before Nicole. Before she joined this sorority. Before all of it.

Now he was passing the first of the terrible landmarks. The stone bench beneath the weeping willow where he'd slipped the amber ring on her finger, and where she'd given him the poem he still kept in his wallet:

> Time may take us far apart,
> But you will always be the lover of my heart.
> I have not given you my body yet.
> But I have given you, forever, What I Am

He stopped, looked at the bench, at the layer of snow accumulating on it, and he was so cold, shaking so hard, that if he hadn't had his jacket zipped, it would have rattled off of him, he thought. He blew a long scarf of frosted breath into the air above the bench before he continued to walk, and he didn't look up again until he'd gotten to the spot where, on Greek Row, you could see the hill from which the brooding Omega Theta Tau house looked down.

How had it gotten so dark so fast?

How long had he been walking?

Craig looked from the house to the sky, where a big blank moon was hanging, and then he looked toward the house again, where, in the light of that moon he saw two dark-haired girls walking down the front steps in puffy winter coats but very short skirts, knee-high boots.

They were still far away, but he could see that they were laughing, tossing shaggy wool scarves over their shoulders as they emerged through a scrim of snow.

He took a few steps toward them. They hadn't noticed him, but they were heading in his direction. When they were less than a block away, Craig rubbed his eyes to be sure, but now he had no doubt:

One of them was Josie.

Craig would have recognized that black silk hair, that pointed chin, anywhere. He could even hear her familiar laughter as she got closer. That high, sharp cackle. "Oh, my God!" she was saying. "You are totally kidding me. Tell me you're kidding."

Craig continued to stand in the center of the sidewalk, watching. They were directly ahead of him, and so close now that their shadows, stretched ahead of them on the snowy sidewalk, nearly touched him, would soon envelope him.

Yes.

He knew without a doubt that the one on the left was Josie, but he had to rub his eyes and blink the snowflakes out of them several times, shake his head, before he could be sure of what he was sure of:

That the second girl, the dark-haired one walking with Josie, was Nicole.

Nicole.

"Nicole," he said.

She didn't hear him, and she hadn't seen him.

He stood where he was and watched her, taking all of her in. The way she walked and the corners of her mouth. The little folds at the edges of her eyes. The perfect little bump on the bridge of her nose.

The silky straight hair was dark now, like Josie's.

But the tilt of her head.

The delicate ear behind which her hair was tucked.

Those were the same.

He'd have recognized them anywhere.

She was wearing a leather skirt. And tights with a silver sheen, and high-heeled boots. More eye makeup than she'd ever worn in—in what? In *life?*—and dark red lipstick. Her skin was pale in the moonlight, but her cheeks were bright, either with cosmetics or the cold, or maybe she'd been drinking. She seemed to stagger a little. She held a hand to her mouth to laugh at something else Josie had said, but Josie's voice shouted over the sound of Nicole's laughter, and Craig was grateful for that, because if he'd heard her voice, her *actual* voice, he might not have been able to stand it.

"Nicole," he said again, and then he was walking straight toward her, saying her name over and over, shouting it, and he was sliding on the slick cement toward them, and then they saw him, and there was no denying it:

Nicole.

She saw him, too. Her eyes filled with alarm. She turned and ran with what seemed like incredible speed back from where she'd come, back up the hill to the OTT house. Craig ran after her, slipping on the sidewalk, stumbling like a drunken man but managing somehow to stay upright, to continue the chase.

But she was so much faster than he was. She did not slip at all. How was that possible? In those high-heeled boots? In his life, Craig had only ever seen a deer run that gracefully, that quickly, that wildly and swiftly and without a backward glance, across the freeway, into the woods, without a sound. He was, himself, a much clumsier, heavier animal, slipping after her, panting, not with exertion but with panic, excitement, ecstasy.

She was ahead of him, but he was closer to her than he'd ever really believed he'd be again. She wasn't within reach, but she might have been. She might be, eventually. If he could only—

But then Josie Reilly had slammed her body fearlessly into his, knocked him to the ground, and then she was on top of him, pummeling him with her fists, straddling his hips with her legs spread, slamming her small, white, balled-up hands against his face, his head, his eyes. She tore off her soft gloves so she could claw at him. "You motherfucker. You asshole. You murderer. Get out of here. Get out of our lives. Get off this campus you fucking bastard." He tasted blood, and though he heard the sound of a bone snap somewhere in his face, and although it seemed to Craig that the whole thing lasted for decades, he felt no pain—and suddenly, just as he was getting used to it, he opened his eyes, and she was gone, and he was alone on the sidewalk, staring up at the moon as it seemed to toss cold white flakes down on his throbbing face.

"Holy shit," a guy in a Red Sox cap said, looking down at him. "You okay, dude? I hope whatever you did to piss her off was worth it."

87

"Oh, goodness. That certainly wasn't the image I intended to show you," Mr. Dientz said. "I'm sorry." He sounded as if he were apologizing, belatedly, for having absentmindedly forgotten to offer someone sugar for his tea.

Perry had come back from the men's room and was standing with his head against the window, looking out onto the Dientz Funeral Parlor parking lot, which was shadowed by the casket-shaped rectangle of the Dientz Funeral Parlor sign.

Both of these things—the parking lot and the sign—he'd passed in cars and on his bike maybe ten thousand times in his life, and yet there was something so unfamiliar, so unreal, about them in that moment that he knew that, if he were asked to, he'd be utterly unable to read the sign, to name the function of a parking lot, to place these things or himself on the surface of the earth. Back in the men's room, he'd rinsed his mouth out, but he could still taste the bile. Professor Polson came up behind him and touched his arm. "Perry." She said it firmly, pulling him back from the window.

"Well, that must have been a shocker for you!"

There was no escaping the amusement in Mr. Dientz's voice, and Perry remembered now Mr. Dientz standing over a table of Cub Scouts in the Bad Axe Elementary School cafeteria chuckling as the Scouts tried to pound nails into boards. What had they been building? Birdhouses? Toolboxes? The pine boards had been thick and incredibly hard, and the Scouts were all under the age of ten, and with every smack of the hammer, a nail would bend over dramatically instead of being driven into the wood. "Hah, hah. We aren't too good at boys' work, are we, *girls*?" Mr. Dientz had teased, and Perry remembered the screwed-up expression on his son Paul's face, the watery glare he kept trained on the nail as he prepared to smack it again with a hammer, and the way, when the nail bent over a fourth or fifth time and his father began to laugh, he didn't throw the hammer down or even drop it, but very carefully placed it next to the boards and walked away as his father watched and continued to laugh.

"*This*," Mr. Dientz said, "is the image I meant to show you, the *post*-reconstruction photo. Very good photo, and nice work, if I do say so myself."

"First, let me see," Professor Polson said, letting go of Perry's arm, and leaving him in the corner of the office.

"You can see, Professor," Mr. Dientz said, "how much work went into this, I hope. There's really no resemblance between the first face and this one, is there?"

Professor Polson said nothing. She was looking intently into Mr. Dientz's computer screen. Perry could see that there was a small line of sweat at her spine, gently soaked through the red silk of her shirt. The blouse wasn't tight, but the material clung to her back, and Perry could have counted the vertebrae from where he stood. The electric glow from the computer illuminated the hair around her face, causing it to look both black and blindingly bright. "Perry?" she said gently, turning toward him. "Do you think you can you look?"

Perry swallowed. He crossed the mauve carpeting again, took the seat beside her, rubbed his eyes, which were watery and blurred from vomiting, and then he leaned toward the computer screen.

"You can see," Mr. Dientz said, "that it's truly like sculpting, the kind of work that has to be done on a face in the kind of condition in which this particular decedent was delivered to me. Luckily, the skull was mostly intact, and provided in its entirety, so that the fragmented sections could be glued back to their original places." Mr. Dientz inhaled, as if reexperiencing the exhausting task in his memory. "I was then able to use something we call mortician's putty to cover the bone, and then of course, because of the burning and discoloration, I needed to use mortuary wax as a kind of masking. But after that, with some cosmetic work, she was really almost finished. The hair needed only some styling and a synthetic addition or two. That was lucky, considering the damage from the fire to her skin. In total, maybe five hours work? Sadly, until the two of you, no one except me has ever seen her."

Perry leaned in closer.

The face of the girl in the digital photograph was like no human face he had ever seen.

She radiated something so purely *radiant* that he wanted to close his eyes and lean forward at the same time, to disappear inside it. He had the feeling that, if he put his hand to the computer screen and touched her, she might wake up. She would be startled, confused, perhaps, but she would be more alive than anyone else in this room.

She had her eyes closed, this dead girl in the photo, but Perry didn't have the sense that she couldn't see. He had the sense that she no longer needed to have her eyes open to be able to see. She was seeing everything. She *was* everything. He had to lean back in the plush velvet chair and close his own eyes, and then open them again, and then he looked from Professor Polson to Mr. Dientz, and back to the girl.

"Perry?" Professor Polson asked.

"It isn't her," he said, shaking his head. "That's not Nicole."

88

She took only the things she'd need for a night in a motel—she couldn't stay at Rosemary's, not with her children there, not in the state she was in—but when Shelly closed the door behind her, she felt an intense moment of grief for the things inside the house: the teacups and the comforter and the prints on the walls and her shelf of CDs, things she felt she might possibly never see again. No one ever knew, did they?

She didn't bother to lock the front door. It was such a safe neighborhood, she'd never bothered—a fact she'd shared with Josie.

Her hands were still cramped and shaking from the shovel, the hard early winter ground. As she buried Jeremy (with a blanket, because it was unbearable to think of him in the cold, in the dirt) and wept, she thought about whether she should call the police, and decided that, if she ever did, it could not be now.

The darkness was pale on the lawn.

The moon was full.

The snow was falling fast, and it made a webby froth on the grass.

There was what seemed to be an unusually large number of students out, walking in small groups or in pairs, girls in ridiculously high heels leaning against one another, slipping around, making their way to bars, she supposed, and parties, where exciting and terrible things would happen to them. There would be kisses, and accidents, and endearments, and bitter words exchanged. Someone would fall in love. Someone would dance all night. Someone would get drunk, get raped, get hurt.

Shelly had to wait for a couple kissing in the middle of her street to break apart (two beautiful blondes, the girl on tiptoes to reach the mouth of the boy) before she could pull out of her driveway. They noticed her taillights eventually, and laughed, and moved with their arms still around each other, to the sidewalk. When Shelly backed up and passed a few feet from them, separated by the rivulets of melting snow on the glass of her passenger window, the girl (whose scarlet lips were parted over her white teeth) gave Shelly the finger, and then the couple let go of each other, doubling over with laughter, slipping around on the sidewalk, headed away, lit up in the moonlight—two incredibly beautiful, pointless human beings with no idea what awaited them—and Shelly had no choice but to drive past them again, trying not to stare, willing herself not even to glance at them in her rearview mirror, but watching them anyway.

They had nothing to do with her.

She knew that.

She could stand out in the snow all night and lecture those two about the fleetingness of youth, the dangers of this world, the accumulating importance of every act in this life, the thin thread, so easily snapped, between death and life, or simply the importance of being respectful of one's elders, and they would never hear a word.

89

G o," Professor Polson said, and handed Perry the keys to Professor Blackhawk's car. "I'm going to stay and talk to Ted Dientz here about possibilities. Identification. That sort of thing. He seems willing to work with us. He seems intrigued."

Perry agreed.

At first, when Perry said that the girl in the photograph was not Nicole, Mr. Dientz had stammered some defensive remarks about how even a miracle worker can't make a girl who's been burned over 90 percent of her body and who's sustained massive head trauma look like she did in life. But when he realized that Perry and Professor Polson weren't questioning his skills as a reconstructionist, but actually questioning whether or not this girl, in this photo, *was* Nicole, he seemed excited.

Perry could imagine Mr. Dientz perfectly, suddenly, as a reader of detective fiction—the kind of man for whom such a mystery offered an intellectual challenge, a thrilling possibility, and who wouldn't think it was necessarily out of the realm of possibility that a dead girl could be exchanged for a living girl, buried in her stead. He at least wanted to entertain the possibility for a little while.

"You know," he said, "stranger things have happened. I won't even go into it, but let me tell you—"

He didn't tell them what stranger things, but he did tell them that, just because so many stranger things had happened, in his years as a mortician he'd begun, years before, collecting the DNA of every body he'd had "dealings with."

"The military paved the way. They developed such a simple system of collecting DNA that, in my humble opinion, anyone who deals with the dead would be remiss not to take advantage of it."

He went on to explain that he made, for each body, a "bloodstain card," and kept them stored and filed in his basement.

"The tiniest drop of blood carries the entire blueprint, you know. All the genetic information for a single being and his or her family going back to the origins of the species!"

Professor Polson nodded as if she knew exactly what he was talking about, and asked, "So, you've kept a bloodstain sample card for Nicole?"

"Of course. All I would need is about five strands of hair from her mother or a sister to positively identify whether or not the bloodstain I have on file belonged to a relative of one of those Werner females. Just get me the hairs and I'll make a call to my pals at Genetech, and for eight, nine dollars, we've got our answer."

Mr. Dientz and Professor Polson talked excitedly about how swift, how efficient, it had become to trace the dead to the living, or to each other. Mr. Dientz was clearly attracted to Professor Polson. Twice, he'd called her "my dear," and when she was looking through her briefcase, safely distracted, Perry had seen him lean over his desk and peer at the place where the buttons of her silk blouse were undone, where a bit of cleavage could be glimpsed. It probably didn't hurt either that, all along, she'd been expressing admiration for his work, for his facility, for his skills. She'd talked to him about other funeral homes she'd visited, a convention of morticians she'd attended, morgues in other states and countries, practices long forgotten and those still in vogue, and she'd compared his favorably to all those. Either Professor Polson knew this would make Mr. Dientz putty in her hands, or she genuinely admired and understood him.

"You know," he told her, not looking over at Perry, "I feel like being honest with you. I don't keep the DNA just for identification—because, honestly, how often does *this* happen. I mean, as I've said, it happens, but not frequently enough to warrant the trouble of keeping the kinds of records I have. You know, it occurred to me when I first heard about the military project: *ah-ha, they have a plan.*"

Professor Polson nodded, and he took a breath.

"DNA can replicate itself, of course, and how many years away are we, really, from learning how to build a human being, a clone, if you will, a replica from only the most microscopic sample? I thought to myself, this is how they'll raise their armies in the future, now that American boys are getting so soft. Why, even my own sons—don't get me started! There's no way those boys could save our butts in a war. We're not raising real men anymore in this country, and the military knows this. No. They've saved the DNA of the military elite, the fighting machines. They will raise their armies out of those as needed.

"And I thought, shouldn't *my* dead have the same advantages? They may not have died heroes, most of them, but a mortician feels an affection for his dead, and, I've felt that, as the last one to whom their care had been entrusted, I owed them the possibility of this raising. Certainly their families were in too much shock and pain to take care of details like this. Plus, it only takes a few seconds. The cards are small. I've only filled one file drawer so far."

Professor Polson's mouth was open, but she said nothing. She blinked, seeming astonished, speechless.

"But!" Mr. Dientz said, "in the meantime, I have what we need to solve this mystery!" There was more color in Mr. Dientz's face then than there had been even when he was discussing the marvels of reconstruction and his passion for the work.

Now he'd disappeared into his basement to find Nicole's card.

Perry took the keys from Professor Polson.

"Go see your parents," she suggested. "But if you feel like you can stand it, could you visit the Werners? Pay your respects, as it were. And— just see. We might need them, you know. Their cooperation, eventually. I'll take care of things here while you're gone, and then we'll see what's next."

"Okay," he said, although he didn't want to go. He didn't want to leave the funeral home, to face his own or Nicole's parents, to drive off into Bad Axe, which, in this new context, seemed like an entirely alien place. But he nodded, and said, again, "Okay."

"And if you *do* visit the Werners, Perry," Professor Polson said, "it couldn't hurt to bring something back. Everyone has a hairbrush, or a comb, or a few strands of hair lying around a bathroom sink. With all those sisters? All that hair? Mr. Dientz said he needed five hairs, but I've heard of this being accomplished with one. I don't want you to do anything you feel uncomfortable doing, but it would save us having to tell them, right now, about any of this, if, until—"

"Yes." Perry nodded.

It was early evening but already pitch-black outside. Snow had been falling all day, and now it looked like shattered glass all over the lawns and the sidewalks and the streets of Bad Axe. No one was out. The only signs of human life Perry glimpsed were behind curtains: shadows in front of flickering television screens, a lamp burning over a shadow's desk. Some people had their Christmas lights up already. Blinking, blinking.

Every house, Perry realized as he passed them, had a story—and because it was a small town, Perry knew the stories. It wasn't always death, but, over there, somebody's grandmother had fought off her meth-addict grandson with a shovel when he came to try to steal her wedding ring. Across the street from that, Melanie Shenk's house was dark. Her mother, Perry knew, had been put in jail for bank fraud. One of the houses on the corner belonged to the father of another girl Perry had gone to school with, a girl a few years older than he was. Sophie Marks. Everyone had pitied her because her parents were divorced and her father had custody and she dressed poorly, and often joked, herself, about not having had an actual home-cooked meal in her entire life. ("How is that different, 'home-cooked,' from, say hot dogs?"), but now she was a flight attendant, married to a pilot, and Perry's mom had told him that Sophie flew her father, a retired postman, all over the world for free these days. "Last I heard he was headed to Singapore."

Before Perry realized he'd done it, he'd driven past his own house without stopping, only glancing at it as if it were any other house on the block—lit up warmly from within, someone's mother carrying a plate of something to a table. Someone's father at the table. They would not be expecting a knock on their door. It would surprise them, concern them, to find their son, who was at college, at that door.

He was, instead, on his way to the Werners'. Left on Brookside. Right on Robbins.

He'd done this drive a hundred times, picking up Nicole for a student council carwash or debate team meeting. He'd had access to a car, and she didn't. It was a small town. No one needed directions to anyone's house. All you had to do was say, "Oh, he's three houses down from the Werners," or "Catty-corner to the Edwardses, and then across the street."

The Werners' house was lit up warmly, too. They already had their Christmas lights up. Blues and reds and whites and greens shone in little points along the eaves. The curtains in the front window of their nice little ranch house were closed.

Perry had been in that house many times. There were only a few bedrooms, he knew, and so many girls. The sleeping arrangements must have changed with the years, as one girl went to college and another girl got a room of her own. The house was small, but it had always seemed warm and clean. Perry had always had the feeling, as he waited in the living room for Nicole, that you could crawl around all day on your hands and knees in that house looking for a speck of dust and never find one. Of course, their restaurant was the same way. You could imagine it being run through a car wash every few hours. Blasted into perfection. Every surface shining.

But the Christmas lights seemed strange.

Had Perry expected black drapery over the windows?

Well, no. But he hadn't expected early Christmas lights. And he was even more surprised to see, beyond the Christmas lights and the gauzy curtains, several female shadows gathered around the broad shoulders of a masculine shadow. They were gathered, Perry realized, after stopping the car in the middle of the street and staring long enough, around the Hammond organ in the Werners' living room.

All the girls played, he was pretty sure, as well as Mr. Werner. Nicole had told him about the all-night caroling that went on sometimes on Christmas Eve.

He turned off the engine of Professor Blackhawk's car after parking it in front of the house, and the whole rattle-trap—chrome, engine, upholstery—shuddered loudly before dying. It was more noise than Perry had expected to make or he'd have parked farther away, and someone in the house, apparently, had heard it, too. He watched as one of the feminine shadows (Mrs. Werner?) turned from the gathering and moved toward the window. Her hand parted the curtains, just at their edge, and he saw a face, silhouetted with the light from behind, peer out quickly before dropping the curtain. She seemed to have said something that made the others turn away from the organ and look at her.

Perry was glad, he supposed, that they knew someone was on the way, glad that there'd been a bit of warning.

He'd hated the idea of surprising them.

Even with their other daughters at home, even gathered around an organ, Perry imagined that the grief of the place would have its own texture—those shadows—and a smell, maybe the smell of the Dumpster in the parking lot behind Dumplings. When Perry was first learning to ride a bike, his father would sometimes take him to that parking lot on a Saturday morning before the restaurant opened, when there was no one there. It had a hill that sloped down into nothing but high grass, so it was a good place to practice turning, braking—better than the street in front of his house, where a car might be coming. Perry used to smell the Dumpster those mornings, and it wasn't a bad smell. Just yeasty, tired, soft disintegration. Wet bread, he thought. And the scraped-off remnants of cabbage some child had refused to eat. Maybe half a piece of black cherry torte some woman on a diet hadn't finished. Gravy in a garbage bag, bones.

Perry got out of the car and slammed the door loudly behind him (more warning), and then he took a slow step toward the door, which Mrs. Werner had opened before he'd even had a chance to knock—and although she looked happy and flushed (just as he remembered her from years before, bustling around her restaurant, bringing special treats of dark bread and homemade jam over to the tables where "my daughters' chums!" sat), she did not look pleased to see him.

Perry glanced beyond her to the place where the family had been gathered, but there was no one in the living room now. Still, he could see a bright red electrical dot glowing over the keys of the Hammond organ.

The Hammond organ was on.

Perry thought he could hear it humming when Mrs. Werner, reluctantly, it seemed, stepped aside to let him in.

"Nice to see you, Perry. How are your folks?"

"They're fine, Mrs. Werner. I—"

"What can I do for you?"

"I just came by to say hello. I—"

"I was just getting ready to go out, but if you'd like to sit down for a second—"

Mrs. Werner pointed to a white couch. There was a sheet of plastic over it, and Perry remembered the long-haired black cat, Grouch, who'd hissed at him once when he'd knelt down to pet it, and how Nicole had laughed like crazy. ("God, he likes *everybody*. He's never done that to anyone! That's why we call him Grouch.") Perry had never bothered to ask her if she was just kidding—if, in truth, that cat hissed at everyone and she was being ironic, or if it was true, that the cat really *was* friendly, and the name Grouch was ironic. Now he wished he knew.

"Do you still have Grouch?" he asked Mrs. Werner—stupidly, he thought, as soon as the words had left his mouth. (After all that had happened, he was asking about their cat?)

"Why do you ask?" Mrs. Werner said, sitting down in a matching white armchair, also covered in plastic, across a glass-topped coffee table from him. Perhaps it *had* been a stupid question, Perry thought, but he was still surprised by her response, and all he could think of to say was, "I remember him."

"Well, yes, we still have Grouch. He's old. But a cat can live for over twenty years."

"Oh, that's great," Perry said.

"How are your parents?" Mrs. Werner asked again.

"They're fine, Mrs. Werner. They're great. I mean, I haven't seen them yet, but Thanksgiving's just around—"

"You came up to Bad Axe to visit *us*?" Mrs. Werner asked, opening her eyes wide, her expression alarmed. Perry thought she looked as beautiful as any of her daughters ever had. Her face seemed nearly unlined, bright with good health. Her hair was gray, but it wasn't the dry gray he remembered from the funeral, the last time he'd seen her. Now it looked soft. It fell in silver waves around her shoulders.

"Well, no," Perry said. "But since I was here, I wanted to say hello."

"Thank you," Mrs. Werner said, and clapped her hands on her knees, as if that sealed the deal. End of discussion. "That's very kind of you, Perry. We always thought a great deal of you, and also your parents. We'll miss them."

"You'll miss them?"

Mrs. Werner looked at Perry curiously.

"Oh," she said. "I assumed you knew, that it was the reason for your lovely visit. We've sold the restaurant. We're moving to Arizona. In two weeks."

"In two weeks?"

"Yes. I know some people think it seems sudden, but we've been considering retirement for a long time. Mr. Werner and I are not spring chickens, and, well—"

"Of course." Perry was being polite. What he felt was confusion, and a strange disbelief. Who was he to question the plans and the motives of these people? But all these generations in Bad Axe? His first school had been Werner Elementary. Now they were moving to Arizona? In two weeks?

Mrs. Werner stood up. She said, "I certainly appreciate this chance to say good-bye, Perry. It was delightful to see you, and if you ever get to Arizona—"

"Where in Arizona?"

Mrs. Werner cleared her throat and said, "That's yet to be determined, Perry. Probably Phoenix. Of course, I'll send word to all the good folks up here when we have a permanent address."

The smile on her face was anxious, but not entirely false. She *was* happy to see Perry, he could tell by the warmth of her embrace, and she was sorry about something, too, but when he asked if he could use her bathroom before he left, the smile evaporated.

She stood looking at him for several seconds, as if she expected him to take the request back. When he didn't, she said, "Well, dear, let me just take a peek in there first to make sure there aren't any towels on the floor. You know, we've gotten sloppy, getting ready for the move, and I wouldn't—"

Before Perry could object, say he really didn't care about the state of their bathroom, she disappeared through a door in the hallway attached to the living room, and when she returned, she said, "It's fine. Go ahead," and Perry stepped past her, closed the door behind him.

There was light blue tile. Seashells on the wallpaper, just like the wallpaper his mother had hung one Saturday afternoon a few summers back (probably bought it at the same store: a sale, a promotion, at the same time). As quickly as he could, Perry got on his hands and knees on the white carpeting and began to search for anything other than black cat hairs (Grouch: they were everywhere). He couldn't find anything. But when he stood back up, he saw it: a hairbrush on the shelf above the toilet tank. A brush with a tortoiseshell handle and white bristles. It was small, the kind of thing he could slip into his jacket pocket. He looked at it and saw that it was a treasure trove: There were long blond strands of hair floating ethereally out of it, and shorter gray hairs mixed in with those. A feminine nest, something made out of silk and breath. He took a Kleenex out of a box on the sink, wrapped it around the head of the brush, and put it into his pocket just before flushing the toilet, clearing his throat, opening the bathroom door, and stepping back into the living room.

"Okay?" Mrs. Werner asked. She held the front door open for him, despite the cold wind blowing through it, and there was no mistaking her fervent desire that, now, he leave.

Perry reached out and extended a hand to Mrs. Werner, who took it in hers and squeezed with genuine warmth, until he looked down, and she must have noticed him noticing the amber ring on her finger (it had not, he felt sure, been there when she'd taken his hand when he first arrived), and then she was pulling her hand back and closing the door without saying good-bye.

He went back to the car, walking as slowly as he could. He wanted to turn back, wanted to think up some good reason that he would. Was there any conceivable thing he'd "forgotten" to say to the parents of the girl at whose funeral he'd been a pallbearer only nine months before? Maybe *We're thinking Nicole is still alive?* Or *We think your daughter may have risen from the dead?*

No.

He had to resign himself to getting back into Professor Blackhawk's car, and starting it up, and driving it off.

But Perry had driven only a few blocks (past the Hollidays'—one of whose sons, the last Perry had heard, was a homeless violinist in Santa Monica—and around the corner on which Mrs. Samm lived with the children of her youngest daughter, who'd been killed in motorcycle accident) when he pulled to the curb again and turned off the engine:

A whole group of girls had been gathered around that organ, which Mr. Werner had been playing, and when they'd realized someone was stopping by, they'd fled.

It was a small house. Three bedrooms? Was the basement even finished? The kitchen was small enough, as he recalled it, to have been called a kitchenette. They had to have gone to the farthest bedroom. They had to have been holding their breaths. Had they sat at the edges of the bed, holding their fingers to their lips to remind themselves to stay silent?

Why?

It would have been crazy.

If they'd wanted to avoid him, all they'd have had to do was have Mrs. Werner say at the door, "We're busy at the moment, Perry, or I'd invite you in—"

No.

They didn't want him to know they were there.

Or was he the one who was crazy?

Perry got out of the car then and started to walk back to the Werners'.

90

Ted Dientz reminded Mira of a gym teacher she'd had, one of the few junior high teachers who'd seemed to really love his job, feel serious passion for his subject. Sometimes, even now, Mira thought of him while teaching one of her own classes, remembering the way he'd stood in front of a slide projection of an illustration of the muscles of the human body.

Rippling, himself, with muscles, Mr. Baker would point out the best ones, the ones that could be developed with "so little work you won't even know you're doing it." The benefits of this, the beauty of weightlifting, sometimes seemed to overwhelm him as he tried to describe it. ("You won't believe it. One day you won't even be able to lift something, and in a short time, you won't even *feel* like you're lifting it.") And although Mira had never become interested in weightlifting, she'd learned something about enthusiasm from Mr. Baker, and how a teacher can convey a sense of it to his students. It was Mr. Baker she'd thought of in her own freshman Latin class upon learning that the word *enthusiasmus* meant "inspired by a god."

In the case of Ted Dientz, there was no doubt that it was the God of the Underworld who possessed him, but Mira understood as well as anyone what that was like. When he brought up the envelope with the bloodstain card from the basement, he said, "You know there's very little that a few blood cells or a strand of hair can't tell us any longer. You could be a master of disguise, but if I could compare a single one of your cells to a strand of your mother's hair, I would instantly know who you are."

He let Mira take the envelope from his hands, and said, "Go ahead. It's in sealant. You can't hurt it."

Mira opened the envelope and slid out the card. It was a little bigger than a business card. The top half of it was white, and it had Nicole's name and birth and death dates written on it in black capital letters, in a felt-tip pen. The bottom half was purple with a dime-size circle in the center, and in the center of that lay a dark and ragged little stain.

Ted Dientz tapped it and said, "That's our girl."

Mira looked at the little stain. Nicole, if it *was* Nicole.

"Everything there we need to know. Everything we'd need to bring her back to life, really, if we had just a bit more know-how. Well, someday!" He chuckled, and then he took the card from her, tucked it back into the envelope, and held it on his lap. It stayed there between them like a third person—not a ghost, exactly, just a presence—as they talked about Mira's research, her book, her travels, and his travels.

Ted Dientz had, himself, as she had, visited Bran Castle in the Carpathian Mountains.

"Of course, my wife and I didn't tell the folks around here that we were visiting Dracula's castle. It would have looked bad for business."

"So what did you tell them?" Mira asked, before realizing it might embarrass him, his lie.

"Well, we said we were on a mission trip. Orphanages and such."

(And indeed he blushed from his necktie to his forehead as he told her.) "But you can imagine my interest! As I can tell you understand, as so few people do, it's not a morbid fascination; it's a scientific one. I'm not interested in vampires, but I *am* interested in legends surrounding death. I have, myself, witnessed some extraordinary things."

Mira nodded for him to go on, while resisting the urge to take out her notebook and pen.

"I've seen, for instance, corpses sit up and sound as if they were screaming. Of course, it's biological. It's utterly explainable. But let me tell you—" He laughed, and so did she. "And there have been bodies that seemed to withstand decay for strangely long periods of time, Professor. Others that disintegrated even as I moved them from their deathbed to a stretcher. And the differences have so little to do with age, with disease. Certainly, a more primitive people would have needed a way to explain this, along with other things, such as the sense one sometimes has of a presence. Sometimes malevolent. Sometimes desperate."

"How do you explain it?" Mira asked.

"Well, I don't," Ted Dientz said a little sheepishly. "It might surprise you to know," he added, raising his eyebrows, clearly hoping that it would, "that Mrs. Dientz and I traveled to Thailand after the tsunami and assisted in the preparation and disposal of bodies. The need for morticians and others in the death arts was extraordinary at that time. It was perhaps the most important work I've ever been able to offer."

It *did* surprise Mira. It was easier to imagine Mr. and Mrs. Dientz of Bad Axe on a travel tour of Dracula's castle than taking a plane to one of the most devastated places in the world.

Ted Dientz went on to tell Mira that during the weeks he'd spent in Thailand he'd met many people who believed they'd seen drowned corpses rise from the waters, walk onto shore, stride past horrified on-lookers, and even hail cabs to be driven away.

"Did they think they were ghosts?" Mira asked.

"Some believed they were ghosts, yes. In fact, most cab drivers re-fused to make their rounds down by the beach in those early weeks, claiming they were being hailed by ghosts, or that they could see the dead tourists on the beach still looking for each other, or playing obliviously in the sea. One told me, 'They think they're still on vacation.' But most people seemed to think these were actually *reanimated* corpses. It's not an unusual belief, Professor, as you know. I have to tell you, you'd think a man like me, having spent his whole life in this business, would find that laughable, but I don't."

She nodded.

She felt her eyes welling stupidly with tears.

The simple honesty of this man, with her, a stranger. He had waited, she felt, a long time to tell someone other than Mrs. Dientz about all this. It meant something to him that she was nodding. He rested his hand patiently on the envelope containing the bloodstain card. He was a man *made* of patience, she thought.

Now she owed him her own story, she felt—or, she realized, too, that she needed to tell it, just as he'd needed to tell someone. So she started, the day she had stayed home from school, the vision of her mother in the pantry, the funeral years later, the strange and terrifying images that had inspired her entire life's work. She had just finished speaking, and Mr. Dientz was nodding, quiet but fully attentive, when Perry came back through the door, out of breath, *gasping* for breath, holding the handle of a hairbrush wrapped in tissue and trailing a little white blizzard behind him.

91

Craig was halfway up the stairs to his apartment when he heard a door open and someone clomping unevenly toward the stairwell. "Oh, hello," he said, when he recognized her, and then covered his face in his down jacket, which he'd taken off, when he recognized the look of horror on her face.

"Holy shit," Deb said, rushing to him, holding the back of his head in one hand and his coat in the other, pressing his face into the jacket even harder, to the point that he was a little afraid that the tiny, goosey feathers might smother him. "What the fuck did they do to you?"

She hurried him as quickly as a girl on crutches could hurry someone into her apartment, pulled the door closed behind him, shoved him toward her bedroom, where, it appeared, she hadn't done anything—changed the sheets, made the bed—since rousing him from sleep there the day before.

"It looks worse than it is," Craig told her, but he knew the words were muffled by his jacket, and that there was blood all over the top of his head, so who knew what she thought he was saying to her?

"Oh, my God," she was saying. "Oh, my God. Oh, my God. I'll be right back. I'll get some towels."

Craig felt bad about it—he would ruin her towels with his bloody nose, he might stain her sheets with the blood running down his neck—but he let himself fall backward, hard, onto her bed, and the room swirled around him like a warm bath. Never in his life had a bed felt this comfortable. It would be fine, he thought, if she came back with the towels, but it would also be fine if someone just came in here and turned off the lights and let him lie like this forever.

"Here!" she screamed, tossing the towels toward him. And then, again, "Oh, my God!"

"It's just a bloody nose, maybe broken," Craig said—although he also knew that with his current nasal intonation, she probably had no idea what he'd said. "No big deal. I've had one before. Just gotta put a bandage on it if it's broken. Maybe I'll have black eyes."

He took the jacket off his face, grabbed a towel, and could tell by the way she inhaled that he must already have black eyes.

"What *happened*?" she asked, and the way she said it was so serious that he felt, somehow, the need to suppress his own laughter. He pressed the towel harder against his face. He could almost hear the snow falling outside. Those flakes, big as little hands, had slapped him upside the head the entire walk home from Greek Row. The whole way there'd been the gasping of girls when they saw the little trail of blood he was leaving in the snow, and the "Whoa, dude" of the guys, and the whole time he'd felt this same urge to laugh right along with the urge to hit someone, to pummel someone, to punch someone in the face, the feeling he imagined boxers had—a profound love and joy and urge to do violence all wrapped up in one profound physical desire.

But he didn't do it. He'd just kept walking. Laughing, and maybe weeping (was that tears or blood, and what was the difference now?) as he kept walking, thinking of her taking one look at him, running. *She wasn't dead. He'd seen her with his own eyes:*

The fucking lying, cheating bitch hadn't died.

She was the one who'd been calling. The postcards were hers. The beautiful girl he'd loved and killed had come back to life.

Deb left and reemerged above him with what looked like a washcloth full of rocks, or ice, and sat beside him on the bed, moving the towel gently away from his face and lowering her little frozen surprise toward his nose, making noises of empathy and disgust as she did it and demanding that he tell her something he had no idea how to begin to tell her, or anyone, because there were no words with which to express such a thing.

92

I saw her, too," Perry said, holding out the brush to them. "At the same time. Here. I saw her with my own eyes."

"Perry," Professor Polson said, taking a step toward him. "What do you mean?"

"I went back there. I left the car, and I got down on my hands and knees, and I crawled through the Barbers' backyard, and I found a window with a little crack in the curtain, and I put my hands up to it—"

At first, he could see almost nothing through that crack, but every other window had a shade pulled so tight he could see nothing at all through those. So he'd stood there with his hands pressed against the pane long after his hands had gone numb, staring at a little place between what appeared to be a china hutch and the dangling chains of a cuckoo clock, watching the shadows come and go against it, listening to the muttering of voices, and a few high notes of laughter, but mostly serious-sounding voices.

Now and then Mrs. Werner passed before him—Perry recognized the gray-blue dress she'd been wearing, and then another female form: Mary? Constance?

There was a soft gray sweater.

There was what looked like a plaid skirt.

He saw one pair of female arms bearing what must have been Grouch in her arms, and a few times Mr. Werner came and went in a yellow shirt. Finally, Perry was about to leave. (What the hell am I doing? he'd thought.) The snow had soaked through his jacket all the way to his skin, and he realized that he was standing in the perfect place where, if one of the neighbors decided to turn on their porch light, he'd be illuminated for everyone to see, and there would be no way to get away except by scaling their picket fence, and then—

And then she was leaning over.

She was picking up something she'd dropped on the floor.

Her hair was the flaxen blond he remembered from elementary school—whispering around her face, curling around the curve of her upper arm.

Volleyball. Reaching up with that arm, to serve, to spike.

His bed.

She'd rolled over and swung it over his chest and said, "Craig would just die if he walked in here now."

And he'd said into the nape of the neck he was staring at now, "And why does that make you laugh?"

And she'd laughed.

Now she laughed. Her familiar laugh. She managed to pick up whatever it was she'd dropped and stick it back into her flossy hair (a comb, a barrette), and just at that moment she turned to the window and fixed him with a look he also knew:

Hide and Seek in the Coxes' backyard.

I see you.

Her lips were redder than he remembered, and her cheeks were flushed—not that different from the flush on the cheeks of her mother—and her eyes seem to flash in his direction, and she tilted back her head toward the ceiling, and when she laughed he could see her teeth brighten in the overhead light, and he could feel through his whole body the sharp stabbing pain of her laugh.

93

A re you fooling around with Perry or something?"

"What?"

"How many times have I passed you on the stairwell just as I'm headed up to the room, and when I get there Perry's either asleep or has just left for the shower?"

"I was up there looking for you, Craig."

They were standing in the stairwell, facing one another, and the late winter twilight from the one little window shone on the linoleum, casting the shadow of its diamond panes across Nicole's pale feet.

She was wearing flip-flops. She wasn't planning to go anywhere outside. Her toenails were painted pink. She rested her hand on the wooden rail and began to smooth it with her palm. Craig looked at the hand. Her fingernails were also pink, and the way she was touching that rail—recently varnished, it seemed, so that it shone, while still bearing under that gleaming shellac job all the nicks and scratches and carved initials of about a million students. He wanted to pull her hand away from the railing. Jesus, how many germs from how many hands was she touching as she touched it?

She licked her bottom lip, and suddenly that familiar little tic (when she was nervous or upset or about to cry) seemed almost obscene to him.

Her cheeks looked flushed against the pasty stairwell walls, and her lips were very red. Craig thought he could smell her, too, even though she was standing several feet from him, and it wasn't her usual baby powder smell, or the smell of her flowery shampoo. She smelled, he thought, like sex.

He looked down again at her hand rubbing the railing, and had to stop himself from grabbing the hand, making her stop.

"I went up there to tell you I've got to do laundry tonight. Josie and I are picking out dresses for the Spring Event."

"But you knew I wasn't there. You knew I was at the lecture I was assigned to attend."

(Awful: An old professor who mumbled into a microphone for over an hour about the Post-Copernican Double Bind and the epistemological consequences of the Cartesian cogito—whatever the hell all that was. The undergraduates had started to file out at the same moment, like a timer had gone off or something in the middle of the lecture, and Craig had followed them, as the professor droned on. He'd hurried back to the dorm, imagining the poor guy still going on and on back there for the benefit of the two graduate students in the front row.)

"I just happened to be back early. You had no reason to think I'd be back in the room yet."

"I'm sorry. I guess I don't know your schedule well enough, Craig."

"But this isn't the first time."

"You're saying you think I'm—?"

Was he? Was that what he was saying? Did he really think she was— what? Fucking Perry? Was he really looking at Nicole and thinking to himself that there was even the remotest possibility that all this sweet virginity business, the promise ring she wore on her left hand—the amber ring, he noticed now, was not on her right hand tonight, but she said she had to take it off sometimes when she did a lot of typing—that it was all a joke? That not only wasn't she a virgin, but she was screwing his roommate?

Perry?

He knew Perry wasn't crazy about him, but they'd been getting along a lot better lately. Perry, the Boy Scout. Even if Nicole would do it, Perry wouldn't.

Still, there was one thing Craig remembered from the lecture that night, and it bothered him at the moment, just as Nicole took a step toward him, and he could see that her eyes were filled with tears, and her blazingly red lips were trembling, and he knew that she was about to put her head on his shoulder, or press her face into his chest—something about Kant. How the human mind orders reality subjectively. The geezer had called it the "relative and unrooted nature of human knowledge."

It was the only thing Craig had bothered to write down.

It was stuck now in his mind like a disturbing image, a catchy song.

But when Nicole lifted her tear-streaked face to his, he shook his head and took her in his arms.

94

For miles hers seemed to be the only vehicle on the freeway. Now and then a truck passed in the opposite direction, its wipers sloshing snow off the windshield with what looked like elaborate, sloppy showgirl boas and sweeps. Shelly imagined the drivers in those cabs. They would be hypnotized by the sound of their own wipers. They might be listening to talk shows, to the voices of strangers phoning in from other corners of the country, asking personal questions or expressing heartfelt convictions. Those truckers might be nearing sleep, or jangled up with caffeine and those energy pills they sold at the counters of gas stations. The snow seemed frenzied, suicidal, tossing itself into her path, but Shelly herself wasn't lulled into any kind of sleep by the sound of the wipers.

She was more awake and alert than she had ever been in her life.

And although she realized that, really, she'd spent all of her adult years alone (or maybe every year of her life since her brother had died and her parents had fallen apart), this was the first night that she was acutely, completely, aware of how utterly alone she was.

She thought of Jeremy.

She thought of the James Joyce story.

The snow falling on the living and the dead.

There was no sense listening to the radio.

It was just more living and dying.

A few more miles, and she passed a truck jackknifed in the center median, surrounded by orange flares, and could see, heading toward it on the opposite side of the freeway, a police car's flashing red and blue lights beyond the heavy veil of what now could only be described as a nearly total whiteout.

She should get off the freeway. If she could have stood to listen to the radio, she knew that was the advice she would have heard. She had just seen a sign for a Motel 6, a Cracker Barrel, a Quik Mart (Exit 49), and although she did not recall ever having pulled over on this particular exit, or being at this particular town (Brighton), she took comfort in knowing exactly what it would be like.

How many hundreds of Motel 6's had she experienced in her life?

How many Cracker Barrels? Quik Marts?

Unlike many of her fellow academics, Shelly actually went to these places. She stayed in them. Ate in them. Purchased her snacks and beverages in them. She loved them for the very things for which her colleagues disdained them. Their kitschy sameness, and the way the girls at the cash registers always said something like, "Hi there! What's up? Find everything okay?"

Shelly could pull off at this exit she'd never pulled off at before in her life, step out of her car blindfolded, and find her way to everything. The laminated menu. The check-in counter. The Slushy machine.

No. She wouldn't pull over yet. Not at Exit 49. She would keep driving, and she did. Exit 49 blurred right past, and then Shelly realized where she'd wanted to go all along—and although she hated other people who scrolled through the addresses in their cell phones while driving in perilous conditions, she did it herself until she'd found Ellen Graham's phone number, and then was hearing herself ask this poor woman, this nearly perfect stranger, if it would be okay if she stopped by (in the dark, in a blizzard) for the second time in a day.

95

A re you okay, Perry?"
Perry nodded. Again, he had his hands against the fan, blowing its feeble attempt at heat on the dashboard of Jeff's car. They should stop and buy him gloves, Mira thought, before leaving Bad Axe. There was a stillness to the air that made the snow seem even colder and more enveloping than it ordinarily would—and of course there was so little heat coming out of the vents that it seemed pointless to be idling in the funeral home parking lot, letting the car "warm up." The car seemed only to grow colder as they sat in it, engine rumbling around them, interior lit up by the white electric Dientz Funeral Parlor sign, as if that pale light were lowering the temperature of everything it touched.

Still, Mira wasn't ready to drive, and Perry had yet to speak since he'd said good-bye to Mr. Dientz.

When he'd first come back from the Werners', he'd spoken so quickly, been so flushed and breathless, that he reminded Mira of the ranting "preacher" who sometimes stood on a bench on campus and shouted at the students as they passed. On every campus she'd ever studied or visited, there had been such a preacher. Always a cheap-looking suit, a good haircut, eyes so pale they seemed to be lacking irises. What this particular ranting man said usually made sense, sentence to sentence, but no sense at all when put together: Lightning was striking cell phone towers. The producers of television shows were trying to read our minds. People in gray coats were hard to see, and could sneak up on you.

Perry had seemed to be trying to hold back that same ranting passion, bordering on mania, insanity, when he came back saying he'd seen Nicole.

He'd seen Nicole, he said.

He'd seen her teeth.

But there was also something about a cat, and Mrs. Werner's hair—how it was more beautiful than it used to be—and a Hammond organ and a game of Hide and Seek, and then he just quit talking altogether, and Mira knew she had to get him out of there. She'd said to Mr. Dientz, "It's time for us to leave."

It had been a day full of shock and awe, and Mira regretted the toll it had obviously taken on Perry—beginning with the horror of Lucas at the morgue, and then the discussion with the woman from the Chamber Music Society, and then the photographs on Mr. Dientz's computer.

It was no wonder it had ended with Perry seeing a dead girl in her parents' house.

Mira looked over at him and thought of the cliché "you look like you've seen a ghost"—but didn't say it. She reached over and took one of the hands that was pressed to the heater and brought it to her cheek.

Poor dear, she was thinking, surprised by how cold the hand was to her touch.

96

"Hey there, Perry. It's me."

"Yeah, Nicole."

"You alone?"

"Well, since you know my roommate's every move, and you know he went to try to score some weed in Ohio with Lucas, I suppose you know I am."

There was a click then, and a hum.

The hum was nothing.

It was the very song of what nothing was, Perry thought, holding the receiver to his ear long enough that he was still holding it when she knocked on his door, and when he opened it, she said, "Can I come in?" and he was breathing into her hair before saying yes, before he'd even taken a breath.

97

Ellen Graham was wearing the same hot pink bathrobe she'd been wearing earlier that day—although she seemed to have tidied the house a little, perhaps because she'd had some warning this time that Shelly was on her way. The piles of catalogs and envelopes that had been lying on the stairs were now stacked in a few loose piles by the front door. The white cat was lying in a pale patch of porch light that was somehow shining through a crack in the closed curtain. Eerily this cat looked a little like the kind of cat who would have avoided sunlight, anyway, in favor of this reflected winter light. Shelly felt a stab of longing, of grief, for Jeremy, poor Jeremy, who had so loved to bask in a pool of sunlight on the bed or on the kitchen floor.

"Sit down," Ellen said, and motioned Shelly to the couch. "I'm glad you came back. I thought about you all day. I wondered if you'd had any ideas since you left, since our talk. Ideas about my daughter, where—"

"Again," Shelly said, shaking her head a little, "I don't want to mislead you, Ellen. I have no proof of anything. But I *have* had some more thoughts."

"You look terrible," Ellen said. "Has something happened?"

Not now, Shelly thought. She could not tell anyone, now, about Jeremy. That would have to wait. Instead, she said, "After I left here I went home, got on Google, and then I found the boy, the one who was in the accident with Nicole Werner. I went to his apartment, and we talked. There was a professor there, and another student who also knew Nicole. They're—"

Shelly stopped herself before saying that they had gone to Nicole Werner's hometown to speak to the mortician who'd buried her because of a suspicion that it might not be Nicole in that grave. Shelly knew that if she were Denise Graham's mother, she would have known instantly what that meant. She took a deep breath and said carefully, "I believe you might be the only one who can institute any further investigation. I'm not saying that it might even lead us to—"

"Finding Denise." Ellen nodded. Her eyes looked somehow clearer tonight. Her feet were still bare, and that struck Shelly as the saddest thing of all. It was so cold out, and even in the house, where the thermostat must have been turned up to eighty degrees, the floors were cold. She tried to look away from the feet, but she couldn't. She thought of *Death of a Salesman*. Willy Loman. *Attention must be paid.*

The toenails were clipped neatly, but the toes looked gnarled, red— the toes of a woman who had, until recently, worn high heels every day of her life. Ellen Graham had been a woman who, proud of her long, slim legs, had probably worn knee-length skirts, too, and silk hose, just to go to the grocery store.

"As I told you," Shelly said, looking from the sad feet to the face, so bright with hope, "I worked at the Chamber Music Society at the university until recently. What I didn't exactly explain earlier today was that my work-study student this year was Josie Reilly—"

Ellen inhaled, as if willing herself not to scream at the sound of that name.

"Yes. I'm sorry I didn't tell you before, but it's complicated by so many things."

Ellen nodded, but her jaw was working on her anger. God help Josie if she ever crossed this woman's path again, Shelly thought, not without some satisfaction. Eventually, she knew, she would have to tell Ellen the whole, sordid story, but it wouldn't help either of them now, and might end with Shelly thrown out the front door and into the snow, having accomplished nothing at all.

Instead, Shelly started by telling Ellen what Josie had told her about the coffin, about the Spring Event. The hyperventilation. The EMT kept on hand for emergencies.

Ellen listened without seeming to be breathing.

She had, of course, like so many other mothers, assumed that the Spring Event was a party, a dance, a princess ball. There would be decorations, and hors d'oeuvres, and pretty dresses, and maybe a bit too much champagne, ending in giggling, and dancing around the OTT house in stocking feet.

Even after all that had happened, Ellen had not yet begun to suspect that this image might be entirely wrong.

"Were you ever in a sorority, Ellen?" Shelly asked.

Ellen Graham shook her head. "I didn't go to college," she said. "I married my husband right out of high school, and I worked as a secretary until he finished his MBA. And then I had Denise."

Shelly nodded. "Well, I was," she said. "It was over two decades ago, but some things are the same. Hazing, and—"

"Hazing is illegal," Ellen said. "We would never have allowed Denise to join a sorority if we thought—"

"I know," Shelly said. "But it happens. And being illegal has made it even more dangerous, even more secretive." She went on to tell Ellen Graham, who held a hand to her mouth now as Shelly spoke, what she knew about the Pan-Hellenic Society and the pressures that could be put to bear by it on a university—a public university, the funding of which was dependent on the goodwill of the taxpayers, which its administrators understood so well.

"I questioned," Shelly said, "how someone like Josie Reilly had come to get one of the work-study positions generally reserved for students who pay their own tuition and who come from fairly disadvantaged backgrounds. As it happens, the music school dean's wife was an Omega Theta Tau sister of Josie's mother. It took only a little bit of research to find out that the two of them are still very involved in the chapter. They would have a vested interest in preventing any scandal related to, say, hazing."

"But what does this have to do with my daughter?" Ellen asked. From the change in her posture, the rigid backbone, Shelly suspected she already knew.

"I was at the scene of the accident," Shelly said. She held her palms open, hands resting on her knees in a gesture she'd been taught to make by her mother when beseeching God to take care of her brother in Vietnam, and which she'd never made again after he died.

She looked down at her open hands then and said to them, "Nicole Werner wasn't visibly injured. She sustained injury, certainly, since she was thrown from the vehicle. She might have sustained terrible, life-threatening internal injuries, but Nicole Werner was not—"

"Beyond recognition."

Shelly could not look up from her hands until long after she'd nodded and Ellen Graham had already spoken again:

"But that boy," she said, "the one who was drunk, why wouldn't he have said something if—?"

"If there was someone else with them?"

Ellen nodded this time, boring her eyes deeply into Shelly's, and Shelly felt an incredible wave of wild energy and bravery emanating from her.

To sit so completely still, with her poor feet pressed together, chapped hands folded sadly in her lap, waiting for Shelly's answer.

"As I said, I spoke to him. Today. Finally. I don't know what took me so long to go looking for him. He doesn't remember anything."

"But *of course* that's what he'd say. They could have put him in jail for *years* for what he did."

"Yes," Shelly said. "I'm a suspicious woman, too, Ellen. I feel I have good radar for liars, cheats, cons—but I don't think he's one. He doesn't remember. He truly does not know. Or he only peripherally knows. Something happened to him."

Shelly went on then to tell Ellen Graham what Josie had told her about the ritual. The tequila, the hyperventilation, the coffin, the girl who would be "raised from the dead." Reborn as an OTT sister. They kept a paramedic on hand. They knew what could happen. Wasn't it possible, Shelly asked, that sometimes the girl did not come back, that the ritual might—?

"Kill a girl." Ellen Graham did not nod this time. She closed her eyes.

"Yes," Shelly said, trying to speak quietly. "And you can imagine the scandal for the sorority, the Pan-Hellenic Society, the university, and the lengths they might go to cover it up. Isn't it possible that an accident might be—?"

"Staged?"

"Staged, or made to happen. Created? *Devised?*"

Ellen Graham opened her eyes now and looked from Shelly to the ceiling.

"Ellen, I was there," Shelly said. "That boy swerved to avoid something, but only seconds later what he'd swerved to avoid wasn't there. And the girl they say was killed, injured beyond recognition, burned with the car, I *saw* her. I would recognize her anywhere. She wasn't dead. There was no fire."

"Why are you telling *me?*" Ellen said, standing up, heading toward a buffet that sprawled in all its shining oaken splendor from one wall of the living room to the other. She yanked open a drawer by a flimsy brass handle and pulled out a pack of Marlborough lights. Her hand was shaking as she put a cigarette between her lips, but she didn't light it. She turned back to Shelly, eyes blinking and blazing at the same time. "Why did you come here? You know so much. Why haven't you told someone who can do something?"

"I've tried," Shelly said. "I called the papers, I called the police, I waited for the police to call me, but—"

"Now what?" Ellen asked, tossing the cigarette back into the drawer with the pack, and heading back to the couch, but not sitting down. "You think that was my daughter then, don't you, in the backseat of that car? Maybe she was already dead? Maybe they set it on fire? Maybe they buried my baby up there instead of this Nicole Werner girl? I'm sorry. I see what this means, what you're saying about what you saw, except, if it was, if you're right, where in the fucking hell is Nicole Werner now?"

Shelly took a moment before she spoke, before she could even consider speaking.

She tried to think of a way to phrase this thing, which seemed so insane, so that it would not sound insane. Finally, she said, "She's still there. She's at the sorority."

Ellen Graham started to shake her head so quickly, so wildly, that, remembering those earrings Josie had snitched, Shelly imagined Ellen wearing them, her face lacerated by jewels, and Shelly held up a hand to try to stop her from shaking her head so violently. In the calmest voice Shelly could call forth from the depths of her own shaken self, she said, "I can't prove anything, Ellen, but I believe they would have sheltered her, Nicole. I know now that they—the sorority, the Pan-Hellenic Society, the university—have enough power to drive the only witness to the accident out of town, to involve a dean in doing so, and who knows—"

"How did Josie drive you out of town?"

Now Ellen stopped shaking her head, and Shelly knew she had to tell her. As she spoke the words of the affair with the girl, of the photographs, of the last conversation she'd had with Josie at the Starbucks, Shelly opened her hands again, looking at her palms, and she thought, for no reason she could fathom, of sheep. Sheep with blood on their fleeces, with flies in their eyes. Maggots in their ears, in their anuses. She finished the story and stopped speaking, and then she brought the hands to her eyes. When she looked up again, Ellen was watching Shelly with a kindness that would have knocked Shelly to her knees if she hadn't been sitting down. It was not compassion, or empathy, or pity. Ellen Graham was simply looking at Shelly as if the story hadn't surprised her at all.

As if she'd been hearing such stories all her life.

After the silence, Ellen said, in the voice of the very competent secretary Shelly knew she must once have been, "Okay, Shelly. They got rid of you, if your theory's right. But the boy was a witness, too."

"Yes," Shelly said, trying to regain her composure, to echo the all-business tone of Ellen Graham. "Yes, the boy, too," she said. She nodded. "He doesn't remember anything. But they are doing things to try to drive him away, too. Postcards. Ghosts."

Ellen didn't ask for elaboration. "Just tell me what to do," she said. "Your story—frankly, Shelly, I hate your story. I hate everything it might mean. I think it's crazy. But it's no worse than all the stories I've invented in my mind. And you're the first help we've ever had. We've gone everywhere, spoken to everyone. The state police, the FBI, the—"

"The FBI," Shelly said, an idea forming. "Speak to them again. Tell them you believe there's been a case of mistaken identity, and demand that Nicole Werner be exhumed, examined. I can't do anything, Ellen. I have no credibility in this at all. But you're the parent of a girl who disappeared. They might listen to you."

98

M ira tried to warm up the car before they pulled out of the parking lot. But even as the fan blew hard, nothing but cold air came out. Beside her, Perry was shivering. In the cold electric light from the Dientz sign, Mira could see that he had his eyes squeezed shut. Could he be shivering in his sleep?

Ted had turned off the lights inside the funeral parlor, but his Cadillac was still parked beside them. He was still inside. Mira imagined him scrolling through more photos on his computer—his before and after images of the many disfigured corpses he'd brought back from the dead.

She didn't blame him. If she had such a talent, she would be proud of herself as well.

She pulled out of the parking lot and headed for the freeway without speaking, and after a few minutes, Perry stopped shivering and seemed to have fallen asleep.

The drive back in the blizzard was slow and treacherous, and at every exit Mira thought, We should pull over. We should get off. There were no cars behind them, none ahead of them, none passing in the oncoming lanes, as far as she could see, as Jeff Blackhawk's car rattled around them, and Mira became more and more vividly aware in the silence of the sound of the slick road just under their feet. Jeff's car gave one only the slimmest illusion of being anything other than what you were: a soft and vulnerable vessel traveling at great speeds over hard ground.

The car warmed a little, anyway—if from nothing but their body heat and breath—and Mira hoped Perry could stay warm enough to sleep until they got back. It had been wrong, she knew, to bring him here. To encourage or include him in any of this. All of this had gone far beyond what she needed for a book. This had turned into something in which, if she'd really felt she had to take it on (for research purposes? to find Nicole Werner?), she should never have involved a student.

But Perry had been so eager, and he had not seemed to Mira to be what she would have called "troubled" or "impressionable." In her years of teaching, Mira'd had many brilliant, troubled students—their brilliance fueled by brief intensities, always ready and willing to follow someone else's lead. They were the kinds of young people who could easily have been seduced by their professors, or inducted into cults, or recruited to build bombs in townhouses for the revolution. But Perry Edwards had seemed different—although perhaps no less vulnerable for it. He had not reminded her of any of those students. If he reminded her of someone, Mira realized, it was herself.

When Ted Dientz had called up the final photo of the dead girl in all her blazing gigabytes, Mira thought instantly of her mother in the pantry that day, so radiantly alive. That image of her mother was with her always, wasn't it? It was a kind of stubbornness. There was never a day that went by that Mira did not feel that if she could just go back to that childhood house at that moment, she would find her mother still there—shining and crying and studying the cans on the pantry shelf, alphabetizing them as she wrapped her brilliant white wings around her, getting ready to fly away.

Perry had that kind of stubbornness. Another word for it might have been *faith*. He believed in something, and he *saw* it. He would be, she knew, an academic. A scholar. A researcher. He would never be able to leave well enough alone, even when it would clearly be better to do so. She'd seen that about him during the very first sessions of the seminar, and already been reminded of herself at that age—how the other students would be headed off to the bars, but how she wanted, herself, to be bent over something dusty in some study room, inventing questions to answer.

Mira rested a hand on his shoulder as she took the exit toward campus. He didn't stir. She vowed to herself that she would talk to him seriously about his academic pursuits, soon. Degrees and programs and courses of study. Soon she'd have to wake him, but not now. Now her only job was to drive them safely to the next stop. Through the whiteout, as he slept on.

99

Ellen Graham's kitchen clock echoed through the rooms of her house as they talked on for hours. In the morning, Ellen would begin to make phone calls—the State Police, the university administration, the FBI—to speak to officials, to lawyers, to journalists, to start her final crusade. But for now she seemed to want company, so Shelly stayed.

Ellen told her about her separation from her husband six months earlier. ("Some couples grow closer with this sort of trauma, they tell me, but most don't. We didn't.") They talked on about their childhoods, their pasts. Shelly told Ellen about her brother—the flag-draped coffin—and then, without intending to, she told her about Jeremy.

Perhaps, Shelly realized even as the story was coming out of her mouth, she'd never intended to tell anyone at all.

Perhaps until this moment, telling it, it hadn't really happened.

But there was no taking it back now, or denying it, after Ellen's reaction:

"Oh, my sweet fucking Jesus Christ," Ellen cried out, and when she leapt to her feet, her own cat, which had sat like a statue through the entire evening, came suddenly to life and ran from the room. Shelly looked at the place where it had been sitting, and felt she could almost see its permanent aura still glowing where it had been.

Ellen began to pace then, and then she went back to the buffet, took out the cigarette she'd tossed into it hours ago, lit it with a shaking match, and dragged on it as if she were trying to smoke it down to the filter all at once. Afterward, she said, "I need a drink, Shelly. What would you like?"

Shelly never had a chance to answer. Ellen returned with a bottle of white wine and two glasses. She poured the wine. They drank in silence until Ellen said, "Your life is in danger, Shelly."

Shelly said nothing.

"You're not going back to your apartment, maybe ever, and certainly not tonight," Ellen said.

"No," Shelly said. "Tonight I thought I'd find a Motel 6."

"Of course you won't," Ellen said. "For one thing, look at the snow." She nodded toward the tiny crack between the curtains in her front window. "You can't drive in that. Plus you have nowhere to go."

Shelly felt the tears coming in to her eyes. *Nowhere to go.* But also the kindness, again, and from someone who'd suffered things Shelly could not, herself, begin to imagine. Such a surplus of kindness. Had Shelly ever met anyone kinder?

"No," Shelly said. "I couldn't."

"Yes. I'll make up the couch for you, sweetheart."

Ellen poured more wine into Shelly's glass then, and touched her lightly on the shoulder. She never mentioned Jeremy or Josie again— another bit of compassion for which Shelly was incredibly grateful.

Mostly they drank their wine in silence.

The wine was so pale it made the glasses—beautiful crystal goblets, surely another heirloom, or a wedding gift—look emptier than they had when they were actually empty.

100

My roommate and I have been calling you the Cookie Girl for so long it's hard for me to remember your actual name. And also, no offense, Deb, but you sort of don't seem like a 'Deb.'"

Deb smiled. Craig liked that there was the tiniest gap between her two front teeth. It was the kind of thing most girls he'd known would have had four thousand dollars' worth of orthodontia work to fix, but it was cute on Deb. She said, "So, what do I seem like?"

Craig shrugged apologetically and admitted, "You seem like a Debbie?"

Her smile faded then, and she looked down into the mug of tea he'd made for her—or, really, that she'd made for herself after he'd nuked the water. When he couldn't find a tea bag, she'd gone to her own apartment and come back with two.

She said, "I used to be Debbie. I changed to Deb when I came here. I thought it might make it a little harder to Google me. The whole story's there, of course, and my photograph right along with it. But Richards is a common name. 'Deb Richards' confuses it a bit, or so I was hoping. At least it would slow someone down."

Craig grimaced. "Sorry," he said. He thought a minute and then said, "Maybe I could call you Debbie, like, in private?"

"If you must," she said. "But can I call you Craigy then?"

"No," Craig said. "Sounds like a negative adjective."

She took a sip of her tea, and then looked at him and said, "You're really smart, Craig."

"Thanks," Craig said. "But you also think I'm crazy."

"No," she said. "I don't think you're crazy . . . exactly."

They both laughed, but then she put the mug of tea on the floor and turned to him. She said, "But I do think you've been through something terrible. Something crazy-*making*. I used to see him around, too, Craig. I mean, I saw him every time I closed my eyes, but I'd catch him out of the corner of my eye, too. Like, at the library. I'd be on one side of the shelves and there'd be someone on the other side, and, you know how you can get a little glimpse between the books sometimes? I'd get that glimpse. This happened more than once, and it was always him. So I quit going to the library in town. I made my mom drive me into the city. I mean, it's different with me. I didn't know him before I—"

She stopped before saying "killed him," but they both knew it was what she was going to say. They'd talked for hours. Never once had she called what had happened to her an "accident," but the one time she'd spoken the words *killed him* aloud, she'd had to run from the room to the bathroom, where Craig had heard the water running in the sink for a long time.

"So it was easy to think that every guy about that age, blond, skinny, was him. And every time I saw a guy on a bike. Even still."

She squeezed her eyes shut. Craig reached over and put his hand on her shoulder.

"I didn't really think it was him," she went on. "I didn't think he was haunting me or anything, but it was like what you described tonight. It would just happen. I'd think I'd seen him, and suddenly everything would be different. Like, the whole world. My whole life. In that second. Instead of being horrified, I was happy, and the universe was suddenly operating with these completely different laws, and—"

Craig said, "I know."

"And all the consequences, they were just nothing. It was like, for those two seconds, I was free, and—"

"I know," Craig said. He was laughing now, despite himself, but she was shaking her head.

She said, "Except that I'd be wrong. It wasn't him."

Craig nodded. He took a sip of the tea. It was minty, green. It tasted to him like something a witch might have come up with to cure a broken heart or a bad case of hives. It tasted like a supernatural garden. He had always hated the herbal teas his mother tried to convince him to drink, but he loved this tea.

He inhaled, looked up from the mug, and said, "Except, Debbie, I'm sorry. I'm sorry, but this is different. I *saw* her. I truly saw her. This *was* Nicole."

Deb gave him a sad little smile. Not happy, but not surprised.

"I'm going to go back there tonight," he said. "If I have to sit outside the OTT house for five years, I'm going to talk to her. I'm going to ask her what the hell—"

Then, Perry opened the door, and Craig stood up, went to him, took him by the shoulders, and said, "I've got something to tell you, man. Something huge."

"Yeah," Perry said, sounding weary. "I've got something to tell you, too."

101

"Hey, Perry."

He could feel it, just like in the clichés, his heart sinking, his heart leaping. Was he ever as aware of that muscle at the center of his body as he was when Nicole Werner stood in front of him?

Now he could feel all four chambers, and the blood traveling in and out of them, and the valves squeezing open and shut.

She was wearing a grungy sweatshirt tonight, like that night he'd found her on the front steps of Godwin Hall feeling homesick, getting ready to cry. Now her hair was in a messy ponytail. Bits of it hadn't been pulled back and gathered with the rest, and they fell around her face—but not artfully, not the way they would if she had, as he sometimes sensed she must have, spent hours at the mirror loosening just the most golden strands.

She wasn't wearing her usual pearl earrings, either, and the tiny empty holes in her earlobes looked pretty, he thought, and strange. He looked at them.

Pierced ears: one of the hundreds of the odd customs of girls. He remembered asking Mary if it had hurt, getting her ears pierced, and how she'd rolled her eyes back, fluttered her eyelashes, and said, "Oh, my God, Perry. I can't even *tell* you how much it hurt."

"Can I come in?"

"Why?"

She shrugged.

"Okay," he said, "come in," and stepped out of the way. He turned, and sat down at his desk, and sighed. She sat across from him at the edge of Craig's bed.

"What's the point of this?" he asked her without looking at her. "Why are we doing this?"

She was silent so long he finally turned around. She was staring at the floor, but he could see that she was smiling.

"Are you sick or something, Nicole?"

She looked up at him then, and seemed to tuck the smile away so he couldn't see it. She said, "You mean, like, mentally ill or something?"

Perry shrugged. "Okay," he said. "Maybe. Like mentally ill."

"Or, do you mean like *evil*?"

"Okay," he said. "That sounds good, Nicole. Let's say evil."

The anger in his voice seemed to make her flinch, and he was immediately sorry, but it was too late to take it back.

She stood up. She took a step toward him. She said, "What about you? Are you? Are you mentally ill, or evil?"

Perry turned his back to her again and put his elbows on his desk, put his head in his hands. As he'd known she would, she came up behind him and put her hands on his shoulders.

He could feel the cool, smooth fingers near his neck.

And his heart—that pleasurable pain, all anticipation and dread.

When Mary had forced him into such places, he'd seen those girls at the mall (what was that store called? Claire's?) having those little pistols held to their earlobes, flinching and crying out, and the stinging tears in their eyes, the smiles on their faces.

He felt her breath on his neck just before he felt her kiss, and when he stood and turned to her, for just a second he thought he saw what it was—in her eyes, in her face. It almost knocked the breath out of him.

He remembered (or was he imagining it?) turning once in the hallway at Bad Axe High. Mary'd had her arm slipped between his elbow and his side, and she was pulling him toward her, but he'd seen a shadow behind them, and for some reason it had made him turn, and he saw Nicole there, holding an armful of books in her arms.

She was just standing there, watching them with what looked like an expression of complete grief on her face, as if she were witnessing her own death, or the death of something she'd loved all her life.

He'd nodded to her, and the expression was instantly gone, replaced with that pretty little smile. Perry had been watching those expressions pass over her face like the moon's phases for as long as he could remember.

And then she'd turned and walked in the opposite direction, and he realized that Mary had spun around to look at her, too. She huffed. She tugged Perry's arm closer and leaned over to whisper to him, "That girl's in love with you. She always has been."

102

D eb said, "This is the worst idea I've ever heard, you guys. You can't go sneaking into a sorority looking for a dead girl. You already know they've got an EMT living there. Who knows what else? I mean, if they're hiding dead girls there, there's got to be, like, a rent-a-cop there, too. There's going to be weapons and alarms and—"

"Yeah," Perry said. "I heard somebody crack a rifle on the porch the other night."

Craig looked at him, but Perry didn't say anything more.

"You mean you've gone sneaking around there in the dark before?" Deb asked.

Perry didn't answer. He was sitting on the edge of the couch beside her, staring into his hands. Craig's heart was beating so hard he was afraid to sit back down. He paced back and forth in front of Perry and Deb, and felt that if he sat back down on the couch, his heart might actually explode from the pressure of trying to slow it down.

"Something's going on here," Perry said, more to himself than to either of them.

"We've got to go to the house," Craig said. "We've *got* to go to the house."

"You guys are crazy!" Deb said. She leapt up and grabbed Craig's arm. "She's not there! She's not in Bad Axe! She's not on this earth because she's *dead*!"

"She's not dead," Perry said with complete calm. "I know. She's not dead. I saw her in Bad Axe."

"No. She's here," Craig said. "You gotta trust me, man. I saw her, too. She's—"

"Let's go, then," Perry said, and stood up, and Craig did not wait even the length of a heartbeat before grabbing his coat.

"Jesus Christ," Deb said, and sat back down, defeated. "Please, just—"

Craig tried to turn and smile at her apologetically—she was such a sweet girl—but Perry was pulling him out the door.

The town, the streets, the lawns, the roofs: it was like a moonscape. As if the thing hanging over them in the now-clear sky had projected its surface onto the earth. No one was outside but the two of them, and the snow had swallowed up all the subtleties, all the edges, all the sounds. The branches of the trees looked heavy, but not exactly burdened, with all the snow with which they were loaded down. They appeared renewed, rejuvenated, by their white cloaks. The shadows they cast were smooth and very still on the ground.

Neither Craig nor Perry said a word until they came around the corner of Greek Row and saw it there on the hill:

Not a single light was on in the Omega Theta Tau house. It seemed to swallow up the light of the snow and the moon, casting no shadow, looking, instead, like a shadow of itself. Something scissored out of the air. A house made of outer space, of silhouette, of time past. They stopped walking and stood looking up at it, and Craig said, "You remember the first time we were here?"

Perry looked over at him, and Craig could see that he didn't.

"Remember? We were here with Lucas? Lucas and I were drunk and screaming and shit, and you were all pissed?"

"No," Perry said. "But that sounds like the way it would have been."

Craig meant to laugh, but it came out sounding like a sob. "I'm sorry I've been an asshole for a friend, Perry," he said, and Perry just looked at him, shook his head.

"You're not," Perry said. "You never really were. Let's go."

Craig and Perry walked on the side of the street opposite to the house, then crossed and trudged uphill along the tree line between the frat next door at the sorority's rear entrance. Craig walked ahead of Perry because he knew the way. He'd been at this back door before, tossed out of it.

Once or twice Craig turned to look at Perry, and saw that his own footprints in the deep snow seemed to be making a ghostly path for Perry to follow. Perry wasn't looking up at Craig, though. He was staring straight ahead, at the house beyond them. Still no lights. Maybe only a tiny glow from one room. Maybe the face of an electric clock, an iPod glowing in its dock, a sleeping computer's screen saver light pulsing.

Craig reached the door and turned the knob, not really expecting anything—or maybe expecting the lights to flash on and sirens and alarms to begin wailing.

The knob turned easily in his hand, and the door opened silently toward him.

God, he thought. All that trouble they went to when they had parties—the bouncers, the girls stationed at every entrance—and now, in the middle of the night, a houseful of beautiful dreamers, and the door was unlocked, like an invitation.

The darkness inside was total. How stupid, he thought, not even to bring a flashlight—and then a bright zero of light shone on the kitchen floor, and he gasped before he realized that it was Perry. Perry had a flashlight. Of course. Eagle Scout. Craig turned, smiled, gave him a thumbs-up, but Perry just walked past him into the OTT kitchen.

It smelled like cookies to Craig. The kind his mother used to bake before she went back to work, sort of, and quit baking. Vanilla, he guessed. Maybe some kind of spice. Nutmeg?

Perry moved the flashlight around on the counters, scanning, and Craig caught glimpses of white china behind glass cupboards—institutional, heavy-looking cups and plates. He could imagine the heft of those. The sound of silverware on the hard, shiny surfaces in a roomful of girls eating salads or noodles or whatever skinny, pretty girls ate when they had meals together. He pictured Nicole—not Nicole as he'd known her then, but this new dark-haired Nicole of now—at the heavy wooden table in the center of the room, sitting down to dinner with her sisters. As Perry's flashlight skimmed over the clean, bare surface of that table, Craig imagined her bright-white empty plate. Would Nicole, now, need to eat? And if she ate, what would she eat? Snow? Petals? The breath of her sisters?

He looked up then. He must have stared at the kitchen table too long because now Perry was gone, already slipped through a doorway and into a dark room. Somehow he'd gotten far enough ahead that Craig could see only the distant zero of the flashlight against the wooden railing of the stairway, and hear the first few stairs make a muffled groaning under Perry's steps before he saw something else there on the stairs ahead of him.

Perry must have seen it, too.

He stopped climbing.

The flashlight froze on it.

Something so pale and lacy it seemed to have been created by the light of the flashlight itself—like something crocheted out of a bit of light there on the air. A nightie sewing itself in complicated patterns around a pale form. The pale form of a dark-haired ghost on the stairway.

A ghost holding something trembling into the beam of light. Holding it up, pointing it. Saying something Craig couldn't hear. A whisper. And then the explosion.

And then the only thing Craig could see was the beam of the flashlight as it bumped down the stairs to the landing, where it blinked out just before all the lights in the house came on at once and Craig could see that Perry was there on the floor in a spreading puddle of his own blood, and the girl with the gun was screaming, "Oh, my God, oh, my God, I shot him, I shot him, I killed the burglar!" as a hundred other girls swarmed down the stairs and through the house and all around Craig in their white nightgowns crying and calling to each other as if they didn't even see him, as if they didn't even notice that Craig was there.

103

Jeff Blackhawk was asleep on her couch when Mira got back to the apartment. His socks were off, tossed on her floor. He had his jacket pulled over him as a blanket. She passed him without stopping on the way to the twins, who were just where she'd hoped they would be: in their cribs, asleep. Matty had his cow down at the bottom of the crib, by his feet. Andy's rested against his cheek. She kissed their heads, breathed in the sweet sweaty scent of them. She closed their door softly behind her.

In the hallway, she hesitated, looking toward the couch. Should she wake him? Let him know she was back and he could go home?

But no one should be driving in this storm anyway, she thought. And, surely, if her opening the door, crossing the room, and clearing her throat hadn't woken him up, he needed his sleep.

She would not, she decided, wake him.

She changed into a T-shirt of Clark's and, after brushing her teeth quickly, got into bed.

Jesus, Jeff," Mira said to him in the morning. Her hand was trembling as she put the phone back on its cradle. "I can't believe this. You're never going to speak to me again. I'm the friend from hell."

"No." Jeff was shaking his head, rubbing his eyes. "It's fine."

"I'll tell him *twenty minutes*. That's it. I'll be back before the twins wake up."

"Believe me, if Fleming hadn't called, I'd still be asleep until then myself. I may never have mentioned this, Mira, but I sleep like the dead."

"Oh, my God," she said, and put her hands over her face. "What does he want, Jeff? Why did he call me in the morning, at seven o'clock? What's he even doing in his office at this hour? Didn't he think I got enough of a reprimand yesterday? He's hauling me back in already?"

Dean Fleming had said, "I need you to be in my office as soon as possible. I would prefer that it be within the hour," and the tone had taken her breath away. She'd started to shake—although, in truth, she'd woken up shaking when the phone rang, with no idea where she was, and only the vaguest awareness that she had run out of bed to answer it.

"The man's an administrator, Mira. He probably sleeps in his office. Or he doesn't sleep. Who knows where administrators go when the lights go out?"

She liked that Jeff was making light of it without trying to make her feel stupid for being worried. Clark would have dismissed it, been annoyed by her "overreaction to every little thing," but Jeff told her he'd be worried, too. "It's creepy."

But he didn't seem to have any guesses, either, about what the dean could want.

Mira did what she could with her hair, her face. She pulled on a white blouse, black skirt, and a sweater. Jeff was asleep on the couch again by the time she closed, and locked, the door behind her.

104

Shelly woke in the morning on Ellen Graham's couch. Outside, the sun had risen fully, and it was as if the volume on the whole idea of light had been turned up. There was so much sun on the snow out there that the curtains couldn't keep it out. In the living room, everything seemed to be shining. The white carpeting, the knobs on drawers, the down comforter Ellen had given her when she made up the couch—and the cat.

That cat.

Had he (she?) simply come back to the chair and sat on it through the night, watching Shelly as calmly and nonjudgmentally as it seemed to be observing her now?

Shelly made the little kissing noise that always brought Jeremy to her side, but this cat didn't move. This cat, Shelly thought, was as still as the Sphinx. She had an urge to ask it a question but was afraid Ellen might be awake, already up and around in another room, and if Ellen overheard she'd think she'd let a truly crazy woman spend the night in her house.

Shelly knew she would have to get up soon and use the bathroom, but for now she felt as if she'd entered some kind of eternity. With that sun reflecting so whitely on the snow outside, Shelly felt it wouldn't surprise her to pull the curtains fully apart and find that everything was gone.

Erased.

Nothing left of the world but herself, and this white cat, and the brightness shining on some motes of dust between them.

The cat continued to regard her. Not even blinking.

This cat was nothing like Jeremy. This cat had none of Jeremy's scruffy skittishness. Jeremy's fur had been rough, and his eyes, unlike this cat's eyes, had been a mottled olive, not this blazing marble green.

But here Shelly was, looking at this cat looking at her, and she felt certain of something she'd once or twice had an inkling of in the past: that each cat is part of some larger cat soul.

That this cat and Jeremy had come from the same place—whatever cat nothingness that was.

Shelly and the cat held that gaze in a trance of that certainty between them, and the incredible comfort it offered, and Shelly didn't even startle and the cat didn't move when Ellen called from the top of the stairs, "Are you decent? I was going to come down and make coffee."

"Thank you," Shelly called.

She would drink Ellen's coffee, and then she would head back to town, find Craig Clements-Rabbitt, tell him this new plan, ask for his help.

105

The campus was empty. The sidewalks were slippery, lonely. The sun had come up on the horizon and turned the untrodden snow—the great mounds and blankets of it—into a blinding moonscape. Now, this was a perfect campus for ghosts, Mira thought. For the invisible. The gone. No one would be able to see them strolling along through this snow. There was no one to see them. The students were all in their beds, asleep. She thought of Perry, dreaming. She imagined his eyes moving rapidly behind his lids—that frantic dancing that was actually complete peace.

It was hard to walk through this much snow, and Mira tried to think but could remember no November snowfall like it in all the years she'd lived in this town. Luckily she'd worn flat leather boots. Although they were cold, with a bad tread, she could march through the snow on the sidewalks, trudge through the slush in the streets. It seemed that a few trucks and cars must have passed already through town, because she could see the tracks of their tires, but she didn't see any vehicles now. At the corner she didn't bother to stop for the Don't Walk sign.

Professor Polson," the man said, standing as she stepped into Dean Fleming's office. She had never seen him in person before, but she knew who he was from the photo on the university website, the photo that came up right next to the gold seal bearing the university's dates and the Latin motto under its name (*Utraque Unum*: "Both and One") every time she double-clicked on Home.

"President Yancey," Mira said.

The dean was standing in the corner, as if he'd been banished to it. He didn't meet Mira's eyes.

"Sit down, Professor Polson," the president said, gesturing to the seat across from him. He held a piece of paper in his hand. "This is very serious. Very serious indeed. Serious complaints have been filed against you by your students—" She sank into the chair across from him. He handed her the piece of paper he'd been holding, which she could only glance at before feeling as if she might faint, recognizing a few names and signatures beside them:

Karess Flanagan. Brett Barber. Michael Curley. Jim Bouwers.

"But the real news of the day," President Yancey said—and there was no mistaking the hysterical little laugh in the way he said it—"is that one of your students has been *killed*. Shot. After a B-and-E at the OTT house—"

Mira was swimming through the initials, and found herself moving her arms at the same time that she stood up. "Who?" she said.

"Sit down," the president said, pointing at the chair she'd just stood up from. "Sit down, now, Professor. I have no doubt you'll be hearing from the police soon enough, but in the meantime you're to clean out your office. In the meantime, you're to tell me in all the detail you can come up with why it is that this student of yours, this Perry Edwards, this student with whom you were working closely, might have broken into a sorority at three o'clock in the morning and managed to walk straight into a terrified young lady with a weapon, and gotten himself shot."

"Oh, my God," Mira said, and fell back into her chair.

"Oh, my God is fucking right," President Yancey said. "Do you have any fucking idea what this will mean, Professor Polson, for this fucking university?"

106

On the drive back to her apartment (snow giving the world the appearance of a moon, another world, an empty, perfect one) Shelly drove by the site of the accident.

Of course, she'd driven by it hundreds of times over the months since, and watched the changes to the shrine it had become to Nicole Werner. The teddy bears were occasionally replaced, the flowers rearranged. The crosses continued to accumulate. There must have been fifty of them out there by now, spread across the spot where the accident had been, lined up along the ditch. At least a dozen had been organized into the shape of an *N* at the edge of the field.

Eventually, Shelly thought as she approached the shrine, the sorority girls who saw to all this would graduate. Things would dissipate, decay. Maybe every year or two a relative would make the trip to town on Memorial Day, leave behind a bouquet.

She would, herself, Shelly thought, try to avoid this spot from now on. She would leave this town, but when and if she returned to it again, she would arrive from the other direction.

She wouldn't even drive by.

Her eyes watered in the snow glare.

She hadn't expected to slow down as she passed. She hadn't even wanted to see it—but she also hadn't expected to see someone out there wading through snow four feet deep, wearing no coat, at eight o'clock in the morning, staring straight ahead as he made his way toward the snowed-over photo of Nicole Werner nailed to that tree.

No car was pulled over anywhere on the road that Shelly could see. How had he gotten here?

His shirt was white, and her eyes were watery, and Shelly wondered if maybe she was seeing things. Maybe this was the kind of hallucination people had in Antarctica when there was so little of anything real left to see. She rubbed her eyes.

No.

This was a young man, and he was talking to himself, or to Nicole Werner's photo, holding out his hands as he drew closer to it, not even glancing up as Shelly's car came closer—although certainly he must also have noticed her slowing down, approaching, as she was the only thing on the road.

When she did slow down, she found herself nearly letting out a little cry, thinking, looking out at him, Richie, her brother, he was—

No, God.

Of course not. What was wrong with her?

Of course not.

It was that boy who reminded her of her brother, the roommate. The buzz cut. The nicely pressed white shirt. What was his name?

Shelly braked. She pulled over as far as she could near the bank of snow that was now the shoulder of the road. Like the first time, the last time, like the accident, she unrolled her window, called out, knowing he would never be able to hear her in the great white space between them— the snow and the white annihilating everything, especially the sound of her voice.

Still, he must have heard her pull over, because he turned around. He looked at her. She opened her mouth as he began to shake his head—a slow back-and-forth *no, no* that made Shelly close her mouth, and put her hand to it. She didn't need for him to say a word to know what he was telling her:

No.

There was nothing she could do for him.

He was telling her to go.

Shelly lifted a hand before she rolled her window up again, and watched him walk away until she could no longer see him at all in his white shirt in the snow.

Part Six

107

Ellen had aged. There was no denying it.

But, of course, so had she. How old must Shelly have looked to Ellen? It had been fourteen years since they'd last seen each other. Still, they managed to recognize one another instantly and simultaneously, and rushed toward one another there in the Las Vegas airport between the escalators and the baggage carousel, with no hesitation.

Ellen tossed down the black leather bag that was slung over her shoulder and threw her arms around Shelly, and said, "I told you so," into Shelly's gray hair. They both began to weep—no sobbing, just quiet tears dampening their cheeks.

Shelly nodded at Ellen. It was true. Ellen had always promised she'd come to visit Shelly in Vegas before either of them managed to die. She'd say it at the end of every phone conversation, jot it at the bottom of every email—and there'd been a million of those phone calls, emails, postcards, notes over the years. Time had seemed to create itself out of those exchanges across space.

It was a short drive from the airport to Shelly's apartment. They were only awkward in the moments of silence, so they kept talking. They talked about Ellen's flight—four hours beside a woman who stopped blabbing only when she was chewing the cuticles of her fingernails. ("I got up to go to the bathroom three or four times, hoping she'd bother the guy on the other side of her, but she was just waiting for me when I got back.")

They talked about Las Vegas. Ellen had never been, and Shelly had lived there so long by then that she didn't even notice how strange it might seem to someone who'd never been out of the Midwest except to go to Manhattan, or France.

It was like moving to Mars, Shelly had told Rosemary on the phone when she first moved. When the plane had landed on the tarmac in Vegas, Shelly had looked through the little plastic window at the desert, and said to herself, I have moved to Mars.

"Good," Rosemary had said. "In Las Vegas, everyone's in hiding. And you have to consider yourself in hiding, Shelly. Don't do anything stupid, like start a Facebook page, okay?"

After that first phone call from her new life, Shelly had hung up, crossed the floor of her fourth-floor apartment, and looked out:

Forever, she'd thought. As in the song, she could see it from the window of her apartment. Forever reached as far as the red-dirt mound of Sunrise Mountain before it abruptly disappeared from view.

And, in all the years, Shelly had never considered moving. Not from Las Vegas (which had become the home she'd never known she hadn't had—sometimes shabby, consistently inconsistent, but full of a beauty that was that much more lovely because you had to go looking for it) and not from the apartment.

She loved the view from her apartment. At night, the moon hovered over Sunrise Mountain as if it were completely empty up there in the sky, shining light down on light, not seeming to be reflecting anything, but holding its own spot tenaciously up there—a gleaming checkpoint, long ago abandoned.

Directly below Shelly's balcony, a prickly pear cactus spread its flowering menace between her view and the parking lot.

Once, years before, some member of the maintenance crew had tried to chop it down, swearing as the cactus ripped its barbs through his flimsy windbreaker. Shelly had hurried and called the landlord, who'd agreed to stop the worker, and no one had touched that cactus since.

Now every spring it bloomed as if it were some sort of simple-minded florist's offering to God. The rest of the year it didn't try to fool anyone. You knew, if you got close, it was going to rip you to pieces.

In Las Vegas, they said, you never saw the same person twice. And it was true, in its way. Not at the library, not at the gym, not the shopping mall. Even the people Shelly worked with at the hospital kept moving and rotating, coming and going, always keeping their distances so well that it felt, even if it wasn't strictly true, that she was surrounded by strangers, new strangers every day. And the people in the apartments around hers never lasted more than a few seasons, were easily replaced by brand-new people completely foreign to her, who also left. Every summer, the heat scoured the streets clean of the past.

Only once in all those years did Shelly gasp and turn around, feeling she'd recognized someone. She'd been walking a sand trail through Death Valley in the shadow of the Funeral Mountains, and five girls were walking toward her, coming from the opposite direction. They were swinging their empty water bottles, and stupidly wearing flip-flops through the tough desert terrain, and little spaghetti strap tops under the blasting sun, Greek letters stenciled against the pastel cloth, bare shoulders turning red. It was ninety-five degrees out. ("But it's a dry heat," everyone in Las Vegas always joked, "like an oven").

They will die out here, Shelly thought. Just by being silly, they will die.

She considered saying something, but as those girls passed, they didn't even acknowledge her—except for one with shining black hair who flipped it over her shoulder and looked at Shelly without smiling.

That girl, in truth, looked nothing like Josie Reilly, except that she was a type. Still, it took all the restraint Shelly had to keep walking, not to stop and say something to this girl, to the whole group of them:

Something about the stupidity of thinking you were bigger than death. That you could walk in the valley of it without even bothering to bring enough water or wear hiking shoes.

But these girls would just turn around and walk right out, Shelly knew. They would survive it. They could, and they knew it, and, after all, that girl was not Josie. Like so many others who had passed through her life over the many years (she was, after all, sixty-three years old), Shelly would be haunted by Josie Reilly forever, and would never see her again.

Shelly had made up the couch in her apartment living room for herself so Ellen could have the bed, but of course Ellen would have none of the bed. "You slept on my couch," she said. "And you put the fight back in me, Shelly."

"I gave you a dead end to follow for the rest of your life," Shelly said. It was something they'd talked about hundreds of times over the years— how much and how little difference Shelly's bits of information had given Ellen. Had they been worth the trouble in the end, since they'd never brought her daughter back?

"No," Ellen said. "It was the only thing anyone gave me. The only thing better would have been if you'd given me Denise."

They talked about Denise, of course, as they so often did. Marveling that she'd have been thirty-five years old now, if she were alive.

"I don't see her anymore," Ellen said. "I still look for her, but I can't imagine her now. She can't be twenty years old to me anymore, but I don't know who she would be if she were thirty-five."

"She'd be like you," Shelly said. "She'd be a mother by now. And a friend. A good one. The best."

108

It didn't matter how many times she wrote it on the board (lie, lay, laid), they always got it wrong.

The students at South Plains College thought Mira was a crazy lady anyway, or just plain misinformed, herself, on the basics of good grammar. She sometimes considered going all the way—writing letters to newspapers and politicians insisting that it was simply time to change the verb tenses. (I *laid down* last night. Tomorrow, since it's Saturday, I plan to just be *laying around* all day. *I lied* on the couch until noon drinking Budweiser.) It would be so much easier to change the grammar than to continue trying to teach these kids to get it right.

She erased the board, and closed the classroom door behind her, headed for the parking lot, got in her car, and drove back to her trailer.

It was September, and the sky was blue and uncluttered by clouds, or anything else. In West Texas you really *could* see forever. You could have rolled a coin on the ground, and there would be nothing to stop the rolling for a thousand miles.

Mira tossed her bag on the couch, grabbed a Diet Coke from the refrigerator, sat down, and booted up the computer. As she'd hoped, there was an email message from Matty, and one just under it from Andy.

The usual sweet things:

Classes were great. They needed money. Matty was in love with a girl, and Andy was just breaking up with one, and that night they were having pizza in the cafeteria, not to worry. They'd be home in a couple of weekends.

She smiled as she opened the photo that Matty had emailed of himself with his arm around the new love object. He was wearing sunglasses and a UT-AUSTIN T-shirt. He was taller, thinner, but there was no way to overlook his resemblance to his father. Somewhere, Mira suspected, she still had a picture like this one of her ex-husband in a T-shirt and sunglasses: Clark with shaggy dark hair, needing a shave, smiling crookedly, an arm tossed over Mira's shoulder the way Matty had his arm tossed over the shoulder of this girl.

The girl was blond. A little chubby. Familiar-looking in the way of so many girls that age.

Or everyone, of every age, Mira thought.

That afternoon, as always, she'd strolled across the quiet campus from her office and to the library, raising a hand to Tom Trammer, who looked to her so much like Jeff Blackhawk (especially in the mornings, before her eyes were clearer and before he looked more haggard than he did later in the day, and older) that she almost called him by Jeff's name as he passed.

And then she said hello to the dean, Ed Friedlander, a nice enough man, doing what he could at a low-budget community college to keep the faculty—a few with serious drinking problems, and the others with a variety of personality disorders—teaching their classes, and the students from killing one another. His resemblance to Dean Fleming was all in the age and the suit, she thought, but the sight of him never failed to unnerve Mira, start up the heart, fight or flight, although she always managed to conceal it, and to smile.

Clark was everywhere, too—although he was always the young husband and father who'd smiled so sadly at her in divorce court, and then, later, nodding solemnly on porch steps as he picked up or dropped off their sons. A depressed man, growing older, seeming to have been expecting something to come, now knowing it wasn't going to.

He'd gotten married again. And that also hadn't worked out. Last Mira had heard, he was in Dallas working in some kind of sports equipment shop. They had no reason to keep in touch now that the twins were old enough to drive themselves from one parent to the other.

And the students, of course.

There was Brent Stone, a nice boy from Muleshoe who wanted to be a gym teacher, and Mary Bright, whose name, unfortunately, did not in any way describe her. These could have been any of Mira's students, in other classes, at other places, and she supposed she could have been anyone to them in return. They looked at her and thought, she supposed, Aunt Molly, Ms. Emerson, my mom.

Types. Ideals. Reproductions. Representations. Nearly exact copies of one another.

Perry Edwards, of course, was everywhere, but Mira was used to that after all these years. Really, she took comfort in it now when Perry passed her on the highway in his pickup, or said, "Hello, ma'am," to her from behind the counter at the grocery store. By now, Perry Edwards would have been the age she'd been herself when she met him—but, instead, he was always the age he'd been the night she said good-bye to him in the snowstorm in Jeff Blackhawk's car.

Sometimes she saw him at a movie, maybe a row or two ahead of her, his arm around the shoulder of some girl who looked like Nicole Werner or Denise Graham, or any of those girls, his hand in the popcorn bag between them. She tried never to think of him laid out at Dientz's funeral parlor. The nice suit. The lovely job Ted Dientz would have done to make him look as if he hadn't been shot a few days earlier by a panicked sorority sister with a gun (given to her by a father who firmly believed every pretty girl on an American college campus needed to have one), who had been up late that night reading a book about Ted Bundy when she heard footsteps in the hallway and came out of her room in the dark to find a stranger on the stairwell of the Omega Theta Tau house.

Mira would have gone to the funeral, to see Perry for herself, but Ted had told her that the family had politely requested that she not come—and she'd also received a letter from the university lawyers saying she was not to speak to the media, the students, or the families of the students about anything that had happened. And she was *never* to write about it.

Mira's own lawyer had said, "No one has a right to establish these restrictions. Last time I checked, this was a pretty free country. If you want to write a book about it, write the book and we'll stick it to them then."

But as it turned out, Mira had no interest in writing about death, ever again.

Over the years, until he died one Christmas morning, Mira had kept in close touch with Ted Dientz. He'd become obsessed, as she'd known he would. (She'd thought they were alike that way, but as it turned out he was much more passionate than Mira had ever been.)

The DNA test had proved ("Incontrovertibly!" he'd shouted over the phone) that the body he'd buried in Nicole Werner's coffin, the one from which he'd taken the sample for his bloodstain card, was in no way related to anyone whose hair strands had been found in the brush Perry Edwards had taken from the Werners' house.

"Unless Nicole Werner was adopted, or that hairbrush was used by someone other than Werner women, there is no way the girl I buried in that coffin was a daughter or a sibling of any female in that family."

By then, Mira didn't care about Nicole—where she might have been, who might have been buried under her headstone instead of her. Perry was dead, her husband had left her, and she'd lost her job in an explosion of accusations and suspicion and hatred.

Still, she told Ted to call her after the exhumation. There would be, she knew, no talking him out of this. He was determined to dig her up. When Nicole's parents couldn't be located, permission had to be granted by Etta Werner, Nicole's grandmother, to exhume the grave. (Etta was a feisty old woman who'd attended nearly every funeral in Bad Axe for the past eighty years, and the idea of digging up a grave didn't seem to bother her at all. She never even asked for an explanation.) And, afterward, when Ted called Mira with the news, she had to sit down to keep herself from passing out when he told her that there was no one, nothing, in that coffin at all.

"Empty," he'd said, sounding empty himself. "And no one anywhere to explain that fact to me, or with the vaguest interest, it seems, in investigating it—except for me."

And although Ted Dientz devoted all the last years of his life to solving that mystery, he never managed to uncover the truth about anything. He closed down his funeral home, wrote letters to newspapers, called authorities and experts everywhere in the world. He became possessed by the empty grave, by Nicole Werner's DNA, by other missing sorority girls all over the state. And then all over the country.

It was amazing how many there were!

They could have formed their own private sorority house somewhere: some large old mansion hidden behind a shadowy hedge, where they built floats out of tissue paper flowers and styled one another's hair and sang songs and took secret oaths for all of eternity.

Ted believed that someone from the university, or from the sorority, or both, had been trying to hide a hazing death and had come in the night and spirited away the remains of the dead girl so that her identity could never be determined. They were professionals. They'd done it with surgical precision. The grass over "Nicole's" grave, the crucifix, the stuffed animals—all appeared to the naked eye never to have been disturbed.

But, later, when none of the hundreds of relatives of the Werners' in Bad Axe were able, or willing, to reveal the whereabouts of Nicole's parents so that they might be told the news that their daughter's grave was empty, Ted came to suspect not only Nicole's parents but the entire Werner clan. (Even Etta: Hadn't there been something almost gleeful in the way she'd given her permission to exhume her granddaughter's corpse?)

He thought most of them knew exactly where Nicole was, and that she hadn't been the girl in that grave.

But there were other possibilities Ted Dientz was willing to consider, especially as the years passed. He had worked with the dead long enough, he told Mira, to know that strange things happened. This world was more than a material thing. Was it impossible that he *had* buried Nicole Werner on her funeral day, and that, somehow, she had escaped from her grave?

What could Mira say?

Ted Dientz died without answers, and Mira had no idea what his wife and children might have done with the bloodstain cards he'd kept all those years in the basement. All those souls he'd wanted to bring back, that army of his dead he'd been waiting to raise—he was with them now, she supposed. There were so few answers in this life, and what few there were often scattered with winds. And only now and then little bits of belated justice.

It took a decade, but eventually some sharp sophomore who wrote for the university newspaper dug up the story of Denise Graham, of Nicole

Werner. The student managed to pass herself off as an Omega Theta Tau pledge for six months, and then to expose the rituals for what they were.

The sorority sisters were not, as it happened, drinking tequila and hyperventilating and passing out before their raisings in the coffin. They were being injected by an EMT from the local ambulance service with Scopolamine, the zombie drug.

At the right dosage, the sophomore reported, as Mira already knew, the drug causes you to sleep and then awake feeling born again. At higher dosages, it makes it impossible to form memories of anything that has happened in the hours before and after the injection. At the wrong dosage, it kills you.

Mira followed the story on the Internet from Texas. She would have been lying if she hadn't admitted that she wanted to see some administrators fired, but they never were. She'd hoped at least that the Omega Theta Tau chapter would be shut down. But it wasn't—receiving, instead, a hefty fine, and its members, counseling.

Mira hoped they might be able to prove that Craig Clements-Rabbitt had been injected, himself, with Scopolamine, and that's why he remembered nothing of the accident. She was herself convinced that the car he'd been driving with Nicole in it had been chased off the road by someone trying to cover up for the sorority, someone who knew that Nicole and Craig had the dead, or dying, Denise Graham in the backseat. Someone who knew that they were trying to get her to a hospital and who was trying to keep them from getting her there.

Craig and Nicole were run off the road, and the car was burned later by those trying to cover up the hazing, the overdose.

Nicole's death was faked. Denise had been her stand-in. Being a good sorority girl, Nicole went along with it.

Craig Clements-Rabbitt was blamed, and he'd taken the blame. He'd been drugged, and he'd been in love, which is its own zombie drug, especially when mixed with guilt and grief.

You could still Google *Nicole Werner*, and still find bloggers who claimed to see her ghost at Godwin Hall.

And there was evidence to be found on the Internet, too, that students had never managed to squelch the fascination with Alice Meyers, either. Every year, there were the cutters. Every year there were fewer and fewer applicants to Godwin Honors College—a fact that would have been officially blamed on the laziness of today's students, Mira knew, but which she suspected was because parents didn't want their kids, especially their daughters, living in Godwin Hall.

But there was always one such hall on every campus, wasn't there? It used to be Fairwell Hall they shunned, as Mira recalled.

Here at South Plains College there was an Alice Meyers, too—a girl who haunted the auditorium where, it was said, she'd hanged herself from the rafters.

And there was also a Nicole Werner:

Here her name was Sara Bain. One day she'd been holding on to her boyfriend's back on his motorcycle, and they'd hit—who knows? A squirrel? A rabbit? A rock in the road? The details didn't matter. Sara Bain was thrown from the back of the motorcycle. She landed in the median, where her boyfriend, dazed and bloody, had rushed to her side.

A small mound of stones ringed a cherry tree in the South Plains College courtyard. Every spring, a group of girls was rumored to huddle around the cherry tree on the night of a full moon to cut themselves, and sing songs, read their poetry aloud. In the morning some horrified faculty member would find blood splashed on the stones. There would be talk of chopping down the tree, of carting away the stones, but no one ever did.

109

Karess got lost somewhere south of Bad Axe, and by the time she found her way off the freeway she was exasperated and wondering why the hell she'd thought this was a good idea, and what it was she'd been hoping to find or lose by coming back to this godforsaken state after all these years away in search of a boy she'd barely known.

But somewhere inside herself she also knew, even as she threw her ruined map (coffee spilled on it, and wrinkled to shit) behind her into the backseat of her rental car, why:

Somewhere inside her Perry Edwards was still alive.

Of course, she didn't think about him every day. That would have been crazy. It had been over a decade. A decade and a half. She'd dropped out the semester he got killed and finally finished up her degree at three different schools on the West Coast. She'd been married, divorced, and she liked her job. She was completely sane. She didn't drink.

But she often found herself thinking, He was the one.

"Of course the one that gets away is always *the one*," her friends would say.

But Perry Edwards hadn't gotten away.

He was everywhere after he died. He was in every guy who turned a corner, or drove by, or asked her to dance, or bought her a drink in a bar.

After he died, Perry Edwards was *the air*. He was everywhere.

"Maybe you should visit his grave," her therapist had said. "It'll give you a sense of closure."

Okay, Karess had thought. I can do that. *Okay.*

So here she was, pulling off the freeway, driving through the kind of town she didn't think existed anymore. A church on every corner. Little houses with little porches. There was an actual dog tied to an actual tree in a front yard. *Jesus, Toto, I don't think we're in LA anymore.*

It took two stops at two gas stations to get directions to the cemetery, and then she started to wonder how she'd ever thought she'd find his grave: there were four times as many people buried here than there could possibly be alive in this fucking town.

She parked. She got out.

It was a typical late September day. Karess remembered, vaguely, these kinds of September days from her freshman year in college in this state. The raggedy leaves. The spooky branches of the trees. The sense of things fading and dying, but springing up crazily one last time before they did—blazing, writhing. *Look at me!*

Shit.

There were rows and rows and rows of Shepards. That must have been one big miserable family, stuck in Bad Axe for generations. And a little circle of Rushes. Mother, Father, Beloved Son. Karess wandered through the old part of the cemetery to the new part. He hadn't been gone that long, after all. Some Owenses. Some Taylors. A crowd of German names. And then she decided maybe she should follow her gut. She'd close her eyes. She'd turn around. She'd let her instincts guide her.

It didn't work.

She found herself under a tree. Like all the others, it was losing its leaves. They were falling all around her. Orange and red. She could smell the earth. The grass. That dampness. Moldy, like old clothes. Loamy. Cool.

She would, she decided, sit down. She would close her eyes for a little while and rest, and when she felt more energetic, she would go back to the entrance—those wrought-iron gates she'd passed through—and start over, and she would kneel down if she had to and brush the leaves off every fucking name, look at every single grave, even if it took her all day.

Even if it took her *days.*

110

There was a sad landmark on every block of that town:

The bench they'd sat on, watching the other students walk by—backpacks, short skirts, iPods. The tree they'd stood under in a downpour, laughing, kissing, chewing cinnamon gum. There was the bookstore where he'd bought the collection of poems by Pablo Neruda for her, and the awful college sports bar where they'd first held hands. It was called something else now, but from outside it looked the same.

There were the pretend Greek columns that pretended to hold up the roof of the Llewellyn Roper Library, and Grimoire Gifts, where he'd bought the amber ring for her—set in silver, a globe of ancient sap with a little prehistoric fruit fly trapped in it forever.

And the Starbucks where they went to study night after night and never opened a book.

Craig's father, beside him, said, "Son, slow down," and Craig said, "Sorry, Dad." His father had been blind for years now, and one of his worst fears was getting into an accident he couldn't see coming.

Craig just wished his father could see it with him. The beauty of it was the strangeness, the familiarity. The girls in their short skirts. The guys with their weird hair.

You won't recognize the place," Debbie had said. She still lived there, worked at the university hospital. She'd become a doctor, and over the years had remained Craig's best cyber-friend. They emailed every week, although they'd seen each other only a handful of times in the last decade, when they'd met up in various places they happened to be flying through. Her husband was a doctor, too. Back in New Hampshire, Craig had a wife and two kids and a little house that backed up to a little mountain. He'd built his father a small, solid cabin on the property.

"Just stay away, Craig. I mean, I'd love to see you. But you have no idea. It'll freak you out—not because you'll remember it, but because you won't."

Craig had a family now. He'd written a book, published it. He'd traveled the world promoting the book, and had never come back here.

Now he was back.

And Debbie had been wrong.

He remembered it all. Not a thing had changed. He could have been blind like his father, or closed his eyes, and found his way to Godwin Honors Hall, or to the apartment he'd shared with Perry.

He'd open the door, and there Perry would be, book open on the table beside a sandwich. Perry wouldn't bother to look up. "Hey, man," he'd say. And Craig, older and astonished, would just stand in the doorway and stare, grateful and terrified at the same time to find Perry still there, still alive.

He drove more slowly now, rubbed his eyes, so he could look around. He was looking for Perry, Craig realized, but on every corner, it seemed, a girl was crossing the street with her arm hooked into a boy's, and the sidewalks were shining and the sky was the same pale nothingness it had always been that time of year, and the old man who had become his father was coughing into a Kleenex, and Craig, forgetting that his father couldn't see, said, "Look," as yet another beauty crossed in front of their car, listening to something on her earphones, mouthing the words to herself.

The motor of the car hummed around them, and Craig's father continued to cough—and there she was, that beauty, flipping her hair over her shoulder, glancing at Craig, making eye contact briefly, and then looking away.

Acknowledgments

For their brilliant editing advice and tireless support, I thank Lisa Bankoff and Katherine Nintzel and Bill Abernethy with all my heart.

For being my best friend in this world or any other, Antonya Nelson.

For the blessing of Lucy Abernethy, my beautiful, smart, strong stepdaughter.

For support above and beyond and over the years: Carrie Wilson, Eileen Pollack, Jill Elder, Nancy Gargano, Holly Abernethy, Andrea Beauchamp, Linda Gregerson, Pastor Doris Sparks, Laura Thomas, Debra Spark, Tony Hoagland, and Keith Taylor.

For trade secrets, fun talks, and being the best student ever, Sara Johnson-Cardona.

Thank you to the University of Michigan's English Department and Residential College and my colleagues and students for generous support and inspiration of all sorts.

And for the perfect plot advice at the crucial moment, thanks to my extraordinary son and fellow writer, Jack Abernethy.

About the author

About the book

Insights,
Interviews
& More...

Read on

An Interview with Laura Kasischke

There are hauntings and somewhat supernatural mysteries in many of your novels. To what would credit your interest in the kind of material you often choose to write about? Are you inspired by experience?

In my family, on the maternal side, every woman I could name for you claimed at one time or another in my youthful presence to have seen a ghost. My great-grandmother told a story of having seen her eldest son standing at the foot of her bed the night he was killed in France during World War I. He was covered, head to toe, in mud and blood.

My grandmother said she saw a cousin of hers, a little boy who'd died of pneumonia, in the house she herself had grown up in. One great-aunt was visited by my grandfather (her brother) the night after his funeral. Another of my aunts met a semitransparent woman in her bathroom one night. And my mother—

My mother saw ghosts *everywhere*.

And all of these stories and many more were passed on to me when I was young enough to believe them.

I myself have had only one questionable experience, but I have no doubt it has haunted me throughout my writer's life. I was five, in bed, and heard something in the hallway, looked toward the door, and saw, standing there, an old woman with long black hair. The old

> " My mother saw ghosts *everywhere.* "

woman looked at me, and I looked at her, and then she turned toward me and began to run. Fast. Faster than anyone could run across such a short space between my bed and the hallway, and then she leaped into the air—a kind of soaring which, had she been subject to the laws of gravity, would have brought her down hard on my torso. I screamed. But she just soared straight over me and disappeared.

My screams woke my grandmother, who was sleeping in our living room on the pull-out couch. I must have told her what I'd seen.

My grandmother stared at me with a look I'd already begun to recognize on the faces of the women I was growing up around—a kind of horror that was more like a *memory* of horror than the thing itself. And even then, at five or six years old, I was more scared of it than of any ghost I might see. I told my grandmother, "It was just a bad dream, Grandma. I'm going back to sleep now."

My grandmother had been spending the night with me because my mother was in the hospital having her gallbladder removed. There'd been "complications" about which I'd been told more than it's probably wise to tell a five-year-old—something about an infected incision oozing yellow pus. In the morning, after my bad dream, my grandmother called my mother in the hospital and told her that I'd seen a ghost.

I took the phone out of her hand and said, "It was just a bad dream, Mommy." ▶

> **" My grandmother stared at me with . . . a kind of horror that was more like a *memory* of horror than the thing itself. "**

But, after being badgered long enough, I gave her the details. The long black hair, etc.

Afterward, not much was said, but at Thanksgiving I overheard my mother talking to my aunts, and they were all agreeing that, yes, it sounded as if, unfortunately, the house we were living in was haunted, but that, despite what was always said, it wasn't always true that children who were visited by "the Hag" died within the year.

Well, I was happy about this last part at least.

And our house, I was sure, even at that impressionable age, couldn't possibly be haunted. Our house, it seemed clear to me, was the least likely house on the planet to be haunted. Aluminum-sided. Two bedrooms. Tossed up hastily in the fifties. Exactly like every other house on the block. No long hallways. Just one short shag-carpeted passage between the bedrooms and the bathroom. No nooks or crannies. For a ghost, what would it have to offer?

Now, of course, looking back, I think, *of course*. It would be, of course, the least likely house that *would* be the one to be haunted. Those Victorian things with the chandeliers, that was too clichéd. Ours would be the kind of house a self-respecting ghost could haunt without feeling like a ghost wannabe.

But at the time I didn't believe in ghosts:

Especially because they all insisted that I'd seen one.

Could you talk to us a little more about your childhood, your mother, your grandmother?

I was an only child of an only child. My mother's parents came to Michigan from England to get married. As my mother was with her own mother, my mother and I were extremely close. I don't think there was a tremendous sense that children were necessarily to be treated any differently from adults, which is probably where the scary stories came in. Maybe that's a function of being the only child around—I really had no cousins to speak of either. They probably just got used to thinking of me as an adult. And actually, for reasons lost to obscurity, their nickname for me was Little Grandma. My own grandmother's childhood was a mystery only alluded to on occasion. It was a fact that she had been taken in as a newborn by the midwife who delivered her, but why was never made entirely clear to me. Certainly, her mother must have been unmarried, but after that there are different stories, one of which was that her father was a sailor who sailed off, the other of which was that her mother cut her throat with a broken bottle—but neither as a child or as an adult can I figure out how you kill yourself and then give birth to your baby (especially in 1901). My mother died when I was in college. My grandmother died a decade later, but she'd long since slipped into Alzheimer's. She never knew that her only daughter had died.

My father was much less eccentric than my grandmother and mother. He was a quiet mailman. He'd spent ten years in the Air Force prior to the post office. His own parents had come to the United States from Germany, and they were faithful, frugal people who never told stories, let alone gruesome ones. My father tried to teach me to play baseball, but I was hopeless.

What were you like as a teenager, as a young woman, and as an adult?

I grew up in Grand Rapids, Michigan. I rather enjoyed school but always felt much more comfortable around my teachers than my peers. I only got in trouble once, and that was for writing a nasty story about my sixth-grade teacher, whom I actually liked. I was trying to impress the captain of the Safety Squad, and I guess I already knew that my best chance at this was going to be writing something. . . .

He was actually caught with the story on the playground, and was only too happy to tell the recess monitor who had written it.

I went from high school to the University of Michigan, where I studied creative writing. After my mother died, I made an unfortunate first impetuous marriage, which ended in divorce. Then I married my present husband, Bill Abernethy, who is a dean at a community college here. We have one child, Jack.

Grand Rapids was a fairly dull place to grow up, and, this being the 1970s, the youth of Grand Rapids dealt with the boredom by drinking a lot. This lead to the likely consequences among my acquaintances of car wrecks and raging fires and unplanned ▶

An Interview with Laura Kasischke
(continued)

pregnancies, plate glass windows
smashed with beer bottles, kids
jumping off moving cars ending
up in wheelchairs, drowning in
backyard pools, that sort of thing,
pretty much constantly.

Somehow, I survived. That was the
only time of my life when drama and
horror seemed fun. Soon after, my
mother was diagnosed with cancer and
died. I never have recovered my sense of
invincibility, and I've never recovered my
sense that risks are fun to take, except in
writing.

*Do you have another job, aside from
writing?*

I teach writing at the University of
Michigan.

Where do you live?

Three years ago we moved from a
hundred-and-fifty-year-old farmhouse
to a newer house on eleven acres. We
have an orchard, a pond, a vegetable
garden, a berry patch, a couple of
pastures.

What do you see from your window?

From one window, I see the pond; from
the other, a stand of pine trees. ⌒

66 That was
the only time
of my life when
drama and horror
seemed fun. 99

Laura Kasischke on Campus Ghosts

A COLLEGE CAMPUS is its own village, full of folklore and traditions and initiation rituals. Like a village, it has its haunted places, its ghost stories. Within the world at large, it takes a couple of decades to usher in a new generation. On a college campus, however, a new generation arrives every year, and every May at graduation, another generation passes away and leaves behind its stories.

Suicidal ghosts and homicidal ghosts roam college campuses freely; Greek ghosts and residence hall ghosts, lovers' ghosts and theater-major ghosts may stick around to haunt the places where they died. Death doesn't skip over a college campus just because its inhabitants are mostly healthy and young, but one could also say that college campuses are haunted not only by the dead. Being, as they are, inhabited by young adults who stay only a short time, and for the most part don't return, college campuses play host to an endless parade of souls through the place, with not much but fading memories of them left behind after their diplomas have been taken away. No matter how vivid those years seem at the time, they're brief and liminal. It's a threshold time. A time between times. A ghost is someone or something that's neither in this place nor the other. What better definition is there of those years between childhood and adulthood that so many spend in college? Return to your college campus ▶

decades later, and see yourself as a ghost on every corner. Every year someone new takes your room in the dorm and wanders the hallway as you did, hurries down the stairwell, waits for the hot water to run in the shower stall, stands in line outside the cafeteria. Here, to be a ghost, you don't necessarily have to be dead.

To me, that's the most interesting thing of all about ghosts: You don't have to believe in them to see that the proof of the intangible world is the way the lives we've lived and the people we've been can pass away while we're still alive. ◡